PLAYING with FIRE

PLAYING with FIRE

a novel by Dani Shapiro

DOUBLEDAY · *New York* · *London* · *Toronto* · *Sydney* · *Auckland*

PUBLISHED BY DOUBLEDAY
a division of Bantam Doubleday Dell Publishing Group, Inc.
666 Fifth Avenue, New York, New York 10103

DOUBLEDAY and the portrayal of an anchor
with a dolphin are trademarks of Doubleday,
a division of Bantam Doubleday Dell
Publishing Group, Inc.

Library of Congress Cataloging-in-Publication Data
Shapiro, Dani.
Playing with fire : a novel / by Dani Shapiro.
p. cm.
ISBN 0-385-26722-3
I. Title.
PS3569.H3387P5   1990
813'.54—dc20   89-77593
CIP

Printed in the United States of America

June 1990

FIRST EDITION
BVG

In memory of my father,
PAUL HENRY SHAPIRO

ACKNOWLEDGMENTS

I am grateful for the support and guidance of the following friends, teachers, and colleagues who helped me find the courage first to write, then to keep on writing: first of all, Robert Brownstein, who helped me beyond measure; the students and faculty of Sarah Lawrence College, most particularly Jerry Badanes, Ilja Wachs, Linsey Abrams, and Esther Broner; the Virginia Center for the Creative Arts, and the Cummington Community of the Arts for their generosity and the clean clear space in which to work; Al Waller, for his wonderful letters full of hyperbole and praise; Dan Halpern, for believing in me; Rachel Simon, for solidarity; Jim Chambers, for lending me a room of my own; Hallie Gay Walden, for gently showing me the way; and my mother, Irene Shapiro, for being there always.

Finally, my most heartfelt thanks goes to my agent, Esther Newberg, for taking a chance on me, and to my editor, Loretta Barrett, who is an integral part of this book, and who I can't believe I have the luck to know in my life.

We found then
in the physical rose
quivering fire
and we used each other
to the point of pain.
we lived,
wounding ourselves.
there, life presented
its tidy essence:
man, woman,
and the invention of fire.

—Pablo Neruda, *Loves:
Rosaura (II)*
(translation: Alastair
Reid)

PART ONE

*T*here are many versions to this story, Carolyn. You have yours, I have mine, he has his. I never meant to hurt you, but this, of course, is a moot point.

You are somewhere in New York City. You are in restaurants, at the opera, in seedy Irish bars, on the subway. Even though I am thousands of miles, light-years away, I imagine I see you on every street corner.

Carolyn, if I never ask you anything else, I must ask you this: is this what you wanted, perhaps from the very beginning?

———

My father's mother has been an invalid for eighteen years, which is as long as I've been alive. She had a stroke at the funeral of my grandfather, the great scholar Jacob Greenburg, when I was six months old. The pain traveled like liquid down the left side of her ample body, coursing down her black-clad arm, through her heart, down her leg, rendering everything it touched useless.

It is not a story my mother likes to tell. (My mother is a superstitious woman; whenever I mention Grandma's name she knocks on wood, throws salt over her shoulder, says "Poo, poo, poo," like a fishwife.) However, my mother is also a modern woman. She's read Dr. Spock, and she knows children are entitled to explanations.

Here is what she told me once, long ago: My grandmother stood pale and swaying for a full forty-five minutes as the chief rabbi of New York eulogized my grandfather. My mother kept nudging my father, who stood next to her in his suit with torn lapels. She whispered, "Joe, look at Mama. She's not well," but my father stared straight ahead, his eyes on the plain, pine box covered with a black Star of David, so close he could almost touch it.

"Death," my mother told me, "death is verity to your father's family. It is life that is illusion."

I imagine this would be the way my father would tell the story. I have never asked him; the answers are there to see. All I have to do is look into his eyes and I see that day unfold like a silent movie. His ancestors walk across his brow, settle into the creases in his forehead. He can never escape them.

His father walked through Central Park on his way home from shul on Yom Kippur, the highest of holy days. It was Indian summer; the fringes of his *tallis* lay damp against his chest, and his feet were traditionally clad in rubber-soled shoes. Beads of perspiration gathered under his velvet yarmulke, a bright remnant of some wedding or bar mitzvah, but he felt lighthearted, and hummed a tune in a minor key from that morning's services. His stomach grumbled at him, as if to say, "How can you be happy on this day of fasting?" But my grandfather swung on, his pince-nez firmly in place; he considered himself a lucky man.

At the end of that day, at sundown, the Book of Life would be closed in the heavens, sealing his fate for the following year. In temple he chanted with the rest of the men: "Who shall die by fire, who by water, who by land, who by sea . . ." He beat his breast with an uncompromising fist, atoning for all the sins of man.

My grandfather didn't make it home. He fell on the crab-grass near what is now called Strawberry Fields. If, in the gathering crowd, someone had stooped to look at the inside of the yarmulke that had fallen off his head, they would have seen delicate gold lettering which read, "Wedding of Leah and Jacob Greenburg, Plaza Hotel, July 9, 1920." My grandfather, above all, was a sentimentalist.

It is considered one of the greatest honors that can befall man. To die on Yom Kippur, I have been told many times, is to be chosen by God.

On the day of Jacob Greenburg's funeral, all of the yeshivas in New York City were given the day off. The streets of lower Manhattan were filled by the Orthodox community. Yeshiva boys, young men holding their sons on their shoulders, old rabbis with waist-length beards spilled out of the doors of the funeral home. My father, Joseph, sat on the hard wooden bench in the first row, between his wife and his mother. My father was the only son of Jacob, and looked uncannily like him: the stately body, both portly and tall, the balding head, the round face.

My father's eyes were fixed on the rough-edged pine box which held the remains of Jacob Greenburg. He fingered the frayed edge of his jacket lapel, which the rabbi had torn directly over his heart. His mother moaned beside him, but he did not take notice. People were moaning throughout the great hall. It was "untimely." It was "a great loss." It was his father. The Hebrew words flew around him like a gathering of black hawks. He was thinking the impossible: inside the pine box, the puffed-up cheeks were sinking, the green eyes were being covered by webs, oh, the perfectly manicured hands. Nails continue to grow in the grave.

My father closed his eyes against the sun streaming through the stained glass windows; the colors were unbearable. Someday it would be he, lying prone, stiff and blanketed in wood. It was then that he heard the sickening sound to his left, and he opened his eyes just in time to see his mother, as if in slow motion, crumple to the floor.

Grandma lives high above Central Park, in the home where she and Jacob lived since my father was a boy. Her bedroom has been converted into a replica of a hospital room, complete with mechanical bed, oxygen, and resuscitation devices.

The rest of the apartment has not changed in seventeen years. In the long marble gallery, twenty-one stories into the sky, the first thing a visitor would notice is the mammoth portrait of my grandfather, painted by his good friend Chagall.

The dining room table is set with service for twelve, although to the best of my knowledge, no one has dined there in over a decade. The living room has the rarified air of a museum, or a country house closed for the winter season; rumor has it that the last person to sit on the crushed-velvet sofa was Jacob Greenburg himself.

The grand piano near the window shines with the blue-washed light reflected off the Central Park reservoir. An early edition of Bach's Three-Part Inventions is always open to the same page; it is a piece I learned as a child, though I am not allowed to touch the piano. The noise might disturb Grandma.

Instead, I always look at the assortment of family pictures, of children, grandchildren, and great-grandchildren she has never met. I am in this assortment. I am surrounded by wan, dark-haired boys in yarmulkes, girls with tightly coiled braids. A gilt-edged frame contains a picture of me from my ice-skating youth; my blond hair is pulled off my face with a thick band, my cheeks are rosy, and I am smiling my buck-toothed smile. This photograph was used by Kodak for its annual Christmas card when I was six years old. I remember seeing it in F.A.O. Schwarz' window, wishing me a Merry Christmas and a Happy New Year.

Remember. We were once eighteen.

When I dream about you now—yes, I still dream, Carolyn —it is at that age. You are wearing tight, faded jeans and that absurd rabbit coat of yours, the one that looked like a nest of dead animals.

Do you still have that coat? Are you still as beautiful? And what is your version of the story. Carolyn, sometimes I think the world may not be big enough for both of us.

My father cannot come to opening day at Smith because it is Saturday, the *Shabbos*. My mother and I make the four-hour trip to Northampton alone; I rest my cheek against the cool glass of the car window, and watch the landscape change. First, it is the Jersey Turnpike. We have turned the air-conditioning on, so the stench from the factories stays on the outside, along with the steaming heat rising up in waves along the sides of the highway. New Jersey gives way to upstate New York, which has the privilege of leafy summer trees and fragrant, freshly cut grass.

The smell of grass prompts me to think of Chris Mulcahy, the boy I am leaving behind. Everything about Chris was forbidden, but especially this: the woods in our neighborhood, which could be reached by a ragged hole in the wire fence, where I kneeled before him in a world which was alien and exotic. The scent is the same. It rushes in through the open windows on the Taconic Parkway.

I want my mother to leave as soon as we arrive at my dorm room. If she stays, I know I will fall to the ground, cling to her knees; my tears will stain her alligator pumps. I have never been away from home for more than two weeks. I once went to camp, but sprained my ankle on purpose in order to come home.

My mother does not leave. She reverently peels cashmere sweater sets out of my trunk, which has not been used since camp, and lines the insides of my dresser drawers with lemon-scented tissue paper. This is a dream of hers. When she went to college, there was a war on. She attended the state university. She envied blond, cosmopolitan debs with matching sweater sets. She envied coeds who had mothers with alligator pumps. My mother stays for a long time.

The door to my new room opens, and in walks the other occupant, the woman with whom I will share living quarters and long midnight talks for the next year. Or so I hope. I think she is exquisite. She is everything I am convinced I am not. She does not have a steamer trunk, but instead carries soft leather luggage in her manicured hands. She has angles everywhere: high cheekbones, a sharp jaw, a symmetrical Japanese haircut brushing her bony shoulders.

"Hello, I'm Carolyn Ward." She smiles, revealing a line of even, white teeth, and offers her hand. Her grip is smooth and firm.

"Hi, I'm Lucy Greenburg," I say, losing my voice somewhere in the middle of that short sentence. I feel myself flush. I have never thought I had the right combination of ingredients, or at least the ones that matter.

Her parents are busy introducing themselves to my mother. This gives me a chance to study them for a moment. Her mother is an older replica of Carolyn, looks more like a sister. She is tanned and somewhat rounder; I hear her telling my mother that she recently had a baby.

The man standing to her right is a giant. He is uncomfortable in this small room. His head brushes the ceiling as he shakes my mother's hand. He is dressed in expensive New England weekend clothes: a beige linen sports jacket strains across his broad back, and he is wearing what must be the largest pair of Levi's ever made. I glance out our window, which overlooks Paradise Road, and see a yellow space-age convertible with doors that open up instead of out. It looks like a vehicle in a Batman cartoon. I assume it's his.

"I'm Ben Broadhurst, Carrie's stepfather." He directs this at me. His voice is raspy, like pebbles sliding down a mountain. He clasps my one hand in both of his.

"I didn't realize this freshman class would have such pretty girls," he says, grinning at me.

It seems Mrs. Broadhurst can't wait to leave. She glances several times at the thin gold watch on her wrist.

"Darling, we're going to be late," she says.

She makes a motion toward Carolyn.

"Bye-bye, love." She brushes her daughter's cheek, and for a moment the two women are indiscernible. Mr. Broadhurst ducks his head and bends his knees as he follows his wife out the door.

My mother holds me close. She smells faintly of mothballs, tweed and a perfume she has worn ever since I can remember, a scent that comes from a delicate bottle with a crystal angel poised on top, ready to take flight.

She breathes deeply, as if she could capture some part of me in her lungs and carry me home, invisible, inside her. She holds my face between her two hands, studying me. Her eyes dart over me; she takes in every inch.

"*Eza bat yesh lee,*" she says, the one Hebrew phrase she knows. Loosely translated, it means: "What a daughter I have."

I am mortified. In my peripheral vision I see Carolyn unpacking. I am sure she is listening to every word. I am sure she thinks we are very strange, and is already conspiring to get a new roommate.

"Good-bye, mother," I say in my most dignified manner. My mother's eyebrows arch, her forehead wrinkles.

"Good-bye, daughter," she says, stifling a laugh, as she backs out of the room.

I have left Carolyn the better bed. It is near the window, and closer to the closet than mine, upon which lies an embarrassing heap of cashmere.

"You didn't have to take that bed," she says, her voice higher than it was moments before.

So she's nervous too.

"It's all right, I like sleeping near the door," I say, realizing that this is true: I am more comfortable with a quicker means to escape.

She inhales deeply, exhales slowly, emitting a sound like a child deflating a balloon. I have a feeling that it is a sound I will get used to hearing.

Carolyn pulls a glass hotel ashtray from the outside pocket of her leather knapsack, which I am already coveting, and shakes a cigarette out of a pack of Virginia Slims.

"Do you mind?"

"No, I smoke too."

"Great!"

She seems surprised by this. I must look like little miss goody two-shoes. She offers me one of hers, but I smoke Marlboros. We plop down on the little available space left on my bed, the ashtray sitting on top of the cashmere pile, and blow perfect smoke rings up toward the beamed ceiling.

Carolyn twirls a highlighted strand of silky hair around her finger, and chews on it.

"The letter they sent me said you're from New Jersey, that you're a pianist, and a vegetarian," she says, more a statement than a question. I've heard that the eyes are the window to the soul, but in Carolyn's case, the shutters are closed, I cannot see in.

"Not a vegetarian. Kosher," I say, "and not even really kosher. I just put that down to please my father."

"What's kosher?" Her mouth fits around the word like it's in a foreign tongue.

"*Kosher*, you know. Orthodox Jewish dietary laws, and all that."

"You're Jewish?" She looks incredulous, taking in, I imagine, my blond hair and blue eyes.

"Yes." I flush, annoyed.

"Lucy, I didn't mean anything by it, you just don't look . . ."

"Jewish," I say flatly.

It's not that I mind, really. This conversation is one which I've had many times. I think of my Christmas card, displayed across the nation, my six-year-old, Scandinavian-looking self.

My father received phone calls from friends in Boston, Richmond, Minneapolis. "Joe, do you know that Lucy is . . ." They would trail off, not knowing what to say, as if it were some sort of sin. Daddy would laugh. ". . . Wishing you a Merry Christmas?" It was a story he loved: "Imagine," I can almost hear him say, "Jacob Greenburg's granddaughter, a regular little shiksa."

My smile fades as I begin to think of the opposite end of the spectrum, the times my father's mouth would set in a frown, and his eyes would all but disappear. This almost always had to do with my first love, Chris Mulcahy. The hole in the wire mesh fence, the tangled white underwear lying in the leaves, the smell of cigarette smoke and freshly cut grass. I hear my father's voice, sense my father's fear. "Lucy, you will have nothing to do with the Mulcahy boy. Nothing. Do you hear me? Lucy?" I left high school a year early to attend Smith. Better to leave, I thought. Better to leave.

Carolyn is watching me. I have been lost in thought forever, and I think she sees right through me. She is smiling a wistful smile.

"Let's go check things out." She bounds off the bed, all elbows and knees, and searches in her knapsack for a moment, before pulling out a pink lipstick. She outlines her mouth without looking in the mirror.

As we walk together through the warm, late August twilight, the humid air seems thick with possibility. Upperclassmen pass us, comfortable in this strange place. There are people playing Frisbee in front of Seelye Hall, an old Janis Ian song drifts out an open window, her familiar voice singing of love and truth at seventeen.

We go to Packard's, the nearest and most popular pub. As we enter, I unconsciously focus my gaze somewhere below eye level. Instead of faces, I am looking at gold chains, shirt collars, stubbled chins. I am doing what is easiest for me in moments of discomfort. If I don't meet anyone's eyes, they will not be able to avert their gaze in a silent snub.

For me, it's always been shyness. My words become garbled, my face as hot and dry as a baked apple. My expression, I know, becomes a cross between a smirk and an apology. I have often been told that the result is perceived as a certain aloofness. Good. Better, I think, than the truth.

Carolyn gets us a couple of beers. The foam rises above the top of my twelve-ounce Styrofoam cup and forms a puddle on the wooden table. The table has carved etchings covering its whole round surface. I examine the graffiti. There is a crack in the wood, around which someone has penciled hair, and drawn a small, distinct clitoris. "What is this?" is written in blue ink underneath. As I begin to survey the responses, we are joined at our table by a pink collar with blond stubble above it. He plunks himself down between Carolyn and me, placing his beer on the table with purpose.

"Hi, William Jones. Amherst College," he introduces himself in Carolyn's direction. "And you are . . . ?"

"Carolyn Ward," she says faintly.

She is looking at him levelly, her mouth slack, eyes cool. I am impressed by her, by this show of utter indifference. I always have to struggle to appear indifferent, even to boors like this one. Especially to boors like this one.

He turns to me.

"And what's your name, little lady?"

"Lucy."

I quickly look up at him, at a shock of white-blond hair and annoyingly sharp blue eyes which immediately remind me of Chris. This guy knows he's in the domain of an all-women's college; I imagine this makes him bolder than he would ordinarily be. He stretches his legs out on the one empty chair, so that every time my legs move under the table, I seem to graze him.

"Excuse me," I say. "Sorry."

He smirks at me. "What for?"

"So . . ." He puts his hands together as if he is about to deliver a piece of thrilling news.

"I didn't know this freshman class would have such pretty girls."

Why does he assume we're college girls? Or more aptly, freshmen?

Carolyn glances at me, conspicuously rolling her eyes. This seems to spur young William on.

"I always come up here a few days early, just to check out the new crop." He then abruptly turns to Carolyn. "Are you a virgin?" he asks.

Before I even know what is happening, Carolyn is on her feet, and her half-finished beer is all over William's lap.

"You're disgusting," she announces in a neutral voice. The only evidence that she is less than calm is a tautness in her pale neck, delicate veins appearing like thread.

William doesn't say anything. Perhaps this is not the first time he has suffered such an indignity. I hear the laughter echo around us as we walk out of the pub. As the door closes behind us, I hear Carolyn sigh. It is the same sigh I heard earlier this afternoon, after her mother and stepfather left. It is the sigh I know I will get used to: a forced expulsion of more air than it seems her small rib cage can hold.

She walks briskly, shoulders squared, arms almost militant.

"I hate that. I just hate that," she gives a quick shrug, trying to get rid of it.

"I know what you mean," I say, but this isn't true. I really don't. Of course, I found it offensive. William was an asshole. But he did pay attention to us. He probably was, as my mother would say, a BMOC. And he did, in his obnoxious way, call us pretty; this is truly all that matters.

When we return to our room, my bed is still covered with sweaters, corduroys, rain slickers and other clothes I have a feeling I will never wear here. I find I have no energy left for unpacking. The beer, the newness, the excitement. I sweep the pile of clothes off my bed and locate a down comforter.

Carolyn sits on her bed, which she has already made; sheets with tiny bouquets of flowers, hospital corners, eyelet pillowcases. She idly holds an emery board, watching me undress. I feel ashamed of my Carter's white underpants, which are not quite bikinis, coming up over my hips, my plain white bra.

She probably wears silk. I turn my back, quickly taking off my bra and pulling my cotton nightgown over my head.

As I stand before the mirror over our dresser, rubbing pimple medication into my face, I see her undress behind me, an elongated shadow. I concentrate on my chin.

We turn out our lights at the same time.

"Lucy . . ." The increasingly familiar voice in the darkness.

"Yeah?"

"Are you a virgin?"

We laugh. The next thing I know, it is morning.

Grandma doesn't understand. She doesn't hear us. Over the years, there have been many "incidents." Strokes, small heart attacks, lack of oxygen. Little deaths. Everything possible is always done to save her. Frantic calls in the early hours of morning. Heroic measures. Ambulances careening down Broadway, in the direction of Roosevelt Hospital.

My father and I used to have a Sunday afternoon ritual. We would drive into the city, have lunch together at Fine & Schapiro, where we would eat turkey, tongue, coleslaw and Russian dressing on rye. Then we would walk up Central Park West to Grandma's house.

"Daddy, Daddy! Grandma squeezed my hand! I was sitting with her, talking to her, and I felt her squeeze my hand. Honest!"

I used to say things like this, a long time ago, when her eyes were still half-open. My father would wearily smile, murmur something to me about motor reflexes, and I would cry.

"Lucy, don't take it to heart," my mother would tell me.

"Death," she would whisper, "death. It is all they think about. But we know better. Your grandmother will bury us all."

Every night at eleven o'clock, a group of my dorm-mates can be found sitting around the living room of Emerson House, playing one game or another. Some nights, they play "Truth or Dare," other nights they play board games like the genus edition of Trivial Pursuit.

Carolyn and I have never paid attention, that is, not until tonight. We are both overtired, and the walls of our room have been closing in on us for hours. Carolyn slammed her textbook shut a few minutes ago.

"Let's go downstairs and see what the Smithies are doing," she said. Carolyn always refers to students here as "Smithies," as if she and I were somehow exempt.

They are sitting around a threadbare rug in a semicircle; everyone is silent. They are all intently looking at one particular girl, a tall girl with a wild mass of black ringlets who I always see wearing a black bomber jacket and enormous silver earrings. Carolyn and I sit down quietly. Finally the girl speaks.

"I never . . . did it on a public monument in a foreign city in broad daylight," she laughs, falling over onto the rug.

She turns to the girl next to her, who has spiked, bleached blond hair and is wearing green zigzag earrings.

"Your turn," she says.

"I never . . . gosh guys, I don't know," she says, turning red.

"C'mon, you have to say something," prods the ringleader, the one who is always organizing these games with a vengeance.

"What are we playing?" asks Carolyn with an amused smile, like an adult talking to a group of kindergartners.

"I Never!" they all chorus.

"And what are the rules?"

"You have to come up with something you've never done," says the ringleader.

"Oh," says Carolyn, leaning back onto her elbows, "I can't play this game, then. I've done it all."

"Fornicated on a public monument in a foreign city during broad daylight?"

"Well . . . not during broad daylight," she says, smiling.

A momentary hush falls around the room as everyone looks at her, trying to decide whether she is serious.

The girl with the zigzag earrings is still trying to come up with something.

"I never . . . did it in the backseat of a car," she says, still bright red.

"You're kidding!" people murmur, and a few minutes go by as everyone compares stories: Volkswagens, Saabs, Jeep Cherokees.

I am next in the semicircle. I don't belong in this room with these girls; it seems I don't belong at the same college, or possibly on the same planet. The only place I've ever "done it" has been in the woods, under a tree. I've never been in a bed, much less on top of a statue, or in the backseat of a car. And as far as "I Never" goes, there is something I've never done that I would rather die than share with this group of young women. It has nothing to do with where. It has everything to do with larger issues, like how and why and to what extent.

————

I think Carolyn slept with William Jones. She hasn't told me, but last night she didn't come home at all. I saw her late in the evening. She was sitting in the library reading *The Naked and the Dead*. He was at the same table, but I pretended not to notice. Amherst boys always use our library, and usually it's not for the books. But when I wake up this morning, she isn't here. Her bed is untouched, hospital corners intact.

This becomes even clearer to me when I bump into them in town before our nine o'clock class. Carolyn and I are both in "The Tradition of Mothers and Daughters in Literature." She is bent over her orange juice, a lock of limp hair falling over the cup. The tip of her nose gets pink when she sees me. William stretches and lets out a loud yawn, affording me full view of his stained underarms. His eyes are bleary and satisfied, like a puppy waking up from a nap.

"Good morning," she mumbles, kissing me right below my eye. "Sorry about last night."

I thought she said he was so disgusting. Bad taste, Carolyn. Bad taste.

"You should have called. I stayed up all night worrying about you. You never call, you never write . . ."

I assume a hangdog expression, wring my hands together in mock despair.

She tries to smile, but her mouth contorts, instead, into a grimace. She looks terrible. Her skin is all blotchy, I assume from William's blond stubble, her hair is stringy and she is wearing yesterday's linen blouse. Linen is one fabric that cannot get through a one-night stand. Which I assume this is. Which I hope this is.

The three of us stand outside, businessmen purposefully walking by us on their way to work. William stage-whispers to Carolyn, "I'm going back to school. I have to take care of the scratches on my back." He leers at me, letting me know that he has said it for my benefit. Carolyn stares at him, expressionless. He laughs as he saunters away.

"Carolyn, what are you doing?" I ask her as we walk back uphill. I link my arm through hers.

She shrugs me away like a gnat. "Mind your own fucking business," she says.

This isn't the first time Carolyn hasn't come home at night. About once a week, usually on Sundays, she just disappears. When she returns the next morning, she looks like she's been through a war, complete with signs of battle. Hickeys on her neck look like bruises, lips swollen as if they'd been punched, dark circles under her eyes; she looks like the lightweight champion of Smith College. I never ask her where she's been. She never tells me. A few hours later, she's always better than ever before. It's as if wherever she's been, whoever she's been with has somehow acted like high-octane fuel does for a sleek, temperamental race car. Her skin smoothes out, her eyes brighten. She is raring to go. Ready for anything.

This transformation is not taking place this morning. We sit at opposite ends of the long table, half listening to Professor Kimble discuss *Mourning Becomes Electra*. This is my favorite class, but today I find myself unable to listen.

"What do you think Lavinia Mannon means when she tells Peter, 'I can't marry anyone, Peter. I've got to stay home. Father needs me.' And Peter says to her, 'He's got your mother.' What do you make of Lavinia responding, 'He needs me more!'?"

I glance at Carolyn. She is studying her fingernails, which are the only part of her that seem undamaged. They are recently manicured ovals, unchipped, deep red.

"Miss Greenburg?"

I can't believe he's calling on me.

"I'm sorry, Professor Kimble. Could you repeat the question?"

"Good morning, Miss Greenburg," the professor says dryly. The class laughs.

I feel myself flush, and look across the expanse of the table, hoping for a show of solidarity, a wink, a small wry smile. Carolyn's seat is empty. I hear the door to the classroom click closed, and I have a feeling I won't see her for a while.

Carolyn is gone. She leaves behind her shadow, the scent of Shalimar, and all of her clothes in the top two dresser drawers. She has been a good student up until now, so she gets away with this. People are concerned. Professors stop me on wooded paths to ask if she's well, friends call to see if she's back. I'm not worried. I know she'll be back. She'll be better than ever.

I don't spend much time in our room. Ever since I've been at Smith, I hate to be by myself. Growing up, being alone was one of my favorite things. I would close the door to my room and push the button on the lock. I would read gothic novels, the most graphic ones I could find. I would crack open my window, sneak a smoke, listening to the crickets in the bushes below. Then I would shake baby powder all over the room to get rid of the smell. But here, surrounded by sounds of people, I feel an almost tribal need to be among them.

I practice piano in the antique-filled living room of Emerson House, while other students study, or talk quietly. It is one of the only places on campus where I feel I belong. I am admired here. I embellish upon Haydn sonatas, adding extra trills where they don't exist. I play Bach Inventions at triple tempo. I work myself into a frenzy.

It is while I am playing that I decide to call Chris Mulcahy. I wonder if he'll be happy to hear from me. An *arpeggio down*. Maybe he won't even come to the phone. *Broken chords up the keyboard*. After all, I'm the one that left. *Minor sevenths*. He never understood. His parents despised me. It was one thing for their son to have a fling with a Jewish girl, but Chris and I had stepped over the line. *Scales, now*. His parents threatened to disown him. My father would have sat shiva for me. He would have torn his clothes and sat on a low stool, mourning me as if I had died. Better to leave, I thought. Better to leave.

I think of the previous summer, the long walks I took with the dog. My parents couldn't believe how much I walked that dog. I would take him out in the morning, and be gone for five hours.

Chris and I had our special place, fifty paces into the woods. He sat in the shade of a sprawling oak tree, leaning back against its thick trunk, a blade of grass hanging out of his mouth. His breath always smelled of summer.

I always held the dog in my arms when I crawled through the sharp wire of the fence. I listened to the twigs snap under my feet and waited for the smell of Chris' cigarette to guide my way.

Once together, we barely spoke. I would tie the dog's leash to a low branch. The earth beneath us became a landscape of freshly washed underwear. I lay on my back; his undershirt was my bed, the flecks of sunlight through the leaves was our quilt, covering us with its dappled heat.

"Come on, Lucy," Chris would whisper in my ear, "come on, baby," he would coax with his long fingers, his tongue, his cracking voice. Eventually he would give up; when he came it was always with a crushing disappointment, as if he were giving something up, something I could not give in return.

"What's the matter?" he would ask, resting his head on my stomach, circling my nipples with the tip of one finger. "Is it something I'm doing wrong?"

We had both been virgins. The first time we made love it didn't hurt. I didn't bleed. I didn't feel anything at all. Nothing had changed since that first time. My nipples always grew hard, I became swollen and wet as if to accommodate.

By the end of that summer my legs were covered with ant bites, and the base of the old oak tree was littered with discarded foil packets which created rainbows when the sun hit them just right. On the day before I left, I picked up all our evidence—cigarette butts, Coke bottles and the foil packets—and threw everything away.

I stop playing. My fingers are limp on the ivory keys. I realize it's been six weeks since my last period. Six weeks since I've been in college. Six weeks since I've seen Chris.

I quickly walk out of the living room. I'm afraid that if I have to speak, my voice will come out in a shriek, I will babble in a foreign language, my tongue will hang out like an epileptic's. Walking up the stairs to my room, I place my hand low on my belly. The five pounds I've gained here take on an abrupt new significance.

I remember August: the tears streaking down Chris' face, dripping off his chin as he lay naked in the leaves like a lost animal.

"How can you leave?" His voice shuddered and cracked.

It was the first time I had hurt someone I loved. Even with no experience, I knew there was nothing I could say to make it better.

"You'll forget me," I told him lamely, ashamed of myself.

"You'll come visit," I lied, as I stroked his freckled back, as white and exposed as a baby's in the sun.

It doesn't make sense. I whisper it over and over, like a mantra, like a prayer. "I'm pregnant. I'm pregnant. I'm pregnant." I think of the diagram from my high school biology class. It must be no bigger than a thimble. Than a fingernail. Than a grape.

It was a game I used to play with my mother.

"Is it bigger than a breadbox?" she would ask me.

"No, but it will be."

"Oh. So it's growing?"

"Faster than you could imagine."

She would look at me, puzzled.

"How big will it get? As big as an elephant?"

"I certainly hope not."

"How long will it take?"

"Nine months, give or take."

I can't call my mother. I assume she knows what went on between Chris and me, but there has always been a mutual silence between us concerning the woods, the hole in the fence, the soiled panties that she must have noticed when she did the wash. If it wasn't spelled out, if she didn't know absolutely, she wouldn't have to tell my father, and at least for the time being, there would be a semblance of peace.

Last year, my father got out of the hospital on his sixtieth birthday. He had just had surgery on his spinal column. On our way out of the city, he told us he wanted to stop at Grandma's. He thought she might be worried. She hadn't seen him in a while.

The sun flooded the white room where Grandma lay, one fleshy arm dangling over the side of the bed, her face crumpled next to it, facing the floor. Dad got down on his knees and looked up at her.

"Mom, it's my birthday!"

Her eyes were closed; she was drooling.

"I'm sixty today! What do you think of that, Mom?"

He looked up into her face, his eyes wide as a toddler's.

He kneeled there for a long time.

When I return to my room, Carolyn is there. I don't think I've ever been so relieved to see anybody in my life. She will know what to do. She is sitting at her desk, hunched over a notebook. She smiles at me when I open the door, as if she hadn't just disappeared for a week, as if she'd been here all along. She looks wonderful. She is tan, and the circles under her eyes are gone. She is wearing a T-shirt that says, "Welcome to St. Croix."

I stand in the doorway, holding my sheet music and a bootleg bottle of Dewars that I bought from a girl downstairs.

"Carolyn, I'm in trouble."

I've always been one for euphemisms.

"What kind of trouble?" She closes her notebook, folds her hands over her chest.

"Trouble, trouble. I'm pregnant."

Carolyn does something totally uncharacteristic of her. She walks over to me, taking the music and bottle out of my hands, placing them on the dresser. She stands behind me, taking off my windbreaker as would a gentleman on a date. Then she hugs me. This is not a brief, sympathetic hug, but a prolonged, sensual embrace. I feel her rib cage, her thighs, her knees against mine.

She takes me by the shoulders and guides me over to the bed, sitting me down. She pours a finger of scotch into a Dixie cup, and sits down next to me, holding my hand.

"What are you going to do?" she asks.

It is the first thing she has said.

"I don't know."

Carolyn rubs my neck, and I start to cry.

She tells me she has had three abortions. This is the first piece of truly personal information she has ever given me. It is an act of generosity. It costs her a lot. She doesn't tell me who the men were. She doesn't tell me when it happened. What she does tell me is how it feels. Where to go. And what to do.

There is a clinic on East Sixty-first Street, in New York. It has plush furnishings, kind nurses and a gentle doctor who looks like Marcus Welby. It will cost me five hundred dollars.

This is a problem. My allowance is fifty dollars a month. At that rate, by the time I save enough money, I will have had a healthy, bouncing baby girl. I am convinced it is a girl.

Carolyn rummages through the bottom of her closet, and removes a shoe box. It is filled with cash. She pulls out a handful, counting out twenty-dollar bills until she has twenty-five twenties: five hundred dollars. She neatly pulls a rubber band around the stack, handing it to me.

I pour myself another cupful of scotch.

"I can't possibly accept this," I tell her, fully aware of my limited options.

"Lucy, it seems to me you don't have much choice."

Her voice is quiet, coaxing. She is going to get me through this.

"I'll pay you back. Every penny."

"Don't worry about it. What am I going to do with all this, anyway?" She motions toward the shoe box, which she then tightly closes and buries back in the closet.

"C'mon," she grins at me, "let's tie one on."

We sit on the floor, passing the bottle back and forth. The scotch makes me bolder, or maybe the intimacy of the last hour, the aching exhaustion. She is back. She is beautiful. She is better than before. I cannot help myself. I want to know her secrets.

"Carolyn, where were you?"

She points to her T-shirt.

"Who is it? You can tell me."

Silence.

"I can't tell you."

"Do I know him?"

"You know *of* him," she says, watching me carefully.

"Is it Teddy Kennedy?"

She laughs, her teeth white against her tanned face.

I pass out at some point during the night. I wake up to find myself curled up under my quilt, wearing last night's flannel shirt, my jeans and socks folded neatly at the foot of my bed.

There is a note next to my head on the pillow: "Gone to class. xxoo, C." I vaguely remember Carolyn unlacing my sneakers, pulling off my socks, sliding my jeans off as I lay semiconscious. She must have tucked me into bed, though I don't remember. She can drink me under the table, or onto the floor, in this case.

My head hasn't felt like this since I had my tonsils out when I was eight years old. The anesthesia had given me such a bad headache that I was sure there was a blind mouse running around inside my head, bouncing off the bony walls. I call the clinic. The woman's voice on the phone is as soothing as butter on a burn.

Tomorrow. I'm scheduled for tomorrow. Nothing to eat or drink after midnight. This is fine with me, I'm sure I'll never eat or drink again. I look at myself sideways in the full-length mirror. In my eyes, my stomach swells beneath my rib cage, my breasts are as heavy and full as balloons filled with water, my nipples hard and chafed. I exhale, naked, pushing my belly out as far as it will go.

Carolyn opens the door. Thankfully, she doesn't laugh at me, doesn't appear to notice. I pull on one of my father's shirts, hiding my new, grotesque self.

"Good morning!" She arches her eyebrows at me.

It is noon.

I wait until four o'clock to call Chris, since he is still in high school, and won't be home until after basketball practice. His mother answers the phone.

"Well, well. College girl!" she says, by way of greeting.

Mrs. Mulcahy, I imagine, includes in her morning prayers gratitude for the early admissions policy at Smith. When Chris gets on the line, his voice is even.

"What do you want?" he asks.

If his mother is within earshot, she must be crossing herself.

"Chris . . ."

"What? What do you want, Lucy?"

The woods, the orange tip of his cigarette gleaming in the dusk, the prickly shock the first time he took off my panties and I felt the breeze hit my bare ass.

"I . . forget it. Just forget it," I mumble.

"You obviously called about something, Lucy. What is it?"

I squeeze my eyes tight; the world turns into a swirl of orange and red.

"I'm pregnant," I say, knowing that it is something I cannot ever take back, that once said, we will both know it forever.

There is silence on the other end of the line. I imagine Chris slumped into an overstuffed floral easy chair, one lanky leg dangling over the side. I can almost see his untied basketball sneaker, the cuff of his faded jeans.

Still, he says nothing. He is waiting me out.

"Chris," I begin, but he interrupts me.

"So what?" he says quietly. If he were in front of me, I would see the high color in his cheeks, the pink tips of his ears. "It's not my problem."

I feel as if I have just been meted out a punishment: an eye for an eye, a tooth for a tooth. I have gotten what I deserve. My heart ricochets beneath my flannel shirt, beneath my swollen breasts, as I hang up the phone.

Carolyn is staring at me. I focus on a small crack, a hairline fracture in the wall above the door. I cannot meet her gaze. She would never understand. I'm sure that nothing like this has ever happened to her. Her life is a succession of trips to the Caribbean, casual flings, garden parties. No man has ever spoken to her as Chris just did to me. She has never watched her hands shake, fought back tears, been rendered mute.

"You're a fool."

She says this flatly, as if there were no question.

"Promise me you'll never do that, never do anything like that again."

Her eyes are gentle, misted over.

"It's us against them, Lucy. You must remember that," she says, wiping my cheeks with her hands.

"I promise." My voice is barely audible.

"What?"

"I promise, I promise."

She will teach me. She will tenderly guide me through the brambled woods of malice, of enmity, of East Side abortions and shoe boxes full of money. She will be the signpost by which I will find my way in a world of darkness. I will listen to her. I will learn.

At the crack of dawn we take the Northampton bus to Springfield, and then the train to New York. The smoking car is filled with businessmen carrying overnight bags. They have been dropped off at the station by their wives, who are all wearing raincoats over their pajamas. I imagine the men getting out of their family-sized cars, giving hasty toothpaste kisses to their women, who will then drive home through the rain, crawl back into their still-warm beds.

Carolyn and I don't talk much during the ride in. The four-hour trip goes by like a long, lulling movie. I listen to the hissing sound of the rain along the sides of the train, and read my child psychology textbook. We're studying Erikson's principles of nature versus nurture. Carolyn sleeps beside me; her mouth, slightly open, looks ready to be kissed. Her wet hair covers half her face as she snuggles deeper into her down jacket.

Every so often my heart does a dance, reminding me of where we're going, and what I'm about to do. What I'm most afraid of is dying. I've heard stories. I close my eyes, imagining the sharp silver scalpel sliding through my uterine lining like a knife through freshly baked bread. The train whistle becomes my scream. I open my eyes as we arrive at Pennsylvania Station.

We take a taxi to Bloomingdale's, where we have an hour to kill. The clinic is two blocks away. We walk through lingerie and cosmetics, where I buy a bright red lipstick which I know, even while pulling out my wallet, I will wear once and discard.

I have dressed for the occasion. I am wearing a kilt, argyle knee socks and a shetland sweater. My hair is in braids. It is the first time I have ever worn braids of my own volition. My mother would be proud. When I plaited my wet hair this morning, I thought of Heidi, or Pippi Longstocking, or any of the braided heroines of my childhood: perfect, hardy, impenetrable.

Carolyn squeezes my hand as we enter the brownstone, which looks like anything other than what it is. She described the doctor accurately; he looks straight out of central casting. His eyes crinkle when he recognizes her. He knows her intimately. They've had this date before.

The waiting room is filled with couples, with nervous men sitting alone, thumbing through recent copies of *Ladies' Home Journal*. I think of Chris. He would be out of place here. He would dribble his basketball on the parquet floor. The tips of his downy ears would burn hot and red. It is early afternoon. He is probably sitting in biology lab, dissecting a frog. I used to dip his frogs into the formaldehyde for him. He couldn't bear to kill a living thing.

"OK, Lucy, let me explain what we're going to do." Dr. Marcus leans across his desk, ingratiating.

My eyes feel pinned open, like mounted butterflies.

"First we're going to attach a vacuum to the opening of your cervix. Do you know what a cervix is?"

I nod yes.

"OK, good. Then we are going to apply suction, and clean out the little problem."

I think he winks at me. I hope it's just a tic.

"Then we will go around the area with a sharp instrument, just to be sure that we didn't miss anything. Any questions?"

"No. No questions."

"Excellent. Afterward, you will go to the pharmacy around the corner, and give them these," he says, handing me two prescriptions. I look down at them. One is for antibiotics, the other is for birth control pills.

"We don't want to see your pretty face back here again," he says, and this time I'm sure he winks at me.

Why did he keep saying "we"? Is this a team operation? Or is he just like the salesladies at Saks Fifth Avenue that I hated when I was a kid. "Do we like this dress? Oh, we look so pretty in it. Let's try on another." Something about obsequiousness. Something about safety in numbers.

I have opted for no anesthesia. If I die, I want to be awake. I want to see the end, the tunnel, the soft envelope of darkness. I think of Carolyn, sitting just a room away. I imagine she is leafing through *Vogue*, marking pages that have outfits she particularly likes. She is thinking of me. She is with me. I will come to no harm.

With one hand I grip the side of the narrow metal table upon which I am lying. With the other, I dig my nails into the palm of a very understanding nurse. It is pain unlike any that I have ever known. It is at my center, a place at my core which no vacuum, no scalpel, no human hand should ever touch. I concentrate on the top of Dr. Marcus' head. He has a bald spot, roughly the size of a half-dollar, skin pink against the rest of his gray, thinning hair. I recite the prepositions backward: "without, within, with, on, off, of, like . . ." The noise of the machinery is louder than the subway. I decide to commit Mozart's Piano Concerto in D Minor to memory. The doctor scrapes in tempo. The strings soar, a swelling crescendo. Before I have reached the end of the first movement, it is over.

The cramps are bad. After napping fitfully for what seems like hours, I hobble out of the changing room and sit down next to Carolyn, who puts her hand on my waist. She tells me it will hurt only for a little while. She wipes the perspiration off my forehead with a monogrammed handkerchief. I look out the picture window into the garden of the brownstone. It is dusk. The day has disappeared.

"We're going out to dinner," she announces.

"Carolyn, look at me. I'm a mess," I say.

She removes the ribbons from my braids, carefully unwrapping them like gifts.

"Look at you. You're beautiful," she tells me in a quiet, gentle whisper.

I look in the ladies' room mirror. My hair springs Pre-Raphaelite curls around my face, which is chalk-white and drawn after the past few days. My cheekbones seem to have popped up out of nowhere. I glide the bright red lipstick over my bottom lip and press my mouth together. I look good. It seems adversity agrees with me. I pinch my cheeks hard, and push up the sleeves of my shetland sweater. Below the mirror, underneath my skirt, I am as hollow and raw as a ditch drained of water.

Carolyn stands behind me, lifting the weight of hair from the nape of my neck.

"So. Where are we having dinner?" I ask her.

I am tough, invincible. I have just undergone and survived a rite of womanhood.

"I called my stepfather," she answers, "we're meeting him in a half hour at La Côte Basque."

She is concentrating on her reflection, expertly applying two layers of black mascara.

"Carolyn . . . Côte Basque? We're not exactly dressed for the occasion."

Secretly, I'm excited.

"It doesn't matter," she tells me. "If we're with Ben, we could be wearing burlap sacks and they'd let us in."

Carolyn hasn't told me much about Ben. Then again, she hasn't told me much about anything. All I remember about him is his enormous size, like a giant from a fairy tale. He phones Carolyn all the time. When I answer, he always calls me "pretty lady." None of my friends' parents talk that way. I never know how to react. So I just giggle, and pass the phone to Carolyn. When her mother calls, it's a different story. "Hello, Lucy, how are you?" she will ask me formally. "How's school? How are your parents? I'm so glad to hear that everything's going well," she will say, without waiting for my answers. It's a standard parent amenity, one which I'm used to.

Carolyn never goes home for weekends. I've gone home three times. Each time I close my bedroom door, sneak cigarettes out the window, reread love letters and old diaries with a terrible thirst. Going home confuses me. On Friday nights, my father sits at the head of the long dining room table, yarmulke in place; he raises the silver goblet of sweet wine, reciting the blessing. He slices the challah into thick slabs, scattering crumbs on the white tablecloth, thanking God for our bread. My mother sits at the opposite end of the table, dressed up in a white silk blouse and pearls the size of marbles, as the maid serves platters of sweet-smelling food. I am in the middle. I stare directly in front of me at a silver tray of colorful papier-mâché vegetables, so real, so lifelike they look good enough to eat.

Carolyn and I bounce together in the back of a Checker cab. She is wearing enormous sunglasses which obscure most of her face. Looking at her, I have a prescience of what she will look like at forty. She will be stunning, all angles and with a smooth, unlined face. She will wear tailored suits, and sunglasses just like these. People will turn on the street, wondering who she is. She will walk as she does now, with her chin aimed in a direction far ahead of her, a destination only she can see.

Our cab pulls up to an awning on East Fifty-fifth Street. We could have walked, but every step I take reminds me of the previous hour, and Mozart's D-Minor Concerto comes roaring back into my head. I wonder whether I'll ever again be able to listen to that concerto in particular, or Mozart in general, with any degree of pleasure.

I have never been to La Côte Basque, though I've heard about it. It's one of my mother's favorite restaurants, a harmony of vivid color, an impressionist collage of flowers and fancy dresses punctuated by somber dots of three-piece suits. Ben Broadhurst is sitting at a center table which I imagine to be one of the best seats in the house. He is the first person I notice as we enter the restaurant. His size, the shock of black hair falling over his forehead, his clunky gold watch—everything about him seems to demand attention. He smiles and rises slightly from his chair, gesturing to us. Sitting next to him is an elfin young man dressed just like him in a double-breasted suit, pocket handkerchief folded just so.

"Carolyn! Lucy!" He spreads out his arms. "Meet George Stein."

We all murmur greetings, shake hands in a complicated pattern across the floral arrangement.

"George is a new associate in the firm," Ben tells us.

"What do you do, Mr. Broadhurst?" I ask him.

"Please . . . call me Ben," he says, resting his thick hand on mine for a fraction of a second. "You mean Carolyn hasn't even told you what I do? Carrie, I'm hurt. You don't talk about me?"

Carolyn holds her wineglass by its stem, swirling it around. She seems fascinated by the rich red color. She doesn't answer him.

"I build buildings," he tells me.

"Builds buildings!" George Stein says excitably. "You know that glass building under construction on Fifty-sixth Street? That's Ben's. And most of the new high rises down by the South Street Seaport, and the renovation on Central Park South, not to mention . . ."

Carolyn interrupts him, her voice strained.

"George, I'm sure Lucy isn't interested in everything Ben owns. We all know he owns half the city."

Ben turns and stares at her.

"Well, not quite half, according to recent estimations," he says. "Anyway, you've never minded until now, little lady. Need I say more?"

His hand is under the table. I see Carolyn wince, as if she'd just been pinched, hard, on the knee. Or the hip. Or the thigh.

George Stein and I sit there like potted plants. We are observers of this little drama. I feel sorry for him. His blush creeps all the way up to his balding hairline. He begins to ask me questions by rote, what he considers to be polite society questions, like "Where did you go to prep school?" and "What does your father do?"

All the while he keeps his eyes on Ben, as if he knows that he is merely scenery, the perfect foil. Ben is clearly a demigod of some sort, as looming and large as the buildings he constructs. George Stein wants desperately to be just like him. He wears the same wing-tipped shoes, drinks the same dry martini with three olives. He wants expense account dinners, a center table, and a stepdaughter who looks like Carolyn Ward.

Carolyn is staring at me. She is flushed, and I see her trying to control her breath. She doesn't say a word. She holds my eyes, probing, questioning. She is challenging me. Her shoulders heave, her mouth is moist with wine. I feel my throat constrict as I look away.

I order langoustine en croûte. I don't know what this is, don't care. Diners throughout the restaurant are turning discreetly to look at our table, and several people have nodded to Ben as they've passed. Carolyn drinks two goblets of wine in rapid succession. She is giddy as a colt, and as gentle, endearing. Her fingernails are perfectly manicured red. With them, she scratches the back of Ben's neck.

I excuse myself, and find a door in the back of the restaurant marked "Dames." There is a black-and-white ruffled attendant inside who offers me an array of Handi-Wipes, deodorants and perfumes. In the stall, I watch the marble floor move under me for a moment before I wretch up an entire plate of langoustine and rich red wine into the pristine, white toilet.

I pull down my stockings. Carolyn's silk panties, which I am wearing, are caked with blood. I remove them, stuffing them into a metal basket on the side of the stall which says in three languages: "Ladies, please dispose of sanitary products here." I place a wad of tissue into my stockings, apply Chanel No. 5, and carefully make my way back to the table.

• • •

Ben's limousine takes us all the way back to Northampton. In the back, there is a television, stereo and wet bar. The windows are tinted, so that we can see out, but no one can see in. They make the night seem grayer and more dismal than it already is. I stretch out on the backseat. The pain has relented into a dull ache, just enough for me to remember that it's there. Carolyn sits opposite me on a small upholstered seat, her back as straight and rigid as an iron pole shooting out of her waist. "A spine of steel . . ." I catch myself thinking, the moment before I see her face.

She is crying. She turns away from me toward the window, her whole body shaking rhythmically to its own beat, a delicate flutter. She doesn't make a sound until she moans when I touch her back, just below where her hair falls. I can see the driver's head above the darkened glass partition, which I miraculously find the right button to close. It glides up soundlessly.

The rain and wet leaves are a million miles away, outside this dark blue limousine speeding along the Taconic Parkway. I trace circles on her back, applying pressure, increasing the circumference each time until no more circles can be drawn.

"Lucy?" she says my name drowsily, turning her tear-stained face toward me.

"What?" I ask, pushing a few damp strands of hair behind her ear.

"I will always be your friend."

Her head drops, resting against the window, her sleepy breath fogging up the glass. In the disappearing mist, with my fingernail, I etch her name and watch until it fades completely.

———

When I close my eyes, I can almost see your scornful face in front of me, cold and white and incomplete, like one of Michelangelo's unfinished statues.

You have become that alien to me. That remote. Some days I manage not to think of you at all. Some days, I go about my business like a woman of the world, one of the millions of women populating the subways of this city, each carrying her own secret behind dark sunglasses, or tightly between clenched knees.

We are not the only ones with secrets. Just walk through a cemetery, or certain wards of any hospital. Look around you. Sometimes I think we are surrounded by nothing but shards and bones, the ashes of lives. Sometimes I close my eyes while walking down the street. This is when I think of you.

———

Grandma is turned daily, like a roast on a spit. It takes two nurses to lift her; she has grown heavy from eighteen years of baby food, but she's never had a single bedsore. Her skin is as smooth and unblemished as an infant's.

I've heard stories about what happened when they took my grandfather's body to the cemetery, though I wasn't there. I was at home, lying on my back in my crib, my feet pedaling the air. I was watching the hazy colors of the mobile sway in the breeze over my head. I strained as hard as I could, lifting up my pudgy arms, but no matter how I tried, I couldn't touch them.

My grandmother wasn't at the cemetery either. She was in the back of an ambulance, breathing into a respirator. She didn't hear the siren wailing, parting traffic on Amsterdam Avenue. She didn't see her daughter-in-law sitting by her side, tightly holding her hand, saying, "Come on, Mama. You can't leave us now."

All she saw was a strangely familiar tunnel; it was dark, yet somehow enticing. "Death," she thought to herself, "death." It was inviting. She saw *Hamalach Hamavet*, the angel of death, standing at the end of the tunnel. Something was wrong. He was waving at her. "Go back, Leah, go back," he was saying. "It's not your time."

"When?" she screamed into the black shaft. "Why?"

"You are not to ask questions, Leah," he whispered.

And then he was gone.

At the cemetery, the story goes, the procession of limousines filled the old Brooklyn street. On the radios inside the limousines, news broadcasters solemnly intoned: "On a sad note, the great Jewish scholar and philanthropist Jacob Greenburg is being laid to rest in Bensonhurst today . . . Mr. Greenburg's wife, Leah, collapsed at the funeral. She is in critical condition upon arrival at Mount Sinai Hospital."

Policemen were on every corner directing traffic, until finally the procession ground to a halt. The pallbearers lifted the pine box to their shoulders. The rest of the trip to the family plot was to be on foot. My father came out of the cemetery office, his coat flailing around him in the October wind. He was shaking his head. The grave diggers had opened the wrong grave.

There was a flurry of whispers. It was the grave diggers' lunch hour. They wanted to eat. This group of old Jews would have to wait. The men set Jacob Greenburg's casket down, resting it on the front end of the hearse. There was a further exchange, this time with a handshake full of money.

The grave diggers set to work. Within an hour, they had completed their task. They motioned to my father, who with five other men hoisted Jacob Greenburg's remains onto their shoulders, and began the perilous walk to the family plot.

When they arrived, there were gasps and a swell of murmurs throughout the crowd. There were two gaping holes in the snow-covered ground, one next to the other. The hole that had been dug by mistake was next to my grandfather's. It had been reserved for his wife, who was at that moment lying on a metal stretcher in the emergency room of Mount Sinai Hospital as her husband's remains were slowly lowered into the crusty ground.

My grandmother's grave has never been properly closed. The men shoveled the earth back in, making the ground as level as they could. But whereas ivy grows in abundance around my grandfather's headstone, no growing thing has ever taken to the land next to it, where Grandma will someday lie. A few weeds sprout up, and whenever we visit the cemetery, we carefully remove them, pulling them out by their roots. Nothing lasts. After eighteen years, it still looks like an aberration, a new grave, a long mound of earth rising slightly out of the ground. Jacob Greenburg's marble head-stone watches over it like a single shining eye.

My crib is filled with the softest blankets, and the sidebars are stenciled with leaves, birds and flowers.

"Death," my father's breath grazes my ear, "death. It is an eternity."

He pulls me onto his lap, turns my face toward his.

" 'O God, before I was formed I was of no worth, and now that I have been formed I am but as though I had not been formed. Dust am I in my life: how much more so in my death. Behold I am before Thee like a vessel filled with shame and confusion. O may it be Thy will, O Lord my God and God of my fathers, that I may sin no more. As to the sins I have committed, purge them away not by means of affliction and sore disease, but in Thine abundant compassion.' "

He brushes my downy cheek, counts ten little fingers and ten little toes. To the left of his shiny head, the mobile slowly revolves: red fades to blue, pink, green, colors I don't yet have names for. I try to focus on his face towering above me. I see the green of his eyes, his pale, unshaven face, so coarse to touch. I hear his whispers, his gentle voice telling me things I do not understand.

Carolyn and I don't see one another over Christmas vacation. This has mostly to do with geography, since she's in Connect-icut and I'm in New Jersey. Smokestacks and barren trees separate us, many miles apart.

It takes me a few days to get accustomed to sleeping alone in my old bedroom. I am used to late-night conversations, her soft voice floating above me in the darkness. I miss the din of the hallways, people pounding on doors, tipsy laughter.

My room at home is unchanged. The carpet is a shaggy

pink, and the walls are covered by orange daisies. There is a poster of a multicolored rainbow hanging above my desk. The black print underneath the curve of the rainbow says: "If you have to get out of town, get in front of the crowd, and make it look like a parade!" My mother gave it to me the summer before I left for Smith.

My locked box full of unmailed letters, rolling papers and pictures of Chris and me is in its proper hiding place underneath my winter clothes, which are packed away in mothballs. I find the box as my mother and I go through my closet, choosing what I will take back to school.

"What's this?" her eyebrows arch.

"Nothing." My cheeks are brighter than the pink of the carpet below me.

"What do you mean, nothing, Lucy. This looks like something they would use at Fort Knox."

"It's private, Mom."

"I read things in the paper, Lucy. You're not doing anything you shouldn't be doing, are you?"

"That depends on what you think I shouldn't be doing."

She doesn't answer. She thinks it's a rhetorical question.

I decide that I will take my locked box back to school with me. My mother will look for it. She will turn my closet upside down, search through my dresser drawers and under my bed. The furrows in her brow will get deeper, she will redden from the exertion. She thinks that with a key she can discover my secrets. They will come tumbling out like pieces to a puzzle. She will understand me, for once and for all.

My father sits on a low stool, dangling by a thin wire from the top of the door. He is in traction. The straps of the mechanism press under his chin, pushing his cheeks up around his eyes. He looks like a chipmunk, hanging there, watching television.

Every few hours, he releases himself to get a glass of water, with which he takes an assortment of pills. I have counted them; there are seven, in all. Three yellow, two blue and two white. After he takes them, he seems to fall asleep with his eyes open. He does not hear me when I talk to him; he is focused on the television. His hands are limp in his lap, fingers curled upwards, as if he were giving blood.

On weekends, he sits like this for hours. During the week, when he comes home from work, he makes a beeline for the family room, where he attaches himself, relieving pressure.

It has been like this for as long as I can remember.

Sometimes I sit with him, quietly watching television. He likes baseball, basketball, football and old movies. I don't like any of these things, but his nearness is comforting as an old familiar blanket, or a favorite teddy bear. He doesn't ask me questions, he doesn't look at me. But I know he likes to have me around.

I think of the big house, of what it must be like when I'm gone. In one wing, Dad would be strapped in traction. In another room, more than a shout away, my mother would be listening to an opera she has taped from the radio, fingers busy with needlepoint. The black poodle is getting old. He has cataracts, making his eyes look almost transparent. He's always loved my father best. He would be lying at his feet, as I do now, his head resting on one giant cashmere sock.

The thought depresses me, so I go outside to smoke a cigarette. I sit on the milk box in my nightgown, with my mother's ski jacket wrapped around my shoulders. I rest one hand on my stomach, feeling its flat surface, hipbones jutting out on either side; it has been empty for weeks. My breath and the smoke mingle in the frigid air. We're all alone, here, in this brick house, so imposing with its expanse of lawn, cobblestone path, Georgian columns lit up by wrought-iron lampposts. Not for the first time, I find myself missing Carolyn. I wish I could be sharing this cigarette with her, this clear night, the Big Dipper outlined so flawlessly in the sky. I could ask her all my questions. I could weep into her shoulder, soaking her nightgown with my tears.

She is probably on some exotic island, wearing nothing but suntan oil, stretched out on a white beach listening to the ebb and flow of the gentle waves. Next to her is a handsome stranger. Their hands are entwined. He is wearing a thin gold bracelet. His arms are strong, tanned and covered by dark hair. He rolls over, embracing her, as the theme song of *From Here to Eternity* swells in the background.

It is the kind of dark night particular to the suburbs. The lights from my parents' house cast an unnatural gleam on the pool, which is closed for the winter, covered by thick plastic. The Jacuzzi next to it is open, steam rising from its light blue depths. There is snow surrounding the condensation, the steady gurgling of bubbles rising up to its surface.

My father likes to take the Jacuzzi first thing in the morning. He says it helps relieve the pressure in his back, his vertebrae pressed against his spine like insects flattened against the glass pane of a window. He pads downstairs in his thick terry-cloth bathrobe and his galoshes, gingerly stepping through the snow. He places his robe and footgear on a nearby table, and wearing only bathing trunks, eases himself into the mist.

I watched my father do this early today. When I heard him creaking down the steps I went to my window, which overlooks the backyard. I watched him make his way through the snow. I watched him sink into the hot water until all I could see was his bald head bobbing like a beach ball in the waves.

After he returned to the house, I heard the rest of his morning noises. The jangle of the poodle's leash, the clicking of the front door. I imagined them walking through the dawn, a big man and his little black shadow. I listened to their return, the clatter of keys, the whistling of the teapot, the rattling of pills in their amber plastic container. There was a brief thumbing through newspaper, probably *The Wall Street Journal,* the opening of garage doors, the whining of a car motor. And then he was gone.

I never feel more alone than when I watch my father from a distance. A few years ago, when I had a day off from high school, I surprised him by arriving at the New York Stock Exchange, where he worked. I sent a note in with the guard, and leaned back against a wall, watching harried-looking men rush around me, pencils poised on little white pads.

After a few minutes, my father came rushing out from the swinging doors.

"Lucy! What's the matter?" He stared at me, panting, waiting for bad news.

"Nothing, Dad. I was in the city, and I just thought . . ."

I stopped speaking when I looked at his face. He was ashen. He placed one hand on the guard's table, steadying himself.

"I'm sorry," I told him. "I should have called first."

Any news is bad news. All surprises are foreboding.

"No," he hugged me close. "No. I'm glad you're here. It's just . . . never mind. Let's go have lunch."

We rode the elevator to the top floor. He kept one arm around me, assuring himself that I was there. Beads of perspiration lingered on his forehead.

"Mickey, I'd like you to meet my daughter, Lucy," he introduced me to an older man wearing a tan jacket, similar to my father's.

"You're both wearing the same jacket," I whispered to my father.

He laughed. "All traders wear tan jackets. It makes us stand out in the madhouse down there." He gestured below him to the huge room which I had seen only in newspaper photographs. He wore an oval name tag, JOSEPH GREENBURG #146, pinned to the pocket of his jacket. I remember being proud that my father had a number, that he belonged.

We walked into the Stock Exchange dining room, which looked like a men's club. The tables were covered with white linen, offset by the mahogany walls, upon which hung stuffed heads of bulls and bears.

"Louie, could you get my daughter and me a table?" my father asked a white-coated waiter who looked like he'd been there for a hundred years.

We made our way to a corner table. "Ulmer, John, Matthew, meet my daughter, Lucy."

My father introduced me all around. Everywhere I turned,

I was shaking hands with suited men as my father stood proudly by my side.

"So, Joe. This is your daughter. I can't believe it! Where'd she get her looks? Must be from her mother."

There was backslapping, hands on shoulders, physical camaraderie between these men. It was a side of my father I had never seen. He was a part of this world, with his jacket, his identification number, his nicknames and beaming boyishness.

I ate a salade niçoise cut up into tiny pieces, the way I like it. I drank brewed coffee, with cream and Sweet 'n Low. I sat back in my soft leather chair feeling safer, more cherished than I ever had. I wasn't just Lucy. I was Joseph's daughter. I would never be alone.

My father walked me to Broadway and Wall, and flagged down a cab. He kissed me good-bye, encircling me in his arms. As the cab headed uptown, I watched him out of the back window. He walked quickly back to work, turning around to wave twice. I watched him recede into the crowd of men until I had lost sight of him completely. I found myself crying, though I didn't know why.

I go back to the Stock Exchange to visit my father as frequently as I can. I love this side of him, so different from the father I am accustomed to seeing at home, hanging in his contraption, watching television with glassy eyes and a pocket full of pills. My father, who masterfully parts traffic to hail me a cab, who gently places me inside with one hand on my elbow, is not the stooped man I see now, who is praying in the living room, facing east through the window, toward Jerusalem, in the direction of the Wailing Wall.

"Daddy, can I talk to you?" I ask him when I enter the house after my fifth cigarette.

"Shhh, darling. I'm davening." He shakes his head. Murmured words of Hebrew rise and fall.

I watch him. His eyes are shut tight, his brow is creased. The yarmulke on top of his head has a bobby pin attached to it. I wonder about this, because my father has no hair upon which to secure the bobby pin. It must be an old yarmulke, maybe from his youth, when blond hair sprung like wheat from his scalp, when a strong breeze might have whipped his hair around his face and his yarmulke would have sailed into the wind, a sort of embroidered Frisbee flying high above the trees in Central Park.

He cradles the prayer book in both hands, but he doesn't look at it. He's known these words since birth. When he was in Leah's womb, she took him to temple. He heard the chants through the amniotic sac, through the red layers of her belly. He kicked as the men swayed. He bowed, in the fetal position.

Whereas Leah took my father to temple in her belly, my mother carried me to the opera. She tells me my favorite was *Madame Butterfly*.

Daddy opens his eyes, blinks twice and looks at me as though coming out of a deep sleep. His prayers for the night are over.

"What's up, shnookie?" He rumples my hair.

"Nothing important. I just wanted to talk." I am still standing in the doorway, ski jacket over my nightgown.

"So, talk." He looks at me. He expects something particular, concrete information, an agenda.

I begin to weep. Tears come without warning, an uncontrollable, salty flood streaming down the front of my nightgown. I wrap my mother's ski jacket tighter around me.

"Lucy, what's the matter, what's the matter . . ." He holds me close, pushing my head into his shoulder with a large hand. My nose is squashed into his soft neck brace, which muffles my sobs. He hands me a clean hanky.

"Sit down. Tell me what's wrong." He takes in every plane of my face, searching.

I look up at him, at his round face, his yarmulke, his eyes alert and frightened. What can I tell him? There are prayers for the sick and wounded, prayers for those fallen in battle, memorial prayers for next of kin who have departed. There is

a prayer for just about anything imaginable, except this un-
nameable fear, this emptiness I carry with me, mute and in-
sidious as a disease.

I do not realize now what it is that I am mourning for. I do
not picture in my mind's eye the microscopic hands and feet,
the illustrations I have seen many times of a six-week-old em-
bryo.

I will have to wait for Yom Kippur, the anniversary of my
grandfather's death. I will beat my chest with a clenched fist.
I will atone for my sins. I will pound my breast again and
again, admitting to every sin that is listed.

"For the sin wherein we have sinned before Thee by breaking off the yoke, and for the sin wherein we have sinned
before Thee by contentiousness; For the sin wherein we have
sinned before Thee by ensnaring our neighbor, and for the
sin wherein we have sinned before Thee by envy; For the sin
wherein we have sinned before Thee by a breach of trust, and
for the sin we have sinned before Thee by terror of the
heart."

The inventory goes on and on. When I was a child, I ada-
mantly refused to recite any of the list.

"But Daddy! I didn't do any of these things," I would tell
him, thrusting out my lower lip.

"You have a lifetime ahead of you," he would answer me.
So I would sit next to him in shul, my mouth pressed tightly
together. I figured that if I didn't admit to anything, it would
never come true. I would never grow up. I would never enter
the adult world of evil and redemption.

"What's the matter, Lucy. What's the matter, honey, what's
the matter . . ." my father repeats, whispering into my hair.

We sit on the sofa, his hand resting on top of my head. He
wants to help me, but he doesn't know how. In another room,
strains of Puccini, of Dame Sutherland's mounting aria
pierce the silent air, almost shattering glass.

Northampton is frozen solid. Icicles hang like swords from every windowsill. Everything is white. The sky, the snow, the paths which students carefully negotiate in their snow boots. I get back to my room early. My parents have given me a car, a 1978 Mustang, straight out of *Consumer Reports'* safe and practical listings. Driving up here this morning, I didn't wear my seat belt. I blared Crosby, Stills, Nash & Young on the tape deck, singing along at the top of my lungs. I smoked cigarette after cigarette, tossing the butts out the window along the snowbanked sides of the Taconic Parkway. I tapped the steering wheel with one gloved hand, feeling more free, more alive than I had in a month. I let the wind in through an open window, and it stung my face.

Everything seems possible today. I unpack my sweaters, pausing to stretch. I push my shoulders back, feeling my neck lengthen and crack. I light a scented candle, put fresh sheets on my bed, beating the down comforter until it fluffs up. Through the window I see Paradise Pond, covered with ice skaters' tracks like wrinkles in an old woman's face. Through the walls I hear footsteps, slamming doors, laughter.

I decide to take a shower in the bathroom down the hall. There are two shower stalls, six toilets and four sinks. I pad down the corridor in my new silk robe, a Chanukah present from my mother. In my arms I hold soft pink towels which smell like home.

The trickles of water make their way slowly down my up-turned face. The water pressure here is almost nonexistent, but it is hot, so I stand still, inhaling the steam. I unwrap the almond-scented soap which I charged to my father's account at the drugstore (along with candles, massage oil and body lotion), and make figure eights around my stomach with its smooth, waxy surface.

I am enjoying having the big bathroom all to myself. I shake my hair, sending drops of water flying. I pull a towel around me, absorbing moisture. I look in the mirror. I have lost weight in the last few months. My legs are thin, and my rear end, which has never been my strong point, is high and firm. I can count my ribs, which I do. I have six on each side.

When Carolyn walks in, I am standing like a stork by the sink, one leg lifted high onto the basin, shaving. She stands watching in the doorway.

"Don't stop on my account," she says, "I should go get my camera."

"Why?" I stop, razor poised in midair.

"You look like an advertisement for shaving cream, or towels, or college bathrooms," she smiles at me, still standing there. "You do wonders for all three."

Her leather suitcase sits by her feet, and a tote bag is slung over one shoulder. She has a new haircut, soft layers falling around her face, framing her cheekbones, making her large, dark eyes seem even wider than before. Of course, she is tan. I have rarely seen Carolyn without a tan. It is as if she was born in the sun. She is wearing a light yellow sweater and tight faded jeans tucked into impractical suede boots.

"Come back to the room," she tells me, and walks away. She has not come over to give me a hug, to kiss me, to say hello. After she leaves, I quickly finish shaving, nicking myself in the process. I encircle my neck with the wet towel, and wrap my robe around me as I make my way back up the hall.

When I walk in the door, she is standing there with camera in hand.

"Take off your beautiful new robe," she says quickly, quietly.

I untie the sash, and my robe falls like a whisper to the floor. I am more naked than I've ever been. My nipples grow hard in the cold, and something deep in my stomach contracts. With one slender finger Carolyn wipes the last bit of shaving cream from behind my knee.

She places her antique quilt over the armchair, arranging it so that the folds hang in even ripples.

"Sit down," she commands me in the same low voice. She chooses a lens from her camera case, twisting it until it snaps into place.

I sit on the edge of the chair, my legs crossed, hands folded over my breasts. My hair lies wet on my back.

"Lucy, that isn't sitting. That's posing. Relax," she tells me, standing in the center of the room.

She adjusts the light, moving the scented candle over to a small table next to my chair. I ease back, feeling the curve of the seat underneath me. The quilt smells like Carolyn: a combination of Shalimar and Ivory soap.

The only sound in the room is that of the shutter clicking. I begin to loosen, layers falling away easily, carelessly, like a child opening a box full of tissue paper, eager to get at the core. I am amazed that I'm comfortable like this, my arms falling to my sides, Carolyn crouched on one knee, shooting up at me. My thoughts seem to come to me through a distant mist; they are diluted. I think everything is fine, finer than it has ever been.

Click. My legs are crossed at the thigh, my arms resting on either side of the armchair. I look down. My breasts seem to float above my rib cage, as buoyant as if they were resting on water. I close my eyes, tilting my head until it falls all the way back. *Click.* I lift one arm above my head, angling it, exposing a freshly shaved armpit. I swivel slightly, jutting one hip slightly toward the camera, toward Carolyn. *Click.* I raise my other arm, cradling my head with both hands. I keep my eyes closed. This is my world: this heat, this quiet, this darkness. I hear the whir of the camera closer to my face. She is to one side of me, then to the other, then directly in front of me. I don't want to see her face. I don't want her to see mine. There is a camera between us, a mechanical, impartial witness, in black and white.

I sink deeper. I think about the day I met her, the firm, cool handshake, the level gaze, the same gaze which is now leveled at me. I think of the train ride, her damp head against my shoulder, the way she held me outside the brownstone on East Sixty-first Street. "I'll be with you," she told me that day. "Nothing will hurt you," she said. "Everything will be all right."

Weekends she is gone without a trace. Many nights her bed

remains untouched. Whole weeks she disappears, returning with a tan, always laughing, "No, I'm not tan," eyes looking directly into mine, defiant, never giving in.

She has secrets. She understands the nature of silence. She knows how to hide, and how never to be found.

The clicking stops. Carolyn is inches away from me. She is kneeling in front of me. I feel her breath on my shins. I begin to shake, an uncontrollable shudder which begins with my toes and spreads upward until my whole body is moving independently, and I can no longer tell it what to do.

"Lucy, look at me." Her voice is trembling. I keep my eyes closed. I see a sort of triptych of purple and blue. My mind's eye absorbs me with its shifting colors. The only undeviating element is the black line running down the middle. There are two distinct sides.

"Open your eyes," she asks me. She is so near that she only has to whisper. I feel her hair brushing my knee.

"I can't," I say. I am in a perfect, weightless moment, a precipice, balanced between going forward and looking back. I am dead center between the purple and blue, the black and white. I am in the middle of the triptych. I want to stay like this, sitting on the line, straddling the fence.

"Why?" She kisses the inside of one knee, gently parting them with her mouth.

"I don't know . . ."

I'm stalling. I want to remain here, in this hour before life shifts imperceptibly, hanging in the balance.

Her tongue is soft. She is tracing a wet line up my thigh. Her hands touch my hipbones, then move higher.

"Carolyn, this can't happen." My voice comes out in a whisper, in a croak.

"Why?"

She doesn't believe me. She is used to getting her way. Her fingers encircle my nipples, which are now hard for reasons other than the cold January air.

I moan. I shake. My hips rise and fall. In one more second I will have no choice in the matter.

"Carolyn, this isn't going to happen."

I force open my eyes. The black line disappears. She looks up at me from between my legs. Her eyes are moist, and her mouth is moister. She is still wearing her light yellow sweater, tight jeans and knee-high suede boots. I am wearing gold hoops in my ears, and a Timex on my wrist.

I focus on the room, its familiar outlines falling into place. The scented candle has filled the air with jasmine. Carolyn sits cross-legged on the floor, her cheek against the side of the chair. I stroke her head, my fingers gliding easily through the layers of her new haircut. She is staring out the window, into the gathering dusk. The fading sunlight casts red shadows across her face. Between us, her camera lies, black and mechanical, like a bomb.

I cover myself with my robe, tying the sash in a double bow. I try to run a comb through my hair, but it is matted from the previous hour. Carolyn comes up behind me.

"Bird's nests?" she asks with her same old smile.

I hand her the comb.

"This may hurt," she tells me, gathering up a few strands of hair at a time, carefully unknotting them.

It doesn't hurt. I don't feel a thing. When she is finished, I turn around. I look at her, I keep my eyes on hers as I move closer and closer to her face.

"Don't close your eyes," I murmur.

She is perfectly still. With every inch, her eyes seem wider. I see flecks of green and gold the instant before I feel her eyelashes on mine, the instant before I kiss her.

The first thing I notice is an absence of stubble. Her cheeks are as smooth and cold as marble. Her tongue feels strangely like my own. I hold her head in both hands as I explore her mouth. We stand like this, eyes open, too close to see anything at all.

I love her. This sentence, the smallest of sentences, forms in my head so clearly that for a terrifying moment I wonder whether I've said it out loud. I look at her, soft and unfocused, and realize that I haven't. I am grateful for this, because I have no idea what these particular words, in this particular context, can possibly mean.

I wonder why it never occurred to me that this would happen. Now that it has, it seems as inevitable as a tidal wave, or an electrical summer storm. It sends me reeling over to my dresser, where I find my long johns and a sweatshirt. I get dressed in record time, and before either of us knows what is happening, I race out the door, car keys in hand.

"I'll be back," I tell her, but she just looks at me deliberately, as if to let me know that she's heard it all before.

I decide to walk into town. The Christmas lights are still up, strung along the streets, showing me the way. On one lawn there is a sculpture of Rudolph and all eight reindeer. On another, there is the baby Christ in the manger. There are wreaths, Christmas trees, multicolored lights.

I walk, in a trance, into Fitzwilly's. It's eight o'clock at night, just past happy hour, and the restaurant is filled with families of four enjoying rib-eye steaks and side orders of onion rings. There are jars of crayons on every table; children brandish them with glee, coloring everything they can get their hands on.

I sit at the bar watching my reflection in the mirror behind bottles of scotch. I am flushed from the cold, and my eyes look wild. I order a Dewars on the rocks, and try to control my shaking hands as I raise the glass to my lips. The bar mirror is stenciled with candy canes and holly, punctuated by glittering white snow. The scotch burns down my throat, warming my empty stomach. I play with the lemon peel, running it along my bottom teeth.

Carolyn's face floats in front of me like a lovely ghost. This can't happen. I still feel her mouth lingering on mine. Carolyn, this isn't going to happen. I have escaped. I have paddled my way safely ashore. I am on comfortable ground.

I order another drink.

"Taking a break from studying?" the bartender asks me.

"Sort of."

He's cute. Thirtyish, unshaven, dark chest hair poking out of the top of his flannel shirt.

"You go to Smith?" he asks.

"Yeah."

"What's your name?"

"Lucy."

"Well, Lucy, this one's on me." He smiles, revealing deep dimples, setting down my drink on a clean napkin.

"Got a cigarette?" I ask him.

He shakes out a pack of Marlboros, giving me two.

The restaurant is full, but the bar is unusually empty. There are two older men sitting at the opposite end, hands curved around the handles of their beer mugs. Weekends, this place is filled with college students, but tonight no one is here. People are back at school doing what I should be doing: unpacking, arranging their rooms, cracking books open that they haven't looked at in a month.

I wonder what Carolyn is doing. Perhaps she is sitting in that very same armchair, her quilt spread over her lap, reading Baudelaire. Perhaps she is smoking a cigarette, as I do now, and is lazily watching the smoke drift up, hovering around her head like a halo. Perhaps she is wondering what I am doing.

Is she frightened? Do her hands shake, as mine do now, as she lowers her cigarette, inhaling deeply? Or is this, as everything else is with Carolyn, no big deal. Will her mouth return to its scornful contours, will she disappear next weekend, will she dare me to inquire as to her whereabouts, her tan, her suitcase full of money? Will her back remain erect, will she pretend this never happened? Nothing happened. Almost doesn't count.

The bartender leans into the bar.

"Lucy, my name's Bobby," he says. He smiles, reaching over to take my hand. He's not wearing a wedding ring; I think he's interested.

He refills my glass, dropping another lemon peel into the amber liquid.

"Lucy, how would you feel about keeping me company until the end of my shift, and then maybe we can go somewhere?"

I stick my finger into the glass, twirling it around the ice cubes. Beneath the bar, my hands are damp.

"That sounds like just what the doctor ordered," I say in an attempt to be cool.

I have never done anything like this in my life, but anything seems safer than the place I just came from.

"Good," he says, mildly surprised, "I'll be off at eleven."

Bobby and I don't talk for the rest of the evening. I catch him looking at me, but he quickly turns away. I wonder if this is a regular occurrence in his line of work, picking up college women at Fitzwilly's.

He seems shy despite the way he approached me. I am somehow emboldened by this. Up until now, the only man I've slept with has been Chris Mulcahy.

Tonight that's going to change. I'm going to go back to Bobby's apartment, wearing my long johns and a Smith sweatshirt. I will ride in his car with him to an apartment he shares, on the edge of town. He will borrow a bottle of something strong from the restaurant, and we will sit on his bed, drinking out of water glasses. He will put his hand on my waist, not sure, and I will unbutton his shirt, making things clear. I will run my hands over his curly hair, down, farther down, until I find what I am looking for.

He will gasp as he grows in my hand. I will bend over him on the bed. There will be no woods, no ragged hole in the fence, no smell of pine needles and sap. There will be only the creaking bed, a rough afghan blanket, Miles Davis playing on the radio.

He will expand inside me, he will come in a ragged rush, and then I will tell him I want to leave. He will silently drive me to the main gate, lightly put his finger on my lips, and mouth good-bye.

———

I get back to the room at four in the morning. I slowly turn my key in the lock, gently opening the door so it won't creak. I tiptoe through the darkness, trying not to stumble, feeling my way toward the lamp on my bedside table, turning it on low.

Carolyn is not in her bed. This is one possibility that hadn't occurred to me.

There is, however, a pile of freshly dried photographs staring up at me from my pillow. I stare at the top of the stack. It is a black-and-white picture of curves and angles, knees and hips. My skin looks alabaster in the light, flecked with shadows cast from the candle, which is still burning, blue wax spilling onto the wooden table.

I pick up the whole pile, which is somewhat warped, the way pictures developed in college darkrooms late at night usually are. I sit on the edge of my bed, holding them as if they were hot, as if they could burn me.

I quickly begin to leaf through them, not pausing to look carefully at any single one, afraid of seeing a suggestion, a hint of what I had been feeling, captured forever on negatives which are nowhere to be found.

There are my thighs, my stomach with a deep indentation running up the middle, as if I had been inhaling, as if I had been holding my breath. There are my breasts, lying wide apart, nipples staring frankly at the camera in a way my eyes couldn't.

Look at me, she had said. Lucy, open your eyes.

There are my arms, held high above my head in surrender. There is a photograph taken from an angle above me, my legs crossed, a triangle of blond hair peeking out from between them.

All of the images are of parts of me: legs, neck, shoulders, knees, ankles, hands, except for the last photograph in the pile. It is the picture I have been waiting for, the one of my face, the one which tells the story, in case memory does not suffice, in case I am able to forget. As I look at it, I feel a trickle of wetness between my legs as Bobby begins to leak out of me.

My head is tilted back, eyes barely shut, mouth slightly parted, shining in the faint light. My hair falls over one shoulder. My neck strains upward. The corners of my mouth are turned up into an unwitting, ecstatic smile.

My dreams are visible. They are etched onto this thick paper, so lifelike that the black-and-white image seems ready to move, to softly moan, to speak another language. The invisible body underneath is writhing, toes clenched, stomach fluttering.

The face defines the unseen body, cut off below the shoulders, leaving everything to the imagination. The full lips become breasts, the cheekbones are hips, the jawline becomes the curve of a thigh. The closed eyes are the secret place, unexplored depths.

It is a portrait of a woman caught in this moment, oblivious to the quiet click of the camera, unaware of everything but the soft hand on her waist, the question suspended in the air. She cares about nothing except for this hand, this question. The furthest thing from her mind is that she is being watched and recorded by an impartial witness, like an exotic bird headed for extinction.

———

I would give anything to understand what began that night. To this day, it is a secret I carry with me, it is something that stands between me and the world in the way that secrets do.

You know about secrets, those words you keep beneath your tongue like melting ice. You know all about the loneliness of silence; I suppose he taught you, in the same way that, eventually, he taught me.

It is a bitter lesson, Carolyn.

I don't suppose we'll ever talk about it, that is, if our paths ever cross again. If we ran into one another on the street, in a European city or a small New England town, we might not even say hello.

I would feel my blood turn thin and cold, rushing downward, in the direction of my feet. My face would flush—no number of years will ever cure me of that—and I might look at you quickly, then away. My arms might raise involuntarily from my sides in a gesture, an offering.

What would you do, if you were me?

———

On the day my parents signed the mortgage papers for their new home, my father asked Jacob and Leah to come see the house and give their blessing. There are snapshots taken from this day, the only pictures I have of my grandfather and me together.

"Family," my father has said to me, "is the cornerstone of life. Without it, things cannot grow. See that pine tree out back? It was a sapling when we moved here. Now it towers above all the rooftops. The rainwater, the careful pruning . . ."

He would smile at me, ruffling my fine hair as if *I* were the sapling, as if his touch would turn me into a mighty tree, strong and unflappable in the wind.

I have the snapshots from the day my grandparents saw the old house. They lie in my top dresser drawer between notebooks and unfinished term papers, their corrugated edges peeking out like ruffled fans. Jacob cradled me in his arms as he walked up the cobblestone path leading to the front door. There is a black-and-white photograph of his face and mine, his pince-nez glinting as he gazed down with enormous pride at this child he would never get to know.

"Now this is *balebatish*," he told my father, voicing his approval. Both men wore seersucker suits and straw fedoras; my grandfather carried an ivory-tipped cane. On the cobblestone street in front of the house, his new light blue Chrysler convertible gleamed in the New Jersey sun.

They can tell me my grandfather was a scholar all they want, and I have even read his books, but I know this: my grandfather was also a dandy.

Leah and my mother walked arm in arm behind them, an older woman with her new daughter-in-law, both wearing pale spring suits and mink stoles. My mother leaned into Leah's shoulder affectionately and called her "Mama." She wanted to belong to this family, where no one did anything without the others' blessings. What in later years she decided had been suffocating, on this sunny day seemed like the answer to all of life's uncertainties.

My grandparents spent that leafy Sunday on the sprawling back lawn, years before the swimming pool was dug and the grass was covered by concrete and plastic garden chairs.

I crawled up Jacob's belly toward the face so much like my father's. I stuck my fingers into his mouth, up his nostrils, trying to grab the pince-nez so precariously balanced on his nose. I rubbed my face against his rough stubble. I drooled on his starched white shirt as he laughed, holding me above him and whirling me around.

My mother has told me I was Jacob's favorite. I was the last of his twenty-five grandchildren, and the only progeny of his son. Perhaps he knew I would be the last Greenburg, or at least the last one he would ever know. Perhaps he had seen a sign, some parting of the clouds before he fell in the park that Yom Kippur. Perhaps he awoke in the early hours of morning to see angels dancing on his pillow, lost spirits descending on one who was near to them, one who would soon turn into nothing more than glittering dust.

In the picture I now keep thumbtacked to my bulletin board, Jacob and I are lying in a hammock. The hammock is to him as his soft belly is to me, an immensely comfortable place. Our profiles, as we look at each other, are oddly similar. His head is bald from age, mine from youth. His smile is the childlike, giddy result of a man who has earned the right to be happy in the world; my uncontained glee comes from not having been in the world very long. We both have double chins: he grew into his, and I eventually outgrew mine.

———

Carolyn doesn't return for several days. She misses three quizzes and the deadline for one paper.

"Where's Carolyn?" This question gets asked again and again by friends, teachers and guidance counselors. As if I should know.

I shrug my shoulders.

"I'm only her roommate," I tell them.

Tonight there's a knock on my door. This is unusual. People generally just barge in. *Rat-tat-tat.* The sound jars me away from my book.

"Come in," I yell, not willing to give up the comfort of the armchair, my afghan wrapped around me. I have retreated in the past few days. I go to class, perfunctorily practice the piano, and otherwise stay in my room reading, and listening to Bach Inventions until I can separate the two melodic lines, exactly the same yet a beat apart.

Carolyn's mother pokes her head into the room. I am stunned for a moment. It is as if Carolyn is back, aged twenty years, wearing a silk suit and carrying a lizard handbag. It is more than a physical resemblance; they both have the same level gaze which only seems to be acquired in finishing school.

This gaze, for the moment, is fixed on me.

"Hello, Lucy," she says, "where's Carolyn?"

Where's Carolyn, where's Carolyn. It's enough to make one crawl beneath the covers, or take to drink, or pick up strange men in bars.

"I don't know," I tell her, rising out of my armchair comfort.

"You don't know?" She looks at me, raising one eyebrow.

I suddenly feel the urge to protect Carolyn. Unfortunately, I'm a bad liar, so this impulse does not carry me too far.

"Um . . ." I stammer, "I think she's in the library."

Mrs. Broadhurst looks at her watch.

"It's midnight," she says icily. "I have been driving for two hours. Where is my daughter. I have been calling for days. No one answers. I want some answers around here." Each word is carefully punctuated, a staccato blast.

I look at her. I am at a loss for words. She is like no mother I've ever known. She is very young. She must be under forty. She is also very beautiful, like a magazine advertisement, full of color and frozen in time. Carolyn will someday look just like this.

"Fine," she bites off, "I'll just wait."

She sits on Carolyn's bed, her back shooting up like a perpendicular arrow.

"How's your family?" I ask her in an attempt at small talk.

"You don't need to be polite, Lucy," she tells me, "don't let me interrupt you. Go back to whatever you were doing. I'll just wait until my daughter gets back."

I pick up my book, but I can't concentrate at all. Mrs. Broadhurst is tapping her fingernails on Carolyn's bedside table. She sighs; the bed creaks as she shifts her weight. The words dance in front of me on the page, rearranging themselves into a senseless jumble. What does she want? Why is she here?

I fall asleep with my book folded over my chest. My piano teacher appears before me in a murky dream, holding a ruler in her hand as she paces the music room, listening to me practice my finger exercises. She walks back and forth, floorboards creaking beneath her in time with the arpeggios and broken chords. I keep waiting for the thwack of the ruler to come crashing down over my knuckles. I play faster and faster in an attempt to escape.

I am startled out of my dream by Carolyn's mother standing before me. When I open my eyes I shriek, scaring both of us.

"I'm sorry!" She backs off, eyes wide.

"It's all right," I mumble, "it was just a dream."

She stares at me, her head cocked to one side, assessing my bleary eyes, sleep-puffed face and tangle of hair.

"How do you stay so thin?" she asks me.

Your daughter, I want to tell her, I want to shake her by the shoulders, so much like Carolyn's. *Somewhere along the line, I decided to be just like her. I decided adversity could agree with me.*

"Cottage cheese," I smile at her, "cottage cheese and bran muffins."

She sits back down on the bed, yawning as she stretches her arms downward. She must have been driving for hours. I find myself feeling sorry for her. The fine lines around her lovely mouth are not from smiling.

"Mrs. Broadhurst, can I make you some coffee?" I ask her.

"Please, call me Liz."

She looks so much like a "Mrs." with her hair perfectly combed into place, her huge diamond ring, her legs crossed, just so, at the ankle.

"Liz, can I get you some coffee," I repeat.

She nods. I pad down the hall in my bare feet. The lights are off under all the doors, and the hall lights are dimmed. There is a stillness to the air in this corridor usually so filled with life. Every noise I make sounds louder than necessary as I stand in the kitchen waiting for the water to boil. The little illumination comes from the open refrigerator door.

The only coffee we have is decaffeinated; if I don't tell her, maybe she won't know the difference. I pour the instant coffee and powdered milk into a mug which says JANICE on it. Janice lives down the hall. She won't mind. I fill the cup with boiling water, and it slops over the brown carpet as I head back to my room.

"Delicious, thank you," Liz says, cradling the ceramic mug. "I'll finish this, and if she's not back, I'll be going," she tells me.

She looks tired, holding the keys to her Mercedes in one hand, jingling them in a silver melody.

"Carolyn's not coming back tonight," I say quietly, half hoping she won't hear me.

"I know," she says, "I know." She searches my face.

"Lucy, do you know where she is? Please tell me," she pleads. Her large brown eyes fill up, threatening to spill over.

Damn her, where is she?

"Honestly, I have no idea. She hasn't been around for days," I tell her.

"Was she . . . was she OK the last time you saw her? I mean, did she seem all right to you?"

She ran her tongue down the inside of my thigh, as soft and deceptive as a trickle of water. I can still feel her hands when a cold wind hits my back.

"Fine," I say, "she seemed fine."

Elisabeth Broadhurst wraps one small hand around Carolyn's bedpost. I watch her knuckles turn from pink to white.

"I think I have some idea where she is," she says grimly, more to herself than to me. She finishes her coffee in several thirsty gulps.

"Thank you, Lucy," she says, composing herself. The mask is back in place, implacable and cool as marble.

She pulls a compact out of her handbag, then brushes fine beige powder over her nose and under her eyes. She barely says good-bye as she shuts the door behind her. Through my window I watch her climb into her car. I hear the whine of the engine as she slowly negiotiates her way down the icy driveway. She will trudge along the deserted, snowbanked streets of Northampton until she reaches the highway, which will curve before her like a black snake. The only sound for miles will be a psychologist answering late-night questions on her car stereo and her low sobs as she speeds her way home.

On my first day of seventh grade, my mother dressed me in argyle knee socks, a kilt my uncle had brought back from England, and a Fair Isle sweater. She brushed my blond hair until it gleamed, fastening yellow barrettes above my temples.

She stood back, holding me at arm's length, examining me with scrupulous care.

"Beautiful. Just beautiful," she sighed.

"Bee-yoo-ti-ful," echoed Bea, her best friend, who was sitting at the kitchen table drinking tea and eating a corn muffin.

"We could have used you in the camps, little blondie," Bea told me.

"Tell me again, Aunt Bea!" I exclaimed. I always loved to hear this story.

"When we were in Treblinka, twelve of us dug a tunnel and escaped into the woods. Six survived. We lived off whatever we could find. But for our bread, we would send a child, the fairest child into the town to beg for bread. You . . . we needed you, little Lucela. The fairest of them all. A regular shiksa, you are."

My mother listened, bending her head toward her steaming coffee. She and my father had not been touched by the death camps: places with thick, unpronounceable names like Auschwitz, Bergen-Belsen, Treblinka. They didn't have numbers burned into their wrists, which many of their friends had removed through plastic surgery. They didn't have thick accents, or eyes which could not help darting to windows and doors, always marking escape routes. As far as I know, they did not hide thousands of dollars in their mattress.

My mother held me tightly to her breast, showering the top of my head with kisses. This day marked the beginning of her part in my education. My father had the first half: elementary school. He sent me to the yeshiva, where I learned Hebrew, the Old Testament, and the Talmud, where I had habits ingrained in me, habits he hoped would last me the rest of my life.

My mother had the second half. This was their agreement. So I was off to prep school, the land of blond-haired people with names like Mulcahy, wearing my preppy coat of armor.

I had some notion of what my mother hoped for, as she wiped a bit of talcum powder off my temple, smiling her widest smile. She knew that no matter what I had learned in elementary school, high school would undo the damage.

My father did not say good-bye to me that morning. He left before I was out of bed. I'm sure he imagined the worst, driving to Wall Street through rush-hour traffic. Perhaps he envisioned a wedding: a tall priest with a crisp white collar stood before me and a nameless, faceless man, our blond heads catching the sun's rays.

"If anyone present knows a reason why this couple cannot be bound in holy matrimony, in front of the Father, the Son and the Holy Ghost, speak now, or forever hold your peace," the priest intoned.

My father tried to scream out, but there was no sound.

"*No,*" his face contorted, but no one could hear him. Silent tears streamed down his face; he made no attempt to wipe them away. They moistened the ground beneath him. He imagined his tears soaking through the earth's center, creating a narrow passage all the way to the Dead Sea, a sea so salty from the tears of Jews that the heaviest object remains afloat.

"A new beginning for my beautiful daughter," my mother whispered into my hair.

"Remember, people will tell you many things you may not understand. Trust no one. No one except for me. Your best friend will never tell you, but I will always tell you the truth."

She looked eagerly into my face, scanning it as if it were a map. Then she nodded, as if satisfied.

"Good," she said. "Go on, now. Knock 'em dead."

Carolyn is going to return soon. I can feel her in the air round me. The deep freeze has broken; icicles drip from their jagged points, slush is everywhere. I walk from class to class wearing only a heavy sweater, relishing the mild breeze, knowing it won't last.

I have an acute case of spring fever. Professors' words float above my head; I carry on conversations, then walk away having no idea what was said. I am filled with sensory pleasures: the sound my boots make in the crackling ice, the lone chirp of a bird, the feel of my hands thrust deep into my pockets.

Every moment seems to herald a new beginning. I catch my image reflected in the clear glass doors of the library, and for a moment don't recognize myself. My blond hair is pulled off my face with a stretchy pink band. My sweater falls just below my waist, and my legs look good, encased in Carolyn's tight, faded blue jeans. I hold a pile of books I'm returning in my arms.

I place one hand against the glass, staring at myself. "Happy Birthday to me," I sing giddily.

I am nineteen.

I spend the afternoon practicing the piano. My teacher has forced me to break down music into mathematics. Everything is logical, a priori. She has told me that nothing happens without a reason. Beethoven was a genius, yes, but not a creative madman. If you remove the romance, you will see that his music is nothing more than building on an original brilliant premise. It requires little imagination. Only a deductive mind.

My teacher, Mrs. Dodd, wears her hair down to her waist and her skirts down to the floor. Her hands are freckled and strong. With her, I diagram Mozart concertos, Chopin nocturnes, Liszt études. I draw lines, turning scores of music into charts resembling family trees.

Until today, the pleasure has been missing. Mrs. Dodd has labeled it neatly and stored it away. Arpeggios have not flown like the wind, but rather, have been named and put in their proper place. Today, my hands leap again over the language of the keyboard. I close my eyes. I play from memory. I play from the heart.

While I am playing I feel a shift in the air behind me. A door has opened; someone is walking through the room. A floorboard creaks under the click of heels, a chair groans, and then there is silence. I do not stop. I am playing a Chopin nocturne, one I've known since I was a little girl. It is a slow, repetitive piece, building to one glorious, dramatic crescendo. I am moments away. I hear the strike of a match, like a sigh. The scent of Shalimar drifts over to me, a genie taking on its own shape. The crescendo thunders through my fingers, octaves climb an intricate ladder to the peak, the dramatic moment which is made more so by the quiet lull, the hush preceding it.

She is back. I turn around slowly, swiveling my legs over the piano bench. She sits perfectly still, leaning back into a brocade armchair. Her legs are crossed, her hands rest comfortably on either side of her, and her eyes are unwavering as she looks at me. Smoke curls around her face in a whimsical mask. She can see out, but I can't see in.

Her tan is deeper. She is wearing a white cotton men's shirt; a diamond pendant I've never seen before hangs low between her breasts. Her nails are painted light pink. She pushes one fist into her cheek, leaning on it as she continues to look at me. She is waiting. Her eyes register nothing. Her neutrality is a challenge. If either of us is going to speak, it will have to be me.

"Where were you?" I ask her, dispensing with formalities, afraid of anything else.

"None of your business," she hurls at me, her eyes now on fire, every muscle in her body suddenly taut—if I touch her, I imagine she would feel inhuman under my hands, as smooth and cold as a stone on a wet beach.

"I was worried about you—"

"Worry about yourself," she interrupts, her voice sharp and thin, like the rest of her.

She rises quickly out of her chair, then strides over to the piano bench until we are standing knee to knee.

"You think you matter to me?" she whispers, an inch away from my face. "You're an infant, Lucy. You don't know a fucking thing."

She is breathing hard. Her breath smells like nicotine and spearmint gum. I feel a hot wave begin in my chest, spreading over my neck until it reaches my face and I feel my cheeks burn. I am determined not to cry. I am going to be just like Carolyn.

"Why are you doing this?" I ask her.

"I'm not doing anything," she says. She's not going to give an inch.

"Carolyn, please. I haven't stopped thinking about you. I haven't stopped asking myself whether I did the wrong thing. I'm all fucked up, Carolyn. I'm not you. I'm not anything like you. I don't have all the answers."

I am pleading with her. I have my hands on her shoulders, and I am shaking her back and forth. Her arms dangle by her sides. She has closed her eyes. She doesn't respond, but she doesn't move away. I hold her like this, afraid of letting go.

She opens her eyes. "The wrong thing?" she echoes, shrugging my hands away, "which was the wrong thing, Lucy?"

She stares at me hard, as if sizing me up for the first time. "Was it wrong to start?" A small smile plays at her lips, she is mocking me. "Or was it wrong to stop."

She steps back and crosses her arms in front of her. She tilts her head and hips to one side, as if resting on air. She is waiting; it is this patience, this endurance, which gives her power. She will stand here all night, if necessary. She will stare at me until I look away. She is holding an invisible string in her clenched fist, a string which is attached to a part of me, a muscle, perhaps, dormant from lack of use. With a flick of her wrist she can send me flying, or reel me in. She knows it, and so do I.

My voice, surprisingly, comes out when I open my mouth.

"Carolyn, I did the only thing I could do," I say.

"Ha!" She draws herself up to her full height, her chest puffs out like an opera singer's. "Ha!" she repeats, shaking her head.

I stand in my original position, inches away from the piano. Something beneath my ribs begins to open like a fist.

"I expect better, Lucy Greenburg," she tells me, reaching out one palm, open in invitation. "Tell me something I don't already know."

My face begins to collapse. I dig my nails into the inside of my left hand, hard enough to stop me, hard enough to draw blood.

"What do you want?" I ask her in my new squeaky voice. I clench my teeth, feeling the muscles bunch in my jaw. "What can I tell you?"

I want her to give me answers. I want her to lift the hair off my damp neck, murmur platitudes into my ear. I want her to tell me about the nature of truth, of love, of danger. I want her to explain it all to me.

"Oh no, Lucy. Oh no," she says wistfully, as if she had read my mind. "There are certain things you have to figure out for yourself."

My knees are about to buckle. My thighs shake as I sit back

down on the piano bench. I lift one leg, resting chin on knee as I look up at her. I am suddenly exhausted. I keep my eyes on hers as silence falls around us like a blanket. Two can play this game.

I think of the woman in the picture, eyes closed, head thrown back carelessly, disregarding the consequences; that woman has taken on an identity separate from myself. In that split second, captured on film, I see a world full of promise. A world in which anything is possible.

I stare at Carolyn until she becomes blurry, features flattening out into an indistinct terrain. She is easy to look at in this amoeba-like condition; her edges are softened. I listen to the ticking of the grandfather clock, the strains of violin scales filtering down the stairs.

Just as I am getting used to this suspended state, Carolyn breaks the lull; she steps back, leans against the wall and sighs the longest, loudest sigh I have ever heard. It sounds like I imagine a plane would, in rapid descent, right before it crashes. She shifts her gaze away from mine, focusing on a portrait of Ellen Emerson, after whom this house is named; she is a truly homely woman, peering down her nose at us like a hawk.

"Why did you stop?" she asks. "I know you didn't want to."

"No, I didn't want to," I say in little more than a whisper.

"It was so lovely," she says, still looking at the portrait. Her neck is angled away from me. I see a thin vein pulsating along the side of her throat.

"Yes," I say.

She turns to me, her eyes filling up. I take two steps toward her and grasp her hair from behind her neck, pulling her face into my shoulder. She doesn't make a sound. Her rib cage heaves as I hold her tight. Her backbones feel as fragile as a bird's wings. Every few moments she lifts her head up slightly, gasping for air.

"Ssshhh," I murmur into the top of her head, as if calming a wailing child for whom I don't know what to do. "Everything's all right," I stroke her hair softly. "I'm sorry," I whisper, again and again.

———

I know I am blind. I know I am possessed of the unique oblivion that comes with the age of nineteen. I know that the flip side of promise is deceit, that the antithesis of hope is despair. I know these things, but I pay no attention to them.

I know there is more to uncharted territory than sheer, unadulterated adventure. There is risk. It marches across your beautiful forehead in shiny gold letters. It glints at me when your mouth parts. You hold its shape in your hand.

Why didn't you warn me? I assumed you knew everything, even this: there are many ways to break a heart.

———

"Happy birthday," my mother whispers into my tiny ear. "Today you are one," she sings into the top of my downy head, covered by peach fuzz.

She tickles the bottoms of my feet, which fit into the soft part of her hand.

"Lucy Greenburg. Lucy Chaya Greenburg," she croons, kissing each toe. "That's you," she points one finger, tracing circles around my belly button, right above my diaper.

"Chaya," my mother says. "Chaya means life." She looks down at my blue eyes, as big as saucers, so different from her own.

She picks me up from underneath my arms, holding me in the air, facing her.

"You, my little one," she tells me, "you are going to have the most wonderful life." She speaks slowly, so that I will understand.

———

Carolyn takes me out for my birthday. Her face is still swollen, her eyes red even after Visine. We walk into town, taking advantage of the mild February night. We link arms as we walk through the dark streets. We don't speak; for the moment, there is nothing left to say. My limbs feel heavy. I push one foot in front of the other, dragging my heels.

"I came back because it was your birthday," she had told me earlier, when her head was still buried in my shoulder.

"I'm so glad," I had said.

"Let's go out tonight," she said, perking up. "Let's go to Fitzwilly's."

I started to laugh. I laughed until my face stung, until I started to hiccup. "We can't go there, Carolyn," I told her.

"Why not?"

"Never mind. You have your secrets, and I have mine."

She looked at me then, with something akin to adoration.

"Well, well," she said, sniffling.

We both laughed, the sound filling the quiet air as we walked through the twilight, back to our room.

We go, instead, to Beardsly's, a fancy French restaurant neither of us has been to before. The maître d' seats us at a front table.

"Pretty mademoiselles should sit where everyone can see them," he tells us with a wink.

The table is covered by thick white linen; a small bowl filled with waxy orchids sits in the center. Carolyn asks to see the wine list, then proceeds to order a bottle of bordeaux in a perfect French accent.

"I didn't know you spoke French," I tell her.

"I don't speak French. I just speak wine lists."

She is nineteen years old. Neither of us is of legal drinking age in the state of Massachusetts.

I lean back into the velvet banquette as the waiter pours a splash of wine into a crystal glass. He hands it to Carolyn; she hands it to me. "You try it," she says.

I lift the glass to my nose, swirling it around, inhaling, then taking a small sip. I have never been in this situation before, and am grateful for a lifetime of careful observation. I think of my father; I have watched him do this a hundred times. I nod once, smiling slightly at the waiter. "Fine," I say.

For the first time today, it feels like my birthday. Carolyn toasts me and we clink glasses, a middle C echoes between us.

She is beginning to look better, and I am beginning to feel better. We order an enormous amount of food: salads, appetizers, entrées.

I think of my mother's phone call early this afternoon. We have the same conversation every year on my birthday.

"I was sitting here thinking of nineteen (eighteen, seventeen) years ago today," she always begins. "It was the happiest day of my life."

I can practically see her face before me, brown eyes inches away from mine, darting quickly all over my face, as if to etch it in memory.

"Your father and I wanted you so badly," she tells me. "More than anything in the world. No sacrifice was too great."

At this point she pauses, and I say what I always say, what is expected: "Thanks for having me, Mom," I tell her.

"You're welcome, dear," she responds, and so the conversation ends.

The bottle of wine is finished before our entrées arrive. Carolyn orders a second one. Her lips are stained red.

"Do you want to know what I was doing this week?" she asks, knowing full well the answer.

I just look at her. The wine has made me less curious; I am surrounded by a comfortable haze. "If you want . . ." I murmur. My eyelids feel heavy, and my stomach is full.

She doesn't seem to hear me. She barely stops for my answer, just continues talking, refolding her napkin with one tan hand.

"I was in Barbados," she says. "I was with my friend." She looks at me, expecting a response. She gets none.

"We flew there on his Learjet," she says flatly. "We stayed at the villa of a prince."

She is reciting this like a list, from memory, like a prayer.

"We snorkled, we swam, we lay on the beach," she says, never taking her eyes off me. "But mostly we fucked."

I take a big sip of wine. Since something is required of me here, I raise one eyebrow.

". . . like bunnies," she continues. "We fucked like bunnies."

She finds this amusing. She is entertaining herself.

"Why are you telling me this?" I ask.

She raises her glass to me. "You want to know, Lucy, don't you?" She smiles a terrible smile, which seems to leave her face and dance in the air between us, a blithe spirit.

My veal is drowned in a brown sauce on my plate. I cut it into tiny pieces, a trick I learned as a child when I wanted to buy time and avoid conversation. I push the pieces around with my fork, counting them, creating designs with the gravy: a flower, a river, a hill. My meal turns into a landscape.

"Is it always the same?" I ask her, meaning several things. Is it the same villa, the same jet, the same man?

"It's always him," she says.

"Who is he?"

I know she won't answer.

"Is he good to you?"

She fingers the diamond hanging by a thin gold chain around her neck, then laughs in a way I've never heard her laugh before. It is a hollow sound, void of any pleasure or amusement. Her mouth curves upward, but her eyes remain wide and unblinking. "Define 'good,' " she says sharply. "Define 'happy,' " she adds. "Define 'love.' "

She sits back, cupping the bowl of her wineglass in one hand. She looks older than she has any right to, with her hair pushed behind one ear, her heavy-lidded gaze, her taut neck.

I imagine her lying on her back, spread-eagled on an enormous bed which is covered by Pratesi cotton sheets. She is not looking at the man who is perched above her, thrusting rhythmically like an animal in heat. She is staring at the ceiling, at a fan which revolves slowly in the balmy island breeze. Out the window, the ocean is a stone's throw away; waves gently lap the shoreline. At a bar down the beach, couples drink daiquiris and listen to a gold-toothed local singing "Yellow Bird."

"Your mother was here," I tell her, changing the subject, which is getting too hot to handle.

Her head jerks back.

"When?" she asks.

"A few days ago."

"What did she want?"

"She—"

"What did you tell her," she interrupts, firing question after question, interrogating the witness.

"What could I possibly tell her, Carolyn? I didn't know anything."

Her face looks pale beneath her tan. I realize that I still don't know anything. In trying to get on neutral ground, I seem to have stumbled into mined territory. Everything I say elicits an explosion.

"If my mother knew what I was doing, she would kill me," she says, incongruously, with a smile. This thought seems to please her.

"I know how to keep secrets, Carolyn," I tell her.

"I'm sure you do."

"So, then tell me," I say. This is my last effort. I am pushing this as far as it will go.

"I'll never tell you," she says gravely.

Whatever this is, it is not a game. Or if it is a game, the stakes are very high: Russian roulette, perhaps, in a smoke-filled private casino room. Her eyes are on the dice.

"Lucy?"

"Yeah?"

"Please never, ever ask me again," she says. "Promise me." She means it.

"I promise," I say, with one hand over my heart. "I promise," I repeat, holding up three fingers in the Girl Scout pledge of honor.

As we leave Beardsly's, linking arms again, and walk back

to school through the now-deserted streets, I know that I will keep my word. I will not talk about it. I will never ask her. As surely as I know this, I also know that someday, somehow, I will learn the truth.

PART TWO

I received the Smith College Alumnae Directory in the mail today, a green, leatherbound affair. I looked up your name before anyone else's. You were not listed. There was no Carolyn Ward.

Where are you? Did you graduate with honors? Or did you not even manage to scrape by. And wherever you are, are you thinking of me?

It is summer. I breathe in the weighty, fragrant air of southern Connecticut, the strange, hot, trapped sense of being nowhere near water. Carolyn's kitchen smells of raspberries, strong cheese and the lilac bushes underneath the open window. She sits next to me on the countertop, swinging her legs like she probably has since she was eight years old. Her gaze is directed out the French doors, past the sprawling patio, over to the tennis court, where her mother and younger sister are volleying.

"Thank you for being here," she says, keeping her eyes on the ball whizzing back and forth. "I don't feel like I can do this alone."

"What's 'this'?" I ask, knowing I won't get an answer. If she responds at all, it will be cryptic, part of the puzzle she half expects me to piece together.

She swivels around, pushes my hair behind my ears and kisses the tip of my nose.

"So many questions," she laughs, eyeing me carefully to see how I have responded to being kissed on the nose.

Carolyn and I no longer touch as we once did, as close friends sometimes do. We have managed to sidestep each other in an intricate dance, coexisting until recently in a dorm room which could not have been more than one hundred square feet. We have had no choice in the matter: when our legs so much as graze underneath a table, or when we brush against one another accidentally, for a moment, both of our worlds stop still. Neither of us can speak. We can afford no accidents.

It is the first time I have visited this place where Carolyn grew up, where she has lived for the past eight years since her mother married Ben. It is set back from the country road, so far back that they use their Jeep to pick up the mail in the morning. Everything about the house reminds you that it's old: the wide planked floors, low ceilings, fireplaces large enough to sit in. It must have been a farmhouse once, when the land still offered food to eat, and animals wandered freely along paths which are now highways.

Perhaps farmers' wives sat in the kitchen where we sit now, gently stacking still-warm eggs into baskets to sell. We are not stacking eggs; Carolyn decided to make a raspberry soufflé today, and we are patiently waiting for it to rise.

She called me at my parents' house yesterday, just as I was leaving for the beach.

"There's a party for Ben tomorrow," she said. "Please

come, I need you here," she told me, practically begging. I could not say no to her. I have almost never been able to say no to her.

She hops off the counter, then places her hands on my knees, which are pink from the sun.

"Lucy Chaya Greenburg," she says, "you look like a dream." Her voice is husky, a sound I know well. Something soft turns in my stomach, flutters downward. In recent months, whenever I've heard that tone in her voice I've run in the opposite direction, or changed the subject.

"Hadn't you better check your soufflé?" I ask, not quite looking at her, knowing if I do she will be smiling her wistful smile.

"Lucy, Lucy," she says, "don't you know that if you open the oven door the whole thing will fall flat? Didn't your mother teach you anything?"

She moves away from me, peeking through the glass door beneath the stove top. The moment has passed. Once again, I am back on safe ground.

There is something I'm not telling her. I saw Chris Mulcahy last week. I went to a high school graduation party, the celebration of the end of a senior year which I missed. I told myself I was going to see all my friends, but the truth is that I have no friends left to speak of from high school; the only reason I went was the likelihood that I'd see Chris. Because the last time I saw him, in the woods, under our tree, almost a year ago, I was still a child.

I wanted Chris to see the hollows in my cheeks which have appeared, as if by magic, in the same way my hipbones are clearly visible, even through tight jeans. I wanted him to notice my painted toes, peeking out through mesh shoes. I wanted his eyes to follow me across the room, astonished at the grace with which I carried myself, all angles and downcast eyes, a visiting dignitary, a homecoming queen.

I wanted him to note my flat stomach, and, with little mental calculation, realize with a sickening shock that nine months had passed. Then he would look at me again, more closely. In his eyes my stomach would expand, my breasts would fill with milk; I would be bursting at the seams. He would see the shadows in my face, the dullness in my eyes, and he would be suffused with a sudden, irreparable sadness —a sadness somewhat like the one I carry with me in a place more private than any other.

I'll never know if Chris thought any of these things. Somehow I doubt he did. We kissed on the cheek like distant relatives, almost brushing air. I nearly didn't recognize him; he had grown his hair longer than mine, and a soft blond beard covered his face. He talked of the Grateful Dead, who he was going to follow around on their national tour, before he "settled into college." I decided not to tell him that going to college doesn't settle anything, that life just gets more complicated as you go along. He told me he'd be going to Princeton in the fall, where his father went, where his grandfather has a building named after him. I told him I expected no less, though I'm sure he didn't know what I meant. Sarcasm is something I developed this year, something I caught, like a virus.

Chris knew something about me which tied me to him in this roomful of people; a secret he never acknowledged, which he conceivably didn't even think about. This secret had nothing to do with East Sixty-first Street, the phone call, the hot tears which dripped off the phone long after the line went dead. It had to do with something more terrifying, and much less concrete.

"Come on, Lucy," he whispered long ago, his head between my legs. "Let go, honey," he said, as the sun was going down.

I shuddered and moaned, as if on cue, writhing like the women I had seen in movies. I contracted my muscles, and released. Contract and release. Simulated motion. A physical lie. I imagined my insides to be white, like a snow-covered field, like a lonely dove, like a sheet of ice.

Afterward, we always shared a cigarette, lying on our bed

of leaves. We didn't look at each other. We admitted nothing. We searched the sky, the perfect deep blue, in the moment before pitch black, for falling stars.

I thought there was something wrong with me, and I believed from the bottom of my heart that you held all the answers. I imagined you had tucked vital information behind your ear, beneath your pillow, under your tongue. I believed that if I stared long enough into your pale, brilliant eyes I would understand everything I needed to.

I was precocious, and I was smart, but I missed the most obvious of clues: your eyes were mercurial. They reflected the color of whatever you observed. When I looked at you, I saw myself as if I were looking into a fun house mirror: chilly and passionless, a body of withered bones.

"Why did you stop?" she asked me once, during a time which seems as distant as an echo. "It was so lovely." A curtain of dark hair covered half her face.

"I can't . . ." I said, but she interrupted me, her voice sharp, a scythe separating wheat from chaff.

"Of course you can. You can do anything you want to do, Lucy," she told me, and for once, she didn't know anything. Not anything at all.

The soufflé is magnificent: lightly browned on top, spilling slightly over the edges of the white ceramic bowl. It smells so good, in fact, that we decide to eat this one now, and make another for the party tonight.

Carolyn slits open the top of the crust, then pours hot raspberry sauce into the middle. We don't bother with plates. The soufflé sits between us as we dig in, greedy and unself-conscious as children licking the icing out of mixing bowls.

Carolyn's mother and younger sister Debbie have finished their game. They walk back toward the house in their tennis whites, two dark-haired, contented young women living a life of privilege: of farmhouses in Connecticut, beach houses in Nantucket, Paris in the springtime. They swing their rackets at their sides. The mosquitoes seem to part, making a path for them.

"Look at this!" Liz Broadhurst says, eyeing our raspberry masterpiece.

"Have a piece, Mom," Carolyn says lightly, in the tone I always hear her use with her mother. It is as if the depth and timbre of her voice vanishes, leaving in its place a thready, high-pitched echo. A child's voice. A child in the dark, afraid of the shadow on the wall, the monster in the closet.

"Oh, I couldn't possibly," Liz says, still looking at the half of the soufflé that's left. "When you get to be my age . . ." she trails off, smiling, wiping the perspiration off her brow with a white terry cloth wristband. She shakes her head, patting the slim curves of her hips.

"Cut it out, Mom," Carolyn says, regaining the voice I'm used to. "You're being ridiculous."

I can't believe what I'm hearing. If I spoke with my mother that way, she would put me over her knee.

"You're right," Liz says, unfazed. She sticks a finger into the side of the bowl, wiping it clean.

"Can you believe it?" she smiles at me. "Three children, and I still fit into the jeans I wore in high school. She runs one finger along the outside corner of her eye, a reflex, feeling for crow's-feet.

Debbie sits at the kitchen table polishing off a hefty piece of soufflé. Her tanned legs stick out from under her tennis skirt, exposing pudgy, sixteen-year-old thighs. I imagine it would be difficult to be a daughter of Liz Broadhurst, a sister of Carolyn Ward, but Debbie is Carolyn's opposite: clear-eyed, smiling, seemingly without a care in the world. She's planning to go on a safari this summer with a group of high school students. In one hand she holds a spoon, in the other a pen, with which she is making a list of things to pack.

"Water bottle, bug spray, Nikon . . ." she enumerates out loud, already half a world away.

Carolyn rolls her eyes at me. She wants to get out of here; she's exhibiting all the signs. Her eyes are dim, her half-smile is set and her fingers click insistently against the kitchen counter. *I need you,* she said yesterday on the phone, *I can't do this alone.*

We go to her room, which is on the top floor. At one time it must have been the attic. Her window faces the front of the house; I look down the driveway at Ben's collection of Rolls-Royces, which are lined up next to each other like racehorses in a stable. I count six. Past the driveway there are treetops as far as the eye can see.

Carolyn collapses into an overstuffed chair, then lights a joint, balancing the ashtray on her thigh.

"Aren't you afraid someone will come up?" I ask.

"No one ever comes up here," she says.

"What if they smell it?"

"They've smelled it for years." She shakes her head at me. "Lucy, why are you so nervous? Isn't it tiring to be nervous all the time?"

Yes, Carolyn, it is. It's a dirty job, but someone's got to do it.

She looks deflated, lifeless, sitting there, as abandoned as the dolls on her dusty shelves. She closes her eyes and her head rolls to the side, the joint still between her fingers. It drops, then begins to smolder on the upholstery beneath her. I pick it up, putting out the sparks with my hand, and place it on her bedside table.

I curl up on her bed quietly as a thief; I lie on top of the covers, my back to the room, watching shadows play against the wall. I hear the chair creak. A moment passes, and then she is lying behind me, her face in my hair, the curve of my back against her. Her arm falls, as if by accident, over my waist. She smells faintly of eggs, herbs, and always, of Shalimar. As I drift off to sleep, I think that we are dreaming the same dreams.

———

Nineteen twenty-nine was a good year for Jacob Greenburg. While his cronies on Wall Street were hurling themselves off the tops of buildings, he was comfortably ensconced in his office downtown, watching the dollars roll in.

He had seen it coming. He had gotten out in time. God was with him.

Jacob took his family to Miami Beach for the winter season. They stayed at the Tropicana, in the height of luxury. It was fortunate that the finest hotel in Miami was walking distance from a shul in the old quarter.

Shabbos, Jacob and Joseph walked hand in hand the two miles to the old Spanish temple, while Leah stayed behind preparing lunch. It was a few years before Joseph's bar mitzvah. Joseph watched as Jacob wrapped the *tefillin* lovingly around his own wrist, winding it up his arm like a black snake.

Together they chanted the morning service with nine other men; ten men were needed to fulfill the requirements of prayer, and Joseph didn't count, because he was too young.

Many years later, my father took us on a trip to Aruba. On the way there, flying high above the earth's surface, my father realized that he would be away for his father's *yahrzeit*, the anniversary of his death. How could he pray for his father? There were no Jews in Aruba; he was sure of it.

"Turn the plane around," he said to my mother, only half joking.

"Joe, you can always fly to Caracas," my mother told him.

It was important enough. The black snake of *tefillin* had wrapped up my father's arm, through his chest, and into his heart. There were no compromises. Things were what they were.

Once in Aruba, my parents sat at the dinner table with other guests of the hotel.

"Tomorrow is my father-in-law's *yahrzeit*," my mother announced to the three couples with whom they were sitting. "My husband is flying to Caracas to find other Jews."

The next evening, at sundown, nine men filed into the living room of our suite. They wore dark summer suits and yarmulkes on their heads. With my father leading them, they faced east, out the balcony and over the blue water, in the direction of Jerusalem.

My hand couldn't reach the doorknob, but I managed to peek through the slats in the door. The murmured words of Hebrew, the swaying backs of the men rose and fell with the tide. My father's voice was the strongest of them all, singing out over the waves, carrying out to the horizon, to the place where heaven is, where the sky meets the sea.

———

The house is filled with flowers. Truckloads of flowers were delivered while we were sleeping. Everywhere I look there are bright, waxy bouquets: on end tables, mantelpieces, above fireplaces which are crackling in the cool June evening.

The guests will arrive in an hour, and the household is moving like a well-oiled machine. The nanny is downstairs with Jessie, the youngest Broadhurst, a maid is polishing the mahogany dining room table until it gleams, and the cook, complete with chef's hat, is in the kitchen overseeing a staff of three.

Carolyn is getting dressed. She slips a silk camisole, the color of a seashell, over her shoulders which are still gleaming with bath oil. She handles everything gingerly, careful not to smudge the clear, wet enamel on her fingernails. She holds a perfume atomizer away from her, sprays the air, then walks into the mist, letting it fall around her, an invisible cloak.

I am watching her. I sit back in a hammock which is fastened to the ceiling by metal hooks. It swings slightly, rocking me; I am still heavy with sleep. She moves lightly through the room, stopping here and there to fasten a bracelet, fix an earring, twist her hair into an effortless chignon. She stands before a lighted mirror, turning her head this way and that, observing herself impartially, critically, as if she were a stranger, as if she were a work of art.

She wraps a pale yellow skirt around her waist, then picks a daisy out of a vase and places it behind one ear. She looks at herself, makes a face, and removes the daisy.

She glances over at me, as if just remembering I was in the room.

"Hmmm. Now what are we going to do with you?" She cocks her head, assessing me.

"I brought a dress," I tell her, halfheartedly. I want to wear something of hers.

Carolyn opens the doors of an antique armoire, revealing rows of shimmering color: evening dresses, cocktail dresses, silk blouses in every imaginable style. It is the wardrobe of a princess, destined for a life of state dinners, of masked balls.

"Take your pick," she says, sweeping her arm out. "It's a black-tie affair, even though it's on a Sunday night. My mother believes fancy parties are the only kind worth having."

I finger a deep blue silk skirt; I don't know where to begin. There are at least twenty pairs of shoes lined up on the floor, ranging from ballet slippers to rhinestone-covered pumps.

She pulls out a silver beaded dress, the most beautiful of all. "Try this one," she says, holding it in her arms.

I quickly undress, throwing my shorts and T-shirt onto the hammock.

"Take off your bra," she tells me, "it'll show through."

I unhook my bra, tossing it onto the pile of clothing.

"Lift up your arms."

I raise my arms above my head, and she slides the dress up and over them in one fluid movement.

She stands back. "Perfect," she declares, smiling as if I were her own invention.

I turn around to take a look, but she blocks my path.

"Wait," she says, fastening something around my neck. "Just wait a minute." She sits me down on a stool with my back to the mirror.

I feel her hands on my face, light as a breeze, then a brush on my cheekbones.

"Close your eyes."

She smooths powder over my lids, then outlines my eyes with a soft pencil. She is gentle; she knows what she's doing. She is at home in the world of beauty, in the world of artifice.

"Look up."

She draws the pencil underneath my eyes in short strokes, then smudges it with the inside of her thumb.

"Look at me."

I blink a few times, until she comes into focus. She looks me over, nods, rummaging through her makeup bag, and pulls out a few pots of lip gloss. She chooses a pale, pale pink. She dips her finger into the pot, then runs it over my bottom lip.

"Press together," she tells me.

She lifts my hair from my temples with two combs, silver-and-black Art Deco combs which perfectly match the dress. She pulls a few tendrils away from the sides, and brushes the back of my hair.

"OK, you can look now," she says with a small, tight smile, swiveling the stool around.

There is a stranger in the mirror. I think she is beautiful; I cannot think of her as me. Her hair glistens gold against her bare shoulders, her cheeks shine through a soft film of rose, her eyes are midnight blue. The silver dress she is wearing falls down the curves of her body, a lovely second skin. Around her neck lies a strangely familiar diamond pendant hanging just below her collarbone, winking, sparkling in the fading light.

I slip into a pair of Carolyn's sandals, which seem to mold to my feet. Strains of Satie float through my head: an oboe, a clarinet, a harpsichord. I spray her atomizer in front of me, and walk through mist finer than a dawn by the sea. I know the scent well. The vision is complete.

"Lucy Chaya Greenburg," she murmurs, an echo of the not too distant past, "you look like a dream."

She is staring at me, flushed, two red spots appearing

through the rouge on her cheeks. "What else do you need?" she asks me.

"Nothing," I sing, twirling around, "nothing at all."

Her eyes are growing dangerously flat, but I refuse to notice, at least not now. I am a spring nymph, I have sprung off a Botticelli canvas.

"Where did you get this gorgeous dress?" I ask.

"It was a gift."

"And the shoes?"

"They were a gift."

"And the . . ." I trail off, aware now of the dangerous, bright flatness, like a desert fire, spreading over her face.

I stop. She is leaning against a wall, as if it's too much for her to stand. She is heading toward the place where I can't reach her, heading for the hills. But she is still here. Perhaps I can bring her back.

"Carolyn, what's wrong?" I ask slowly, quietly, as if talking to someone on a ledge, ready to jump.

She says nothing. She shakes her head, staring at me as if she were looking into a window, over and beyond this moment, into the past.

"Talk to me," I whisper. I take a step forward. She slides away from me, still leaning against the wall.

"Lucy, don't come any nearer," she says in a low voice. "Do you know what will happen if you touch me?"

It is my turn to say nothing. My voice is swallowed, somewhere deep in my stomach.

"If you touch me, I will touch you back," she says, "and this time I won't stop." She keeps her eyes on mine like a cat does, unblinking. Her lids are half-shut, and she is smiling the same small, tight smile. "You can keep your eyes closed, you can tell me all about how this can't happen, you can even scream if you want to. But I won't stop."

She reaches over to her bureau, pulls a pack of Marlboros off the top, then shakes one out and lights it with one hand.

"Do you understand?" she asks me, exhaling smoke in my direction.

• • •

Do I understand? Carolyn, I don't understand any of this. I am standing here in your clothes, bathed in you from head to toe. There is no part of you that isn't touching me already. You are like the breeze, like the ocean, like a multitude of angels. You are what I see when I close my eyes.

"Do you understand?" she repeats. She is not going to give this up. She wants an answer. I cannot give her one. If I open my mouth a snake will come out, vermin, a host of maladies. She will recoil, gasping with horror; she will realize the stakes, stop playing the game, and we will be lost forever.

"Do you think I don't know, Lucy?" she asks in a singsong voice. "I know everything about you."

She is being cruel as a child, testing the waters, not knowing any better, afraid of nothing.

"I can take you to a place you've never been," she tells me, "but you don't want that, do you."

Not here, not now. From dust we come, and to dust we return. No one tells us what exists in between. Clay, wood, marble, granite. I don't know much, but I know this: I am soft as air, as fine as sand, as pliable as the damp earth. What will I become in your hands?

"Tell me you don't want this," she says, slowly moving toward me, "tell me and I'll go away."

My mouth opens, but my voice is strangled into a sigh. My head is filled with salt.

How does she know? She has taken a gamble, and she has won. I am torn between embarrassment and fear.

"Tell me, Lucy." She is inches away.

I am praying. A language I have not spoken in years rushes into my mind like a long-forgotten song. The prayers have no significance; the words mean nothing. They are foreign to me, as if I had never learned them, as if they were someone else's legacy.

"Tell me," she whispers, a gust on my lips. With her thumbs, she moves down my rib cage. Her hands span my waist.

I can see out her open window from where I stand. The guests are beginning to arrive. Rows of expensive cars line the cobblestone courtyard. A jazz version of Pachelbel's Canon floats up with the breeze, the clink of glasses, of gin and tonics.

"Tell me," she says, guiding me backward, over to the bed, warm and light from the setting sun.

She lifts the dress above my head, and I feel my blood, like sand, rushing from the tips of my fingers, downward. My legs are bare, except for the glittering sandals on my feet. She unzips her own evening dress, and it falls to the floor; she steps out of it as if stepping out of the ocean. My head rests on a crisp white pillow. I am floating, I am hanging from the rafters watching two young women settle softly into the depths of a bed, preparing to begin the most elaborate dance of all.

———

In my Christmas card I am playing with a wooden train. The train is green, and the toy men sitting in it wear red hats. I hold one of the men in my small fist as I look to the left of the camera. I am looking at my mother, who is standing there next to the photographer, coaxing me.

"Smile, honey," she says, sticking her fingers into her ears and making a funny face.

I stare at her, stony-eyed.

"Give us a big smile, sunshine," she pleads, stretching her mouth wide, showing me how.

Nothing. No way.

"I'll take you to Rumpelmayer's later," she says, resorting to bribery.

Not even the promise of an ice-cream sundae is going to get me to do something I don't want to do.

"Fine, Lucy," my mother says, "be that way." She doesn't understand. She thinks I should be grateful for this attention, for these blinding lights reflecting off the top of my white-blond head like a halo.

My mouth quivers. My eyes grow wide as pennies, shiny and unblinking. In this moment, the flash goes off, and blue stars dance before my eyes, Orion's Belt, the Little Dipper, and I am suddenly safe in my father's arms.

"Look, shnookie," he would say to me, holding me above his head, resting me on his shoulders. "Look up there. It's Grandpa Jacob winking at us. Don't you see him?"

I would search the sky for the brightest star. "I see him, Daddy, I see him!" I would softly say, in awe at the love transcending millions of miles, bridging the gap between heaven and earth, between men and angels.

In my Christmas card my eyes are the bluest blue, and a small, grown-up smile plays on my six-year-old lips. I am looking beyond this room, far away from here, to a place where I am just learning I can go. The blue stars swirl before me, luminous in their distance, but I know better. Through my open eyes I can see anything I want, touch anything I want. The possibilities are endless.

———

Her mouth is as luscious as a peeled green grape. With the tip of my tongue I trace its outline, her full lower lip.

Is this what she wanted, perhaps from the very beginning?

"Tell me, Lucy. Tell me you don't want this," she mumbles through hot breath, a tangle of hair.

"Shut up," I say, nudging aside the sheet between us. Our hipbones touch like bird's wings.

Through the open window, gravel crunches beneath car tires, doorbell chimes play the first bar of the national anthem.

I run my finger around the elastic of her panties, but she pulls my hand away, nudging me onto my back.

"No," she whispers, "not me."

Her hands are Rubinstein's, Heifetz', Ashkenazy's. She plays me. I am a Steinway, a Stradivarius. Her foot is on the soft pedal, her fingers barely brush the keys. They are sure, her fingers. They memorized me long ago. They read me by sight. Nothing is too difficult, nothing is impossible.

I am looking into gold, amber, green, black. The closer I get, the more I can see.

"Your eyes are the color of the woods," I tell her, "an endless forest."

She smiles. "And your eyes are the color of the sea."

"Which sea?" I ask, her hand inside me, softer than moss.

"Not the Caribbean," she says, "not the Pacific. Nothing tropical. Your eyes are the color of shoals off the shore of Nantucket, in winter, when it is snowing."

"Ice," she says, and something melts.

Carolyn, I am a tunnel, I am a grave, I am something finite. I begin and end. Your hand, tracing outlines on me in the same way as you must, in the dark, by yourself, makes me feel I can go on forever. Carolyn, I am the sky, I am a stream, I am an endless stretch of white sand. Do you hear me?

She will not let me touch her. I move my hand up her stomach, towards her breasts which I have watched, beneath silk blouses, lacy bras, cotton bathrobes for almost a year.

"No," she murmurs, "not me."

"Why?"

"Ssshhh."

"Please."

"No. Not me."

Beneath us, on the lawn, a chamber orchestra has begun to play. Next to us, on the clock radio, Joe Jackson is singing. His voice cracks, a saxophone, diminished sevenths.

I am falling deeper. *I can take you to a place you've never been.* Her eyes are wet, the bed is damp, we are covered by dew. A single tear falls down my neck, over my collarbone, and hangs on my nipple until she licks it off.

"Oh," she whispers, burying her head in my shoulder.

———

"Come on, Lucy," he said, the dappled sunlight painting leaves on my body. "Come on, honey," he said, but he was wrong. He didn't understand. We never had a chance.

———

So it happens, for the first time, that life hangs in the balance. We are on a journey, she is behind the wheel, I am sitting next to her. There is nothing to do but pray. The embankment is covered by painted faces, carved figures, it tells a story: a fresco, the Uffizi Doors.

Her mouth.

At the end of the journey there is only white. The clouds, you know, will hold you aloft, if you let them.

My hips rise up, an arc, an offering, and she slips a pillow beneath them. "Show me," she says.

No, Carolyn, it is you who are showing me.

There is the white of the sun, the white of a tombstone, the white of a piano's keys: Rubinstein, Heifetz, Ashkenazy.

———

Were you possessed of supernatural powers? Did you imagine my terror, did you smell it, did you sniff it out the way animals do? Did you read my mind, did you know that I believed myself to be paralyzed from the waist down, that I thought my insides to be as frozen and translucent as bits of prehistoric life caught forever in amber for all the world to see?

You knew about heat, unrelenting hands, tireless mouths. You were aware of the distance which always needs to be traveled between consciousness and desire.

It was a journey I had never taken. How did you know that? And when, exactly, did you determine that you, and only you, would take me there?

———

Cocktail hour is over. The music has died down, and guests are standing by a long buffet, helping themselves to poached salmon, haricots verts, ice-cold Puligny-Montrachet. On the flagstone terrace overlooking the grounds, tables have been set with floral cotton, sterling silver, lanterns glowing yellow.

Beautiful People mill about, satisfied with this backdrop, aware they are being shown to advantage. The air smells of Havana cigars. The trill of a woman's laughter rises above the crowd, then recedes. There are bare backs, elegant wrists, cigarette holders. The women are colorful; the men are in black and white.

Carolyn had a faint pink smudge on the back of her neck, which I wiped off before we walked onto the terrace. My lipstick is reapplied, and her silver beaded dress falls again, to my knees. We both have the same scent: bath oil, Shalimar, a light film of sweat; but Carolyn has something more, on her fingers, on her lips. I'm sure everyone knows.

If men smell like freshly cut grass, women smell like the bottom of the ocean.

"Where have you two girls been?" Liz Broadhurst asks. Calling us "girls" is an attempt to diminish us. She is upset by what she sees, though she doesn't know what it is. There is a feeling she has, looking at her daughter, magnificent, shoulders gleaming in the light of the moon.

Carolyn doesn't answer. She smiles, and asks the bartender for a glass of champagne. She has something to celebrate.

"Lucy, you look beautiful," Liz says, looking me up and down. "Where did you get that gorgeous dress?"

I start to speak, but Carolyn interrupts me.

"It was a gift, Mom. From an admirer." She looks at me quickly, a gesture as clear as kicking me under the table.

"Must be quite an admirer," Liz says, arching her eyebrows, arching her mouth. She is a queen of small talk, of hidden meanings, the double entendre. She wafts away, leaving us alone.

Carolyn hands me her glass of champagne. The rim is imprinted with her lipstick, a soft pink half-moon.

"Drink up," she says.

I can't imagine what champagne will do to me tonight. I feel drunk already. My knees are weak, my thighs quiver. My rhinestone heels sink into the moist summer earth. She looks at me hard, starting with the top of my head, ending with my toes, which peek out from the sandals she fastened to my feet just a few moments ago.

I want to go back to that moment. I want to go back upstairs and sink deeply into her bed. I want to feel her hair fall gently over my face, covering it, until everything is dark.

She smiles at me. She knows exactly what I'm thinking, she is aware of every inch of me beneath the silver beaded dress. There is a chill in the air, and I shiver, hugging myself. She reaches out a hand, and cups my chin in her long fingers.

"I have to circulate," she murmurs, and then she disappears into the crowd, her head erect, a polite smile settling into its proper place. The etiquette bred into her at Miss Porter's has paid off; none of these guests would ever suspect that Carolyn Ward had just spent the previous hour enveloped in damp Porthault sheets, wrapped in the arms of her college roommate.

Of all the control one human being can possess over another, did you have any idea to what degree I was yours that night?

You could have told me to jump off the Tappan Zee Bridge, and I would have.

You could have asked me to climb on top of the buffet, surrounded by smoked salmon, oysters on the half shell, Caesar salad, and strip in front of two hundred guests to the music of Cole Porter, and I wouldn't have given it a second thought.

They say we shouldn't live in the past, but I think it's all we have. There is something I still want to know: was I the only one?

She is dancing. Her head rests on the broad shoulder of the governor of Kentucky. They swirl around the dance floor in a perfectly elegant waltz. People clear a path for them; they are that good, that perfect, that elegant.

Her dress floats around her, the same dress that drifted above her waist, over her head and shoulders just a little while ago. There is a path on my body that her tongue left behind. I watch her. Her head is thrown back; I see the delicate veins in her neck, the simple chain, the sparkling diamond.

Her stepfather cuts in. "May I?" he mouths. The governor bows out with a small, Southern smile.

Ben places one hand on the small of her back. His other hand clasps hers. Her head reaches to the middle of his chest. She turns, resting her cheek against him. The music changes, this time, to an orchestral version of "Feelings." The saxophone plays the vocal line.

He holds her gently; she looks tiny in his arms. He whispers something in her ear, and she laughs, looking up at him. Slowly, the polite, strained smile begins to dissolve. She moves gracefully, thoughtlessly through the music, the wailing sax.

I watch them. I lean against a redwood table, holding a stuffed mushroom which has grown cold in my hand. Their mouths move constantly; they have not stopped talking. The music grows imperceptibly faster, more embellished. His hands drop to her hips, and she wraps her arms around his neck.

She shakes her hips. Only Carolyn can make this kind of dancing look refined, as if it really belongs in a drawing room. Only Carolyn can make the difference between a drawing room and a bedroom seem vague, an inconsequential point.

They are surrounded by other dancers, bare-backed women, men in starched white shirts, their tuxedo jackets flung carelessly over wrought-iron lawn chairs, but I watch them, only them. It is as if there is a spotlight trained on Carolyn and Ben; this is a movie, and all the guests are extras.

Her laugh glides over the heads of the other dancers until it reaches my ears. She reaches up on tiptoe, he bends his head toward her, and she says something quietly, her eyes trained on me.

His head jolts back, and his eyes widen. Carolyn has managed to say something to Ben which has taken him completely by surprise. I imagine this is no mean feat. Then, as if the music had stopped, a deadening quiet fills my head. Ben slowly turns on the dance floor, Carolyn still in his arms, and stares at me. They both stare at me. I look at her. She is smiling a triumphant smile.

Perhaps I was seeing things. Perhaps I imagined the whole incident. I had always known that there was a side of you which was capable of anything, and I believed with all my heart that I was somehow immune to that part of you. I believed that you would protect me with your strong, graceful arms, that you had wings which would carry me away.

If I were in a burning house, would you rush in to save me? Never mind. Do not answer that question.

I feel incapable, at this moment, of conversation. Perhaps I should have attended boarding school. I wander around the side of the house, holding the thin stem of Carolyn's champagne glass.

There is a low stone wall separating the patio from the garden. I place my glass on it, then hoist myself up, hearing the metallic clatter of silver beads. Behind me, there is a cacophony of voices, of forks scraping against plates.

It is a clear night. The sky is white with stars, but I don't look at them. Tonight is not the night to talk with Grandpa Jacob. I hope he isn't looking at me. If he sees this scene, this elegant gathering, perhaps he overlooks the young woman huddled on a stone wall, emptying the last drops of champagne from her crystal glass, trying to stop her head from spinning, trying not to think.

He cannot help me. He is a million miles from here. He keeps an eye on things, an interested observer, watching the last Greenburg make her way in the world. Does he see me? Can he see through the roof of a farmhouse, into an attic room, beneath a patchwork quilt, through an intricate network of skin and blood, into the heart?

Grandpa Jacob, your belly was the softest place I had ever been. We touched each other once. I reached out for you, my fist as small as a silver dollar. I have your eyes, I'm told, and the shape of your face.

Your eyes. Do you wear your pince-nez in heaven? *The color of shoals off the shore of Nantucket, in winter, when it is snowing.* Perhaps my eyes have simply replaced yours, a light blue window with which to see the world.

Wink if you hear me. I'm not looking. No one will know.

"What are you doing out here, alone in the dark?"

The voice, like gravel, in the night. I can barely make out his face, but I would recognize the deep voice, the remarkable silhouette, anywhere.

"Mr. Broadhurst," I say.

"Lucy, I've told you this before. Please call me Ben. 'Mr. Broadhurst' makes me feel too old," he says.

"Ben," I repeat faintly. I am grateful for the thick darkness surrounding us; I am sure he cannot see my flushed cheeks, my mortified expression. I do not have a face which contains its secrets well.

"So . . . aren't you going to answer my question?"

"What question?"

"What's the belle of the ball doing all by herself?"

"Thinking."

"Thinking," he repeats. "Well, I'm sure you have a great deal to think about."

He smiles at me, delighted. I have given him the precise opening he needs, a well-lit path for his innuendo.

We fall silent for a moment. I imagine that if you put our thoughts together, they would form a composite of the same image, of the same young woman who is undoubtedly dancing at this moment, one hand resting on her partner's shoulder, the other loosely holding yet another glass of champagne.

"Would you like a drink?" he asks abruptly.

"Yes, I'll walk back with you," I say. I do not want to be alone for another moment with Ben Broadhurst. I gather my cigarettes and matches from the stone wall. I push myself off and he grasps me in midair, holding me around my waist, gently easing me to the ground. The wall is not very high; there is no need for this, and we both know it.

He stands back, looking at me.

"That dress looks familiar," he tells me. "You do it justice."

"Thank you."

"You're blushing," he says into the crisp air, his words evaporating first into white steam, until they disappear. Everything is quiet. Crickets clamor beneath us.

He places his dinner jacket around my shoulders.

"What are you doing?" I ask.

"You look cold."

"You're being very nice to me," I say.

"I'm nice to all my stepdaughter's friends. You are her friend, aren't you?" he asks, placing a special emphasis on "friend," eliminating from my mind any doubt as to what Carolyn whispered into his ear on the dance floor.

We walk back to the patio; my eyes burn as I look for her. As always, she is nowhere to be found.

Hundreds of candle-lit lanterns spread out before us, glowing like yellow stars on the dark green expanse of lawn.

Ben reaches under the floral tablecloth covering the buffet, and pulls out a dusty bottle of wine.

"Private stock," he says, winking at me. He holds the bottle between his rib cage and upper arm as he expertly uncorks it. "This wine is older than you are," he smiles, handing me an inchful in a large wineglass. "Château Margaux, 1958. Taste it," he says. "We must make sure you approve."

The dark-red wine looks like poison to me as I swirl it

around the deep bowl of the glass. He wants to kill me, I think to myself, as I take a sip.

"It's good," I say, looking somewhere below his eyes.

"Yes," he laughs, "it's good."

We stand quietly, watching the dancers. Liz drifts by, on the arm of a bald man with an ascot.

"Wing Sayles," Ben murmurs, "interior decorator extraordinaire."

Liz has taken off her shoes, and taken down her hair. It falls around her shoulders, and she looks years younger. She dances barefoot. I notice behind me, on the steps into the kitchen, a pair of pale suede Charles Jourdan pumps. I marvel at this show of impropriety until I hear Ben chuckle by my side.

"My wife," he says, "is four sheets to the wind."

Where were you? As I stood there, your stepfather's proprietary hand against the small of my back, I remember scanning the dance floor. You were outside my line of vision. I did not hear your laugh, your perfectly musical laugh rising above the crowd. I did not see your sardonic smile, the upward tilt of your chin. You were as invisible to me than as you are now.

Isn't it amusing: I wanted you to rescue me. At the time, I did not acknowledge the fine, logical point which stared me in the face. I did not deal with the fact that it was you who had choreographed the whole situation; it was your masterpiece. He and I stood there, dancers in your own private, dangerous drama. I could not begin to understand the temptation in the air, the palpable tautness between us, which grew as if it were a living thing.

You could not have done a better job if you were behind a velvet curtain, pulling the strings.

This is how I have come to think of you: in my dreams you are a puppeteer. You attempt to control the world with your delicate, manicured hands. Your hands: they are capable of anything.

———

She appears out of thin air. One minute she wasn't here, and now she stands before us, swaying slightly in the breeze.

"How are my two favorite people?" she asks the space between us. Her breath could inebriate an entire army.

It is a chilly summer night. I am cold even with Ben's jacket wrapped around me, yet she stands in front of me, bare-shouldered, flushed, a trickle of perspiration falling down the side of her throat. She has wrapped her hair into a loose knot; she is disheveled, at her most beautiful, willful self.

"Fine, Carolyn," I say quietly, hoping she will look at me and recognize that this is not a time for drunken irony; I don't want to be toyed with, I don't want to be flirted with. I want a word from her, a sign that what transpired between us in the attic of this farmhouse, during the fleeting hour of dusk, was more than a deft move in a perilous game.

"And you, Ben, darling? Are you enjoying your party?" she asks, lurching forward, almost losing her balance. She turns to me. "Ben's parties, you know, are famous worldwide! Isn't that true, Ben? How many magazines are covering this one? Mother will be so disappointed if we don't make *Women's Wear Daily.*"

She smiles in my direction, but she doesn't really see me. She has lipstick on her teeth.

"Ben, have you been telling Lucy all about yourself? Or are you too dazzled by her. She is beautiful, isn't she," Carolyn says, tilting her head to the side, appraising me. "Wouldn't you just like to—"

"Stop it!" he growls, then reaches out and grabs her upper arm. "Get a grip on yourself, Carolyn," he says, barely opening his mouth.

She looks up at him. "Well it's true, isn't it?" she says. She laughs and laughs, an awful sound reverberating around the three of us, glancing off each of us as if we were in our own, private, empty room.

When he lets go of her arm, there are red welts where he

held her. They swell up instantly, taking the shape of his hand.

The orchestra is playing something I don't recognize, something with a precise rhythm. I count as I walk away: *one* two three, *two* two three.

"I'm never going to be buried in this place," my mother told me as we entered the Brooklyn cemetery gates. "I'll come to visit, to pay my respects to Jacob, but to lie here for all eternity? Never," she said, pulling into a parking space. "Remember that, Lucy. When my time comes, I want to be buried on a hill with a view."

I hopped out of the car, my sneakers sinking into the steamy gravel. You've never seen the sun shine until you've visited a cemetery on a bright day.

"What difference will a view make?" I asked. "You won't be able to see it."

"How do you know?" she snapped. "Have you ever been dead?"

We walked up the paved road to the family plot. On either side of us, tombstones told stories: Aaron Levy, 1932–1942, lived for ten years, the same age I was. He was described as "A Son." I suppose that's all he could have been at the age of ten; in the same way, walking beside my mother, I was acutely aware of being a daughter. Isadore Abramowitz, MD, who lived to a ripe old age, was inscribed in marble as "A Doctor." Minnie Abramowitz's tombstone next to Isadore's simply said, "A Doctor's Wife."

When my mother and I reached the family plot, we both gasped in unison. At the foot of the plot, there was a brand-new grave, no more than twelve inches in length. An infant. A small marker poked out of the mound of earth like the instruction tab for an African violet. In longhand, in the handwriting of a woman, was written, "Jeremiah Brody, 1980. God Needed Another Angel."

Christians place flowers on graves. Jews place stones. I picked up the smoothest, smallest pebble I could find, cool from the dark under a bench. I laid it next to the marker, hoping it might become an eye, hoping that Jeremiah Brody might somehow see this world; there were no hills, no grassy knolls, only the El train rumbling overhead, and the wild dogs who were rumored to patrol the cemetery late at night. Still, seeing something was better than seeing nothing at all.

"Promise me you'll never bury me here," my mother whispered into the top of my head, holding me to her. We rocked together. She felt clammy, chilled in the hot July air.

"You're never going to die, Mommy," I said.

"No, I'm never going to die."

We held each other for a long time, listening to the sound of our mingled breath, aware that the ground we stood on was populated by Aaron Levy, Isadore and Minnie Abramowitz, Jeremiah Brody and countless others. We were the only human beings standing in a castle of white.

———

There is nowhere to go. There are people in every direction, smiling, nodding, dancing, fully absorbed with themselves and with this perfect evening, this perfect party. Liz Broadhurst will have nothing to worry about: though I have no experience in these matters, I imagine this party will hit the top of every social column up and down the eastern seaboard.

Once again, I walk around the side of the house. There is a couple standing there, a blond woman with her crinoline skirt bunched up around her waist, a man with his hand thrust into her panties. She is wearing, I notice, a black garter belt. They turn away as they hear me, muffling their laughter. They do not stop doing what they're doing.

I walk in the other direction, back through the party and toward the driveway, in hopes of finding my car. I now know what I should do: I will drive home. I will leave all my clothes in this house, strewn over the armchair where I left them. I will leave everything behind.

I brush past Carolyn without saying a word. I barely see

her. She has faded into the landscape, an evil, leering gargoyle.

"Where are you going?" she asks, putting out an arm to stop me.

I keep moving. I realize I don't have my car keys, so I walk into the kitchen, past the battery of cooks, and head up the circular staircase. I turn on the landing, and continue up the second, narrower set of stairs until I reach her room. My pocketbook is flung into the corner, where I left it earlier today.

I survey the room. Carolyn's clothes and mine are strewn across the room, lying on top of each other, intermingled; they look as if they belong to the same person.

Her vanity table is covered by cosmetics, silver brushes, spilled talcum powder. An open crystal flask of perfume sits dangerously close to the edge of the vanity. Everything smells of Shalimar.

The only evidence of what happened in this room is in the unmade bed: the kicked-off patchwork quilt, the barely visible indentations in the crumpled sheets where we lay, inexplicably, during a time which seems distant and untouchable, as history often does.

"What are you doing?" I hear her voice from behind me; every word is enunciated too clearly, an attempt to disguise her condition.

I throw my jeans, shorts and bathing suit into a Bergdorf Goodman shopping bag. I can't find my bra.

"Lucy, what are you doing?" she asks again, moving around to face me.

I look at her, and for a moment, she has lost her power, she is an ordinary mortal just like the rest of us.

"Leaving," I say.

"But I love you," she says in a tiny voice, so small that it's almost possible to pretend I didn't hear it.

Her skin is luminous in the yellow light of this room. Her hands are bunched into fists at her sides, contracting and releasing rhythmically, like two twin hearts.

No you don't, I think.

"I'm leaving," I repeat for emphasis, because if I say it enough times, it will be so. I sling my pocketbook over my shoulder and lift the lavender shopping bag full of clothes. I am ever so careful not to brush against her as I walk out of her room. I imagine at this moment, with all the ingenuousness in the world, that I am walking out of her life for good.

———

There's a Five-College joke that's been going around. I wonder whether you've heard it. It goes like this: at a Five-College lecture, the professor says, "Good morning, class."

The Amherst students say, "Good morning, Professor."

The Smith students write it down.

The Mount Holyoke students giggle.

The Hampshire students say, "What?"

And the U. of Mass. students ask, "Is this going to be on the exam?"

I am just writing this down, Carolyn. I am just trying to get all this down.

———

Monday morning I wake up to the nauseating smell of freshly squeezed orange juice. My mother is waving it cheerfully under my nose.

"Rise and shine!" she says.

My eyes feel glued shut, and my pillowcase is damp. I peek at her through my eyelashes and groan loudly, hoping for sympathy. My mother has never had a hangover; I am certain she has never had an experience which in any way resembles last night.

"We didn't expect you home until tomorrow," she continues, as if sleeping past noon is something I do on a regular basis.

I roll over, pulling a pillow over my head.

"Up and at 'em," she says, "you've already had a few phone calls. I'm not your secretary, my dear."

This is one of my mother's favorite lines of reasoning: "I'm not your maid," she likes to say, or "I'm not your psychiatrist," or "I'm not your chauffeur." One of these days, I'm waiting for her to say, "I'm not your mother."

She pulls the covers off. I climb out of bed, and feel the floor move beneath me, as if I were on a ship. It seems I do not have a tolerance for fine red wine, wine poured from the weathered hands of an older man, wine which is older than I am.

Again, I smell the orange juice.

"Get that stuff away from me," I say, my voice pushing its way out of my throat.

I walk tentatively to the bathroom, where I dunk my face into a sink full of ice-cold water. Then I head downstairs, past my parents' newest acquisition of modern art, a Paul Jenkins painting, angry clashes of red, yellow and black.

There are two messages for me sitting on the pink-and-white Formica counter. They are written on office memo pads.

TO: Lucy
FROM: Mother

Carolyn called. Please call back.

TO: Lucy
FROM: Mother

A man named Harry Wheeler called. He says he was referred to you by Ben Broadhurst. He's from the Wheeler Group, Inc. (My daughter the big shot!)

I pour myself a cup of coffee. Who are these people, and how did they get into my life? I ponder this question through the diminishing haze, the gradual clearing in my head. And who is Harry Wheeler?

On the wall opposite the counter where I am sitting, there is a panel with two small black buttons; this is what is referred to by my parents as the "panic switch." Its purpose, I have been told, is just in case Charles Manson or the equivalent finds his way into the house at 645 Maple Avenue. Once pressed, it cannot be turned off. I feel like pressing it now.

I dial the New York number. A mellifluous voice answers the phone.

"Mr. Wheeler's office."

"Is Mr. Wheeler in?" I ask, having no idea what kind of office this is. Is it a brothel? Nothing would surprise me.

"Who's calling?"

"My name is Lucy Greenburg. I was referred by Ben—"

"One moment, please," she interrupts me.

Very little time elapses. I hear four bars of Beethoven's Variations in G before Harry Wheeler picks up the phone.

"Lucy Greenburg," he says, more of a statement than a question.

"Yes?"

"I've heard a lot about you from my good friend, Ben Broadhurst," he says.

"Oh?"

"Ben seems to think I should meet you. He called me first thing this morning," he continues.

"Mr. Wheeler, I'm sorry, but I have no idea what this is about," I say.

He pauses.

"Is this some kind of joke?" he asks.

"What do you mean?"

He takes a deep breath, then his words come out in one long rush.

"Miss Greenburg. I am the president of the Wheeler Group, which is a talent agency. Ben Broadhurst told me that you wanted to be an actress, and that I should call you up."

My head is reeling.

"I never said anything like that to Mr. Broadhurst," I say, "and I've never thought of becoming an actress."

Harry Wheeler laughs.

"Typical Broadhurst," he says. "Well, he must have had a reason. Why don't you come on in, anyway. Ben says you're a sight to behold, and we're looking for a young girl your age for a big film they're casting out of LA."

A film? I can just imagine what kind of film.

"So, what do you say?" Wheeler asks me. "Can you be in New York tomorrow morning, say, around ten o'clock?"

I don't say anything. I am trying to think; everything is happening too fast for my poor, wine-soaked head.

"But I don't know anything about acting," I say.

"Miss Greenburg, why don't we start this conversation all over again," he says. "Hello, I'm Harry Wheeler."

"How do you do," I say, laughing.

"I'll tell you what: I'll send a car for you," he says, taking my silence for reticence.

"Is there any nudity in this film?" I ask him suddenly, even surprising myself.

"Of course not," he says without missing a beat. "Miss Greenburg, this is a completely legitimate operation. We are one of the largest and most respected agencies in the business. But if you don't want to . . ."

"No, I'm interested in finding out more," I say. Then I give his secretary directions, and hang up the phone.

There are two telephones side by side on the kitchen counter. The black one is ostensibly for outgoing calls, the white one for incoming calls. Only a few people have the number for the black phone.

As I stare out the window at the elaborate bird feeder hanging from the elm tree, the black phone rings. I answer it, forgetting for a moment that Carolyn is one of the few people who has this number. She has access to every part of my life; there is no escaping her.

"Hello," she says. She does not identify herself.

"What are the birds called," I say absently, "the ones with yellow speckles on their beaks?"

"I don't know," she says.

"You don't know, Carolyn? There's something you don't know?" I ask. The sound of my own voice surprises me. It is flat and affable. It is a voice just like Carolyn Ward's.

"Lucy, I need to talk to you," she says.

"About what?"

"I don't want to talk over the phone."

"Sorry," I say, "I'm very busy these days."

"I need to explain what happened last night," she says.

"These are the most amazing birds, Carolyn. Are you sure you don't know what they're called? I only see them in June."

My voice trembles slightly. She is beginning to defeat me, but I pull myself back. I focus on a framed poster on the kitchen wall that says, "War is not healthy for children and other living things."

"Please," she says.

"No."

"There's something I need to tell you. I've never told anyone before . . ." she trails off, faltering.

I stare at the pink memo in my hand. Carolyn called. Please call back. I try to conjure her image before me, but I can't. I strain, but all I see is a jumble of parts: her eyes, a fistful of hair, the base of her neck. I crumple the memo into a tight ball and aim for the garbage can. I miss by a few feet, and hit the poodle instead.

"Did you hear me?" Her voice floats through the wire. She is far away from here. "Lucy, please let me talk to you. You don't have to say anything, you don't have to do anything . . ."

Something snaps.

"That's right, Carolyn. I almost forgot. You don't like me to do anything," I say, and I suddenly see her face before me: her lips part as she blows a stream of cool air down my clavicle, farther down. Her eyes are light with desire. Does she only have a passion for what she can control?

"Stop it, please stop it," she whispers into the phone. She has said "please" more times in this conversation than in all the time I've known her.

"Meet me," she says.

"No."

"Lucy . . ."

"I said no."

"The Empire Diner," she continues, "at four o'clock."

"Carolyn, I won't be there," I say, but she has already hung up.

I should call her back, but I am afraid that if I do so, I will lose my resolve. It has taken everything I have to say no to her. I imagine her sitting at a sidewalk table, waiting for me to appear from around the corner, staring expectantly at every blonde walking toward her, outlined by the harsh sunset. She will glance periodically at her watch, and halfheartedly read an old copy of *The New Yorker*. Eventually, she will walk back to her borrowed fire-engine-red Porsche, and press the gas pedal to the floor as she screeches out onto Tenth Avenue.

Maybe not. Maybe she will slouch, instead, into a poolside chair in Connecticut, balancing a frozen margarita on the curve of her stomach. When four o'clock rolls around, she will think of me, and toast me in a silent salute. "Only one of us can be a fool," she will think to herself, "and it's not going to be me."

———

Would you really have told me? Was that your plan? If I could change one single piece of the past, it would be this: I would have run to meet you at the Empire Diner that afternoon. You see, the truth would have saved both of us a whole lot of trouble.

But would you have told me the truth, then, or another fantastic invention, woven so tightly that I would not have been able to see through it.

Whatever you would have said, I would have looked you in the eye and believed the most inconceivable story, the most preposterous lie. But perhaps you would have broken through the acropolis surrounding your heart, perhaps you really would have told me the one thing you had never told anyone before.

It was that simple. It was our only chance.

———

It is *erev* Yom Kippur, the afternoon before the highest of holy days, and my father's hands are tight on the steering wheel of his Citroën. The narrow streets of Brooklyn are filled with women balancing sacks of groceries on their gen-

erous hips, hurrying home to prepare the evening meal before the fast.

"Do you know why we go to the cemetery right before
Yom Kippur, Lucy?" he asks me, keeping his eyes on the road.

"No, Daddy," I answer in a small voice. It is the first time I
have visited the cemetery, and I am scared.

"Yom Kippur is the Day of Atonement. At the end of the
day, God writes in his book, sealing the fate of each and every
man. We go to the cemetery because it is a *mitzvah*, a good
deed. And because it may be the last time we have a chance to
visit, to pay our respects to Grandpa Jacob."

"Why the last time?" I ask, watching his profile.

"We never know what tomorrow will bring, Lucy. Only
God in his infinite wisdom knows our fate."

"Daddy, you're scaring me."

"Don't be frightened," he says, patting me on the knee,
"it's the same for all of us."

At the family plot, my father pulls a weather-beaten prayer
book out of his trenchcoat pocket.

"Come here, Lucela. Recite the *Kaddish* with me," he says,
pulling me close.

Together we recite.

The words look funny to me, and I begin to laugh. I laugh
so hard that tears leak out the corners of my eyes, and I wipe
my nose on my father's sleeve. I laugh so hard I think I will
die.

There are empty patches of land all around us, surrounded
by gleaming white headstones, etched with words of Hebrew.
I realize that these are graves which have not yet been filled.

"Who are these for, Daddy?" I ask, after he is finished placing a small pebble on each grave, an offering.

"It's first come, first serve, Lucy," he tells me. Then he
smiles, hoisting me carefully onto his shoulders, and carries
me away.

———

A limousine arrives promptly at nine o'clock. A uniformed
driver rings the doorbell; I count eight chimes, the first four

mirror images of the last four. I've been trying to get my parents to change that tune for years.

My father called New York early this morning, and when he got off the phone, he sat down heavily at the dining room table.

"Well, this Harry Wheeler is who he says he is," he told me, shaking his head. "You're running with a pretty fast crowd, Lucy. It's up to you. I don't want to tell you what to do."

My father has never told me what to do. "Do the right thing," he always says, assuming that I'll know what that is. His world is divided into clear, delineated sides. There is always a right choice and a wrong choice.

My father is making a mistake here. He thinks I am living in the same world.

"How exciting," my mother says, cinching a belt around the waist of my white suit. "I always knew you were destined for greatness, my dear daughter. Imagine your face, larger than life. . . . On the silver screen, you live forever."

She pulls a pin out of a mouse-shaped pincushion, then pokes it through the back collar of my blouse.

"No gaps," she says, smiling at me. "Now remember. All you have to do is relax and smile. Tell them about your Christmas card!"

She nudges me down the stairs, and walks me out the front door, down the flagstone path to the dark blue limousine. My father stayed home today. He is framed by the doorway as he stands there, waving. In the bright sunlight I cannot see his face, only his large shape, stooped shoulders, fingers spread as if he had just thrown something, by accident, away.

The drive to the city takes forty-five minutes. We pass all the familiar landmarks: oil tanks, landfills, the Budweiser plant. Through the tinted glass I watch other drivers turn their heads, trying to see who's in the back of the stretch limousine. I am at an advantage. They cannot see in. I feel small in the backseat; there is nothing to read, only copies of *Crain's New York Business* and *The Wall Street Journal*. This is the car of a mogul, and this is how moguls live. There are crystal decanters filled with clear and amber liquid, four shot glasses lined up next to them. There are a few tapes: Neil Young, Willie Nelson, Debussy's "La Fille aux cheveux de lin." I opt for the radio, flipping to WINS, "You give us twenty-two minutes, we give you the world." There is a drought in Cambodia, a fallen concrete block has killed a Brooklyn woman, and there is an update on the young girl whose finger was sliced off by a subway train.

The world seems terrifying, and large. I imagine the Lincoln Tunnel will cave in above us, water from the Hudson River will pour down in a flood of biblical dimensions. The crystal decanters will shatter, implanting microscopic shards of glass into my skin, through my bloodstream; they will pierce my heart.

Images of children with swollen bellies, of a female skull split open, a gutter filled with blood pass before me until I can see nothing else. Privilege frightens me; these soft seats, this glass womb, windows tinted to make the grayest skies look blue. Everything is illusion. Nothing is as it seems.

I roll down the glass partition.

"Where, exactly, are we going?" I ask the driver.

"Midtown, miss," he says.

"Where, though?"

"The offices are on Forty-eighth and Broadway," he says.

"Do you drive a lot of people for Mr. Wheeler?" I ask, trying to engage him in conversation.

"Some, miss."

"People like me?" I ask.

He pauses.

"I really couldn't say, miss."

This isn't going to work. I'm on my own. I read the stock market report; the Dow Jones average is up three points. I have no idea what this means. My father has spent his life in the financial world, but he's never explained it to me. "It's just work, Lucy," he always says, "a means to an end."

———

"How much money does Daddy make?" I used to ask my mother from time to time, before I realized I'd never get an answer.

"More than the President of the United States," she would invariably say.

But the President has an unlimited expense account, free travel, and weekends at Camp David. He has bodyguards and spies, people who walk ahead of him, in case a concrete block falls, in case a starving child should wander into his path. The President is impervious to disaster. He has fall guys. He has virgin eyes, and feet as soft as wet sand. He will die a timely death, in his nineties, in his sleep, and will be buried in an airtight, soundproof mahogany casket. Tourists will visit his gravesite for the next millennium.

We pull up to a monolithic building on Broadway. The driver hops out to open my door, but I beat him to it. I walk around a drunken man who is sitting on the sidewalk, and put a quarter into the empty coffee cup in his hand.

"Ooohh," he mumbles, "baby come back!"

"Thirty-sixth floor, miss," the driver calls out after me.

The lobby is covered with mirrors. Wherever I look, I see myself in triplicate. In the elevator I swallow hard; my ears are popping. The doors open soundlessly, and my high heels sink into thick carpet as I approach the receptionist, who is sitting behind a horseshoe-shaped desk.

"Yes?" she asks, looking somewhere to the left of me.

"I'm here to see Harry Wheeler."

Now she looks me up and down.

"What's your name?"

"Lucy Greenburg."

She scans a sheet of paper in front of her with a pointy red fingernail. "Don't see any Lucy Greenburg," she says.

"Mr. Wheeler made the appointment with me yesterday," I say.

She looks up at me, then down at the sheet in front of her.

"Not here," she says. She is taking pleasure in this.

We stare at each other. Finally, with a sigh, she picks up the phone.

"Mary, is Mr. Wheeler expecting a Lucy Greenburg?" she

asks, as if inquiring as to whether Mr. Wheeler is expecting a giant chimpanzee with a ribbon tied around its neck.

"Oh. I see," she says, dejected. "Have a seat, he'll be with you shortly," she says to me.

I clear my throat. I seem to have lost my voice; it has hidden behind a chrome corner, a mirror, a leafy green plant. The receptionist disappears down a long hallway, and I sit on a suede sofa which plumps up around me. Everything surrounding Harry Wheeler is designed to be so soft you can barely feel it at all.

The paintings lining the walls have been chosen according to color and motif. Pastel horses—mauve, lavender, rose— gallop through the frames, or graze in light green pastures. Pink cows peer through a yellow haze. An aqua swan cranes her neck.

"Do you like the paintings?"

A man who must be Harry Wheeler walks toward me, hand outstretched.

"Very much," I lie. I shake his hand.

"My wife did them."

"Lovely," I say, pretending to study them. How much can you say about a pink cow?

"I hate them, myself," he says. "Let's go to my office."

I follow Harry Wheeler down a long corridor, past islands full of secretaries, more pastel paintings. His wife keeps busy. He is the type of middle-aged man who plays tennis three times a week, gets rubbed down at the club, spends fifteen minutes a day under the sunlamp. He has a full head of gray hair, and is wearing a European double-breasted suit. His loafers shine like beetles against the pale pink carpet.

He puts his feet up on his desk, then picks a cigar stub out of an ashtray, pulling in his cheeks as he lights it.

"Perfection," I think I hear him say through a haze of smoke.

"Sorry?"

"Broadhurst was right. You're a real beauty," he says.

I flush at the notion of the two men discussing me.

"Innocent. You look so innocent," he says, "you're perfect. That'll be my nickname for you. 'Perfect.'"

"For what, Mr. Wheeler?" I ask, half expecting him to say, "Call me Harry," as they all seem to do, but he says nothing, just sits behind his desk appraising me.

"For a lot of things," he says, "but I'm specifically thinking of this one project being cast right now. Broadhurst was right," he repeats as if mystified, standing up and coming around the side of his desk.

He takes my hand, pulling me out of my seat. His palms are soft.

"Let me take a look," he says, circling me. "You look gorgeous, Lucy, but that suit's no good," he says.

"For what?"

"For the screen test I'm going to send you on this afternoon," he says, flashing his teeth at me. "You can't wear white on camera, it reflects the light. Also, it's a suit. We're not looking for a career woman here. This character is young. Innocent. Virginal."

I try not to laugh. He looks so serious.

"Do you have anything else with you to wear?" he asks.

What is he asking? I don't normally carry a change of clothes with me.

"No," I say.

"Saks is three blocks away. You have to be at One Gulf & Western Plaza in two hours. Have Jimmy drive you over to Saks, and pick yourself out a dress. Mail my secretary the receipt and the company will reimburse you. I wish I could go with you, but I have too damn much to do. Get something blue. Light blue, to match your eyes. Silk, maybe."

"Mr. Wheeler, I can't take your company's money."

"Don't be silly, Perfect. It's a small investment," he says. "Go on. And remember, nothing too sexy."

"No, really," I say. My mother always told me never to accept candy from strangers; this feels like an extension of the same theory, magnified into adult proportions.

Finally it occurs to me that I have a choice in the matter.

"I can't go today," I say. "I'm sorry, but I need a little time to think about all this."

"Time? I'm giving you an opportunity most actresses would kill for," he says.

"But I'm not an actress," I remind him.

He consults a large desk calendar which is full of pages of intricate notes.

"The only other available time is noon on Friday."

"Fine, and Mr. Wheeler? I'll buy a dress myself," I say, hoping the credit card my mother gave me when I began Smith, to be used in case of emergency, is still somewhere in my wallet.

"As you wish."

"Don't I need to know anything about what's going to happen? I've never done this before," I remind him. "How do you know I can act?"

"Just be yourself. You're exactly what they're looking for," he says, patting my back as he maneuvers me out the door.

"Oh, and Perfect?" he calls out after me. "I'm sending you over as 'Lucy Green.' Greenburg is too ethnic, OK sweetie?"

He winks, as if he had just told me an inside joke.

I think about walking straight out of Wheeler Group's offices into a taxi, then down to Penn Station, where I can catch the next train back to New Jersey and pretend this just didn't happen. I think of Harry Wheeler circling me, not in the same moist-eyed way Ben Broadhurst had, but as if he were a benign grandfather who had just bought me a new outfit. I think of the two men discussing me. "A real beauty," they had said.

I smile a small, uncomfortable smile at Harry Wheeler's driver, and fold myself once again into the backseat of the stretch limousine.

"Where to, miss?" he asks.

"Saks," I say as we pull away from the curb.

I wander around Saks Fifth Avenue in a stupor. I buy a pink blusher, three pairs of argyle socks, and a lambswool vest for my father before I even approach the better dresses department.

I see it immediately; it is cornflower blue. I silently thank my mother as I pull a stickpin out from the collar of my blouse and tighten the waist, which is two sizes too big. It has a scoop neck, puffed sleeves, and I try to feel like Rebecca of Sunnybrook Farm as I twirl around the dressing room. Young. Innocent. Virginal.

The rest of the week drifts by slowly, each day weighed down by the notion that my life is about to change drastically. I have found out that Harry Wheeler is one of the biggest talent agents in town. Why is he so interested in me? And why did Ben Broadhurst make that initial phone call? I wonder if Carolyn knows, and if so, what she thinks. I can almost see her forehead tighten, her mouth go slack with feigned indifference. *Do what you want, Lucy,* she would say, her voice higher than usual, *I couldn't care less.*

I stare at myself in my bathroom mirror for what seems like hours. I think I look like a lot of women; I have fair skin, light blond hair, and eyes which readily change from blue to green. I look at my profile. My nose is straight. My bone structure, I've been told, is fine.

I stand on the lid of the toilet, so I can see myself full length. I have a small waist, small breasts, and legs which require what my mother calls "maintenance," like a car's wheels. My spine is long, and I have delicate, almost childlike hands and feet.

None of it has ever seemed like a big deal to me, not until now. I don't understand it. I have always believed that I looked somehow incomplete. I thought there was a vital, essential part of me missing, a leg, perhaps, or a shoulder.

Now I am being told not only that there's nothing missing, but that I'm perfect. The notion of perfection puffs me up like a helium balloon. I do not think about the fact that a pinprick would be all it would take to send me flying, in pieces, into the sky.

Each night I sit quietly with my parents at dinner. We are all aware of the tension mounting, the clinking of silverware, the grating sound of knives and forks scraping against each other.

"So when's your audition," my mother asks me brightly, for the twentieth time.

"Tomorrow," I say.

"Tomorrow!" my father repeats, looking up from his meal, which has kept him fascinated for the past half hour, "tomorrow is Friday, my dear, in case you've forgotten."

I look at him.

"The Shabbos," he says, as if he needs to remind me.

"I know, Daddy."

"Well then?"

"I'll be back by sundown," I say.

At precisely noon the next day, I walk into the casting offices, which are filled with pastels, chrome, potted plants. At first I think there are mirrors. Everywhere I look I see young blond women wearing blue dresses. Their hair color is the kind that comes out of a bottle, and they all look like the picture on the front of the box. Their powdered skin is flawless, their eyes are rimmed with pencil, applied with an even hand. Their teeth are large and white.

"Can I help you?" asks the receptionist. "Are you here for the call?"

"For the film," I say woodenly.

"Right. Just fill in this card with your measurements, addresses, phone number, service number, agent's phone number, social security number, and your SAG number," she says.

Numbers, numbers. I wonder whether the root of "numbers" is "numb." I have no idea what she's talking about.

"I don't know my social security number," I say.

"You don't know your social security number?" she repeats, incredulous. "Where are you from?"

I hear tittering behind me. I turn and see one of the girls cover her mouth with her script.

I might as well get this over with. "I also don't know what

a SAG number is," I tell the receptionist, who I hate with all my heart.

"Oh, honey," she says with a fake Southern drawl, "is this your first time out?"

"Yes. As a matter of fact, it is," I say.

"Who sent you here, to this big, bad place?" she asks.

"Harry Wheeler," I say. I lean over her desk. "Please stop doing whatever it is you're doing," I tell her in a new voice, one which slices the air between us.

"What's that?" she asks.

"Stop condescending to me," I say, "you don't even know me."

She throws her hands into the air, a mock surrender. "OK, OK, take a seat." She thinks she's won the battle. I walk to the end of a row of chairs, looking straight ahead, hoping my makeup covers the redness I know is spreading over my cheeks.

A young man pops his head out of a door and calls, "Sunny Hopkins?" The woman next to me stands up, smoothing her skirt. She hands me her script.

"SAG stands for Screen Actors Guild, honey," she says with a quick smile, then walks into the next room.

I take a deep breath as I glance at the script. The first page is entitled "Character Breakdown," which seems to be exactly what's happening to me. I feel like I'm shrinking, here in this roomful of clones.

The character I am auditioning for is named Joan. She is described as "vulnerable, yet tough, innocent, yet worldly, beautiful, yet simple." I can't get past the first page. It is a scene in which Joan's father tells her he's going to die, as she kneels at his bedside, her head nestled in his shoulder.

How long do they give you? she asks.

A year. A year if I'm lucky.

The young man keeps popping his head out like a jack-in-the-box, calling names. There are just a few of us remaining. Each of the women who has gone into that room has come out with cloudy eyes, a set mouth, and a chin pointed high. The longer I sit, the more nervous I become. This thing that I didn't care about, this lark, this piece of luck has suddenly become important to me. I want to be different. I want to be special.

———

"Marilyn Monroe," my grandmother said to me, the one who could talk. "You were born on the day Marilyn Monroe died. It's a legacy, Lucela. Don't you forget it."

"But she killed herself, Grandma," I said.

"It doesn't matter. It won't happen to you. On the silver screen, you live forever."

———

Where's Carolyn? I have not seen her since the night of the party, which seems an eternity ago; I have not spoken with her since that stilted phone call the following day. I imagine she is lying by the Connecticut pool, wearing nothing but a thin, gold ankle bracelet, the clasp made of two entwined hearts. Her eyes are closed. Lemon wedges cover her nipples. Next to her is a tall, cool drink of water.

Perhaps I am wrong. Perhaps she is soaring through the air in a bird-sized plane, dipping through the clouds on her way to an exotic port, where she will sit in the shade, sipping a strong aperitif, waiting for her lover to arrive. *Show me*, she will say. *No, Carolyn, it is you who are showing me*. She has cut her fingernails short. The balls of her fingertips will gently knead his back; outside, on a hibiscus-filled porch, she will massage suntan oil into his lateral muscles. He will purr like a kitten; she will smile like a cat. Her eyes will narrow. *Tell me you don't want this. Tell me and I'll stop.*

———

"Lucy Green," the jack-in-the-box pops out. I shake his hand. I am developing a firm handshake.

"Hi Lucy, I'm Bob Stone, the assistant casting director," he says. "It's been a long day. Sorry to keep you waiting."

He leads me into the room. "Lucy Green, meet Sheila Perkins," he says. There are two men also seated in the room, but

I am not introduced to them. I have more opportunities to practice my handshake all the way around.

Sheila Perkins is clearly the big shot in this group. She rises slightly out of her seat as she greets me. She is the largest woman I have ever seen, wearing a dress that looks like a rain poncho. Her arm is the size of a newborn infant.

"Harry Wheeler speaks very highly of you, Lucy. How long have you known him?" she asks.

"I met him earlier this week," I answer.

Her eyebrows arc like two birds. Somehow, I don't think honesty is the best policy here.

"Oh. Well, tell us something about yourself. How long have you been in the business?"

"I'm not in the business. I'm a sophomore at Smith," I say.

"Good school," she says. "Have you done any acting there?"

"No."

"What's your major, then?"

She is getting confused by this. The direct approach is working.

"Music. I'm a music major," I say. Fact is, I haven't yet declared my major, but this woman is perplexed enough.

Her eyes light up. "Piano?" she asks.

"I've played for fifteen years," I say.

"How old are you, Lucy?"

"Nineteen. I started playing when my fingers could reach the keys."

She smiles at me, suddenly maternal. "My daughter started at that age, too," she says.

"Does she still play?"

"No," she answers. Her eyes cloud over.

My father never wanted me to stop practicing piano. When the sun was going down, and I wanted to go out to the driveway and shoot baskets, he said, "Lucy, you have a gift. A God-given gift. Your fingers are golden. Play that Chopin again. The slow one. The one I love."

He sat back in his easy chair, and I, with my back to him, began to play. I imagine he looked out the window at the snow-covered pines, allowing the repetitive, minor bass chords to take him back to a time long ago, when he was a towheaded boy, shooting baskets as the sun set over the low buildings of Brooklyn.

"That was beautiful, honey," he said to me when I turned around. "Play it again."

"Joan is a pianist," Sheila Perkins says.

"Who?" I ask.

"The character, dear. The part Harry sent you over to audition for."

I hear her tap her foot impatiently.

Is this the audition? Am I auditioning now? I am being observed by four sets of eyes, from every possible angle.

"Well. Shall we get started?" she asks, hoisting herself up and moving around to the front of the table. "You'll be reading with Bob. Go stand on the X," she says, motioning to crisscrossed white tape on the floor of the next room, visible through a glass window.

A cameraman wearing headphones opens the door for us. I walk over to the X and stand there, arms dangling by my sides. The lens of the motion camera is an evil eye, glinting and glistening black like the bottom of a lake. I stare into it; I don't know what to do.

"When I give you the sign, state your name," the cameraman says.

"What does that mean?" I ask.

"Just give the camera your name, and smile when you say it."

Oh. I'm introducing myself to the camera. How do you do, Mr. Camera.

He signals thumbs-up.

"Hi. I'm Lucy Greenburg," I say, feeling my eyes flutter as I try to smile.

"Cut!"

"What's wrong?"

"What's your name, Lucy?" says a voice from behind the window.

Oh. OK. I forgot I had a new name. Simple. Virginal. Innocuous.

He signals again.

"Hello. I'm Lucy Green," I smile.

"Who's your agent, Lucy?" Again, the disembodied voice.

"The Wheeler Group."

"And how old are you?"

"Nineteen," I say.

"Cut!"

Now what's wrong?

"Say you're seventeen, Lucy."

"Rolling!"

"And how old are you?"

"Seventeen," I say, looking directly into the bottomless lens.

The camera clicks off. I haven't exactly passed my first test with flying colors. At nineteen, I'm already over the hill, and my name's all wrong. What am I doing here?

"OK. Now the camera's going to keep rolling, Lucy. Just take your time. Have you had a chance to study the script?" I hear Sheila Perkins' voice coming from the next room.

Study the script. Why would I want to do that? I'd have no idea what to do with it.

"As best as I could," I say. Now I'm really getting nervous. I feel a cold trickle of perspiration run down my armpits, pass my ribs and dissolve when it hits my waist. My right eyelid is trembling, keeping beat with my heart. I'm about to make a fool of myself. I'm sure of it.

"I think I want to kneel," I say. "Would that be all right?"

Joan kneeling at her father's bedside. That's something I might be able to pull off.

"Do whatever you want to do," she says.

I glance at the script, creased in my sweaty hand.

How long do they give you?

A year. A year if I'm lucky.

Bob sits on a low chair, and I place my cheek on his knee, facing away from him, toward the camera.

What am I going to do without you?

No one lives forever, Joan. Look up in the sky. Whenever you need me, I'll be there.

"Rolling!"

––––––––

"Look up in the sky, shnookie. It's Grandpa Jacob winking at us. Don't you see him?"

"I see him, Daddy! I see him," I whisper into the top of my father's bald head.

He swings me down from his shoulders, holding me in the air in front of him, as effortlessly as if we were in water.

"We're never alone, Lucy. The sun is *ha-Shem*, the sun is God. The moon is his bed when he sleeps at night. And the stars? They are hundreds of millions of souls watching over us. They see us even when we can't see them. The sky is a city of angels."

He sets me down, and I hold on to his leg. I look up into his eyes, which are as glassy as the black puddles beneath our feet. We stand on the front lawn, his shadow made huge by the light cast from the house. It covers mine until we are one. My feet dig into the cool grass as we wave wildly at the sky.

––––––––

"How long do they give you?" I almost whisper, my cheek against Bob's knee.

"A year," he says. "A year if I'm lucky."

My father's face appears before my open eyes, but it is transparent, like a ghost's.

I begin to cry.

"What am I going to do without you?"

Tears spill over my cheekbone onto Bob's linen pants.

"Look up in the sky, Joan," he says, stroking the ends of my hair. "No one lives forever. But whenever you need me, I'll be there."

I look down at my script.

"Are you in pain?" I ask him. "Is there anything I can do?"

"Pray with me," he says, gingerly moving down to his knees. He crosses himself, then takes my hand and repeats the motion.

My father's eyes are bloody sockets. His fingers bleed, and his mouth contorts with pain. *Help me*, he mouths, but I am too far away.

———

"No," my father tried to scream out, but there was no sound. *"No,"* his face contorted, but no one could hear him. Silent tears streamed down his face. They moistened the ground beneath him. He imagined his tears soaking through the earth's center, creating the narrowest passage all the way to the Dead Sea.

———

"Cut! Lucy, come back in here," Sheila Perkins calls, her voice rousing me from my trance.

Bob helps me up, his hands shaking. I am still crying. I lower my eyes to the floor, and instantly Carolyn is there. *Lucy, stop it*, she says so softly only I can hear it, *don't you know it's only a game?* Her mouth expands into a smile, coaxing me. *It's all only a game; get it together*, she says.

My legs are filled with sand. I walk slowly into the other room, feeling as if I had just been observed in the deepest sleep. What have I given away? The click of my heels on the painted wood floor reverberates in my ears.

When I enter the room, they all stare at me.

"You say you've never acted before?" Sheila Perkins asks.

"No. I haven't."

Was this acting? It seems an invisible hand has reached into my mouth, down my throat, into red turbid depths and pulled out some essential organ, something without which I cannot live. It is on display now. Ugly, throbbing, indispensable.

"It seems impossible," she says, her face softening into its folds.

"That was a wonderful audition," she continues, "and the camera loves you."

I say nothing. If I speak I will undoubtedly fall apart.

"Would you like to see the tape?" she asks. "We can rerun it for you right now."

I nod. Even though I'm not sure this is such a good idea, curiosity overwhelms me. The camera loves me. What does that mean? What does it see that I don't?

She clicks on a television monitor on the console, then signals to the cameraman in what looks like sign language. In a moment, my face appears on the screen, larger and more colorful than in life.

How long do they give you? My voice trembles, my eyes are filled with tears. *What am I going to do without you?* My shoulders heave.

I watch myself genuflect on camera, and it is as if the gesture is something I have learned through a lifetime spent in churches with stained glass windows, a motion fraught with the intensity of historical momentum: Christ's open mouth, Saint Peter's stricken eyes, collection boxes jangling with coins, Handel on the organ.

"You see?" Sheila asks, "Lucy Green, or Lucy Greenburg, or whatever you want to call yourself, you are the kind of person who comes along and makes my job easy. They're going to love you."

"Who?" I ask her.

"The director, the producers, everyone who matters. I'm the casting director. I just tell them what they ought to do, and they either do it or don't do it. In this case, I think they will. I've seen over fifty girls for this part, Lucy, and you're the first one who's right for it."

They are all smiling. If Sheila's happy, everyone's happy.

Shiny white crescents of smiles bounce off the walls. I, on the other hand, am barely here. Their voices are echoes; they reach me moments after the spoken words, which are not sinking in at all.

I am in the habit, lately, of doing the unexpected, doing what I think I don't want. *Tell me, Lucy. Tell me you don't want this*, she had said. *Tell me and I'll stop.*

Her face floats before me again, a delicate phantom. *Are you crazy?* She whispers now through white lips. *This could be the best thing that ever happened to you.*

Or the worst, Carolyn. Or the worst. Everything has a price. But I guess you don't know that.

"I'm going to call Harry and tell him what we think of you," Sheila says, rising out of her chair. "Are you signed with him?"

"What does that mean?"

"Clients have exclusive contracts with their agents. Harry's the best. It would be a good idea for you," she tells me.

"I'm not even sure I . . ."

"OK, then it's all settled," she says. Apparently she didn't hear me. "Assuming things go as I think they will, you should be hearing from me within the next few days."

"But—"

"Lucy, if you get this part, although it's a relatively small part, your fee will be fifty thousand dollars," she says. "We probably won't be able to get you a percentage the first time around, but it's not a bad place to start."

Fifty thousand dollars.

———

"How much money does Daddy make?" I asked my mother.

"More than the President of the United States," she said, watching me out of the corner of her eye.

"Marilyn Monroe," Grandma said.

"But she died, Grandma!"

"So what? One day, Lucela, you will learn that there are many kinds of deaths."

"Explain to me what you do, Daddy," I asked my father.

"It's boring, Lucy," he said, smiling at me indulgently. "It's just work. A means to an end."

Harry's driver, who has finally let me know his name is Jimmy, is waiting for me outside the office building.

"Mr. Wheeler asked me to drive you home," he tells me.

I am grateful for this. The audition has exhausted me, and the world suddenly seems like a huge, unwieldy place.

He looks at me through the rearview mirror as we approach the Lincoln Tunnel.

"How did it go, miss?" he asks.

Asking this question is a big step for him. His spirit has been slowly trampled by years spent driving people to places where their lives change, while seeing the same black stretch of highway in front of himself every day, the same traffic lights switch from green to red.

"Oh, I don't know, Jimmy. I guess it went well," I say. "I'm scared about all this."

He glances at me quickly.

"A young girl like you, miss, got a whole life ahead of her to be scared. Don't let the good things scare you," he says.

Good things have a price. No news is good news. All surprises are foreboding. Again, fear overtakes me. This car suddenly feels like a deathtrap, the tires waiting to explode. The factory pours dark gray smoke into the air; take one wrong breath and your life is over. A carload of kids waves from the next lane. The car will swerve, sideswiping us. I will be thrown from the backseat, through a thin pane of cloudy glass, onto the other side of the highway, directly into the path of an oncoming truck.

None of these things happen. We purr down Route 22. In five minutes, I will be home. Puccini will be playing on the stereo, my father will be hanging in traction, watching the six o'clock news. In the kitchen, on the stove, a pot full of boeuf en daube will simmer. The alarm system will click as I open the front door. I will make it home before Shabbos. We will all be safe forever.

———

"Lucy, what happened?" my mother greets me at the door. She wipes her hands on her starched linen apron.

"Let me sit down first, Ma," I say. I walk into the kitchen and stare at the contents of the refrigerator, which have not changed much since I was six years old: glass milk bottles, blueberry yogurt, Kosher salami, tightly sealed leftovers.

I pour myself a glass of skim milk and sit on a white plastic chair, circa 1962. "Your parents' house is perfect 1960s Jewish decor," Chris once said to me. I look at the walls. Ben Shahn, Larry Rivers, Milton Avery stare back at me.

"Lucy, you had a phone call," my mother tells me, "from that Harry Wheeler."

My heart thuds. What happened? For him to call me so soon, something bad must have happened. Maybe they really hated me. It was just an act, to let me down easy. "Well, it was a good try, Lucy," he'll say. "Don't call me, I'll call you."

My mother is talking, but I haven't been listening to her. She is saying something about the end of August.

"What about the end of August?" I ask.

"That's when you're supposed to start filming," she says as she lifts the lid off a pot of steaming vegetables. I cannot see her face.

"What about school?" I hear my father's voice behind me. "That's the most important thing," he says. "What you hold in your hands, you can lose. What you hold in your head, no one can take away from you, Lucy."

"I haven't made a decision to do it, Daddy. I just found out this second," I say. I feel like I'm in a movie already, this all seems so unreal.

"It's not your decision, Lucy," my father says.

My heart pounds once, like the sound of something dropping. I glare at my father. He glares back.

"Fifty thousand dollars," I say, turning to face him.

He does not look impressed. He tosses two yellow pills down his throat, swallowing them without water.

"Big time, Lucy," he says, turning on his heels and walking down the hall, away from me.

"He'll come around," my mother murmurs, "he always does."

But I know better. The thing my father is most afraid of is losing me. His definition of losing me is different from mine. You will have nothing to do with the Mulcahy boy, he had said. Nothing. Do you understand? He would have torn his clothes; he would have sat shiva for me. Never, never for the rest of his life would he have looked up at the stars.

Chris could be kept a secret; this can't. If I proceed with this, my moving image will be captured in shiny tin cans, projected onto the screen, larger than life, immortal, unmistakable, irredeemable.

"Joe, isn't that Lucy?" my father's friends will ask. "I saw her name in the paper."

"Lucy who?" he will answer. "I have no daughter."

I have always tried to follow his rules. I have seen the world through his eyes: I have observed everything, and at the same time, nothing at all. That is, of course, until recently, until the world started spinning more quickly; I have had to learn to run, just in order to keep going.

What are you afraid of, Lucy, she asked me once. *Was it wrong to start? Or was it wrong to stop.*

I follow my father into the den, where he has hooked himself up to his hanging contraption. The straps under his chin push the folds of his cheeks up toward his eyes, making them small green slits. He doesn't look at me.

"Daddy, I can still go to school," I tell him.

He says nothing.

"I'll arrange the schedule around my classes," I say, having no idea whether this is possible. "I promise."

"Don't make promises you might not keep," he says, straining his jaw open.

"I'll never let it get in the way," I continue, but he shifts his eyes toward me, and I stop. I realize I have already made my decision.

"Never say never, Lucy," he says.

————

"Your father loves me so much," my mother tells me, "that he always wants me around. He wants me here in the morning when he leaves for work, and he wants me to greet him at the door at the end of the day."

She dices vegetables with a heavy knife: carrots, onions, zucchini, preparing for Shabbos dinner.

"When I married your father I had a career, Lucy. I made more money than most women I knew. *Vogue* magazine did a feature article on me. I still have it somewhere if you ever want to see what your mother did when she was young."

She sniffles as she wipes her teary eyes with the bottom of her apron.

"Ma, why do onions make you cry?"

"It's not the onions, Lucy," she says.

"Why did you stop working?"

I hope she isn't going to say, "Because you were born."

"Your father didn't want me to work," she says. "Your father loved me so much he wanted me all to himself."

At Shabbos dinner I watch them. My mother waves her hands three times over two burning candles, reciting the Hebrew words which welcome the Sabbath. A cloth napkin rests on top of her head. She covers her eyes with her hands, and her wedding ring glows yellow in the light of the twin flames. She does not know what the words mean: she has memorized them phonetically.

My father stands at the head of the table, watching her. He is proud. Everything is in its proper place. When she is finished, he sings the blessing over the wine. The small silver goblet in his hand was given to him by his great-grandfather.

The names of his family are finely etched into the silver, so faint and worn they are almost invisible.

My mother whispers something to me, and he looks over at us, frowning. "Ssshhh," he says. It is wrong to speak during the blessings. Perhaps God will get confused; he will not be able to hear us.

He slices the braided challah with a special knife, scattering breadcrumbs all over the white embroidered tablecloth. My mother rolls her eyes, but he doesn't see her. He hands each of us a small piece of the bread, an offering.

Your father loves me so much, she had said.

Once the ritual is dispensed with, he sits down, smoothing his yarmulke on top of his head. His face breaks into the broadest smile as he looks at my mother.

"Honey, what's for dinner?" he asks.

The phone rings, and as usual, I am the one to answer it.

"Hello, is this Lucy?" says a familiar voice, but I can't place it.

"Yes, who's this?" I ask.

"You can't tell?"

The voice sounds amused.

"No," I answer.

Maybe I'm wrong. Is this an obscene phone caller?

"Who is this?" I ask again, sharply.

"It's Ben. Ben Broadhurst."

Oh. Oh boy.

"Lucy, who is it?" my mother calls from the dining room. She hates to be interrupted at dinnertime.

"It's for me, Ma," I call back, not answering her question.

"Yes," I say into the receiver.

What do you want? Go away. My life is getting more complicated every minute.

"How are you?" he asks, his voice even deeper over the telephone.

Has he called to make small talk?

"I'm fine, thank you," I say, for lack of anything better.

"Good."

And then there is silence. It is during moments like these

that I find it impossible to say anything. If someone puts me on the spot, there I stay. But I am learning. I am learning by example. I take a deep breath, summoning up courage.

"Ben, what can I do for you?"

I hear him laugh. That definitely came out wrong.

"I was wondering if we could meet sometime," he says. "Perhaps I could buy you a drink, or dinner, or something."

Or something. I can't believe this.

"Is there something in particular you want to discuss?" I ask him.

"As a matter of fact, there is," he says.

"Can you tell me over the phone?" I ask, crossing my fingers and my toes.

"No," he says.

"Does it have to do with Carolyn?" I ask.

He pauses.

"Yes," he says, "it does."

And so continues, I think, an education in antinomy: the brambled woods, the mystery of silence, the keeping of secrets. I have something else, now, which I cannot tell anyone. It stays between my lips, under my tongue. I think that I will die with it.

I am meeting Ben Broadhurst for dinner Thursday night. Cafe des Artistes. Eight o'clock. "Lunch's no good. Dinner's better," he said. In candlelight, everything is softened. Does he have something to tell me? Maybe so. Perhaps not. Perhaps there is something I have to tell him. Does he want something of me? Or is it I, who wants something of him. And how do we begin, now that we have begun?

"Lucy, your dinner's getting cold," my mother says, walking into the kitchen, her voice on edge.

I sit back down at the table. My father's plate is empty, my mother's plate is half-empty, and my plate, sure enough, is full. I cut a cube of beef into tiny bird-sized pieces, and eat slowly, one at a time.

"Who was that?" my mother asks.

"Carolyn," I lie.

"Oh, how is Carolyn," my mother says, rounding her vowels, sarcastic.

My mother has not taken a shine to Carolyn. Whenever she speaks of her, it is with disdain. If only she knew.

"Why don't you like Carolyn?" I ask.

I am treading in dangerous waters.

"That girl's no good, Lucy," my mother says.

"You hardly even know her!"

I look at my father for help, but he is closely examining a wine stain on the tablecloth.

"I know enough to recognize one when I see one," my mother says.

"One what?" I ask.

What does my mother see?

We glare at each other until my father looks up from the tablecloth. "No fighting," he says quietly. "No fighting on Shabbos."

———

Late at night I sit on the milk box, smoking my customary cigarette. The dog next door barks at me, and I will him to be quiet; smoking is forbidden on the Sabbath. I can almost hear my father tossing and turning in the guest room above me. He has taken to sleeping in this airy room with a yellow doughnut inlaid into the pale blue floor. Long ago, this room was my nursery. My mother sits in the living room listening to her arias, but I'm not worried about her. She doesn't care whether I smoke or not. She will stay up very late, sipping Muscadet and reading a bestseller. When she is tired enough, she will tiptoe upstairs to the master bedroom, where she will spread herself over the width of the bed and sleep a dreamless sleep.

In the course of one weekend I have become a lover, an ingenue, I have been both betrayer and betrayed; in short, I think I have become an adult. I watch the smoke unfurl from the orange tip of my cigarette, opaque, then vanishing into the night sky. I follow it all the way up. By force of habit, I find myself looking for my grandfather amid the dense night clouds. In the shifting patterns, I imagine I see the great scholar Jacob Greenburg; in my mind's eye, he is frowning.

———

"What did you wish for?" my mother once asked me on a birthday long ago.

It was the first time I had blown out all the candles on my own.

"I wished to be a grown-up," I told her, smiling wide, showing all my missing teeth.

She never told me. No one ever told me that if you tell your deepest wishes, if you expose yourself altogether and truthfully, your wishes just might come true.

———

Ben is sitting at a corner banquette in one of the few restaurants left in New York that allows you to smoke cigars. He bites off the end of one, picking the brown paper from the tip of his tongue, and deposits it in the ashtray.

He rises slightly as I approach the table.

"You look gorgeous," he says as the waiter pulls out my chair, "just gorgeous."

"Thank you," I say, keeping my eyes on the floor.

I have never known how to accept a compliment.

He folds his hands behind his head and leans back into the banquette. He looks at me. He has no intention of speaking. Around us, the quiet clatter of china and crystal, the low hum of voices intensifies, as if someone had just turned up the volume.

I look everywhere but at Ben. The walls of the restaurant are covered with murals of cherubs, winged cupids, naked women dancing. On top of the bar there are hard-boiled eggs arranged in a circle. Do people eat these, and if so, how?

Businessmen with loosened ties sit at the bar stirring their drinks. Three women stand in a cluster, intent on one another. They are dressed alike, in flowing silk, and they are all wearing the same gold and platinum watches. What are they doing here on a quiet Thursday night? I look at their long necks, and imagine they are dancers. They are modern versions of the mural behind them, draped in pale silk, tossing their heads.

"What do you feel like?" Ben asks me.

"Sorry?"

"I was asking what you might like for dinner," he says, as he smiles with half his face. The other half is perfectly serious, perfectly still. It is as if he wants me to know that this is only half a joke.

I have no appetite. The steaming smell from platters passing us is making me ill. All around me, I see people's mouths moist with food.

"Actually, I'd like a drink," I say.

He signals a waiter, and I order a screwdriver with Absolut vodka, as I've seen Carolyn do so many times.

He continues to smile his bizarre smile.

"You're a quick study, little Lucy, aren't you."

I feel myself flush. Red seems to be my permanent color around Ben. What does he want? And why does he so enjoy putting me on the spot? Maybe because he knows he can. I resolve to make this more difficult for him. Two can play this game.

I take a gulp of my drink, capturing an ice cube in my mouth. I hold it under my tongue until I am numb from the cold.

"Why did you want to meet with me, Mr. Broadhurst?" I ask.

He stares at me: his practiced, I-can-see-right-through-you stare, which has won him houses in every corner of the world, a plaque from the mayor and, I imagine, countless women.

"Aren't you enjoying yourself?" he asks.

Enjoying myself. Am I enjoying myself? My heart is beating faster than usual, and there is a lump in my throat, as if

I'm about to cry. I swallow hard, and the vodka slides around it.

"Why did you want to meet me, Mr. Broadhurst?" I repeat.

His eyebrows rise like two gulls. Oh, he is thinking, she's going to give me a hard time.

"Didn't you want to come?" he asks.

"I was curious," I say.

"That's all?"

I don't respond. It is taking everything I have just to look him in the eye.

He shifts back on the banquette and plants his elbows on the table. His eyes are absolutely unwavering. Ben Broadhurst never blinks.

"You weren't really surprised to get my phone call, were you?" he asks. He smiles at me, a conspiratorial smile.

The lump in my throat is growing bigger by the moment.

"No," I say. My voice shakes over the one syllable.

"I told you, Lucy. I like to get to know my stepdaughter's friends. And you are certainly a very special friend to Carolyn," he says.

At this moment, by what I imagine must be divine intervention, we are interrupted.

"Ben Broadhurst," I hear a man's voice exclaim from behind me."

Ben looks up calmly, as if there's no awkwardness, no problem in his being recognized dining in a restaurant with a woman other than his wife.

"Hello, Steve," Ben says, reaching a hand over the table, beyond me.

I swivel around. The voice belongs to an older man, perhaps a few years older than Ben, with graying temples and the dense, well-kept body of a former athlete.

"Steve, meet my friend Lucy," Ben says.

We shake hands. Ben's excluding our last names makes me feel almost invisible, as if this conversation isn't really taking place.

"I've been meaning to give you a call, Ben. That was some incredible job you did in San Diego the other night. I think we came close to the million-dollar mark. I really want to thank you for all your help. And of course, your lovely wife did wonders with the decorations," says the mystery man.

At this he glances quickly at me.

"A pleasure," Ben responds.

The two men shake hands again, after making plans to meet at the New York Athletic Club the following week.

Ben waits until Steve moves a few feet away.

"Do you know who that was?" he asks me.

"No."

"He just bought a basketball franchise," Ben says, still watching Steve's back recede into the crowd. "He constantly gets me involved with all these goddamn charities. What an asshole."

The captain deposits our menus in front of us. He informs us of an extensive list of daily specials, all of which I forget even as they are being recited. I want to ask him to join us, to please not leave us alone at this table.

I take another sip of my drink, surprised to see my glass is almost empty. Ben signals the waiter for another round. He is drinking Perrier.

"I would have asked Carolyn to join us, but she wouldn't have liked the idea of my seeing you," he informs me.

Everything he says is predicated on an agenda only he knows, an agenda he follows as if it were an architectural plan: he is pursuing me with the same determination with which he lays down orders for a concrete foundation, central air-conditioning, fire stairs.

He runs the tip of his finger down my nose. His touch feels like rubbing alcohol on a fresh bruise.

"Do you know what I told Carolyn, the first time I saw you at Smith?" he asks.

I don't want to know. You have nothing to teach me. You are too slick, too smooth, you are larger than life. And you are Carolyn's stepfather.

I say nothing. I chip sesame seeds off a bread stick, one by one, brushing them into a little pile on the tablecloth.

"I said, 'Carolyn, your new roommate is the most beautiful

girl I have ever seen.' Carolyn got upset at that. She doesn't like anyone to be better at anything than she is."

I bend forward as he lights my cigarette, my hands visibly shaking. I have never thought of myself as beautiful, and now, in the course of one week, I have been redefined. I feel like I'm in a movie, the part where the music swells. My words are scripted; they belong to someone else: someone with lanky legs, a husky voice and hair falling over one eye.

"Do you always go behind Carolyn's back like this?"

"Only when I have to," he says.

"Why do you have to?"

He doesn't answer. He leans back into the banquette, stretching his arms out. He never takes his eyes off me. This is a business transaction, a win or lose proposition. I don't know what the stakes are, but I know they're high. Ben Broadhurst does not believe in defeat.

"Stop it, Lucy," he says, and for a moment he sounds just like Carolyn. "We both know why we're here."

"No," I say. "No."

He smiles at me.

"What are you saying no to, Lucy? You don't know what's going on? Or you don't want it to happen."

"What are you talking about?" I ask. My words sound to my own ears like a faint echo, a refrain from a familiar song.

His voice is like gravel crunching underfoot: heavy, throaty, uneven. He clasps my hand in both of his.

"So, other than learning to drink the best brand of vodka, what else has my stepdaughter taught you?" he asks, and his eyes slide over my body, extracting from me the same unwilling effect had his hands traveled the identical path.

We are not really seeing one another. We both see Carolyn in each other's eyes.

––––––––

"Look at me," you asked once, icicles dripping a steady rhythm onto our windowsill. "Lucy, open your eyes."

"I can't," I said.

"Why?" The camera swung away as you kneeled by my side.

When a duckling opens its eyes for the first time, whatever it sees is imprinted on its memory: a goose, a lake, a face in a cloud, the man in the moon. A farmer once made sure he was the first image a flock of ducklings saw when their eggs cracked open. In his old age, they followed by his heels, never leaving his side, a winged, white shadow.

"Lucy, open your eyes," you pleaded, your voice rising and falling with the breath of your hands.

Beneath my closed eyes a galaxy of blue stars formed intricate patterns, always in motion, a mute language.

"I can't," I told you, but I was wrong.

Rubinstein, Heifetz, Ashkenazy

His hands are a man's hands. They clasp mine.

"Did you hear me?" he asks, perfectly still.

"Yes," I say, but I am shaking my head no. I am like one of the wooden toys I played with as a child. Weebles wobble but they don't fall down. Nothing is shocking. Nothing is peculiar. All this has been here for me to see, and now I am opening my eyes.

I was never a child who stared at the sun. My mother always said it would blind me. I never touched the stove. I knew it would burn me. I never accepted candy from strangers. And here I am. What we don't know eventually catches up with us.

Sometime during the past half hour, Ben Broadhurst told me he is falling in love with me. He said it in the same exact tone in which he ordered the asparagus wrapped in smoked salmon. He said it with the lack of drama which usually accompanies an undisputed fact.

"I'm falling in love with you," he said. Please pass the salt.

"When I was just a bit older than you, I went out with one of the most beautiful movie stars in the world," Ben says. "You remind me of her."

"Who was it?" I ask.

"It doesn't matter."

I imagine a young Ben with an assortment of famous actresses: Faye Dunaway, Lauren Bacall, Catherine Deneuve. I try to picture him walking next to any one of them—even in the highest heels, none could lean her head on his shoulder. I imagine him lighting a cigar, as he does now, and blowing thick gray smoke around them like a velvety cape.

In the flickering light of this room, his face softens. His large brown eyes are really quite beautiful, I think. I can understand what Faye (or Lauren, or Catherine) saw in him. I watch his forearms flex as he reaches for his glasses, then picks up the wine list, studying it.

"Champagne," he says, handing the list to the waiter, "your best."

His neck looks as strong as an animal's. His tie constrains him like a leash. He does not belong in boardrooms, skyscrapers, expensive restaurants; I think he should be sweating somewhere, in a field, ax in hand, under the sun. His manicured hands look ridiculous. There should be dirt under his fingernails, calluses, the smell of horse manure. But this is not the case, and his touch, under the table, is almost as soft as his stepdaughter's.

———

"So tell me about Carolyn," he says.

"What about her?"

"Oh, come on, Lucy." His smile is easy, controlled.

"What?" I repeat.

"You're blushing," he says.

"I am not," I say stupidly.

His eyes don't waver. I watch in fascination as his lower lip drops slightly. His hand creeps up my thigh.

"Stockings," he says, "I love stockings."

So it happens, like an echo, like something that happened long ago, that I am lost. I am in a car traveling down a country road, my foot to the floor, going as fast as can be. There are cliffs to the left of me, and to the right there is a drop to the sea. I ignore everything. The speed is what matters.

"Oh," they will say when they find me, "she must not have been looking. She must have lost her way."

They will pick pieces of me out from the rubble. An arm here, a leg there. The face will be unrecognizable.

"So tell me," he says, as he signs the American Express receipt without checking the addition.

What do you want to know? And somehow, anyway, don't you know it already?

"I can't," I say.

"Trust me," he says, pushing his chair back from the table, "you won't be sorry."

The width of his hand covers the small of my back as he guides me out onto West Sixty-seventh Street, and into a dark blue limousine waiting at the curb.

———

There is a photograph of you I saw that night hanging in the living room of the Broadhurst apartment. In it, you are standing in front of a children's clothing store on Rue Saint Sulpice, in the heart of the most fashionable district Paris has to offer.

Your hair is pushed off your face by dark sunglasses, which rest on top of your head like a crown. You look as lovely as always. Your forehead is wrinkled slightly, your eyebrows pulled together in the quizzical expression you love to adopt whenever you are the center of attention.

I imagine those wrinkles will someday be permanent, you are the center of attention so often.

But it is none of these things which capture my interest. You are wearing ridiculously expensive clothes, the kind that are bought only in couture houses near the Place Vendôme. They curve around your angles like a lover's hands: the cashmere jacket with the gold buttons, the high-collared silk blouse, the short suede skirt which wraps around your narrow hips tighter than a corset.

It is almost possible to see the reflection of the photographer in your bright, shining eyes. This is what astonished me: the hands that held the camera, the voice that coaxed you to smile. You are looking directly at the photographer, entranced, adoring, mindless, as if you would follow him to the end of the earth.

―――――

"For the sin wherein we have sinned before Thee by breaking off the yoke, and for the sin wherein we have sinned before Thee by contentiousness; For the sin wherein we have sinned before Thee by ensnaring our neighbor, and for the sin wherein we have sinned before Thee by envy; For the sin wherein we have sinned before Thee by a breach of trust, and for the sin we have sinned before Thee by terror of the heart."

―――――

The city is spread out like a quilt below us. French doors open onto a rose garden in the sky. The late evening breeze rustling in through the open doors is beginning to wake me up, clearing away the residue of vodka, champagne, cognac.

I almost got sick in the car on the way over to Ben's apartment.

"I don't feel so good," I moaned, wondering how long Ben would still profess to love me after I threw up all over the backseat of his limousine.

"We're almost there, darling," Ben had said, rolling down the window.

Darling. I had never been called Darling before. It floated in the space between us, the most adult, exotic word. The roundness of it—the rich, full timbre—like the echo of champagne glasses lightly touching, or of stiletto heels clicking against a marble floor.

I leaned my head against Ben's shoulder. I stared straight ahead at a yellow sign which read No U-turns, watching the U move back and forth like a snake.

"Tell me about Carolyn," he says, rubbing my shoulders as I look out into the night. His touch is oddly familiar, as if he had been part of a dream, as if he had touched me in my sleep.

I turn to him, and am surprised by what I see: he looks like a young boy now, his face soft, almost formless. He is a magician; I see what he wants me to see.

"There's nothing to tell," I lie.

He pauses just long enough to grin at me, a dimpled, devilish, please—you-can-do-better-than-that grin.

"You're a different girl than the one I met a year ago at Smith. You've grown up. What happened?"

"Nothing happened."

"Liar," he says softly. He means it as a compliment. I have taken another sure footstep in a world of darkness.

He bends down to kiss me; I feel his rough stubble against my cheek, his lips, then his tongue tracing my mouth. I close my eyes and wrap my arms around his neck for a moment, feeling his hands press against the small of my back.

I open my eyes, and a wave of shock hits me as I realize what I'm doing. I feel as if I've just woken up in a field, or under a rock, in a cave. I don't belong here. He is Carolyn's stepfather.

I try not to think about how I got here, and concentrate on getting out. I have a terrible sinking feeling that a good deal of damage has already been done.

"I'm sorry. I have to leave," I tell him with a smile. No matter what circumstances I find myself in, I am always polite.

His eyes widen. He really did not expect this.

"Why?"

"I never should have come here in the first place," I say, and for the first time this evening, I sound like myself, or at least the self I'd like to be.

"Don't lie to yourself, Lucy. You wanted to come here."

"No. Not really."

Before I know what is happening, he brushes a hand against my breast, and I feel my nipple rise to his touch.

"Tell me you don't want this," he says, as if that proves something; he thinks my mind and my body are the same thing.

Tell me you don't want this, Lucy. Tell me and I'll go away.

"Don't touch me," I whisper as I back away from him. His touch has ruined me; I will never be clean again.

"I love you," he says, incongruously, for the second time this evening.

"How can you love me? You don't even know me."

"I know you better than you think. I know more about you than you could possibly imagine."

"I have to go," I say.

"Is this because of Carolyn?" he asks.

"Yes," I say, finally tired of playing "Truth or Dare."

He pauses. "But this is all right with Carolyn," he says.

"What?"

I can't imagine I heard him correctly. My palms grow immediately damp.

"I told Carolyn I was seeing you tonight. She knows, Lucy. And she knows how I feel about you."

My God.

"You're disgusting," I say. It is the first time in my life I have ever said anything like that to anyone; in doing so, I have used one of Carolyn's favorite words. For once, I am angry beyond politeness, beyond perfect self-control. "How could you do that to me?"

He smiles, shakes his head back and forth. "I thought you said there was nothing between you."

I stare at him, helpless with rage.

"If there's nothing going on between you," he repeats, "what difference does it make?"

He grins again, delighted. He has me cornered.

"You're married to her mother!" I sputter.

"So? I don't believe in labels, Lucy. And you'd be better off if you didn't, either."

He shakes his head again. "There's so much you have to learn, little girl," he says, but I barely hear him. I am groping for my bag, groping for the door.

In the elevator, I collapse into a corner. Black mascara streams down my face. The old man operating the elevator digs into his pocket, then hands me a handkerchief. I take it from him. I have no pride.

"It'll be all right, miss," he tells me.

I have a feeling this is not the first time he's seen a woman leave the Broadhurst apartment in tears. But he does not understand. I think I have just lost my best friend.

————

"Carolyn, it's me," I say in the morning, when she answers the phone.

"What do you want?" she asks in a voice so brittle I could snap it in two.

"We need to talk."

"There's nothing to talk about."

"I know you know that I—"

"I don't know anything. I don't care," she says flatly.

"Carolyn. I just want to explain."

"When I wanted to explain to you, you didn't give me the time of day," she says.

I expected this from her: a rare moment in which she is predictable.

"Please."

She is quiet.

"Please," I repeat, "it was a mistake."

"This afternoon at three o'clock," she says.

"Where?"

She thinks for a moment.

"The Water Club," she says.

I agree, not knowing where or what the Water Club is, and hang up as quickly as possible, before she has a chance to change her mind.

• • •

I am beginning to feel like a commuter. I ride the PATH train to Manhattan on an almost daily basis, auditioning for countless television commercials, industrials, a few scattered voice-overs and soap operas. Since the day I met Harry Wheeler, I have barely had a minute to spare. My mother will not let me drive my car into the city. She thinks it's dangerous. Little does she know.

This afternoon, I drive my car to Jersey City, parking it at the station next to my father's Citroën. There's a certain symmetry in his big foreign car sitting next to my little American one; it reassures me, as if the sleepy headlights of the Citroën were my father's eyes watching over me. I tap my hand on the hood as I pass, for good luck. I have a feeling I will need it.

Before meeting Carolyn, I have a callback for a Meineke Discount Mufflers commercial.

"I'm not going to pay a lot for this muffler," I say into the camera a half-dozen times, each time with a different expression, an emphasis on a different word.

Harry has told me that if I leave a commercial audition feeling like an idiot, I've probably done a good job.

I think I have done a particularly good job today.

She is sitting outside, under a Cinzano umbrella. Her sunglasses are perched on top of her head, drawing her hair back artlessly, as always. She is wearing a yellow tank top; the sun dances on her collarbone.

When she notices me walking toward her, she pushes her sunglasses back to the bridge of her nose. The metal chair scrapes against the sidewalk as I sit down.

This is a fashionable restaurant, and there is the requisite, fashionable pitcher of frozen slush on the table between us. I pour myself a glassful as I try to steady my hand. I pull a cigarette out, then search in my bag for matches, not noticing the matchbook lying on the table.

I light the cigarette, then blow pathetic smoke rings into

the humid air. Anything to busy myself. I cannot bear to look at her.

Finally there is nothing left to do. She is staring at me, haughty and unblinking. Her nails drum on the table, shiny red castanets.

"Why?" she says, still staring me down.

It is the first word either of us has spoken. One word can really sum it all up.

"I'm sorry," I say, looking at the leather strap of her pocketbook, a crack in the sidewalk, anywhere but into her shielded eyes.

"That's not an answer," she says.

I look up at her.

"Do you have all the answers?" I ask her, noticing for the first time her bare, puffy lips, the chapped skin on her cheeks.

She takes a long sip from her half-melted frozen drink.

"I hurt you, so you hurt me? An eye for an eye? Is that it, Lucy?" she asks quietly.

"No, that's not what I—"

"He'll eat you alive," she says suddenly, incongruously. "He'll eat you for breakfast."

Her mouth twists into a little smile. She enjoys this notion.

What about us, I want to ask her. What about an afternoon just a few days ago, a certain yielding between two best friends?

"About what happened before the party . . ." I begin, but she cuts me off halfway through the sentence, as though she had been anticipating this from the moment I sat down.

"I don't want to talk about that," she says. "Some things are not meant to be talked about."

I agree with this in principle, but think that afternoon falls into precisely the opposite category.

"I don't think we can be friends anymore," she says.

I realize that we each have committed an act that, to the other, is utterly unforgivable. I also realize that I am the only one doing any apologizing, but this doesn't stop me. I want to rewrite history.

"Carolyn, haven't you ever done anything because—"

"Because what?"

I recall the first feeling, the one before disgust set in, the one before propriety took over. I remember looking into his moist brown eyes and wanting to hold his face in my hands delicately, like the most beautiful and fragile of objects. It was an insane thought, like wanting to stab someone on the street, or hurl oneself in front of an oncoming subway.

"Carolyn, I didn't sleep with him," I say.

"You think that matters?" she snaps at me. "Are you really proud of yourself, Lucy?"

I promise her I will never see him again. I tell her I found him quite revolting, and watch as she tries to contain her glee. I tell her I despised it when he kissed me, his huge hands pressing against mine.

She will run to tell him this, but I don't care. I have betrayed her, and I want her back. This is all that matters.

It does not matter that I realize I am lying. Although I don't understand it, I know that I wanted to look longer into his eyes, I wanted to get lost in the width of him, I wanted to wrap my arms as far around him as I could.

"Carolyn, I will never see him again," I say, and I know that this had better be true. I know that if I see him again, I will not walk away.

Sartre once said you can live your life or tell a story. For the time being, I am choosing to tell a story, because I don't know what living my life means.

She insists on paying the check, a wry smile playing at her lips as she signs the credit card receipt.

"No, allow me," she says in a light tone, as if to let me know that money is the easy part, that money is the least of it.

For the first time since we've known each other, we do not hug good-bye. As she stands by the curb, her tanned arms crossed over her chest, hips jutted out to the right, I have an almost uncontrollable urge to touch her; I want to run my hand across her shoulders, I want to feel the hollow of her throat.

———

Why didn't you tell me, then. Why didn't you tell me that I didn't have all the correct information, that the gun I carried was loaded with silver bullets? Children shouldn't play with firearms, you would have said, a small, cryptic smile flitting across your face.

It was both of us playing with fire, Carolyn. And only one of us knew it.

———

"It's not fair that everybody dies, Daddy," I say to my father. We are lying on the tall grass, our backs damp against the ground.

"I know, shnooks, I know," he sighs. He is not talkative lately; the pills dull his sense of humor, his sense of play.

"Why does it have to happen?"

"The Almighty, blessed be He, has His reasons," my father says.

We stare at the stars.

"But you know, Lucela, if we lead lives full of good deeds, full of *mitzvot*, we will all meet again in the *Gan Eden*, the Garden of Eden," my father tells me, absently stroking my head.

"What if we don't lead a life full of *mitzvot*, Daddy? What if our bad deeds and our good deeds even out?" I ask.

My father is silent. He's cooking up an answer for this question, which the Bible doesn't answer.

"Shalom Aleichem told a story once, Lucy. He told of a poor soul who stood at the gates of heaven. He was told that in order to enter the *Gan Eden*, he had to produce three gifts for the Almighty, blessed be He.

"This soul went back down to earth, where the first thing he saw was an old Jewish man being robbed. The thiefs were trying to open a dresser drawer, and the old man shouted, 'No! Not there!' Well, of course the thiefs assumed that there was something of value in the drawer, so they forced it open. Inside, they found nothing but dirt. This dirt was special earth from Israel, which the old man was saving to be put under his head when he died. The thiefs threw the dirt at the old man, killing him.

"The next thing the poor soul saw was another old man running through a group of Cossacks who were taunting him. The old man's yarmulke fell off his head, and he turned back to retrieve it. When he bent down to pick it up, the Cossacks killed him.

"The third thing the poor soul saw was an old Jewish woman who was being lifted onto a wagon, high up for all the world to see. The woman took two pins from her pocket and pinned the fabric of her skirt right into her legs, so that her skirt would not fly up with the wind. Modesty was one of the commandments.

"The poor soul went back up to heaven bearing these three gifts: a handful of earth, a yellow yarmulke, and two rusted pins. The doors to the Garden of Eden swung open, and he was welcomed into the open arms of his family, with music and laughter, wine and song.

"So you see, Lucela, we try to live a good life, we try to do the right thing. But if we fail, and we become one of the many poor souls who have sinned, there is still hope for us. There is always hope for us."

My father swings me into his arms, holding me as we look up at the sky. He feels better now; his story has revived him. We search the sky for Grandpa Jacob. We know that he is one of the lucky ones. I imagine he is watching over me. He will guide me throughout my life. He will allow me to do no wrong.

———

"I don't think we can be friends anymore," she had said. Friends. Is that what we were? In any event, things are no longer the same. There is a gulf between us larger than the span of words.

She graces me with an occasional phone call; she is lilting

and distant. She is going back to Smith in a few weeks, and I am not.

"Good luck with your new career," she says to me, her attention far away, on the other end of the telephone line. Perhaps she is filing her nails, or reading *Vogue,* or doodling drawings of arrows shooting through hearts.

When I ask how she is, she tells me she's fine, always fine, her voice rising and falling with cool amusement.

We get together, only when she feels like it, only at the last minute: dinner, the new Woody Allen movie, screwdrivers with Absolut. When I touch her arm, the fabric of her trench coat, she moves away and I am left with an outstretched hand; my body knows this gesture. Sometimes I think I was born with my hands reaching out into territory where I could never belong.

Each day I embark on an education, a lesson about this strange new world of video cameras, blond actresses, air-conditioned offices in towering buildings on Broadway or Fifty-seventh Street.

I am beginning to look like an actress. I dress in crisp, colorful shirts, which will look good on camera, and tuck my recently acquired eight by tens into a leather knapsack.

I have learned to speak directly into the black lens of the camera, as if I am chatting with my best friend. I talk about Palmolive, or Getty motor oil, or Grape-Nuts with equal enthusiasm. I state my name for the camera with a wide, even smile.

"Hi, I'm Lucy Green," I say, knowing the tape will be viewed in a conference room by the corporate clients, that my face will be one of fifty or sixty faces they see.

Ben calls me every day: five times, ten times. It's getting to the point where every time the phone rings, I assume it's him.

"Lucy, it's for you," my mother calls from the cordless phone. She is out by the pool doing halfhearted leg lifts.

My parents do not understand what's going on with me. They sense they are losing me in this vast abyss of phone calls from New York City, the onslaught of unfamiliar voices and strange men.

When I come to the phone, each conversation is, in effect, the same.

"Hello?"

"Lucy, don't hang up."

"I have nothing to say to you."

"Well, tell me to my face. All I ask is that you tell me to my face you never want to see me again."

"No."

"Why?"

"Sorry. Good-bye."

My mother has asked me about the man who keeps calling. "The one with the deep voice," she says, looking concerned. And I tell her it's business.

Lately, Harry's office has been calling me all the time, setting up auditions almost every day. They ask for Lucy Green, these high-voiced young assistants. They are unflaggingly cheerful as they tell me what to wear for the various roles: a flannel shirt (for the outdoorsy look), a one-piece bathing suit (the California look), a Victorian blouse (young and innocent) and so on.

But no one calls as much as Ben. I know my mother does not believe me. I keep wanting to tell her the truth, but something stops me. I carry this information in my chest just above my heart, like a pacemaker, hidden and unnatural.

He writes me letters in a surprisingly fine script: black, bold and gracefully rounded. The letters are written in iambic pentameter; Ben Broadhurst is sending me sonnets. The mailman pushes them through the brass slot in our front door several times a week, and they hit the floor like guided missiles.

I imagine him sitting in his corner office, high above midtown Manhattan, at an enormous desk littered with newspapers, yellow pads of paper and empty cans of diet soda. He cradles a thin gold pen in his hand and stares out the window at the electronic weather forecast on top of the MONY building.

His brain is very large. He is able to manage untold millions, several children, wives, ex-wives and half of Manhattan's commercial real estate, and still think of me. My face floats on silver wings outside the open window. He smiles, waves his left hand, blows a kiss. Around him, on end tables, there are photographs in tortoiseshell frames: Liz, Carolyn, Debbie, the baby. There is even one of Ben, standing next to a sailboat at a pink, sandy harbor. He is holding a rainbow-colored fish by the hook coming out of its mouth. The fish's eye stares at the camera. Ben's teeth glint in the sun.

In today's mail there is no sonnet, but there is an engraved invitation with my name on it. I turn the envelope over, startled when I see the return address: the Connecticut farmhouse. Carolyn.

Come celebrate Carolyn Ward's nineteenth birthday, it reads, on the Broadhurst yacht, Sag Harbor, New York.

———

After twenty-seven auditions, I have booked my first national television commercial. It is for Coca-Cola. It's being shot at an old Spanish Harlem nightclub with a cast of one hundred extras, but I have a principal role.

I close my eyes as the makeup artist whisks her sponge under my jawline. I stand still as Wardrobe pins the back of my blue, flowing skirt. I raise my arms above my head so they can powder my underarms. I am the center of attention, the center of the room.

I am also the least important person here.

Once I am made perfect, I sit perfectly still in a ladder-back chair, filling a metal ashtray with butt after lipstick-stained butt. I drink coffee until my teeth grind together. There's nothing to read here except the *New York Times*, and they won't let me touch it, God forbid I should get newsprint on my manicured hands.

The scene is late at night. The windows of the nightclub are blackened with heavy curtains. My role is that of a girl dancing in the smoke-filled room. I don't speak; I haven't spoken all day.

All around me, technicians, cameramen, grips, production assistants carrying clipboards scurry about. They have work to do, setting up this scene. The extras sit on the floor in a designated area, smoking, drinking coffee, picking each other up. Everyone looks bored. They watch the clock tick. Every hour brings them closer to overtime, when they will make time and a half.

I know the story well: Harry got me several extra jobs so I could begin to learn my way around a set. I now know what it is like to get paid $150 a day to sit in one spot like a piece of furniture. What I am doing today is not all that different, except for this: I will get paid a lot more.

"You look familiar," a deep voice says. I turn around and find myself staring into a face so handsome that it is incongruous in real life; it is the face of a man who had no choice but to become an actor.

"No. I don't think I've ever seen you before," I say.

If I had, I would surely remember.

"I'm David Cates," he says, offering his hand. "I believe we're dancing together shortly." He smiles a blinding smile.

Of course. David Cates. Now I understand the incongruity of seeing him in person. He has been in tons of commercials as well as on the soap opera of choice at Smith. I remember laughing with Carolyn about him. "Now there's your kind of guy, Lucy," she said to me, referring to the sinewy, fair young men I always glanced at twice on the streets of Northampton.

The technicians are going over the Isley Brothers tape which is going to play in the background. Suddenly their music fills the room.

"Do you want to practice?" he asks, and without waiting for a reply, he pulls me out of my chair, then whirls me around the room, dipping me easily so my hipbones touch his leg, balancing me as my back bends toward the floor.

My parents didn't believe in teaching me anything useful; I speak fluent Hebrew, ice-skate fairly well, understand a good deal of Talmudic theory—but I have never taken a dance lesson in my life. I'm not a very good dancer. David Cates realizes this. We look at each other with instant camaraderie. He will cover for me. He's not going to give me away.

During the callback for this commercial, I was asked if I could dance. "We're not looking for a professional dancer," the casting director said, "just a girl who can move well."

And I nodded my head. "Sure," I said. "I can do that." It seems lately to be the motto of my life: say yes, then worry about the consequences.

He dips and twirls me around, doing steps I've never heard of. I am breathless, laughing, nervous. This is where I should be: in the arms of a man, a young man, hands strong against the small of my back. He reminds me of Chris Mulcahy all grown up, with a real beard instead of peach fuzz covering his face. His teeth shine in the dark of the nightclub.

Through the music, I hear the director asking for the talent on the set, and our names being called over a megaphone, even though we are only a few yards away. They are ready for us after hours of perfecting each detail. Crisscrossed fluorescent tape covers the floor, indicating where we should begin, where we should dance, and where we should end. I remember the first time I stood on fluorescent tape just like this, during my audition for Sheila Perkins. It seems another lifetime as I stand here, feeling the makeup artist's soft brush powdering my shoulders one more time.

The music begins. The slate snaps down like a gunshot. The assistant director calls out, "Take one!" and the air is filled with crisp, effective action. We dance in a throng of people, but the camera is trained on us alone. I throw my head back, knowing what my hair looks like, the cascade of curls, the shimmering gold highlights created just for today. I look into his eyes, this most handsome young man who is staring down at me, undressing me with his eyes. His hands rest on my waist. He moves my hips back and forth. I have to remind myself that we are acting.

We are acting. Outside this smoky nightclub it is really daytime in upper Manhattan, probably about three in the afternoon. Boys hang over fire-escape rails, spitting on the heads of passersby. Their fathers stand in the shadows of buildings whispering in soft, stained voices, "Black beauties, speed, got speed here," like auctioneers wielding gavels. Going once, going twice.

Outside it is dangerous, but not in here. This is something I have begun to learn: as long as I'm performing, I feel completely safe. This character, this young, breezy blonde moving on the dance floor has inhabited my body. I discover, to my astonishment, that I can dance after all. I decide she must have a name that ends with a vowel: Candi, Laurie, Marci. She wipes her prettily perspiring brow with an icy can of Coke, never breaking step. She is used to this, she comes here every night. She stares boldly back at her male counterpart. All is well in Spanish Harlem.

When it is over, after the nineteenth take, a Winnebago takes us back downtown. I am exhausted, and I drank more Coca-Cola today than some people drink in a lifetime. My teeth are sticky, and my stomach pushes against the waistband of my skirt.

David Cates slaps me on the back. "You did good work in there, kiddo," he says, crunching his face into a wink. "What do you have lined up next?"

I'm not sure what he means, so I tell him I'm going home for dinner. He laughs at me.

"No, I didn't mean tonight. I meant, what are you doing workwise?"

I feel myself quickly blush, as I always do when I've put my foot in my mouth. "Well, I'm supposed to be doing a film in a few months . . ."

"Oh yeah? Great, that's just great," he says. "What, some kind of *Halloween VI* or that sort of thing?"

"No, I don't know that much about it, but it's a feature film—"

"What's it called?" he interrupts, and suddenly I don't want to give him any more information. His face is tight, a plastic, greedy mask. Everything has changed now that he thinks I can do something for him, now that he thinks I'm "somebody," too.

I shrug my shoulders. "I can't remember," I tell him as the

trailer pulls up to the production office. We hop down the two metal stairs into the first chilly night of the season. He pats me on the back again, pulling me close into an impersonal hug.

"Keep in touch," he says, pressing a card into my hand.

As I walk away, toward the tubes which will take me back to New Jersey, I look at the card and see two different versions of his face staring at me in black and white. In one, he is wearing the obligatory crewneck sweater with a plaid shirt peeking out from underneath, and he is smiling his famous smile. In the other, his hair is slicked back; he is wearing wire-rimmed glasses I'm sure he doesn't need as he gazes soulfully into the camera. This is his I'm-really-too-smart-to-be-an-actor look.

I rip the card right down the center, separating the two faces, and toss them into a garbage can. As I continue walking toward the PATH station, a phrase, like a mantra, turns over and over in my head. That will never be me. That will never be me.

_____

Carolyn's birthday party is next week. Celebrate with us on the Broadhurst yacht. I have carried the RSVP card in the outside compartment of my pocketbook for days now, eyeing it once in a while, wishing it would just go away.

"Carolyn, I'm sorry. I can't possibly come," I tell her, the receiver cold against my shoulder.

"Why not?" she asks.

I can't see her face; I don't know what she is thinking.

"Carolyn, I can't see him," I say.

"Why not, Lucy, if you found him so revolting," she says evenly.

"I don't want to see him," I repeat.

"I don't see what difference it makes."

"Please."

She pauses. "He won't be there," she says. Her voice rises and falls over miles of telephone wire. "Hold on a minute, I'll have my mother give you directions."

• • •

I outline my lips in soft pink, then pull my hair off my forehead with a wide ribbon. I wear a purple satin dress, black mesh stockings and very high heels. It is raining outside, the night of the party, but vanity always wins out over the weather.

"Lucy, you look beautiful," my mother tells me, holding me at arm's length. "Turn around. Let me get the full effect."

I turn around, awkward and self-conscious the way only my mother makes me feel. I can be uninhibited in front of hundreds of people when I am acting, but scrutiny from my mother makes me turn bright pink as I stammer, "Come on, Ma. Enough already."

"Take Mother's car," my father says, clearing his throat. "The weather stinks tonight."

I turn, surprised to hear my father's voice. He hasn't been talking much lately. I know he has upped his daily intake of painkillers; I know this because I count them. He looks at me with confused eyes, as if not comprehending how this young woman came to be standing in his house, in his kitchen. He wanted to keep me his little girl forever. He thought if he prayed hard enough, it might come true.

My father clears his throat again. "Call when you get there," he says gruffly, then turns on his heels and leaves the room.

I drive my mother's Audi down the black tarp of the Long Island Expressway. The rain pours onto the windshield in thick drops. My heart beats in time with the windshield wipers: fast, faster. I am tense. I tell myself it's the weather.

An hour goes by, two, and I have listened to the entire "Pathétique," "Moonlight," and "Waldstein" sonatas, until finally I am in Sag Harbor, in front of a marina which looks ready to overflow, opulent yachts bobbing like ducks in a bathtub.

I slide my way up the dock, which has been covered by a narrow awning and strung with lights. Arrows indicate the way to the Broadhurst yacht, though it wouldn't be hard to pinpoint. Carolyn has always referred to it as "the boat," which appears to be the understatement of the century.

I have never been on anything but a Camp Wakanabe canoe, so I didn't know what to expect, but this is more like a floating mansion. I step onto the brightly lit deck. Bruce Springsteen wails "Jersey Girl" through powerful speakers, and I wonder whether it's a coincidence, or an inside joke.

There are narrow portholes on either side of the door. I look into the swirl of the crowd; the first person I see is Ben. A butler opens the door before I have a chance to consider the option of turning around and leaving. My heart ricochets under the creamy satin of my dress, and I feel my cheeks burning red. I know I have been betrayed, but I am not sure by whom.

Carolyn sidles over to me. She looks like a princess, replete with silk, pearls and pumps. She gives me a musky hug; I breathe into her neck and smell gin.

I grab her elbow and steer her into a corner.

"You told me he wouldn't be here," I hiss at her.

"That's what I thought," she says in a lilting voice. She looks at me as if puzzled, as if she doesn't understand what the problem is.

I wonder what her skin would feel like under my hand if I slapped her. She smiles at me, as if daring me to go ahead.

"How could you do this to me?" I ask her, holding on to her sleeve.

"Let me get you a drink," she says, and walks away.

I decide that the most dignified thing to do is to pretend he isn't here. I begin, with great difficulty, to circulate; I am terrible at small talk, at introductions, at balancing drinks, canapés and conversation all at once. I don't see anyone I know here. There are lanky European couples lounging on tapestried love seats, elegant older men in tweed suits, with pocket watches and pipes. I don't recognize anyone in a roomful of Carolyn Ward's friends.

She hands me a Negroni. This is a drink I have never heard of, and will never want to hear of again after this evening.

Her youngest sister trots over and stares up at me through a haze of blond ringlets.

"We're wearing the same dress!" she squeaks.

"Hi, sweetie," I say, momentarily forgetting her name, "you look so pretty."

"Where's your boyfriend?" she asks.

"Definitely not here," I say, trying not to laugh.

"I have lots and lots of boyfriends," she says.

"That's great, Jessie. Do you have a favorite?"

"My Daddy," she says. "He's the cutest boy here."

The storm has ended. Polished teak doors are opened, guests wander onto the rain-soaked deck, and a cool breeze floats through the yacht's interior. Ben is wearing soft gray trousers and a cashmere sports coat. Amid the glow of candles and light reflecting off the bay, there is a proprietary air about him, as if he owns almost everything and everyone present, which to some extent is probably true. I am a little woozy from two Negronis. I think it might be nice to be owned.

He leans one hand against the wall, standing over Carolyn; both are talking intensely. Her beauty is pale and brilliant as the moon tonight, and like the moon, she is illuminated from a source outside herself: her whole face shines as she looks at Ben. Then she bows her head down, and I think I see a tear fall off the ledge of her cheekbone. She looks up at him again, her eyes flashing in a way I have seen only once in the year I've known her.

Tell me you don't want this, Lucy. Tell me and I'll go away.

Liz Broadhurst darts in and out of the crowd, waving hello to everyone she sees with a perfectly manicured hand. She seems quite busy, though there's nothing for her to do. I have counted at least ten waitresses, three bartenders and the butler at the door.

Something looks different about Liz. After studying her for a few minutes, I realize what it is: she's had a face-lift. Her skin is stretched tighter over her cheekbones, and along her hairline I see tiny, crescent-shaped scars. This face-lift has done nothing for her. She is a striking woman, and until now she looked quite a bit younger than her age, which I imagine to be bordering on forty. Now she looks older, and her smile is careful, plastic, as though if she smiles too hard, her face will shatter.

I close my eyes, resting my head on a wooden door frame. The room is swaying back and forth.

"I'd offer you a drink, but I see you already have one," he says.

What did I expect? I was not going to get through this evening, this party, without hearing his voice directed at me. There is a certain symmetry to this, the logic of the netherworld, and when I look up into his enormous eyes, it is clear this was going to happen all along.

"Thanks. Yes, Carolyn's been taking wonderful care of me" is all I can muster, my feeble attempt at sarcasm. I raise my glass to him and take a sip.

"Yes, Carolyn has certainly thrown us together," he says with a small smile.

"What do you mean?"

"Lucy, she told me you wouldn't be here," he says. "She told me you weren't invited."

I look at Carolyn across the expanse of the yacht. She is standing by an open door, the breeze lifting her dress as she laughs with a group of strangers.

"What do you have on under that?" Ben asks, his mouth tight, moving as if he were chewing something.

"Excuse me?"

"I said, what do you have on under that?"

His voice is hoarse. I look up at him, and the room stops dead still.

"Not very much, thank you," I say, and even as my lips part, even as the words fly across the space between us, they seem the work of a ventriloquist; I cannot believe my own ears.

———

I've been reading up on ancient Jewish mysticism. I'm sure this is a subject you—with your Miss Porter's education and your twice-yearly church visits—know or care nothing about.

These mystics believed that in the beginning, when God created the heavens and the earth, sparks of light fell from the divine realm into the lower depths. The sky rained fireflies for seven days and seven nights. These bright yellow sparks were buried in the netherworld, deep beneath the ocean, burrowing miles into the earth. In this way, good elements of the divine order came to be mixed with vicious ones; even in darkness, there was light.

I have now lived long and hard enough to understand the mystics' theories. They taught me this: it is the obligation of those who seek a life of true understanding to find the buried shards of light, to recover them, to bring them forth, like Shalom Aleichem's gifts, into the world: a yellow yarmulke, a handful of dirt, two bloodied pins.

It is written that we must degrade ourselves in order to go forward, it is said that only in our humiliation will we find the truth.

Sparks and Husks

*I*n the very beginning, I believed he was going to save me. I believed that I was drowning, I was dying, and only he could reach a strong arm into the swirling depths and rescue me. I believed this not in the metaphysical sense, but that my death would be a tragic one: cataclysmic, immediate and wasteful.

Sometimes I still come across his picture in the newspaper, or in one of the many business magazines floating around this country. Occasionally, while waiting for the subway, I will catch his face on the cover of *Forbes,* or *BusinessWeek.* It is a wonder, than, even to myself, that I do not dive onto the electrified tracks, that his eyes do not destroy me like lasers when staring down at me from the distance of a magazine cover.

Why am I telling you this? You already know it. You, after all, will never be rid of him. He is married to your mother, for better or worse.

Have you moved to Sri Lanka? Have you joined a commune, the Hare Krishnas, have you been born again?

The first time we made love was in your family home in Nantucket. (Do you want to hear this?)

It was fall. The leaves had already dropped off the trees, and the house was surrounded by bare, sea-dampened branches. We drove there from New York in Ben's sports car, going eighty, ninety miles an hour, yet I was so relaxed that my bones felt loose in their sockets. We left the city at midnight; by the time we arrived in Hyannis and took the ferry to the island, we had listened to every Willie Nelson song ever recorded, and it was dawn.

The house was all closed up. The shades were drawn, the heat was turned off, there was no phone and no cooking gas, yet it felt warm and inviting. Ben went into town and bought coffee and muffins, and we sat on your living room floor eating breakfast. Afterward, he changed from his business suit into jeans and a fisherman's sweater, and I put on a long knitted jacket of your mother's, and we went out for a walk on the beach.

I am sorry, but this is how it was. You see, it wasn't all bad in the beginning.

There was no one on the beach. We lay down on the smooth, untrodden sand, my head resting on Ben's stomach. Sea gulls walked within inches of us; we were that motionless. After a little while, I began to shiver. He sat up, pulled off his sweater and wrapped it around me.

"You'll never be cold as long as you're with me," he said as he engulfed me in his arms until I stopped shaking. Then he picked me up like I weighed nothing at all, and I rode on his shoulders to the ocean's edge.

We stood there for a long time. I was higher up than I'd ever been. I watched the churning in the distance, the waves crashing white against the weather-beaten dock. His bare shoulders beneath my legs felt as solid as if I were sitting firmly on the ground, and not six and a half feet up in the air, riding on top of a man who was about to become my lover.

The salty wind whipped my hair around so hard it stung my face, my eyes squinted in the pale, thin light of early morning, and I remember thinking that this was how I wanted to live: I wanted to be high up off the ground, safe in the middle of nowhere, pressed against the bare shoulders of a giant who would never let me go.

He carried me to bed. He held on to me all the way back up the beach, through the dunes, down the narrow, weed-filled path which led to your house. He opened the back door, ducking so we both would fit in, and kept walking; he knew where he was going, and so did I.

The bed in the master bedroom was enormous, with a pink chenille spread lying across it just so (but I guess you know this). We toppled onto it, and I clung to him. I dug my nails into him and held on as if I were drowning, which I suppose in some sense I was. There was more of him than I could see at once; his legs were the size of my whole body. He touched me with all the knowledge stored in his experienced fingertips. He kissed me with all the urgency of a man who had not touched his wife in years.

And my body was like a sheet of ice. I felt nothing. I went through the motions with a detached interest, as if my arms, my legs, my tongue really belonged to someone else. I began acting, the same way I had danced in a smoky nightclub with David Cates, the same way I had cavorted on a Caribbean beach in a swimsuit, promoting M&M's. I shuddered and moaned, I undulated my hips. I closed my eyes, forcing a halfwitted, ecstatic smile. I thought I was giving the performance of a lifetime.

You see, this is what I had done my whole life, except for one particular afternoon, in an attic bedroom of a farmhouse, once long ago.

When I was finished with my little drama, I looked up at him. He was still hard, still inside me, and in his dark eyes I thought I saw such gentleness, such complete understanding that I began to cry, right then and there.

"Lucy, don't do that," he quietly said.

"What?" I cried, burying my head in his shoulder. I knew I was caught in a moment of profound embarrassment, a moment capable of bringing me closer to him, closer than I intended to go.

"Don't lie to me, ever again, at least not in bed," he said.

And then we began, in earnest, once more.

He taught me everything I know. We began that weekend, and we never stopped. Even when I hated him, even when I couldn't stand the sight of him, the feel of his hand against the small of my back could make my knees go weak. I learned about peaks and valleys, quivering stomachs, filthy whispers late at night.

A year later, even across a roomful of people, if I saw the muscles in his jaw bunch in a particular way, if he gave me a certain hard, sexual smile, there was no stopping me; I would follow him anywhere. We made love in airplane bathrooms, in the backseats of limousines, on the beach, in other people's bedrooms. He stuck his hand into my panties under the tables of restaurants, he reached under my blouse for my breasts in theatres, at the opera, when it was dark.

I told myself it was harmless when it began, as harmless as it could possibly be to sleep with the stepfather of a woman I had slept with, my college roommate, my best friend. I did not know where it would lead. (I never meant to hurt you, but this is, of course, a moot point.)

But it grew like a lesion, there was no stopping it. By the end, we bordered on the edge of the world, the edge of the bed, the perverse side of sexuality.

I would have done anything he said.

I dreamt about you. In my dreams we were together, no, more than together. Our limbs had somehow merged, becoming a conglomerate of parts: your hair and my face, my breasts and your legs. When he and I made love, you were always in the room. You stood in the doorway, you floated in the air around us. At times it was I, standing at the edge of the room. You were inescapable. You still are.

I learned to close my eyes, and suddenly the whole world became possible. In acting, it's called the fourth wall. You block out the audience. You pretend they don't exist. In bed with him, I was in your company, and the company of your older counterpart, your mother. You lay to either side of us, and I triumphantly rode him as you stared at me with envy, with hatred, with greed. You reached up for my breasts, she stroked my belly as I writhed in the darkness.

When it was all said and done, I always looked down at Ben, and through the murky haze, the hot tangle of breath between us, I knew with utter certainty that our minds were like dancers, twisted into a dangerous pas de deux.

He had brought you into the bedroom as much as I.

He had been thinking the exact same thing.

It seemed we went on like this forever, as I sank deeper and deeper into the ground, in search of sparks and husks. And if you wish the worst for me, think about this: once you have exchanged fantasy for reality, nothing ever seems real again. Once you have chosen depravity, it is nearly impossible to go back.

I will never be the same.

Where are you? Are you married and living in Beverly Hills? Do you have any children? Does he come to visit every Christmas, and if he does, do you lock your children's doors at night? I hope so. I hope you have learned by now that enough is never enough.

———

PART THREE

*T*his is my life: in the short span of a year, I have become fairly successful at being an actress, and highly successful at being the mistress of a married man. I live on both coasts, where I have homes that are, in fact, hotel suites. In Los Angeles we live at the Beverly Hills Hotel, and in New York we live at the Carlyle. Nothing is permanent, but everything has such a high gloss to it that it's almost possible not to notice. If you look hard enough, you can see yourself reflected in everything you look at in a sort of muted, glamorous way. Hotel lighting is designed for this, as is the lighting for television and film. Here, it is truly possible to see only what you want to see.

Each day I wake up at seven in the morning and glance through either the *Los Angeles Times* or the *New York Times*, which are left outside my door. I eat a room service breakfast of cappuccino and a bite or two of a croissant. When Ben is with me, we usually end up back in bed with a DO NOT DISTURB sign hanging on the outside doorknob.

The Wheeler Group generally schedules my auditions for the afternoon, when possible. I suppose they have figured out that morning is not the best time for me to be seen, especially when Ben's in town. Three or four mornings a week, I curl my hair and put on my heavy television makeup. I line my eyes and lips with cosmetics which look terrible in daylight, but wonderful on camera. I sit on hard benches in rooms with other women who all have perfect faces and makeup which does not match the skin on their necks.

The rest of the time I spend with Ben. He has given me keys to the Carlyle apartment, and a standing reservation for a bungalow at the Beverly Hills Hotel.

"Consider these your homes," he says to me, "until one day we can have a house of our own, together."

So I fly back and forth between both coasts, both homes. Sometimes he is with me, more often he meets me in the middle of the week, and we have a few nights together in the candlelight of fancy restaurants and the dark, draped silence of hotel rooms.

It is our second winter together when we arrive in California on the day after Christmas.

As usual, we wait on no lines, we stand in no crowds. We are whisked from a black limousine to a private plane to a white limousine. I feel as though I am living in an air bubble; everything around me runs on its own, orchestrated time, and other people are seen from a hazy distance, as if they really don't exist at all.

The Beverly Hills Hotel is pink. Everywhere I look there are pink marble floors, pink stucco walls, pink sunburned faces. Standing in the middle of the lobby is a white tree covered with pink tinsel and plastic reindeer. Canned music fills the halls, and the bellboys beam cheerful holiday smiles. Pockets jingle with silver.

This is the place that feels like home. Christmas in Los Angeles, the city of angels.

I sit naked in a wrought-iron chair on the patio of our bungalow. The late afternoon sun beats down on my pale body as I take a sip of a watered-down Bloody Mary and leaf through *Town & Country*, glancing at photographs of models who aren't really models but are, in fact, blue-blooded princesses, daughters of bluegrass horse country or Arabian royalty.

A black-and-white picture captures my attention: Elisabeth and Ben Broadhurst, the caption reads, at the Gold and Silver Ball, Lexington, Kentucky, on October the Fifteenth.

They are dancing. Her smooth, uplifted cheek rests firmly on his chest as if it were the most natural thing, as if in the dark of their bedroom she might rest her cheek against him in the same way. She looks fragile, tiny next to him. She is a small woman, smaller than I. I have recently dieted my way down to a size four, but Ben has informed me that his wife wears a size two. Her arms are graceful as a dancer's, her ankles are slightly thick with the birth of three children.

I observe these things like a clinician, marking them off one by one. I have traced the woman's round, dusky eyes, her wide mouth, her delicate jaw so many times in my sleep that I can conjure her to mind with no effort: if you show me a blank wall, I will show you her face.

"What are you doing, darling?" he asks, walking onto the patio. He is naked too, except for the gold watch which he never takes off, and his glasses, perched on the end of his nose as he peers over them at me.

"Reading about your active social calendar," I say sweetly, handing him the magazine.

He holds it close to his face, peering at it as if he can't quite make it out. Then he chuckles.

"Liz won't much like this picture," he says. "She'll think it makes her look fat."

"You didn't tell me you were going to Kentucky," I say, trying to clear my head. I had three drinks on the flight, and am sipping another so I don't get hung over.

"Lucy . . ."

"What?" I ask.

"Come inside and look at your presents, darling. It's Christmas!" he says, then walks back into the bungalow.

The living room is filled with shopping bags and boxes: Elizabeth Arden, Neiman-Marcus, Giorgio. Ben Broadhurst has discovered Rodeo Drive.

———

My first year in prep school I came home humming a tune which stuck in my head after choir practice. The words were Latin, I couldn't remember them, but the music was glorious. My father asked me what I was singing, and I told him I didn't know. He asked me where I learned it, and I told him Mr. Baldwin was teaching us songs for the Christmas recital.

"Christmas is not for us, Lucy," he told me. "Christmas is for the goyim."

I asked him what a goyim is. Until that moment, I believed the world was populated only by Jews.

Later that evening I pressed my ear to the keyhole of my parents' closed bedroom door, the metal knob cold against my cheek. They were whispering, so I could only hear snatches of sentences, like "No child of mine," or "You see, I told you this would happen." I leaned into the keyhole so hard that I almost fell against the door. I heard my mother say, "Joe, she will have to learn. We can't protect her forever." My father's answer was very quiet, so quiet I almost couldn't make it out: "Why not?" he asked, and I imagined him shaking his head. "Why not."

He would have built me a glass house if he could. He would have kept me at home, hired scholars and tutors to fill my mind with only the highest values. He would have killed for me. He would have died for me, if only to keep me innocent, if only to keep me untouched.

———

"Look out the window," he says as he sits down in a white wicker chair. He is grinning, his cheeks crinkling into folds.

Behind him, a palm tree on the wallpaper looks like it's sprouting from his head.

I walk to the bay window in the bedroom, which overlooks the patio.

"Not that window," Ben says, "the living room window."

The living room window overlooks an expanse of lawn, leading to Crescent Drive. As I walk toward it, I already have some notion of what I'm about to see. I part the shades and squint through the glass into the bright sun. Sure enough, there is a car, not just any car, but a ridiculously ostentatious fire engine red sports car with a ribbon the width of my body wrapped around it.

"I can't," I say to him.

"Of course you can, Lucy," he says. "Not only can you, but you *will*."

I have seen this car before. Earlier today, on our way to have lunch in Santa Monica, we saw it parked in front of an antique car dealership.

Ben whistled low, and ran his hand over the fender as if it were my thigh. "This is a beauty," he said. He has an appreciation for fine, flashy things. I nodded and smiled vaguely.

"I can just picture you sitting in the driver's seat," he said. I looked at him and realized he was serious.

"Ben, no," I said, and it sounded like an echo. I tell him no all the time, and the word goes right through him, he seems not to understand. I said no to the pearls which hung around my neck; I said no to the fluffy white coat I was wearing; I said no to the ring, which is not a diamond, glittering madly on my newly manicured hand.

It's no wonder he doesn't listen to me.

The gift-wrapped car winks at me from down below; it is one of many shiny sports cars parked along Crescent Drive, owned mostly by middle-aged men with foreign, unpronounceable names.

"Let's take it for a spin," he says as I stand still, looking out the window, willing it to disappear in a puff of smoke.

"Ben, I can't drive a stick shift," I say.

"I'll teach you," he says, smiling at me benignly. This is the role he loves, and I have given myself over to it completely. The theme song from *To Sir with Love* brings tears to my eyes whenever I hear it on the radio. I am grateful for everything he is teaching me, whether how to make a white sauce with his wife's recipe, or how to know exactly what he wants in bed, like a well-trained concubine. I think these things make me an adult.

I do not yet know that he will teach me more than I have ever bargained for.

We drive to Laurel Canyon and find the steepest hill. Ben parks there and tells me to get behind the wheel. I am frightened, but he tells me not to worry. He tells me that as long as I'm with him, I will be safe. The Santa Ana winds whip the hair around my face as he lowers the top of the car.

He tells me there is a magic place, an exact point of pressure on the clutch, that I can control the car if I find that place, right on the brink of going forward or rolling back.

The first time, I stall out. The car begins to move backward, downhill. Ben pulls the emergency brake.

"Try again," he coaxes.

Again and again, I move my foot too quickly, feel the car sputter and die.

"I can't do it," I yell at him.

He laughs. "Of course you can. This is exactly how I taught Carolyn, and now she zips around like a pro."

Carolyn. Her name sits in my stomach like a heavy meal. Her fragile spirit descends between us, invisible, straddling the gearshift.

None of us says a word.

———

Carolyn, who is it? You can tell me.
I can't tell you.
Yes you can.
No I can't.
Do I know him?
You know of him.
Is it Teddy Kennedy?

By the time we return to the hotel room, I have mastered the art of the stick shift. There still remains, however, a pile of gift-wrapped boxes to conquer.

"Open the biggest one first," he says.

I untie ribbon that is beautiful enough to wear, draping it around my neck like a garland. I unfold tissue paper printed in wreaths and holly.

"But I didn't get anything for you," I tell him. "I'm still not used to celebrating Christmas."

He reaches out his hand, running it down my breast, over my ribcage, resting it on my waist. "You're going to get used to a lot of things with me," he says, his tongue quickly darting over his upper lip in a gesture I have seen many times in the past year and a half. It makes him look like a guppy. At first I found it revolting, but now I find it endearing. I believe adulthood is about acquiring tastes; I have recently learned to love sturgeon, oysters and Ben. This has happened slowly, imperceptibly. Like waiting for water to boil, like watching the dawn break, it wasn't here and now it is.

"Take a look," he cajoles me. He's more excited than I am.

"Kiss me first," I say.

He nibbles on my lower lip. His hands roam my body. He cannot keep away from me.

"You are so beautiful," he mumbles into my ear. "Open your presents, my girl," he says.

The tissue paper falls away, uncovering yards of fuchsia silk. An evening dress. A perfectly elegant, unbearably sophisticated evening dress. The price tag is still attached. I carefully tear it off without looking at it.

"Try it on," he says.

I hold it up to me. "Not right now," I say. I am suddenly tired. I want to nap before dinner.

"Now," he says. "Please."

I shake my head.

"Open this one, then," he says, thrusting forth another box.

I wade through more tissue paper until I feel silk again.

This time it is a white dress covered with a design of red roses. There are ruffles everywhere: along the neck, the sleeves, three tiers of ruffles bouncing along the hemline. It is suitable, perhaps, for a garden party, but only if the garden happens to be Versailles.

"Try it on," he says.

"I'll try on the other one," I say.

These dresses will hang in the back of my closet for years. I can already count the times I will wear each one. I will be invited to three garden parties, and two black-tie affairs. On these rare occasions, I will also wear the silvery rhinestone heels which Ben refers to as my "fuck-me pumps."

I carry the evening dress into the bathroom. Something about changing from my tennis shorts and T-shirt into this fuchsia extravaganza makes me modest. I have never worn anything like this in my life, never thought I would.

The neckline plunges to my waist. It is meant, I suppose, to reveal a stunning décolletage. However, the ten pounds I have recently discarded has left me less than voluptuous. A size too big, the fabric folds where my breasts should be. I feel like a child trying on her mother's clothing; now, all I need is an oversized pair of high heels to teeter around in.

"Lucy, what's taking you so long?" Ben calls from the living room of the suite. I hear the muted pop of a cork. Champagne at six o'clock. We have champagne at six o'clock every evening we are together.

"I'll be right out," I call, frantically adjusting my shoulder pads. I loosen my ponytail. My hair spills over my shoulders, blond against the deep pink of the dress. I want to look good for Ben. I want to look better than ever, better than Liz, better than all the women, better than the nameless, faceless movie star.

I walk out of the bathroom on tiptoe, so I will look taller.

He turns to me, champagne glasses in hand, and lets out a low whistle.

"Come here," he says as he puts the glasses down on the coffee table, then lowers himself onto the sofa, never taking his eyes off me.

I stand still before him. He reaches his hand into the opening of my dress, his fingers rough against my skin. In his eyes I see ten thousand days and nights, one hundred sighs, countless women.

My dress is over my head, his mouth between my legs. He is saying something, but I can't understand him. It sounds like another language. I want to ask, I need to know, but I cannot stop him. He is rough with me, moving me this way and that. My legs buckle around his ears. He is adept at this, as he is at anything in which he uses his mouth.

Later I ask. He cups my cheeks with his hands, tears fill his eyes.

"I said, I will never let you go."

———

The world of night is filled with angels. As far as my father and I can see, there is a population of white lights filling the sky. I am eight years old, he is forty-five. We are lying on a heap of pine needles in our New Jersey backyard. When I prop myself up with my elbows, I see my father staring glassy-eyed at the night sky.

"Which one is Grandpa Jacob?" I ask my father.

He doesn't answer.

"Tell me, Daddy," I say.

Still nothing.

I think he is playing a game; he wants me to guess for myself.

I scrutinize all the stars until I settle on the biggest, brightest one. "There he is," I say, nudging my father.

It is then that I realize he is cold.

I look into his eyes. His pupils are so small that his eyes appear green, ghostly. I poke him, and it is like touching a log, a sleigh, a piece of driftwood.

I scream until I see wisps of air escaping through his nostrils like puffs of smoke, and I realize he is alive.

Later, after the flashing red strobe of the ambulance, in the washed-out light of the emergency room, I watch the doctor's back as he hunches over, talking with my mother. My feet hang over the edge of the plastic chair; I am still wearing my bedroom slippers. On the end table there is a medical chart full of words which are too big for me to understand. I mouth them, phonetically: "Valium," "codeine," "phenobarbital."

———

Harry Wheeler knows I'm out here with Ben. For the longest time I tried to keep it a secret from him, but last week, when I called the agency to let him know I'd be in L.A., Harry told me he already knew.

"You're going to be out there with Broadhurst, right?" he said.

I was shocked.

"How did you . . ."

He laughed.

"Did you really think Broadhurst would keep you a secret?" he said. "You're the best thing that's happened to him in years. You keep him young, Perfect."

"How long have you—"

"Oh, I knew from the first time I saw you."

Harry tells me I'm his favorite client. The film wrapped a few months ago, and now it is plastered on billboards along Sunset Boulevard, scattered along Route 1. The stars' names are above the title, and just beneath, in smaller letters, my name is spelled out for all of California to see: AND INTRODUCING LUCY GREEN, it says. The first time I saw it I nearly plowed into the car in front of me.

Whether I'm in New York or Los Angeles, I audition for television pilots, soap operas, commercials, even theatre. Harry wants me to be as exposed as possible.

Evenings, I take acting classes in a dimly lit studio behind

Carnegie Hall. I am studying with a small, carrot-topped genius, a man respected and feared by the entire theatrical community. He hops up and down as we all sit in the bleachers
listening to two actors perform the repetition exercise.

"You look tired," the boy says.

"I look tired?" the girl answers.

"Yes, you look tired."

"Yes, I look tired?"

Carrot-Top interrupts them, jumping up from his desk.

"No, no!" he screams. "There's no reality! You are not in
the moment!"

He holds up a pencil, pointing to the very tip of the pink
eraser.

"This is all it is possible to know about acting," he shouts.
"You'll be lucky if you ever know this much!"

The class is filled with beautiful boys and girls. There are
models trying to break into acting, soap opera actors trying to
make the shift to prime-time television, and occasionally
there are well-known actors and actresses who study with
Carrot-Top during their hiatus.

All these people were born to be seen, and are learning to
be heard. Every week we do scenes, famous sections of plays
such as *A Hatful of Rain* and *A Streetcar Named Desire*.

I usually try to meet my scene partners at their apartments,
or even in Central Park, when the weather permits. I try not
to tell them I live in the Carlyle.

In the beginning, I avoided at all costs the risk that any of
my fellow actors would meet Ben, but eventually that became
impossible. Someone would be having his apartment painted,
it would be raining outside, and after a while, my private life
became public knowledge.

"I'll meet you at your place," one of my scene partners said.

"Meet me at the Carlyle," I told him, finally out of excuses.

"No, I'll meet you at your place," he insisted.

"That is my place," I said.

And so it began, that I was no longer simply another face
in the bleachers, another young actress trying to make it; I

was Ben Broadhurst's mistress. Pretty soon, everybody knew it.

Ben makes fun of my classes, mimics the repetition exercise whenever he has the opportunity. He has nicknames for all my scene partners, derogatory names. He says acting is self-indulgent and silly, but I think secretly, he's threatened by the parade of handsome young men with whom I work on some of the greatest love scenes written by O'Neill, Williams, Odets. He is afraid, but he will never admit it.

Instead, he whisks me away. Whenever possible, we travel. He seems to be able to take vacations whenever he wants to. He has scores of employees ready to jump at the opportunity to mind the store for him, the chance to show him their stuff.

"I do all the thinking work," he has told me. "No one can do that as well as I can. But once that's done, the buildings practically build themselves."

We go to Monte Carlo, St. Barts, Cozumel. We fly in Learjets equipped with leather seats and Murphy beds. I pack just enough to fit under the seat; all I really need is a bikini and a diaphragm.

We shop, we dine, we make love. The world is reduced to sensory pleasures, the texture of suede, the icy glide of oysters, hot dry fingers and cool tongues. We burrow into the king-sized bed like squirrels into a nest. We sleep all day and dance all night in clubs where we are not members. We sneak in, stealthy in designer black and Ray-Bans. We can do what we want. We are invisible. We are protected by a one-way mirror; we can see out, but no one can see in.

This evening, in California, we stay inside, both of us finally exhausted. We are lying in bed, a room service tray of smoked salmon, eggs scrambled with caviar and crème fraîche between us. A bottle of sauvignon blanc is almost finished. Ben doesn't drink much, just keeps refilling my glass, and lately I have been able to polish off a bottle of wine with ease.

I flick on the television, and it is like looking into a mirror; there I am, over a year younger than I am right now, dancing with David Cates in the smoky nightclub, soda bottle in hand. The Isley Brothers are playing in the background. The camera closes in on me as I tilt my head back, taking one long swallow. When I am finished, I toss my hair around, smiling a big, white, vapid smile.

This is not the first time I have seen myself on television. I have seen pictures of me watching myself, holding on to the bars of my crib as my infant face filled up the black-and-white screen. The commercial was for baby food. My mother has told me I was cast in this commercial because I was the most even-tempered baby they had ever seen.

I feel anything but even-tempered now as I balance a plate of eggs on my stomach and watch myself attempt to dance on national television, my bare arms encircling David Cates' neck. I am having trouble connecting myself to the girl on the screen; I turn to Ben, nudging him, but he has drifted off to sleep. I look at myself again. I remember how I felt that day, the fear and the longing, and see none of it in the face on-screen. I see, instead, the face of an aggressively carefree spirit; this is not the Smith College student I can barely remember. This is not the young woman who sits next to her father on the High Holy Days, beating her chest to keep time with his own pounding, atoning for sins both real and imagined.

It occurs to me as an afterthought that I am being projected into living rooms across the country. Perhaps Mrs. Mulcahy sees me. Perhaps she is sipping cognac and nudging her husband. "See?" she says, "I told you that girl would come to no good."

I turn to Ben, who is softly snoring, his cheek pressed hard against the cotton pillowcase. It seems like a self-fulfilling prophecy. Mrs. Mulcahy may have been right all along.

I imagine Carolyn is watching. She is wrapped in a patchwork quilt, sitting on an antique sleigh bed next to her mother. They are both knitting furiously. Their dark heads bend together, white necks exposed, fragile as wishbones.

Liz Broadhurst looks up and catches my face on the screen. "Isn't that your friend?" she asks her daughter.

Carolyn smiles, pushing her knitting needle into the soft palm of her hand just to the point of pain.

"That is my best friend in the whole world."

I flick the television from channel to channel. I wonder if I'll catch myself in another commercial. Since my Coke commercial, I have booked four other national spots: Ivory soap, Sweet 'n Low, Breck shampoo and M&M's. The roles have all been the same. I never speak, always smile, and my hair is curled into a mass of ringlets.

In other words, I have been typecast as a bimbo. But nonetheless, I am the bimbo of the moment. "Get me Lucy Green," the casting directors say. I have been told that the next phase is "Get me a Lucy Green type," and then after that, it's "Who's Lucy Green?"

I look again at Ben, who is now snoring loudly. His chin, pushed to one side, makes his whole face look skewed. His arm, slung over my body, is as large as my thigh. The stubble on his cheeks is a dark shadow tinged with gray. His reading glasses are squashed against the bridge of his nose, and the business section of the *Los Angeles Times* is trapped under his arm. I gingerly remove it. With a sigh, he rolls onto his back, narrowly missing me. I remove his eyeglasses, then place them on the bedside table.

"Thank you, darling," he says in his sleep. I wonder if he has any idea to whom he's speaking.

I quietly get out of bed. I tiptoe into the sitting room, where our luggage sits, still half-packed. My soft green carryon which I've had since summer camp stands, incongruously, next to Ben's hard-edged designer luggage. His briefcase lies on the coffee table next to an ice bucket filled with water and an empty bottle of champagne.

I know exactly what I'm about to do. I knew before I even got out of bed, though I told myself I was just coming in here for a glass of water.

I am capable of pretending, even to myself.

I am stealthy as a burglar, skilled as a locksmith. I have done this many times before. I should be wearing black gloves, a headlight. I slide the gold lock open effortlessly, careful not to let it snap.

His briefcase is filled to capacity. I immediately divide the papers into "irrelevant" and "relevant." Irrelevant is anything that has to do with business (I haven't figured out that usually files labeled "business" are the most telling of all). Relevant is anything that has to do with Ben's family, with Ben himself, or with me.

Like a child, I begin with the most forbidden: first, I unearth photographs. I have looked at them so many times that I know them by heart. They are zipped into the inside pocket of the briefcase. There is the obligatory family snapshot: Ben, Liz, Carolyn, Baby Jessica and Debbie are cleverly arranged in a semicircle on the beach outside their house in Nantucket. I recognize the house. Their dog, a Rottweiler, sits in the center of the crescent, its tongue lolling out.

I wonder who took this photograph. Did Liz stop someone, a jogger on the beach, and hand him her Instamatic with a strong, graceful hand? Did she cock her head and ask, "Do you mind?", knowing what a lovely picture it all would make?

I stare into her face for clues. Her eyes give nothing away; her smile is the carefully arranged smile of a woman past forty who is more concerned about wrinkles than spontaneity. She is wearing a soft pink dress cinched at the waist by a floral sash, and flat leather sandals. Around her wrist is a gold watch. It looks like the same style and brand as the watch Ben gave me for my last birthday. Mine is inscribed To L., with all my love. I wonder how hers is inscribed. I would give anything to see the delicate gold engraving rubbing cold and soft against the inside of her wrist.

Carolyn is standing next to Liz, holding her baby sister's hand. She is dressed in gym shorts and a man's undershirt, a red bandana tied around her neck. Her tanned legs shine with oil. Her hair streaks across her face, so that only one cheekbone and the corner of her mouth are visible. I do not need to see her face; I would recognize the angle of her hip, the lean, upraised arm, even in total darkness.

Ben towers over all of them, a giant among elves. He alone is not looking at the camera. His head is turned away from his family, in the direction of the ocean. Perhaps a steamer is passing by. Perhaps a sea gull has swooped down to the water's edge. Whatever it is has his undivided attention.

I continue to sort through Ben's briefcase. There are more pictures: Liz pregnant with Jessie; Carolyn holding Jessie; Debbie and Carolyn on a snow-covered mountain in front of a sign which points to the expert slopes.

I am not a part of this picture-perfect family; I am one of the skeletons in the closet. I am one of the things they pretend does not exist, something referred to, delicately, as a "situation." I am hunched over a briefcase in a strange hotel room at one in the morning, poring over evidence of a family of women to whom I do not belong in any way.

"Lucy?" Ben calls from the other room. "What are you doing?"

My heart pounds in my head. I can move faster than he can. I zip the compartment closed, almost tearing one of the snapshots in the process. I leave the briefcase just at the angle I found it, then snap shut the gold lock.

"Coming," I say, running the faucet in the wet bar to cover the sounds of deceit.

When I reenter the bedroom, he is sitting up in bed, a bleary-eyed bear. His hair falls into his face, and he squints at me without the benefit of his glasses.

"What were you doing?" he asks in his raspy voice.

"Getting a drink of water," I say.

"I missed you." He smiles, holding out his arms, and I fall into the warm, fleshy abyss which has begun to feel like home.

———

Here are some things he taught me: how to drive a stick shift, how to read a wine list, how to press crisp bills into a maître d's waiting hands. I learned that money can really buy almost anything. I learned about Nantucket in the winter, Paris in the springtime; I learned that it is possible to spend weeks on end in Italy without visiting a single museum.

Here is something he didn't teach me: it has taken me a long time, but I am finally learning to forgive myself.

When a tree is cut down, you can estimate how many storms it has weathered by counting the rings encircling its trunk. If the insides of women were like the insides of trees, I would now appear to be very old, if you were to cut me open.

I was nineteen when we began, and twenty-two by the time it was over, but I am speaking only chronologically.

How old are you inside? You had many rings wrapped around you, even years ago.

You no longer speak to me. Your silence is imposed, immediate, and perhaps irrevocable. My phone calls go unanswered, and I, when I answer my own phone's ring, often hear a click on the other end. I never meant to hurt you, Carolyn, but this is, of course, a moot point.

How did you find out? One day, while walking down the street, did your heart suddenly turn to ice? Did your fingers curl inward, into claws? Did you look in the mirror and see a double vision? Or perhaps he told you. Perhaps over a glass of wine at a Columbus Avenue cafe, he came out with it. *I'm seeing Lucy now,* he may have said.

You are somewhere in New York City. You are in restaurants, at the opera, in dark bars, on the subway. Even though I am thousands of miles, light-years away, I imagine I see you on every street corner. Wilshire, La Brea, Stone Canyon Road.

———

Most afternoons when I'm in Los Angeles, I go to the UCLA track. Late in the day, when the heat begins to ebb, it is possible to spot famous movie stars and athletes-in-training running around and around its quarter-mile circumference.

I look at the students who pass by. They are eighteen, nineteen, twenty years old—my age—yet I feel old enough to be their maiden aunt. They clasp books to their chests, they crop their hair short and dye it green, they talk intently and illogically about Kant, or Rimbaud.

If I were at Smith, I would be a junior. I would have declared my major by now. I would be sitting in a circle on the living room floor of Emerson House, playing "I Never."

What would I say I'd never done?

Sometimes I miss it all with a palpable longing, as if it were an amputated leg, something irrefutably absent that I can fool myself into thinking is still there. I close my eyes and picture the Northampton campus, the icicles dangling from every windowsill. I crave the notion I once had, however mistaken, that all the parts of my life fit together in a logical, coherent way. I miss my parents, who I talk to over the phone in stilted, weekly conversations. And always, I miss Carolyn.

When I return from the track, I strip and lie in the sun on the back patio of our bungalow. I shut my eyes, absorbed in the patterns the palm trees make against my closed lids, the steady din of cicadas.

I can't help thinking of my parents. The sun beating down against my bare skin, the sound of splashing in the background reminds me of every summer of my childhood, where safe within the picket fence surrounding our property, I would lie aimlessly in the sun.

My mother would serve iced tea in tall, frosted green glasses, leaving a pitcher on the table, full of melting ice cubes in the noontime heat. I can barely remember my father from those humid, late summer days. His car would pull into the driveway at six o'clock, and the next thing I knew he would be hanging in traction, watching the news.

My parents' faces have been slowly fading over the past year, their voices are becoming unfamiliar to me. When I speak to my mother once a week, my father does not come to

the phone. I am living a life which goes contrary to everything he knows, everything he has ever tried to teach me.

We have barely spoken since a lunch in New York, many
months ago.

"Tell me, Lucy," he had said, straining toward me across
the distance, "would I approve?"

I thought about lying, but I knew there was no point.

"No," I said quietly, "you wouldn't."

"Tell me, who is it?" he asked. "Nothing can be worse than
my imagination."

I didn't answer him for a while. I knew my answer would
forever change the way my father loved me.

"It's Ben Broadhurst, Daddy," I finally said.

He got up to go to the men's room. When he returned to
the table, his eyes were dry and his nose was red.

Suddenly there is a shadow over me. I squint my eyes open.

"Hello, bubelah," I hear Harry Wheeler's unmistakable
New York accent.

I immediately sit up, pulling an enormous T-shirt over my
head.

"My God, what are you doing here?" I ask him.

"Would you believe, I'm out here to visit my favorite client?" he asks.

"No."

He laughs.

"Actually, I do have an audition lined up for you, Perfect.
How would you feel about doing a little theatre? It's a new
Horton Foote play, and they called us asking if we had any-
one who could play the piano as well as a concert pianist.
And I thought of you."

Harry smiles at me, the dazzling, conspiratorial smile
which always makes its recipient feel like his only client, the
only person he thinks about. Harry's smile, I am certain, is
the key to his success.

"Sounds interesting," I say.

"Yeah, and you have to learn Chopin's 'Revolutionary' Étude by tomorrow at noon," he says.

"Harry, Chopin's 'Revolutionary' Étude? That's one of the most difficult pieces of piano music written!"

"So?" he says.

"So nothing," I grin at him. This sounds like a challenge, something to get my sluggish blood circulating.

Ben rounds the corner, and his face turns hard and angry as he sees Harry from behind, talking to me. He doesn't realize who it is, and he thinks some other guest of this hotel is trying to pick me up. I watch Ben, seeing the part of him that grew up on the south side of Chicago, and fought street fights with jagged pieces of broken bottles. I have seen this side of him several times, in restaurants, on the sidewalks of New York, in the aisles of theatres. He doesn't like anyone looking at me. His face remains tense for a good few minutes even after he realizes it's Harry.

"Wheeler, you gave me a scare, there," Ben says. "Thought you were trying to move in on my lady."

The two men spar with each other the way all men seem to, no matter what their age. There is an invisible shield between them, unacknowledged but impenetrable. What do they think would happen, I wonder, if they were able to reach across the divide?

"Wheeler, join us for dinner tonight," Ben says. "I'll make a reservation at Chasen's."

"I'd love to, but Lucy has work to do," Harry says.

"Work?"

"I got her an audition tomorrow."

"Oh. That's great," Ben says, not even trying to mean it.

"Young lady, we've got to find you a piano," Harry says. "Throw on some clothes and let's go up to the Polo Lounge."

Ben pouts. His lower lip literally thrusts out into an expression he has probably been perfecting since the age of four. He is not accustomed to being outvoted, overshadowed. Somehow, I know he will make me pay for this.

• • •

The "Revolutionary" Étude is one of the more dramatic pieces Chopin composed, a series of dissonant chords and breathtaking arpeggios. I sit in one of the conference rooms of the hotel struggling with the complex series of notes, which are a bit too technically difficult for me. Why can't I just play a nice Mozart sonata?

"Just learn the first page and a half," Harry said, which seemed a ridiculous idea two hours ago, but now, as the evening is getting late and I am still on the first page, I am growing tempted to throw in the towel. I have small fingers, I tell myself. They cannot span these chords larger than an octave.

But something makes me continue. This is the first opportunity I have had not to be typecast. A new Horton Foote play is an important event, and its first run is here in Los Angeles. It could not be a better break.

I play until two in the morning. When I get back to the room, Ben is gone.

———

Look at Grandpa Jacob. Each shooting star reminds me of him. Why is everyone so afraid of death? I imagine death must be liberating: to be a part of the multitude of angels, to fall freely through the sky.

Look at Grandma. She lies prone in her hospital bed, year after year like a bright, translucent parabola. Her skin is thin with agony; her eyes are dead, but her body glows with the pale blue fire of martyrs and saints.

Everyone does their damnedest to keep her alive.

"We know she can feel pain," they say, "so we must acknowledge the possibility that she can feel joy."

I've been visiting Grandma almost every week for my whole life, and I've seen her cry plenty of times, but I've never seen her smile, or laugh. Not so much as a twinkle in her eye.

I have felt a special kinship with Grandma all these years,

because I have been trapped in my own body. She is fed, and clothed, and bathed, and so am I. Each year I become lighter, more incandescent as I find new paths to pain. I am not unlike the woman who lights matches under her own fingertips, or presses a cigarette lighter to the soft, white inside part of her wrist.

I seek out my own undoing as if it were something tangible and concrete; I want to cup it in my hands like an ember.

I want to be like you. I want to have enough pain to last a lifetime.

———

Ben stumbles over the doorstop at three-thirty in the morning, as he flicks on the light switch. It is the first time I have ever seen him drunk. He is holding an almost-empty bottle of Glenlivet in one hand, and the stub of a cigar in the other.

"Hello," he lurches forward.

I sit up in bed. I have been unable to sleep, torn between concern and anger.

"Where have you been?" I ask, feeling more like an irate wife than the mistress I really am.

He burps.

"Out," he says.

"Did you drink that all by yourself?"

"No," he says, "I drank it with a friend. I do have friends out here, you know."

He walks into the sofa, and then somewhat gracefully vaults himself over the armrest and lands with a thud on the plush cushions.

He clamps down on his cigar, eyeing me, waiting for me to ask him more questions.

I say nothing.

"Well?" he says.

"Well what?"

"Aren't you going to ask me why I'm all wet?"

I look at him through the haze of fury, noticing for the first time his damp hair, his rumpled clothes.

He grins at me.

"I went skinny-dipping," he says, "with my friend."

He puts the same emphasis on friend as he did when he referred to me as Carolyn's friend. He leans hard into the word, makes it sound like fuck.

I spend the rest of the night crying. Ben snores on the couch, still dressed, and our bungalow is infused with the sickly sweet smell of scotch.

In the morning, I sit before the ornate vanity and pull my hair back off my face. My skin looks sallow in the harsh Beverly Hills light. I imagine I see wrinkles. When I look more closely, they disappear. Ben has told me that women begin to lose their looks after the age of twenty-five. I figure I have five good years left.

I drive my newly acquired sports car to the audition in Sherman Oaks, my sheet music and pocketbook sitting on the passenger seat next to me. I negotiate the L.A. freeway, aware of people in other cars turning their heads. Whenever I have been with Ben in my car, he says, "See darling? They're all looking at you." I know this isn't true. It's the car they're looking at, red, flashy and unbelievably expensive. Any beauty I possess pales in comparison.

I park around the corner so no one will see it, and walk toward one of the many low-lying buildings which house casting directors and production companies. I should not be here. My eyes are slits, my face is swollen and there is a long, angry scratch traveling down the left side of my cheek.

Ben tried to climb on top of me last night, and I pushed him away. The more I fought him, the more he fought back. He was laughing, drunk and giddy. He thought it was a joke. He smelled of whiskey, and an unidentifiable perfume.

He stopped after he accidentally clawed my face. He was contrite, and cupped it in his hands, suddenly sober. He called the concierge to ask for an antiseptic at four in the morning. He told me he was sorry in the same way he always tells me he loves me: repetitive, hypnotizing, like the ticking of a clock.

"What happened to you?" the assistant casting director asks, looking down at my eight by ten and then back up at me.

"My cat scratched me," I say, "and I'm allergic."

This is a response I have been composing since leaving the outskirts of Beverly Hills.

"Well, come on in," he says, shaking his head.

In the inner sanctum, there are only three people: the casting director and two older men.

"Lucy Green, this is Horton Foote and this is Joe Trapani," the casting director says.

Horton Foote! Joe Trapani! I feel like I've hit the big time.

We shake hands, and then I am directed to a piano in the corner. My fingers feel stiff from being curved tightly around the steering wheel. I flex them a few times before I begin to play.

The thunderous first chord brings me directly into the piece. The sheet music is propped up before me, but I barely look at it. I studied it so hard last night that it is in my fingers' memory.

All my life, this has been my downfall with the piano. My memory is insistant, and irrefutable. I memorize music the moment I read it. I memorize my mistakes, and then it is impossible for me to unlearn them.

A few moments after I begin to play, during a section which calls for parallel scales racing down the keyboard, I run out of keys. There simply are not enough keys.

I turn around.

"This isn't a piano," I say to them, "this is a spinet."

We all begin to laugh. We laugh as if it's a very good joke that they have asked several actresses to learn Chopin's "Revolutionary" Étude, and then not provided them with a piano on which to play it.

I laugh my way out the door, then cry my way home.

• • •

Harry stops by early the next afternoon. He is wearing tennis whites, with a light pink terry-cloth band encircling his forehead.

"What's the matter with you?" he asks as he comes around the side of the bungalow. Harry does not believe in announcing himself, nor does he believe in privacy.

He stops short when he sees me.

"You look like shit," he says.

"Thanks."

"They called me, said you're a wonderful pianist but that you look like you're about to keel over and die. And they don't seem so far off the mark."

He looks at me closely.

"We're going to order you some room service. You've got to eat something, get some meat on your bones."

"Harry, I'm not hungry," I say.

I'm never hungry. I live on white wine and small bites of each meal.

"I don't care," he says.

He watches me as I take bite after bite of Cobb salad. He waits patiently as I eat a whole wheat roll. He insists I drink an entire bottle of Perrier.

"Is this because of Broadhurst?" he asks.

I nod.

"Get away from him, Lucy. You're not cut out for this," he says. "You look the part, but it's not in you to play it."

"I love him," I say.

Harry shakes his head slowly from side to side.

"Oh, little girl," he says, "now that's a big mistake."

When Harry leaves, I go into the bathroom and lock the door. I stick my fingers down my throat, moving them rhythmically until I retch my entire lunch into the toilet. I do not stop until my throat is raw.

———

Rumor has it that though the great scholar Jacob Greenburg was a learned man, he also enjoyed the occasional fox-trot, or a jaunt to Atlantic City.

Although those who knew him well roll their eyes in an indulgent sort of way when speaking of Jacob, there is only one word they use to describe Grandma: she was a saint.

Grandma was a beautiful woman, the queen of her circle, the Orthodox royalty of Manhattan. Jacob was proud of her. He draped her in furs, cloche hats, lizard bags and alligator shoes. He was proud because not only was she a beauty to look at, but she was a good woman as well.

My grandparents believed in the Talmudic definition of charity: contributions to those less fortunate were only worthy, only truly considered *mitzvot*, if these contributions were made anonymously.

Legend has it that every year, in the spring, at the time of Passover, my grandmother would have the chauffeur drive her to the outer boroughs of the city. She would travel to the Williamsburg section of Brooklyn, as well as the Jewish neighborhoods in Queens and the Bronx.

My father would go with her. He was just a little boy, wearing knickers, a starched white shirt and a felt beret. He sat next to his mother in the back of the big car. He loved to be near her, nestled against her generous hip, inhaling the scent of her powder and of the hot meals they were carrying to deliver to the poor people.

They pulled up in front of the first apartment house. Grandma handed my father a warm plate, covered by tin foil.

"Joey, go up to that building and ring the buzzer that says STEIN. Then just leave the plate in the doorway."

She nudged my father, who was suddenly shy, out the car door. When he returned, he was flushed and breathless, grinning from ear to ear.

"I did it, Ma!" he said, excited at his secret mission.

"That was a *mitzvah*, Joey. You just did a very good thing," she said, smiling down at him.

They went from house to house. My father rang doorbells, then quickly skipped back to the car. Finally, they had only

one meal left to deliver. They pulled up in front of a dilapi-
dated row house in Bensonhurst.

"This is a very special man, Joseph," my grandmother said,
"an old rabbi who lives alone. He is not as fortunate as we
are. He doesn't have enough food to eat."

My father looked at her, wide-eyed. He could not understand how God would not take care of his own children, how
God would not take care of a learned man of the Torah, of the
Bible. He had been raised to believe that if he did all the right
things, he would be rewarded in kind.

He rang the rabbi's bell, dropped the meal on his doorstep,
then turned to run back to the car.

"Wait!" He heard a thunderous voice behind him. "Who
are you?"

He stopped still, shaking in his boots.

"I can't tell you," my father said, turning around to address
the intimidating voice. "It wouldn't be a *mitzvah*."

He was looking into the wisest, most ancient face he had
ever seen. The face folded into a thousand wrinkles, revealing
a toothless smile.

"I know who you are," said the cavernous mouth, "you
must be a Greenburg."

My father's mouth fell open. "How did you know?" he
whispered.

The old rabbi leaned forward, then kissed my father on
both cheeks.

"You have the face of a Greenburg," he said. "You have the
face of your father and your grandfather, God rest his soul."

My father stared into the rabbi's yellow eyes, entranced.

"And don't you worry. It's still a *mitzvah*, young man. To
be born into your family . . . what a blessing on you," the
old rabbi said as he picked up his meal, looked deferentially at
the limousine parked by the curb, the pale face of the woman
inside, then shuffled back into his simple home.

When I was a little girl, my father told me this story at bed-
time. While other children were listening to "Goldilocks" or

Winnie-the-Pooh, I was listening to the Greenburg history. I never tired of it.

Nestled between crisp cotton sheets, lying on one side as I listened to my father's soft voice, I wanted to grow up to be just like my father, just like Grandma; I wanted to deliver hot meals to the poor, I wanted to be recognized by my face. There goes a Greenburg, I wanted them to say with all the awe and love of having sighted a guardian angel.

———

Ben has a New York apartment, but we have never stayed there. I cannot stand the thought of sleeping with him under the watchful eyes of the Broadhurst family portrait; I prefer the anonymity of the hotel, where I am known both as Lucy Green and Mrs. Broadhurst. I imagine I see Liz, the real Mrs. Broadhurst, everywhere. We go to the same hair salon on East Fifty-seventh Street. I have recently cut my hair into a pageboy, swinging straight to the nape of my neck. I told myself, as inches and inches of hair fell to the black marble floor of the salon, that this was a more grown-up style, and that it would help my career, but in fact, it is really just the same style that Liz and Carolyn have worn ever since I've known them.

I have begun to get manicures, pedicures and facials. I shop in specialty boutiques. I wear a brown mink coat which Ben bought me on our third date. My eyebrows are thin. I wear silk camisoles, lipstick liner and foundation.

I was dressed like this on the blustery New York day, late last fall, when I saw Carolyn. It was the day before Thanksgiving, and I was coming out of Lobel's Butcher Shop on Madison Avenue. I had just picked up a ten-pound turkey for the holiday.

Ben and I had worked out an agreement. He would have an early Thanksgiving dinner with his family, I would have an early dinner with my parents, and then we would have a second holiday meal together. I remember thinking that I had never cooked a turkey before, and had no idea what to do with it.

She was walking up the avenue. I cannot forget how she looked, she was dressed in a short tweed jacket fitted just to her waist, a full, gathered skirt and low boots. Her skin was shining. She was wearing sunglasses.

I'm not sure which of us was more surprised to see the other. She covered it better than I. I stood there, rooted to the spot, with a turkey in my arms and a moronic smile on my face.

First she walked by me. The only sign she recognized me was the drawing back of her head, the slight flaring of her nostrils. Then she stopped. I remember this vividly. She stopped, turned around, and looked at me from head to toe in that inimitable way she has, as if we were the only two people on the sidewalk. Rush-hour pedestrians jostled by both of us, walking between us and around us, sighing, elbowing.

I saw myself through Carolyn's eyes. I was wearing the mink coat over blue jeans and cowboy boots from Smith days, a white tuxedo blouse tucked neatly inside an extravagant silver belt. My hair was highlighted and swung in a perfect line to my chin, just like hers, but that was the only similarity between us. She looked, essentially, like the college junior she really was, and I had the strained, precious look of someone who was about to wind up on the front page of the *New York Post:* STARLET FOUND SLAIN IN CARLYLE, or COED JUMPS TO DEATH ON UPPER EAST SIDE.

How had it happened? I had somehow taken up from where she left off, decided I was going to be bolder, go further, play harder at the dangerous games I didn't even know existed until I met her.

She looked at me through her sunglasses.

"What are you doing here?" she asked me.

"I live here," I said.

She took two steps toward me, then grabbed me by both arms and shoved me with all her might into the newspaper dispenser on the sidewalk.

"Whore," she said, a loud, bleating sound.

People's heads turned.

"You're a whore," she repeated, then she turned and walked away.

I barely saw the passersby who had stopped to watch this scene with incredulous smiles on their faces. I watched Carolyn's back recede farther and farther into the holiday crowd, and wondered where she was going.

All my life I have wanted to be an adult, I have wanted to be further along than wherever I was. When I was ten, I wanted to be a teenager. When I was fifteen, I wanted to be in college. When I was in college, I craved something larger, something grander, something unspecified. And here I am. This is not what I had in mind.

———

He holds me. I am perched on top of him, riding him as he holds on to my hipbones, moving me back and forth. His tongue pushes out of his mouth into the air as if it has a mind of its own. I feel the pressure of his stomach against me as I begin to swell inside. I raise my arms above my head because I know he likes this; he likes to watch me, my breasts falling easily, floating in the space between us.

It is this balance: I am both here and not here. I am acting, but I am fully involved in the part I am playing. This is the part that can take me all the way to the top and back again.

"Look at you," he rasps at me.

I smile at him. I know what he is seeing.

"You are so young," he says. "How old are you?"

It is a game that we play.

"Twenty," I say.

"Twenty," he repeats, "a twenty-year-old piece of ass."

I move on top of him, I never stop moving.

"Who do you wish was here right now?" he asks, grabbing me from behind, pushing me harder, faster.

I say nothing.

"Who?" he repeats. He is grabbing whatever flesh he can, hard, harder.

"You know who," I whisper, looking at him. We both know the power I have at this moment.

"Answer me," he grits his teeth, he calls me names.

"Carolyn," I say, and the very word makes my back arch, makes me fall on top of him, until we both disappear.

————

My father is in Los Angeles. He is staying at the Biltmore, according to the message slipped under our door early this morning. Please call Joseph Greenburg, it said, with the calculated distance my father has adopted toward me ever since I left Smith and embarked on this strange new life.

When he answers the phone, his voice brings tears to my eyes as I realize how much I've missed him.

"What are you doing out here, Dad?"

"Business," he replies tersely.

"Will I get to see you?"

"Lunch," he says.

"Today?"

"Fine."

I am surprised he has called me at all. I have gone against every one of his wishes: I dropped out of college, I am involved with a non-Jewish, married man, I am living on the other end of the earth.

My mother handles me gingerly, as if I were some highly attuned, skittish scientific concoction about to blow up in her face. She speaks to me slowly, carefully. She calls every Sunday evening at six o'clock and we stay on the phone for precisely five minutes. I'm not sure if this is for my sake or for hers. But my father is a different story. The few times I have heard his voice, or worse, when I have looked into his eyes, I know he sees my desertion of him as the final disappointment in a life full of compromise and faith.

I think my father has given up. His little yellow pills have chipped away at him, polishing his insides into a huge, vast wasteland. He still places his yarmulke on his head every morning and says the appropriate prayers, still wraps his *tefillin* around his arm with the practiced gestures of a lifetime, but the light behind his eyes has gone out. He is going through the motions. There is nothing left.

He rises when I walk into the restaurant, and waves me over to the table.

"Hello, shnookie," he says, slipping into his old nickname for me. He hasn't called me that in a long time, not since the day I sat down with him and explained that I was accepting the film offer.

He looks tired. There are green shadows beneath his eyes. He has lost weight, and instead of his skin springing back to the bone, it hangs loosely like a stretched-out sweater. His smile is the same, and it makes me want to jump into his lap and stay there forever. It is the smile that takes me in, despite what I have done. It defies Orthodox tradition and everything he has always believed; it says, "You are my daughter no matter what."

"I've missed you," I say, after moments of silence.

He says nothing. More time passes, and I am acutely aware of people at other tables carrying on conversations, laughing, ordering from their menus. My father and I sit quietly, miserably.

Finally, he speaks.

"Where did we go wrong, Lucy, for you to be living like this?"

I look at him. He is not saying this in an attempt to make me feel terrible, although he manages to do this quite successfully. He really wants to know. His chin sinks, then puckers into a thousand tiny dimples: my father is about to cry.

"Daddy, no," I say, reaching for his hand underneath the tablecloth. I am torn between telling him that it's not so bad, the way I'm living, and telling him that it's not his fault, but all I manage to say is no, again and again.

He is crying now.

"We only wanted the best for you," he sobs.

"I'm sorry," I say.

"Maybe we made some mistakes."

"It's not your fault."

He uncovers his eyes, and I look at his tear-stained face,

incongruous against his stark blue business suit, his paisley silk tie.

"Oh, Lucy," he says. "You were the apple of my eye."

The rest of lunch passes by in a blur. My father orders Dover sole, the only thing on the menu which is kosher, and I pick at a salad and drink an iced coffee. There is a void between us, an acknowledgment that we live in different worlds and have little to say to one another.

There is a part of me that wishes my father would pick me up like a sack of flour, throw me over his shoulder and carry me out of the restaurant, onto a plane and back to the house on Maple Avenue, where I would be nursed back to physical and emotional health. This does not happen. I have been acting like an adult for so long now that he has finally begun to treat me like one.

When the check comes, he looks at it with a wry smile.

"This on you, big shot?" he asks me.

"Yes," I say, surprised, my cheeks burning as I reach to take it.

"Don't be silly," he says, grabbing it first, "I was only kidding."

We say good-bye outside the restaurant. He hugs me close, the same hug I have been receiving all my life, which knocks the air right out of me.

"I'll be in town for a week," he says, a concession. "Call me if you want to get together again."

I walk away from my father, back to the car which I have parked out of sight, around the corner. The door handle is burning hot, as are the leather seat, the steering wheel and the gearshift. I ease myself in, then sit still as the radio plays an entire half hour of uninterrupted music. There is not a cloud in the sky. It is the kind of thin, glaring Southern California day in which the light casts no shadows. I do not know where to go.

————

Why you? Why Ben? Why any of it, Carolyn?

For the sake of argument, let's just say I had not gone to Smith. Say I had chosen, instead, to matriculate at Barnard, or Vassar, or any of the other colleges that sent me thick letters of acceptance.

Would I have met a woman just like you, a woman with the longest, deepest sigh, a way of walking as if she carried the weight of the world on her narrow shoulders, and the most beautiful hands I had ever seen?

I don't think so. There is only one of you.

If I had gone to Barnard, I might have majored in political science, cut my hair short, and upon graduation, landed a plum job in the mayor's office. Had I gone to Vassar, I might have become a sculptress, carving realistic heads of jaguars onto the long bodies of women. As it is, I went to Smith, as we all know, and I am still trying to sort it all out.

When I think I flipped a coin by way of deciding where to go to college, I nearly lose my mind.

———

Ben bursts in the door at five o'clock, returning from a business meeting which lasted all afternoon. He is wearing a navy blue suit almost identical to the one my father had on at lunch.

He is in high spirits.

"Hello, love of my life," he practically sings, grabbing me around the waist and whirling me through the room.

We dance over to the sofa, where he pulls me down with him.

"I have just closed one of the biggest deals of my career, and we are going to celebrate," he says.

"What happened?" I ask, breathless from dancing.

"We're going to rebuild Manhattan Beach from the ground up," he says. "It's going to be so hot, tourists will go to Manhattan Beach instead of Los Angeles. We're building five new hotels. The whole entertainment industry will move a few miles southwest—three of the major studios are already in on it—they won't know what hit them!"

"That's great," I say, trying to muster up enthusiasm for Ben's business deals, which seem to be abstract architect's renderings of office plazas and high rises which will not be built for years.

"Great," he says, "you don't know how . . ."

The phone rings, and he gets up to answer it. He is humming a tune from a song I've never heard, probably popular before my time.

He speaks into the phone in monosyllables.

"No," he says, then "yes," then "we'll see." I am attuned to this, because his voice sounds different than it usually does on the telephone; this clearly isn't a business call.

"Well that's just tough shit, my dear," he says, his voice rising.

He pauses for a moment, his head cocked to the side, eyes focused up at a corner of the ceiling.

"That's tough shit," he repeats, and slams down the phone.

He walks once around the perimeter of the living room, his euphoria squashed like a hornet.

"That was Liz," he says, sitting heavily back down on the sofa.

"How did she know you were here?" I ask, my heart pounding.

"She didn't," he says. "She just kept trying hotel after hotel in city after city until she found me."

Ben stares at a hotel ashtray brimming with cigarette butts. I stare at his blue-suited knee. We are thinking the same thing: the world is beginning to close in on us.

"My father is in town," I say brightly, by way of changing the subject. "I saw him for lunch."

"Really? We should all get together," he says.

I laugh.

Ben looks at me, raising his eyebrows.

"What. No really," I say, still laughing.

"Why not?"

"Getting together with my father is about as good an idea as having high tea with your wife."

He nuzzles me.

"I'd like to see you and Elisabeth Broadhurst slugging it out over high tea," he says, nudging me onto my back, "I'd like to see that a lot."

Later, dusk shadows filter through the window, falling over a corner of the bed like a kicked-off blanket. I run my fingers through his chest hair, which is beginning to turn gray, as are his sideburns, and the tips of his beard when he doesn't shave.

"I love you," I say into his neck, but he is asleep. He turns onto his side, then throws his arm over me. I am trapped. I stare at the painted white beams on the ceiling of our bedroom, trying to regulate my breath, slow, slower: I do not want to wake him.

Someone is knocking at our door. Ben stirs, rolls away from me and sighs. The knocking stops, then picks up again. I get out of bed and locate a terry cloth robe, property of the Beverly Hills Hotel. I wrap it around me as I walk toward the knocking.

"Lucy, who is it?" he calls from the bedroom.

"I don't know," I yell back.

I peer through the peephole, and the floor seems to drop from underneath me. My father is standing there, carrying his briefcase, the *Los Angeles Times* and a bouquet of flowers.

I move back from the door and run into the bedroom. Ben is asleep again. I yank the covers off him.

"Get up, my father's here," I say, nudging him.

He rolls over with a groan.

"I mean it, Ben, get out of bed," I say.

I pull on a pair of shorts and a sweatshirt, then slam the bedroom door behind me as I race back to the front door. I unlatch the safety chain and swing it open.

My father is still standing there in the same position. He ducks his head when he sees me, as if he's the one who should be ashamed, and not I. He thrusts forward the bouquet of flowers, pink, yellow and white.

"For you," he says hoarsely.

He clears his throat.

"Come on in," I say, standing aside to let him pass.

As he walks into the bungalow, I see the living room through my father's eyes, not as the inside of yet another hotel suite, but as a profoundly opulent example of what money can buy. It is decorated like the living room of an English manor house might be, full of chintz, mahogany, paintings of fields, horses and hunting dogs. There is a mirrored wall on the far end of the room, and I see our reflection: an older father in a business suit perched on the edge of a sofa, and his daughter, healthy and tanned, wearing cutoffs and a Smith College sweatshirt, offering to get him a drink.

This looks like a picture out of a women's magazine. This looks like anything other than what it is.

My father glances at the closed bedroom door, holding his soda glass, jiggling the ice.

We both hear the shower running, the sound of water splashing, of soap under arms.

"I decided it was time to meet Ben," he says.

His mouth curves forcibly around the name "Ben," as if it were in a difficult foreign language.

"I'm glad," I say, not sure if this is true.

He pauses, musing, takes a sip of his soda.

"I saw your picture on a billboard today," he says. "It gave me quite a shock!"

"Where was it?"

"On La Cienega. You were dancing, or something . . . I went by it so fast."

"Oh, the Coke advertisement."

They have immortalized David Cates and me even further, asking us back for a photo shoot which has been plastered all over billboards and magazines. I hope David's happy, and I also hope I don't have to work with him anymore. The more successful I become, the wider his smile gets whenever he sees me. David is what's known in my acting class as an "attache actor": one who carries his talent around in his briefcase, trapped on the black-and-white surfaces of his eight by tens.

"Lucy," my father's pale green eyes beseech me, "your mother and I love you very much."

His arms reach out to me, I am about to go to him when Ben opens the bedroom door and strides out, hand outstretched.

"Ben Broadhurst," he says, as if anyone present did not know his name. His hair is wet against his neck.

My father stands.

"Ben," he says, shaking his hand. I know my father has an iron handshake, and have no doubt he's using it right now. I watch Ben's eyes flicker.

"Sorry to just drop in on you like this," my father says, sitting back down.

"That's quite all right, our pleasure," Ben says, pointedly using the plural.

Both men are lying through their teeth; no one's happy with this situation, no one's sorry, and it is most certainly no one's pleasure. We sit quietly, the three of us, my father and I on one sofa, and Ben on the opposite sofa, facing us across the coffee table.

On the table there are piles of magazines and papers: *California Homes and Lifestyles*, *Avenue*, the *Herald Tribune* and *Back Stage*.

"I've wanted to meet you for some time now," my father says, addressing Ben.

"Yes, I've wanted to meet you too, Joe," Ben says.

My father blinks, startled by the assumed familiarity. Although Ben is quite a bit younger than my father, he is still unquestionably a middle-aged man. He is hardly going to call my father "Mr. Greenburg," as my friends have always done.

"I'd like to know . . ." my father begins, but Ben interrupts him.

"I'm sure you want to know what my intentions are regarding your daughter," he says smoothly, taking charge of this situation the same way he controls board meetings, and the skylines of most major cities.

"Yes, I—"

"I love your daughter, Joe. I've never felt about anyone the way I feel about her. You've been married to your wife for . . . what is it . . . thirty years . . . I'm sure you know what it is to love someone like this."

My father pushes himself to the edge of his seat.

"Don't you dare compare this . . ."

He has no words for it. He gestures around him, arms flailing, as if the very furniture, the brass chandelier were an affront to his sensibilities.

"I'm not comparing anything, Joe," Ben continues, "I'm just trying to establish a common ground here."

"We have no common ground. We have nothing in common," my father says excitably.

I have been watching the two men, my head swinging back and forth from one to the other, as if watching a tennis match. Finally, I can't bear being discussed this way, as if I'm not even in the room.

"Would you please just stop it," I say.

"Quiet, Lucy," says my father, "just stay out of this."

They stare at each other across the coffee table. Ben's eyes are challenging, probing, full of energy and fire. My father's gaze is flat, unblinking, almost transparent. I wonder whether he's taken tranquilizers; his pupils are small.

Ben lights a cigar. This process takes quite a few moments: he rummages through the humidor, selecting one with the same degree of expertise with which certain women pick ripe fruit in the supermarket. Then he breaks off the end, lights one match, then two as he circles it around and around in his mouth, pulling in on it. When he finishes, and the unmistakable Havana smoke fills the air, he is ready to speak again.

"I intend to marry Lucy," he says. "I would not be robbing

her of these important years if I didn't believe that someday we would be able to legitimize our relationship."

He looks at my father with the same kind of unswerving intensity I imagine he's had all day. This is going to be another deal he makes, another deal of a lifetime.

My father sits back once again.

"Most men say the same thing. Why are you any different?"

My father is asking the question I have asked myself a thousand times. We both look at Ben.

He pauses, sighing deeply, a Carolyn sigh. He puffs on his cigar.

"Joe, let me try to put this to you, man to man. There is a lot involved here, as I'm sure you can understand. There is a great deal of money, and there are children."

"That's not Lucy's problem," my father says, "you should have thought of that a year and a half ago, before you implicated my daughter in this mess."

Ben nods slowly. The only sign of nervousness or irritation is his lower leg swinging back and forth madly between the sofa and the coffee table. I learned to read his body a long time ago, because I knew I'd never be able to read his mind.

"That's true," he says, "and you've got to realize that it breaks my heart . . . just breaks my heart to see Lucy involved in this situation, and to know I'm the cause of it."

His hands are clasped in front of him; his eyes threaten to fill up with tears.

"Things are going to change, Joe. I've consulted a divorce lawyer—"

"You have?" I interject.

"Really?" my father says at the same moment.

"Yes, and he's looking over all my papers. He's warned me that it may take quite a while, though. It's going to be very complicated. As I said, there's a great deal involved."

My father is pale, and he hasn't touched his soda. His glass sits on the mahogany table, ice melting.

"That's good to hear," he says.

He's running out of steam.

"Trust me, Joe. Your daughter's in good hands," Ben says, leaning forward earnestly.

"Well then, I'd better be going. I'm catching the red-eye back to New York." My father sways slightly as he stands up.

"I thought you were staying out here for a week," I say.

He hesitates.

"I changed my mind."

"Dad, stay for dinner," I say, "you have plenty of time."

Ben shakes his head at me from across the table, and mouths "no."

"Thanks, honey, but I'd rather get a head start."

"Please?" I ask, hearing a hysterical note in my own voice; I'm afraid for my father to walk out the door.

"Lucy, I'm going home now," he answers me quietly.

He shakes Ben's hand again, probably with a less vise-like grip this time. Then he kisses me on the cheek gently, and lets himself out into the humid California night.

When the door clicks shut, I turn to Ben.

"Divorce lawyer?" I say.

"Lucy, I don't want to talk about it," he says. "Please try to understand."

I lost my father that night. I didn't want him to permit this. There was a code of ethics I associated with him, as much a part of him as the yarmulke on his head, the strict adherence to ritual, the charity he gave silently, without mention. I knew that my present life had nothing to do with this code of ethics; I had abandoned it as if it were something evil, something that had sullied me. I wanted him to take me under his arm like a package and carry me home. But he just walked away. I never knew his reasons. I never asked why.

I thought he didn't love me.

How could I not have understood what it meant for my father to sit quietly on that chintz sofa in the soft, pink twilight of that Beverly Hills night, watching his only daughter slip through his fingers like a greased-up diver, plunging gracefully through the water to the bottom of the sea.

———

My father's mouth is set in its perpetual scowl, but as soon as he sees me waiting on the other side of the guard's desk, his whole face lifts into the widest, happiest smile.

I am wearing a kilt, argyle knee socks, Wallabees and a plastic yellow barrette in my hair. I think I am the height of sophistication. I am thirteen.

We enter the Stock Exchange dining room like royalty; everyone waves at my father, everyone loves him and, by association, me. We sit catty-cornered at a large table under the stuffed heads of a bull and a bear, white linen napkins covering our laps like tents. He orders Dover sole, broiled, and a side order of broccoli.

He has quit smoking, and he is on a diet.

I order fettuccine Alfredo. I have yet to begin smoking, or worrying about my weight.

There is one thing my father has not quit, however. Two tiny yellow pills, the color of Sweettarts, perch on the side of his bread plate. He thinks I don't notice. One thing my father has never learned about me is that I may not say much, but I notice everything.

Halfway through the Dover sole, my father puts down his fork. His face grows pale, and a thin film of perspiration dots his shiny head.

"Daddy, what's the matter?" I ask.

"Nothing, shnookie," he says, lifting two fingers to his throat, to the place right below his jaw where he can feel the rhythm of his blood, the beat of his heart. He holds his pocket watch in front of him, then counts six seconds.

He returns the pocket watch to his vest. He smiles, patting his head with a soft white handkerchief. "Everything's fine," he says, more to himself than to me. He pulls me to him in a bear hug. He hugs me tight, tighter; I cannot breathe.

———

We are in Paris now, though it doesn't matter. We could just as easily be in London, Tokyo, Tel Aviv. The insides of hotels are all the same: the hot towels, gold faucets, Godiva chocolates resting on the centers of crisp pillows. Whenever life gets too complicated, we fly away. We travel as if the thin air in the pressurized cabin of the Concorde will suck the pain right out of us. We are running away in the fastest method humanly possible, faster than the speed of sound.

We dine only in the fanciest of restaurants, where large franc notes are passed discreetly into the soft palms of maître d's. Tonight we are at Tour d'Argent, ensconced at a window table overlooking Notre Dame. The candle on our table is reflected in a gilt-edged mirror, the pitch-black sky, the Seine flowing by below us. The whole room is ablaze, but I have eyes only for Ben.

He smiles and raises his glass to me.

"To us, darling," he says.

I smile at him vaguely, taking a sip of wine.

"Lucy, where are you?" he asks, squeezing my hand.

"Sorry."

"Look at your plate," he says, motioning to a salad plate the waiter must have set down when I was lost in thought. I was thinking about a particular morning spent on Nantucket, over a year ago, when being in Ben's arms still made me feel safe. We lay on a cold, damp beach, staring up at the sea gulls. I remember Ben's fisherman's sweater wrapped around me, and the way he stood up, bare-chested in the November air, and carried me on his back to the ocean's edge.

"Look down at your plate," Ben repeats.

There is a small velvet box. It is midnight blue. It can mean only one thing.

"Open it," he prompts me, and I do.

The diamond is heart-shaped and larger than any I have ever seen. This does not impress me. I have been with Ben long enough to expect that whatever he owns will be the biggest and the best.

He is grinning at me, proud of himself.

"It's an engagement ring," he says.

"I know," I say faintly.

"Well, aren't you happy?"

I pause. I'm not sure how to answer this question.

"Don't you need to be divorced before you can marry someone else?" I ask.

"Don't start with me, Lucy," he says.

"Why are you giving me this?" I ask, putting the ring on the table between us.

"I love you," he says.

"I love you, I love you, I love you," I mimic him, my voice rising just to the edge of proper decorum for this fancy moment in this fancy restaurant.

"Enough, Lucy," he says sharply. This is how we talk now: every conversation, every romantic dinner centers on these deep, tense moments which are embedded under my skin like needle tracks.

"Never mind, I shouldn't have bothered," he says, scraping his chair back and striding across the restaurant toward the men's room. While he is gone, I hold the ring in my palm, warming it as if it were a moonstone. Then I slip it onto the fourth finger of my left hand.

Once, on the shores of Nantucket, I felt safe. Now there is no place far enough away.

———

Amsterdam, Milan, Geneva

———

People often ask me what I saw in him. They are well intentioned when they assume that I was young and naive, that he swept me off my feet in a motion so fast I could not see what was happening.

They shake their heads mournfully when they hear the story. It is a good story, full of all the essential elements: beauty, wealth, obsession, glamour. But that was not it. I know it, and so do you.

I wonder if deep in your heart you really blame me. You have always understood Ben's special gift. If he were to paint an abstract self-portrait, or submit to a Rorschach test, he would imagine himself as an island, a safe haven in the center of a dark, tempestuous sea. He truly believed that the world was evil, and he was the only man who could save it. He believed he had never hurt anyone in his life. He made me believe it too.

People laugh at me when I say this, but you and I know the truth. Ben Broadhurst walks around with no doubt in his mind that he is an upstanding citizen of this world. When asked to describe himself in television interviews and newspaper profiles, he often uses words like "philanthropist" and "moralist." He believes he can do no wrong.

Where are you? Do you sleep in women's shelters, do you eat in soup kitchens, or do you volunteer in them with a gracious smile, a thin gold band encircling your wedding finger? I can almost see you lifting the lid off a pot of simmering vegetables. The steam rises. I cannot see your face.

———

In our apartment at the Carlyle, I often pretend to make dinner. I buy precooked Rock Cornish game hens, wild rice and stuffed mushrooms from one of the many gourmet places lining Madison Avenue. I am always sure to remove all telltale wrappers and cooking instructions before Ben gets home. He arrives to a set table, an open bottle of cabernet sauvignon and the sight of me in an apron.

How is he ever going to leave his wife, I think, unless I show him I can do a better job in every single area? I am obsessed with Elisabeth Broadhurst. She has replaced her daughter as my notion of the perfect woman, the perfect wife. I picture her driving her Mercedes along the snowbanked streets of her Connecticut village, sunglasses in place, waving to passersby who treat her with respect and deference, as if she were visiting royalty.

She knows the secrets of womanhood. She has passed them along to Carolyn like heirlooms, and I want them too. I want an older woman to come along and explain to me the nature of silence, of guarded smiles and unspoken words. Perhaps she might discuss how she lives with the knowledge that her husband is spending half his time with another woman, a woman young enough to be her daughter.

She does not throw herself in front of train tracks, or hurl herself out a twenty-sixth-story window; she does not even toy with the notion. She wears her private nightmare like a public banner of grace under pressure, of noblesse oblige.

I want her to turn me this way and that, until I am finally headed in the right direction. I am tired of wearing my heart on my sleeve; I want to be a part of the army of women marching down the streets of any city, armed with a legacy of mistrust and betrayal which coats them like a fine, invisible mist.

In the meantime, I pretend to cook. Tonight we are dining on roast leg of lamb, curried rice and young vegetables, courtesy of the Silver Palate. Two champagne flutes are filled with Dom Perignon. We are toasting our second anniversary.

It has been two years since we lay on the beach in Nantucket, two years since Ben told me that as long as I was with him, I would be safe. His presence still makes me feel safe, despite the absolute knowledge I have buried just beneath my skin, the certainty that one day he will leave me.

I wear the heart-shaped diamond on my left hand. When I go to my aerobics class, I know the other women there look at me with envy; I wish I could tell them that there is nothing to envy. They see that I'm thin, but they don't know about the diuretics I take every day, the hunching over my toilet bowl late at night. They see the engagement ring shimmering on my finger, and they do not know that it was given to me by a married man. The surface of my life is a brilliant apparition, and everything beneath the surface is falling apart, dissolving as surely as if my insides were filled with a lethal chemical solution.

Ben smiles at me, and I smile back. He is a handsome man, with the kind of weather-beaten face that gets better with each year. His shirt is perfectly pressed, and he is wearing a new pair of cuff links, which I imagine are a gift from Liz.

Liz knows her husband is having an affair, but I am quite certain she does not know with whom. She is responding to this with shopping sprees and short vacations to distant, exotic places. Every night Ben spends with me costs him thousands of dollars. He seems to enjoy this; it raises the stakes.

He raises his glass to me.

"To my darling," he says.

I have begun to think that he calls me "Darling" in order to avoid any potentially embarrassing moments, like calling me Liz instead of Lucy. We recently bought a dog, a Yorkshire terrier, who travels back and forth between the two coasts with us. We named her Crillon, after the Paris hotel. Ben recently let it slip that he also has a terrier named Crillon living in the Connecticut farmhouse. He believes in simplifying things; he is beginning to have a hard time keeping names straight.

"How's Carolyn?" I ask Ben as he carves the leg of lamb.

She has been on my mind, as always, lurking just beneath conscious thought like a secret.

He stops carving.

"Why do you ask?"

"I've been thinking about her," I say.

"I'll bet you have," he says, and we look at each other for a startling moment.

We have never really discussed it, and we know we never will. He resumes carving the meat without answering my question.

"Have you seen her?" I ask.

"Of course I've seen her, Lucy. She's my stepdaughter," he says.

"Well, how is she?"

He pauses.

"Fine," he says, and in that weighty moment of silence it is clear to me that he is lying.

"What's wrong?" I ask him. My heart thuds once in my chest, like a heavy object falling.

"Why do you assume something's wrong?" he asks carefully, keeping his eyes on the leg of lamb.

"Cut it out, Ben. What's happened?"

He looks up at me.

"Don't use that tone of voice on me, young lady," he says, sounding disturbingly like either one of my parents.

I grip the stem of my champagne glass so hard I am surprised it does not shatter in my hand.

"What is wrong with Carolyn," I say slowly, measuring the space between the words.

He sighs, a trick he has for biding time. He places the carving knife on the table with a flourish, as if to let me know I am testing his patience too much for him to be holding a sharp object.

"Lucy, Carolyn is in the hospital," he says.

"Why?"

"There was an incident—"

"What do you mean, an 'incident'?" I interrupt him.

"Let me finish."

I am silent, and so is he. The sounds of New York City seem intensified despite the double-paned windows of this hotel apartment; I hear a car screeching to a halt, an ambulance, a dog barking. Ben is trying to weigh the importance of this news he is giving me; for once, he has gotten into something, and he doesn't quite know how to get out.

I do not have much patience left. Just at the moment I am about to scream at him, he speaks.

"She tried to kill herself, Lucy."

We stare at each other across the table. The leg of lamb, the curried rice, the tossed green salad suddenly look like the awful remnants of some sacrificial ritual, disembodied rotting parts lying in a forest.

"When?"

"Two weeks ago."

"Two weeks ago?" I finally scream.

"Lucy . . ."

"Why didn't you tell me?"

"Why should I have told you," he says. "You haven't spoken to Carolyn in two years."

"You know how much she means to me," I say, but I realize this isn't true. Ben and I have never talked about Carolyn; she has been considered off-limits, the one card neither of us has been willing to show.

"Where is she?" I ask.

"I can't tell you that."

"Ben, don't play games with me," I say, moving around the table. What am I going to do? Beat him up? Knife him?

"I'm not going to tell you, Lucy."

"Why not?"

"I don't want you to see her."

"Why?"

"Don't you think you've done enough damage already?" he asks as he picks up the knife to resume carving. As far as he's concerned, this conversation is over.

I run straight at him, burying my fists into his stomach. I pound my hands against him, and it is like hitting the hard edge of a highway divider.

He laughs at me, grabbing both my wrists in one hand. The knife clatters to the floor, narrowly missing his shiny black loafer.

"Cut it out," he laughs, indulging me as if I were a difficult child.

"Damage?" I gasp up at him.

He continues to hold my wrists just hard enough for me to hurt myself if I move.

"Lucy, Carolyn is a very confused young woman," he says, enunciating each word slowly, as if I were also confused.

"What are you saying?" I ask, although a dim knowledge of what he is implying is already sinking in.

"It would be hurtful for you to see her," he says. "In fact, the doctors think it would be best if you never see each other again."

"The doctors . . ."

"A team of psychiatrists."

"Is she all right?"

"She will be," he says. "Now Lucy, enough. I don't want to talk about this anymore."

"Fine," I say as I walk over to the closet and pull out my pocketbook and long woolen coat.

"Fine," I repeat as I remove my apartment keys from a shelf near the front door.

"Where are you going?"

"Out."

I do not look at Ben. I do not want to see his stupefied expression, I do not want him to even try to talk me out of this. I think if he says another word, I will kill him.

"That's not such a good idea," he says.

"Go to hell," I tell him as I rush to the door.

"Lucy, it's pouring out."

"Thank you for your concern," I say.

"If you leave, don't come back," he yells after me.

I turn around and look at him for the first time. He is standing by the dining room table, looking as ill at ease next to the delicate white linen, the antique candlesticks as a bear might, having stumbled in from the Central Park Zoo. Everything around him is shining, a resplendent candlelit glow.

"Don't worry. I won't be coming back," I say.

The door clicks behind me loudly, like the snapping down of an assistant director's slate: take one, take two.

The elevator operator smiles when I enter the elevator, then his expression gels into place as he takes a good look at me. He does not ask if I'm all right, or whether there's anything he can do. He studiously watches the lights change from floor to floor as we descend to the lobby. The staff at the Carlyle has been trained not to blink at any sight, or any request. There is an air here, on upper Madison Avenue, of having seen it all.

———

Grandma and Jacob founded schools all over Israel. The Greenburg Institutes are scattered across that barren land like water holes in the desert.

The purpose of the schools is to maintain both secular and Orthodox tradition in a country more concerned with struggling to keep itself alive. Each yeshiva is peopled with Talmudic scholars, rabbis, learned men and even women.

This was Grandma's contribution.

From what I am told, she believed that it was important for Jewish women to understand the tenets of the scriptures, to be conversant with the laws and the reasons behind them.

For this, she fought Jacob, as my mother had to fight with my father many years later.

"It is only important for the woman to keep the home," Jacob thundered the first time Grandma raised it.

Women were not allowed to read from the Torah, from the Bible.

"Jacob, it is important for women to understand. With no understanding, the laws mean nothing," Grandma said.

For years they fought, until ground was broken in Bat Sheva, and the first Greenburg Institute was built. Grandma and Jacob flew to Israel to oversee the work being done.

The entire village came out to watch. Hordes of children stood there, dark and wide-eyed, staring at the strange machines, the odd American couple. They were beautiful, the children. They reminded Jacob of a time and place he had long forgotten, the ghetto in Poland where he had been a child; the children were irrepressible despite all the poverty, like flowers which sprout up through the concrete cracks in sidewalks.

A little girl of six or seven came up to him, holding in her hand a sand dollar. He smiled and crouched down so that he was looking right into her face.

"Thank you," he said in Hebrew.

She grinned at him, revealing two teeth. She was holding a pencil in her other fist.

Jacob dug into his shirt pocket for a small pad of paper he always kept there.

"Here. I want another present from you. Can you write your name for me?" he asked her, holding out the pad.

The little girl's eyes filled with tears. She shook her head from left to right, and back again.

He brushed her hair out of her eyes, but the little girl hung her head.

"Don't be ashamed," whispered Jacob. "We'll teach you to write."

She looked up at him then, and clasped her thin arms around his neck as if he were a tree she was swinging from. He stood up, holding her in his arms, and walked over to his wife, who had been standing there watching.

"You win, Leah," he said to her.

Grandma looked at him, stifling her amusement at this difficult man, her husband. She had always known he would come to this decision in his own time, and now he would act as if it had been his idea all along.

Years later, at dinner dances in New York City hotels, Jacob Greenburg would give heartfelt speeches promoting more equality between men and women in Orthodox Judaism. Grandma always sat in the front row, smiling demurely. At appropriate moments, she clapped.

———

There is no one on Madison Avenue. The street is lined with gated windows, closed boutiques, darkened bookstores. Usually there are Upper East Siders milling about, tired young women walking home from a late night at the office, or tuxedoed men on their way to a function at one of the many private clubs east of Fifth Avenue.

Tonight it is pouring, the icy November rain just on the verge of snow. If it were a few degrees colder, we would be in the middle of a blizzard, but I don't even feel the rain soaking through the back of my coat as I run to a phone booth on the corner of Seventy-seventh and Madison.

I don't know where to begin. Lucy, Carolyn is in the hospital, he had said. Where? I decide to try Northampton General

Hospital first. I use Ben's company phone credit card to make the call.

She is not listed.

Next, I begin with New York City hospitals. There is a method to my madness: I start with the farthest uptown hospitals and work my way down. She is not at Columbia-Presbyterian, Mount Sinai or St. Luke's. She is not at Lenox Hill, Roosevelt or New York Hospital. She is not at NYU, Bellevue, St. Vincent's or anywhere in between.

There is no Carolyn Ward.

I try finding hospitals in any of the towns I can think of near the Connecticut farmhouse: Westport, Wilton, Weston. I'm informed by directory assistance that there aren't even any hospitals in these towns.

The rain is unrelenting. In the hour I've stood in this phone booth, only three people have walked by: a couple holding one yellow slicker over their heads darted across the street, and a homeless man, barefoot, walked slowly through the downpour. I hope he was on his way to the Park Avenue Armory, where there is a shelter.

I do not know where else to look, what to do or where to go. I brought no money with me, no raincoat or umbrella. I decide to run back to the Carlyle, grab my wallet and check into a hotel somewhere. Ben and I have had fights before, but this one seems to require further action; I cannot bring myself to stay with him tonight.

Riding back upstairs in the elevator, I find myself afraid to see him. Don't come back, he had said. He has a way of looking at me when he's angry, a swift, disdainful sweep of his eyes in which he discards me completely. It is a familiar expression; I know where his stepdaughter must have learned it.

I turn the key as quietly as possible, then swing the door open. The living room is dark, lit only by the candles still burning on the dining table. I blow them out. The leg of lamb is exactly as I left it, carved and uneaten, surrounded by a colorful assortment of baby carrots, zucchini, yellow squash. The salad has begun to wilt. I pick up the whole platter and cover it with a tent of tinfoil. I resist the urge to send it hurling through the glass, out the window onto East Seventy-sixth Street. Instead, I place it in the otherwise empty refrigerator, where I imagine it will rot.

The bedroom door is closed, but from under the crack I see that there are no lights on. I open the door. Ben is in bed, asleep. He never has trouble falling asleep; he often says that he can do so at will, that everything in life is mind over matter. On the small table next to him lies a new spy novel, his glasses, and his small, black address book.

I lift the address book off the table as if it were a diamond in a museum. It is that valuable. I think it will tell me what I need to know. I keep my eyes on Ben as I tiptoe back out to the living room, watching him until I shut the door between us.

I turn on a lamp, pour myself a glass of now-warm champagne and sit by the reproduction of a Louis XIV desk which seems to be a fixture in any furnished four-star hotel apartment. I am looking forward to reading Ben's address book, cover to cover. At the moment, it appears the most fascinating piece of literature since *War and Peace*. It is a well-worn book, purchased at least five years ago. There is a front section for addresses, and in the back there are pages and pages of notes scribbled in Ben's fine, bold longhand.

This is where I begin.

Mostly there are lists and doodles. The lists pertain to domestic chores, a part of Ben's life I know nothing about.

1.) Call Levy's Hardware re: halogen lamp

2.) Call Manhattan Motors re: Mercedes repair

3.) Tuesday 6:00 meeting with Montessori school

These lists are surrounded by intricate drawings: abstract squares within squares, circles bisecting triangles, strange amoeba-like shapes. Ben always doodles when he's on the phone; he has an abundance of energy. He can't keep his hands still.

I flip slowly through the pages, not sure what I'm after; I'm trying to get to the bottom of the mystery, to connect all the fragments of sentences, all the pieces of Ben's life until they form one simple truth.

In these notes, he refers to Liz as L.B., and me as L.G., for example, "L.B. to Philharmonic Friday night," or "L.G. dinner at La Grenouille 7:30 Saturday."

I try not to think about these new discoveries; Ben told me last Friday he was on an overnight business trip to Boston. I imagine him at the Philharmonic with Liz, holding her elbow, guiding her through the crowds at Lincoln Center. I imagine Liz handing him her opera glasses so he can get a better look at the blonde playing cello in the second row.

I dismiss these thoughts. I am searching for Carolyn. Where is she? I can almost see her face floating before me, as white as the hospital bedsheet pulled tightly up to her chin. The intravenous fluid drips slowly into her arm; her veins are so thin that the inside of her elbow is black-and-blue from the pressure. She is probably staring at the television hanging from the ceiling. There is a commercial break. I hope she does not see my face filling her screen, larger and far more confident than in life, trying to sell her something sugary sweet: Coca-Cola, M&M's, Betty Crocker cake mix.

Finally I find what I am looking for. I almost pass it by, because it is written in the finest, lightest pencil. C. —Room 24—Silver Hill.

Silver Hill. A private sanatorium which I've heard of only because a wealthy, anorectic Smith student was sent there a few years ago. I remember that Carolyn and I shuddered about it at the time. Imagine, she had said to me, they lock you in your room.

I try to envision her there. I have been thinking along the lines of regular hospitals, hospitals where medical doctors fix whatever is wrong and send their patients home with orders for bed rest. It had not occurred to me that Carolyn would be in a mental hospital, under careful observation, being walked along lush, manicured grounds by a white-coated orderly.

But of course this makes sense. Carolyn tried to kill herself. I have no comprehension of what this means; it has not sunk in. All I can see is the determined set of her chin, the way the muscles in her jaw clench as they do whenever she really concentrates on anything.

How did she do it?

I close my eyes against the thought, and at that moment I hear Ben rustling in the bedroom. I jump up from the desk, taking his address book with me, then grab my raincoat from the hall closet and race out the door.

It is ten o'clock at night. It is still raining, though not as hard. Ben's car is parked in a garage just a few blocks away, and I walk there, my heart pounding at what I'm about to do.

The attendant recognizes me immediately.

"Where's Mr. Broadhurst?" he asks.

"I'm on my way to meet him," I say, slipping him a five-dollar bill.

"I'll bring it right around, Lucy," he says.

Liz is called Mrs. Broadhurst. I am called Lucy.

I have never driven this particular car, one of the half-dozen cars Ben owns. It is a newer version of the sports coupe he was driving the first time I met him in Northampton. It is a red, dangerous-looking machine with doors that open up instead of out, giving it the appearance of an enormous, shiny lobster.

I hop inside, then the attendant closes the door in an elaborate effort.

He grins at me.

"Some machine," he says.

I try to smile back, but I can't. There seems to be nothing in this world to smile about.

"Let's just hope I can find my way out of it once I get where I'm going," I say to the attendant through the rolled-down window. The inside of the car looks like a cockpit.

"Don't worry, Lucy. Mr. Broadhurst will help you," he says with a wink.

With that, I find first gear, and screech my way out of the garage and onto the sparsely trafficked avenue.

I head west, driving all the way across the city and then uptown on Riverside Drive, armed only with the knowledge that Silver Hill is in New Canaan, Connecticut, and Connecticut is north.

For the past two years I have never known where I was going. It is not a new feeling for me to be lost. As I edge my way onto the Henry Hudson Parkway, it occurs to me that I don't know how to find Silver Hill, but for the first time in longer than I care to remember, I know that somehow, I will get there.

———

Were you waiting for me that night?

Perhaps beneath your tranquilized eyes, you saw me speeding in a red blur along the Merritt Parkway. The car simply would not go fast enough as the highway unfolded itself before me like an endless black ribbon.

I'd like to think that your ears were burning. Or is that just one more old wives' tale, something we tell ourselves in order to believe we are not alone? After all, when the blood was pouring out of your wrists and into the bathwater, where was I? Most likely at Bergdorf Goodman's, trying on yet another pair of Maud Frizon lizard pumps.

Oh, Carolyn.

I should have known when you first threw your arms around me that it was you who was drowning, not I.

You wanted me to save you, but you missed the most important clue: I didn't know I had the power to save anyone, least of all myself.

———

I sit in the parking lot of Silver Hill waiting for the sky to change from pitch-dark to dawn. The ashtray has slowly filled with cigarette butts, and the car is littered with empty

Styrofoam coffee cups from the 7-Eleven. I am grateful, to-night, for the invention of the all-night convenience store.

Ben left an assortment of tapes lying near the back win-dow: Cat Stevens, Carly Simon, the Boston Pops. I listen to Carly Simon sing "You're So Vain" a dozen times, reversing the tape at the end of the song and going back to the begin-ning bars, the ominous, tapping drumbeat of the opening.

I wish I had a picture of Carolyn, something concrete to run through my hands like worry beads. I cannot see her face this morning as I sit here so close to her. I think I am afraid of imagining her, of dreaming her up. The perfect facade I have envisioned over the past two years has been shattered as surely as if she were a piece of priceless, delicate crystal.

At about 6:30 in the morning, cars begin to pull up, lone bleary-eyed drivers and carpools full of people who work at Silver Hill. I hunch down in the driver's seat until enough people have gone inside; I know I need to be inconspicuous, though it is difficult to go unnoticed in a bright red space-age sports car.

I pull my hair back into a ponytail, tie the belt of my rain-coat tightly around my waist, and fish in the bottom of my pocketbook for my darkest sunglasses. Looking at myself in the rearview mirror, I think I look like a bad imitation of a private detective, but it's the best I can do.

I look old. Old, tired, and worn out. My nails and teeth are yellow from cigarettes, my eyes are dull and my skin is tinged with gray. With no makeup on, it occurs to me that my face looks like a blank palette. I need a makeup artist to paint some color into my cheeks, make my eyes sparkle, help me look like a young woman again.

I have been living so fast during these past few years that it seems twenty years have gone by. At least once in our lives we see ourselves as we truly are; this is that moment. I am afraid to walk through the doors of Silver Hill. They may want to keep me there.

I walk past the front desk and straight up a winding stair-case which I hope leads to the patients' rooms. C.—Room 24 —Silver Hill. No one tries to stop me. I look like I know where I'm going. I keep my eyes focused straight ahead of me, shoulders squared, and swing my arms back and forth like an East Coast version of a soldier. I am prepared to break down walls, if necessary. The lack of sleep, the bright remnants of champagne, the industrial-strength coffee have made me bold. I will do whatever I have to do.

There are no visible room numbers. I poke my head into one room, then another. The beds are stark white, and empty. There is a bulletin board hanging halfway down the hall, with posted notices about group therapy, meetings of Alcoholics Anonymous, folded notes from one patient to another. My heart is pounding in my chest; I imagine that any minute, I will feel a strong hand on my shoulder, a deep voice saying, Come with me.

I almost don't see her. I almost walk right by her, but she sticks an arm straight out, stopping me. There she is, leaning with one foot against the wall of the corridor like a schoolgirl lounging against the side of a brick building on a crisp fall morning.

I look down at the arm. All I see is yards and yards of gauze bandages. I look up, expecting to meet the eyes I remember, but instead I find myself staring into twin black pools. Her pupils are so dilated there is no color; it is like looking into the eyes of an animal, trapped and unblinking.

"Hello," she says thickly.

"Carolyn," I say.

"Won't you come to my room?" she asks, gesturing to a door immediately to her left.

We walk into her room. Her arms dangle to either side of her, useless and white, like a snowman's.

She has lost weight. Her face is pinched and there are yellowish bruises by her temples. Her fine hair is brushed back. She sits in the only chair, an orange upholstered chair found in rooms like this one. She motions me to sit on the bed.

I look around the room. There is nothing in here with which to kill oneself, even with all the ingenuity in the world. There are no sharp objects, nothing small enough to swallow, nothing to lift and climb out the high window.

She clears her throat.

"Got a cigarette?" she asks.

"No," I lie.

We fall silent again. She runs her hands nervously through her hair, tugging on the ends and pushing them into her mouth. I cannot keep my eyes off her thickly bandaged wrists. I imagine her slicing her veins vertically, in order to facilitate the flow of blood.

It must have hurt. I want to take her into my arms and rock her until she feels no more pain. I want to kiss the insides of her wrists, licking her wounds, as animals do. Please, just let her be all right.

I am striking a bargain with God: if he makes Carolyn better, I will quit smoking, quit drinking, quit Ben. There was a time I would have jumped off a bridge for her; that time is back. I would do anything.

"Why?" I ask her, the word coming up through my throat like a cough.

"Why what?"

"Why did you do it?"

She smiles at me then, a shadowy reminder of her old smile fighting its way up past her morning dosage of tranquilizers.

"I certainly didn't do a very good job, did I?" she asks, holding her bandaged arms out to me, evidence of her failure.

"Thank God you didn't," I say quietly.

She looks at me, her eyes glassy with tears. She is slumped down in her chair like a life-sized Raggedy Ann doll.

"Don't tell me you care, Lucy," she says, "not after everything."

She bends her head into her lap and begins to weep.

"I want to die," she says, and the muffled words are clearer to me than anything I have ever heard in my life.

I move in two steps from the edge of her bed to the chair where she is sitting. I kneel on the floor next to her, and reach around until I am holding her awkwardly, cradling her as she cries.

"I want to die," she repeats over and over again, each time a bit more softly until there is no more sound. We are quiet. I rock her gently back and forth as time floats around us. We could be in our old dormitory room at Smith, or in the back of a limousine, or on a New York City street corner, but we are not. We are here at a mental institution, she has slit her wrists, and the only thing I know for sure is that life will never be the same again.

She has fallen asleep. She leans back into the chair, her head falls to one side. I see the dark length of her eyelashes, the thin veins along the side of her throat, her tiny, perfect ear. She looks ten years younger, lying there, both innocent and world-weary, like the kind of haunting picture of a battered child sometimes seen on the evening news.

I brush her hair behind her ear, I stroke her head, feeling the shape of her skull as if it were a map, as if I might understand her by tracing the ridges and bumps caused by bicycle falls and minor mishaps so many years ago.

Her eyelids flutter; she is dreaming. I want to crawl inside her dreams and shape them. I want to control her in her sleep as I have never been able to when she is awake. Mostly, I want to take her pain in my hands, packing it together tightly as if it were a snowball, and throw it with all my might into the sky.

"Who are you?" I hear a man's voice from behind me.

Goddamn. I was afraid this was going to happen. I swivel my head around, trying not to disturb Carolyn, and find myself staring not at a version of Dr. Jekyll, but at a small, surprised-looking older man with warm blue eyes which seem to say, "Tell me everything."

"I'm Lucy Greenburg," I stammer. "I'm an old friend of—"

"I know who you are, Miss Greenburg," he interrupts. He walks over to me and shakes my hand.

"I'm Dr. Martin Sheidler," he says. "I was just checking in on Carolyn during my morning rounds."

Then he stands there, his head cocked to one side as if he were listening for something.

Carolyn, in her sleep, lets out a sigh.

He smiles at me.

"You know, I'm not surprised to see you here," he says.

"Really?"

"Carolyn has talked about you a great deal. You are a very good friend," he says.

I hear faint traces of a European accent in Dr. Sheidler's voice, though I can't detect the country of origin. There is a musicality, a rising and falling of his words which I find comforting, particularly as it begins to really dawn on me that I am kneeling on the floor of a hospital room in the middle of Connecticut with Ben's car in the parking lot out back, Carolyn asleep in a chair in front of me, and her psychiatrist standing over me asking questions.

"How did you find out she was here?" he says.

I don't know how to respond to this, so I decide to tell him the truth.

"Her stepfather told me she had tried . . ."

I falter.

Dr. Sheidler smiles at me reassuringly.

"Go on," he says.

"Anyway, he wouldn't tell me where she was, so I went through his notebook and found the number for Silver Hill."

"Ingenious," Dr. Sheidler says, continuing to smile.

Carolyn moans, and shifts her weight.

We both look at her.

"You have very strong feelings for Carolyn," Dr. Sheidler says quietly.

"I always have," I answer.

"You live with Mr. Broadhurst?" he asks.

"In a manner of speaking," I say.

"Yes," he says, "I'm sure it's an extremely complicated situation."

Our eyes meet for a moment; we are each wondering how far to go, how much information to withhold, what the other one knows.

He makes a professional decision, an educated guess. We have already talked too much.

"Well, Miss Greenburg," he says briskly, "it has been a pleasure. I think it would do Carolyn a great deal of good to spend time with you. I hope you come back and visit her. Of course, only if she wants."

"How long will she be here?" I ask.

"Oh, Carolyn will be here for quite some time," he says.

Quite some time. What does that mean? Weeks? Months?

Dr. Sheidler begins to leave the room, then turns back to me.

He hesitates for a moment.

"She nearly succeeded, you know."

I rest my hand on her arm, feeling the slight swaying of her body with each breath. I look at her sleeping, a tangle of dark, chewed-up hair falling over her cheek. The tension is gone; her face, though all thin, gaunt angles, is somehow softened. She is a ghost of the old Carolyn Ward, a transparency of bones and shadows, but she is alive.

"I will do whatever I can to help her," I say.

He smiles at me, an understanding, psychoanalytic smile.

"I would wager a bet," he says, "that in whatever ways you help Carolyn, you will also be helping yourself, my dear friend."

With that, he pads quietly away, closing the door behind him. I remain kneeling by Carolyn's side. My legs and arms ache from the uncomfortable position, but I do not want to move.

As long as she is asleep, I am not afraid. When she awakes, I know I will again ask her the question I cannot get out of my mind.

Why? I will ask, and she will answer me flippantly, as always.

Why not? she will probably say.

But this time, I know I will push her and push her until I get past the small, brittle smile, until I go beneath the perfect facade which I believed in from the day I met her.

I want answers. Not easy answers, but truthful ones, and I will patiently wait until I get them.

I know Dr. Sheidler is right. Carolyn's fate and mine are tied together as surely as if we were mates on a sinking ship. The thing that almost killed her has been slowly killing me, and if we survive, we will survive together.

———

You wanted to be dead.

You sat on the edge of a Smith College bathtub filled with lukewarm water and opened your wrists with a razor blade bought especially for the occasion.

You locked the door. You did not make a phone call. You did not leave a note. There was no one to whom you wanted to say good-bye.

If your suite-mate had not come back to her room early with a bad case of stomach flu, you would have gotten your wish.

How long had you been thinking about it?

A week? An hour? All your life?

Sometimes now, when you walk down a city street on a yellow-bright fall morning and feel the wind lifting your hair, or see children pushing each other on their way into a playground, are you glad things didn't go quite your way?

I am not asking if you are happy.

You are living out your life.

Where are you? Sometimes I imagine you live in a lazy shoreline village, on Long Island or perhaps on the coast of Italy. Other times I can only picture you in one of the major American cities, surrounded by people as tightly wound as two-dollar clocks, other citizens with secrets, with private, shielded hearts.

You almost died.

Are you glad that you're alive?

If you are, just send me a telegram. You don't have to say anything. Just yes, or no.

She wakes up. Her eyes blink open hesitantly; she is not sure she wants to leave the world of sleep, where thoughts drift around her quietly.

She stares at me, remembering.

"How long have I been asleep?" she asks.

"A little more than two hours," I say.

She stretches, arching her back.

"All I do is sleep, sleep, sleep," she says, disgusted.

"It's the medication," I say.

"Fuck the medication."

She glares at me. This is the Carolyn I am used to.

"So you've just been sitting here?" she asks.

"Yes."

"Sitting here and sitting here," she says. "Why, Lucy? What do you want?"

"I just want to talk," I say.

I feel the back of my throat closing up.

"Talk," she repeats.

She echoes everything I say in an attempt, I suppose, to make sure she's hearing it correctly.

"Carolyn, I want to understand."

"Isn't it a little late for that?"

"Can't we try?"

"Let me ask you something," she says, her eyes flashing at me, focused like lasers. "Are you still with Ben?"

I pause. I'm not sure how to answer this question.

"Answer me," she says sharply. She is sitting very still.

"Yes," I say.

She stands up more quickly than I thought she could, and walks over to the window. I can only see a sliver of her face, her straight, tense back.

"I thought so," she murmurs.

We are quiet for a few moments. I watch the minute hand of her clock move three times.

She turns to me then, her eyes pink.

"Remember, back at Smith, you always wanted to know

where I went when I disappeared, and who I was with?" she asks, her voice rising into a wobbly, hysterical pitch.

Carolyn, who is it? You can tell me.

I can't tell you.

"Yes, I remember," I say.

"Do you still want to know?"

Deep inside my ribcage, something curls up like a snail, trying mightily to build a shell around itself.

"Yes, I want to know," I say.

She pauses, staring at me. She knows that no matter what happens from this moment on, life is going to be different.

"I was with Ben," she says, and her words angle toward me with all the speed and impact of a physical blow.

I am holding tightly on to the edge of the bed, concentrating so intently on not dissolving into thin air that I almost don't hear the rest of it.

"Lucy," she says almost gently, as if she's sorry, "I've been sleeping with Ben since I was fourteen years old."

Where You'll
Find Me

*I*t began in Paris, where so many illicit affairs begin.

Your whole family was supposed to take a European holiday together, but for one reason or another, no one could go but you and Ben. No, your mother wasn't on the trip, you told me with no discernible edge to your voice, something came up.

You stayed at the Crillon.

You shared a suite.

You were fourteen, and he was forty.

Late the second night, you woke up with a start, and for a moment, you didn't know where you were. The room was pitch-black, illuminated only by patches car lights swooping up from the Place de la Concorde. The sounds were different from the ones you were used to: there were no crickets, no rustling grass, no clink of glasses from a party downstairs.

You were frightened, until your eyes grew accustomed to the dark, and you saw Ben sitting on the edge of your bed. You'd just had a nightmare, he told you, he had heard you screaming.

"Let me give you a hug," he said in a new, husky voice, "and I'll make it all go away."

He pulled aside the sheets and crawled into bed with you.

You were wearing nothing but one of his enormous Brooks Brothers shirts, which fell halfway off your shoulder. It was pin-striped, navy-and-white, with a solid white collar. It was buttoned only in one place, right above your navel.

You rested your head on his chest, as you had so many times, in the farmhouse, in Connecticut.

"I'm scared," you told him. (It was the last time in your life you ever told anyone how you really felt.)

He was not your first, you told me, as if that could possibly make a difference.

You didn't try to stop him, no, not at all.

He guided your head down his belly just like he wanted, and you held him in your mouth like the biggest secret you'd ever have to keep.

You rather liked it, you told me, eyeing me carefully to see just how many of the sordid details I could possibly take before I would bolt out the door.

You underestimated me, Carolyn. I wanted to know every single moment intimately, I wanted to see it in living color. For the rest of my life, I wanted the image of you and Ben entwined together in a Paris hotel room to supersede everything within my line of vision like a scar embedded on the delicate tissue of my cornea.

It went on for years.

When we were freshmen at Smith, he was the one you

would talk to, in code, on the hall telephone. When you disappeared and came back with a tan—*No, I'm not tan*, you laughed and laughed—he was the mystery man with whom you had flown to some remote Caribbean island.

I was with my friend, you told me. *We stayed at the villa of a prince. We flew there on a Learjet. We dined, we danced, we lay in the sun. But mostly we fucked.*

You did the one thing you weren't supposed to do, the one thing he somehow didn't bargain for.

You began to need him.

You began to get used to it.

Do I dare use these words? You began to fall in love.

Fridays, you'd both take the afternoon off—you from high school, Ben from his business—and you'd meet at a prearranged location. This was usually a Connecticut inn, though sometimes it was a New York City hotel room.

You had a note signed from him, which you gave to your high school principal, explaining your absence. (It wasn't until several years later that you discovered the contents of that note: Ben had written that you were emotionally disturbed and had a weekly psychologist appointment on Friday afternoons.)

You would spend from two o'clock until six o'clock in bed with each other on Fridays, but as the years went by, he began to take more chances. When your mother went out grocery shopping, he'd pull you into one of the guest bedrooms. While she and Debbie were playing tennis outside, he'd grab you from behind, cupping your breasts in his large hands.

He couldn't wait for you to go off to college, where you'd finally be free.

Our first semester at Smith, that's exactly what happened. All his wishes came true. At the drop of a hat, you'd be off together to St. Barts, the Florida Keys, the coast of Scotland.

Carolyn, in my wildest flights of fancy, in my worst nightmares, I could not have dreamt this up.

Who is it? You can tell me.

I can't tell you.

Is it Teddy Kennedy?

• • •

No one knew. You had never breathed a word of it to anyone. Not your teachers, not your sister, and most certainly not your best friend.

It wasn't until that crisp fall afternoon in New Canaan, Connecticut, sitting on the floor of your hospital room, that the words began pouring from you in an endless, unstoppable stream.

You didn't look at me. The whole time you spoke, you stared at the white-painted windowpane, the streaks in the sunny glass. You were not looking beyond the window, at the view of the changing leaves. You were like a domesticated animal, staring listlessly at the bars of your cage.

I didn't utter a word for hours. At some point, Dr. Sheidler poked his head in the door, but he took one look at us and walked quickly away.

What must we have looked like, I wonder? The tension in that room was like a living, breathing thing, with you staring at the window, and me staring at you.

You talked and talked. I could recount every word you said, every place you mentioned, every nuance.

You told me about trips you had taken with him, and I knew them well; they were the same trips I took with him four years later.

You described long walks on the beach, the way you would feed the sea gulls out of a large plastic bag, and how they seemed to swoop down right at you, beaks open, fearless.

You told me how he liked to lift you around your hips and plant you right on top of him so that you were sitting up straight, and he would watch you as you moved on top of him.

He always said your name when he climaxed.

Sometimes he didn't get all three syllables out. *Caaa*, he would moan, like the bleating of a sheep.

"When did you stop sleeping with him?" I asked you.

"When you started, Lucy," you said, and your old cynical smile flitted across your face.

"You were my replacement," you said, trying to hurt me, searching for the place where I wasn't protecting myself.

You looked at me then, out of the corner of your eye.

"What do you think of *that?*" you asked me.

I cleared my throat, but there was nothing there, I couldn't speak. All I could see was Ben's face across a candlelit table, his hand raising a wineglass, his eyes gazing deeply into mine.

You lashed out at me then, hurling across the room before I knew what was happening, pummeling me with your bandaged arms, your hard, angry fists.

I grabbed you by your elbows.

"Stop," I whispered harshly to you, "just stop."

I was afraid a nurse would come in, and I would be asked to leave. We still had not finished. (Perhaps we will never be finished.)

You were out of control. You tried to hit me with the little strength you had, and I tried to stop you with the little strength I had. We must have been quite a sight, Carolyn, two ninety-eight-pound weaklings.

"How could you?" you cried, your face twisted with pain. "How could you have done this to me?"

"I didn't know," I said quietly.

"Didn't know . . ." you spit back out at me. "Does it really matter? Wasn't it bad enough that you were sleeping with the stepfather of your best friend?"

"I didn't have all the answers," I said to you as my defenses, which had been in place since seven o'clock that morning, started finally to crumble.

As I began to cry, you immediately became stronger; you sat back down in your chair, rubbed your forehead for a moment, then looked at me with the old direct gaze which had unnerved me from the day I met you.

"Lucy," you said, "you were the only person in my life who mattered to me."

I looked at you, not sure what you were saying.

"You had no idea," you said, your eyes fixed on me, "you had no idea that I was going off with Ben every week?"

"No," I said.

You shook your head, incredulous.

"You and the rest of the world," you said. "If things look all right, then they must be all right."

"No, that wasn't it . . ."

"So what was it, Lucy?"

I didn't answer you. We were quiet for a while, and for the first time since I had known you, there was nothing in the air between us; it was time for no more secrets.

You see, there had been something left unsaid during these past few years, fragments of sentences, words which had lodged just beneath the surface of my skin like microscopic splinters.

Occasionally, when I least expected it, these words would enter into my consciousness with all the fanfare of a parade, and announce themselves so clearly that for a moment, I couldn't deny them.

"I was busy falling in love with you," I finally said.

That was the sentence I always thought would end my life.

What did I think would happen?

The world did not implode, you did not laugh, or bolt out the door. Instead, your eyes softened for just an instant.

"So was I," you said quietly.

Your voice still floats through my head from time to time. I can be standing in line at the dry cleaners, or picking out fresh bread at the bakery, and I will suddenly hear you. *I loved you once*, your voice will say. Sometimes you sound gentle, sometimes angry, sometimes resigned.

Whenever it happens, all I can think is this: I wish I had known it, Carolyn, during a time when I still could have made a difference. I wish that instead of seeing only what I wanted to see, I had looked at what was there.

I still wonder how it all began.

Were you too frightened, did you push Ben and me toward one other like magnets, knowing that it was the only way you could escape alive? Or were you just playing another dangerous game, supplying all of us with enough ammunition to destroy ourselves.

There are sins of action, sins of silence, and sins of omission.

What would have happened, do you think, if we all had taken the biggest risk of all, and simply told each other the truth?

You have disappeared. You are somewhere in New York City, or perhaps you are in Italy, walking silently along the shores of Lake Como, or in Istanbul, hidden deep inside a cave, or a fragrant opium den.

Wherever you are, I will not go looking for you, Carolyn. If you need me, come to the Upper West Side of Manhattan, and walk slowly up Broadway; look into the windows of novelty stores, card shops, outdoor cafes, dance studios.

Look for me in a crowd of people crossing Seventy-ninth Street, or piling into the subway in the early hours of morning. Do not look at the girl on your television set, or on the movie marquee. She is not who she appears to be; she is simply a glistening shell who has somehow survived the churning of the ocean in one piece.

Search instead, through the countless faces marching uptown, going about their business like solid citizens of the world. Look for the people who tuck their pain away in their purses, or store it neatly underneath their bus seats on their way to work.

Look hard, Carolyn, and don't be fooled by appearances, because that is where you'll find me.

PART FOUR

PART FOUR

I have often wondered about the difference between you and me. What was it that allowed you to disappear into thin air, while I stayed right where I was, with my feet soldered firmly to the ground?

I have begun to think it was this: people with families cannot disappear. I have roots which attach me to the soil, a history which weighs me down like an anchor.

My great-grandfather came from Vilna in the belly of a cargo ship, with a knapsack on his back and a few crazy dreams. What's left of him now is an old crumbling footstone etched with simple words of Hebrew at the head of the family plot.

At the Brooklyn cemetery, I have noticed that recent Russian immigrants have their faces stenciled into the black marble of their tombstones, so that the relatives left behind will not forget them.

I need no such reminder.

I will never be allowed to forget.

————

It is eleven o'clock by the time I leave Silver Hill, and midnight before I finally decide where to go and what to do. I cannot go to the Carlyle, I can't call my parents. I have no home.

There is only one place in the world where I'll be safe.

Grandma's apartment is as quiet as a crypt, sealed off from the late-night traffic on Central Park West twenty-one stories below. I remove my raincoat and soaking-wet shoes as soon as I enter the door, then hug Myrtle, her nursemaid, who is wearing a quilted bathrobe and a head full of pink curlers.

"Miss Lucy!" she exclaims. "Goodness, I haven't seen you in years."

I am called Miss Lucy, my father is called Mister Joseph, and so on. This used to bother me, but now I find it comforting; I want Myrtle to throw an arm around me and lead me into the kitchen. I want to perch on the countertop and have her feed me milk and cookies.

I have been trying so hard to be an adult, and now I just want to be a child.

"I'm sorry I woke you up," I say.

"It's all right, but what are you doing here?" she asks.

"Myrtle, I'm going to stay for a few days, if that's all right," I say.

"Of course it is, dear," she says. She takes a close look at me then, and decides not to ask any more questions.

We walk into Grandpa Jacob's study, where there is a foldout couch, covered with protective plastic. The study is my favorite room in the whole apartment, with its gold-and-black wallpaper, walls full of Hebrew books and an old mahogany wet bar near the window, still stocked with bottles of scotch and ancient Russian vodka.

Myrtle brings me sheets, a heavy blanket and two towels.

"Call me if you need anything else," she says in her soft Jamaican accent. She kisses me on the forehead, then walks quietly out, shutting the door behind her.

I pull back the gold-and-black brocade curtains, winding them around two brass hooks attached to the sides of the large window. Central Park is dark, the reservoir full from days of rain. There are no pedestrians at this hour, only a few cars winding their way down the Park Drive South.

I wander into the dressing room across the hall and find a large silk robe hanging in the corner; I wonder whether it was Grandpa Jacob's. It would not surprise me if it hadn't been thrown out, twenty years after his death. I take off all my clothes, folding them neatly into a pile on an armchair, and wrap the robe around me. Then I walk back into the study, over to the wet bar, and pour myself a glass of room-temperature scotch.

I stand by the window, staring at the Manhattan skyline lit up like a postcard in the night, and wonder how much it has changed since Jacob stood here in his bathrobe, nursing his drink so many years ago. It must look like a different city; this is, in part, due to Ben Broadhurst, who likes to say that he built the city up from the ground.

This is not that far from the truth.

What did I expect? A man capable of building whole cities would most certainly try to build women, inventing them and reinventing them until they changed before his very eyes and became whatever he needed them to be, conforming to architectural structure, to his notion of perfection.

Ben. When I think of him, I want to hurl myself right out of this twenty-first-story window and free-fall through the night for the thirty seconds it would take before I hit the ground, at the corner of Ninetieth Street and Central Park West.

They say what we don't know won't hurt us.

For over two years I have been walking around with pieces to a puzzle; I have been searching in all the wrong places for clues, for the missing link. And now I am faced with information that is almost too much for me to bear. I knew I had been carrying a loaded gun for these two years; that prospect thrilled me, and I got out of bed each morning with a pounding in my chest, wondering whether it was all about to blow sky-high. What I didn't know is that on a daily basis, I was unwittingly firing directly into Carolyn's heart.

Whore, she called me on Madison Avenue, some time ago.

I should have listened to her. She was right.

Tonight, standing in Grandpa Jacob's study surveying the world below, I feel I have more in common with the people on the fringes of this city, who get from day to day solely on guts and instinct, stepping over each other, stripping watches off limp wrists and money out of pockets, doing whatever they have to do in order to survive.

I stare at the diamond on my finger, an engagement ring, and seriously contemplate tossing it out the window, aiming for a park bench below. No, I decide, this is not a moment for grand gestures. Or pointless ones.

I sit down on the plastic-covered couch. I am facing a portrait of one of the many rabbis in my family, a great-grandfather I never knew. He is wearing a black robe and black ceremonial hat. He is a stern-looking man, dark eyes peering down his nose; a long, gray double beard travels almost to his waist.

We do not resemble one another.

I feel less like a Greenburg, less a part of the legacy given to me at birth, than I have ever felt in my life.

I wrap Grandpa's robe tightly around me, and walk out of the study and down the long marble hallway to Grandma's room. The door is open a crack, and the light spilling out from the opening is a mechanical green glow from the various life-support systems surrounding her.

I push the door open. She is lying there in her hospital bed, larger and paler than I remember; her left arm is still dangling off the side of the railing, and I imagine it hasn't moved since I last saw her, over two years ago.

I used to visit Grandma every week.

What happened to me, what was so important that I

couldn't get myself to the Central Park West apartment even once during the past two years?

I wonder if she has missed me. I used to talk to her all the time, even after everyone else had given up. You see, I was the only one who never had known Grandma as the woman she once had been; the living, breathing mountain of flesh lying in the bed was all I had ever known, and so I was comfortable with her.

I pull up a chair to the side of her bed, and grasp her hand.

"Grandma," I whisper, even though I know I could yell and it would make no difference.

"It's Lucy," I say.

Her head falls from right to left, so she is facing me. Her eyes are half-open, the famous green eyes which have turned brown over these years, like fall leaves.

"I've missed you," I say.

She breathes in and out. Through the window I hear the distant sound of a car alarm beginning to ring.

From the time I was a little girl, I always told Grandma stories. I told her about piano competitions, tennis matches and being first runner-up in the spelling bee. I told her about my friends, and later, my boyfriends.

Tonight, I rest my head against Grandma's arm and begin to tell her the only story I know anymore, a story that, if she could hear me, I imagine would appall her. I tell her of Carolyn Ward, of Ben Broadhurst, and of the strange new world I entered when I walked in the door of Emerson House at Smith College just three years ago.

I wonder if she feels my tears streaming down her arm, whether she hears my sobs, my body heaving next to her.

It is dawn before I leave Grandma's room. My face stings from tears, and my throat is hoarse. Through the venetian blinds, I see the sun beginning to rise, lighting up the city from east to west, from York Avenue to Riverside Drive. It is the second dawn I have seen in as many days, but I am not tired. I feel as though I have awoken from a long sleep. There is too much to do.

My days settle into a routine. In the morning, Myrtle wakes me up with coffee and an English muffin, setting a tray down on Grandpa's desk. She seems to understand the kind of shape I'm in, and she has been taking care of me, making sure I have exactly what I need: healthful food, peace and quiet.

I have talked to no one except Harry. He knows where I am, and he knows not to call me for any kind of work right now, that no one in his right mind would hire me for anything. The film is finally set to be released next month, and he wants me to be ready for that. I have already done an enormous amount of pre-publicity. Harry found me a press agent who has placed me within the covers of magazines such as *People, Mademoiselle* and *Seventeen*. Sweet 'n Low, for whom I did one commercial, has offered me an exclusive two-year contract, and I suddenly have more money than I ever dreamed I could make on my own.

And none of it matters.

Every afternoon I get into my car and drive to New Canaan. Visiting hours are from two to four o'clock; Dr. Sheidler has made an exception for me, so sometimes I stay and have dinner with Carolyn.

Dr. Sheidler has been very kind to me, because he believes that I am helping her. But there is one thing Carolyn hasn't told her psychiatrist, the one piece of information he needs to know in order to have any chance of helping her: he does not know about Paris, the Crillon, the thing that began when she was fourteen and will haunt her for the rest of her life.

She has made me promise I will never tell a soul.

"Swear it, Lucy," she said that first night, "if anyone ever finds out, I will kill myself, and this time I'll do it right."

At the end of these afternoon visits, sometimes Dr. Sheidler asks me to come into his office, and we talk for a while. He wants to know what went on between Carolyn and me, but more than that, I think he is trying to uncover the secret she carries with her, the veil of mystery which surrounds her, even now.

"Miss Greenburg," he sighs uncharacteristically, "Carolyn is deeply, deeply troubled, and I'm trying to find out why."

And I say nothing, because I believe Carolyn's threat. At the moment, life doesn't mean very much to her; she thinks it would be easier for her to die than to live.

In spite of this, she is beginning to heal. The bandages around her wrists are thinner, and she has been moved to a different wing of Silver Hill where patients have more privileges; she is no longer considered at great risk.

We do not really have conversations. She talks for hours on end, and I watch her, listening, marveling at how I never really knew her, not until now.

She is allowed to smoke cigarettes and walk around the grounds. We walk and smoke. Sometimes, I talk to her. She wants to know if I've seen Ben, and I tell her no, I haven't, and I don't intend to.

She smiles at me, then.

"Lucy, do you really think it's going to be so easy?"

"What do you mean?" I ask her.

"Hasn't he ever told you that he'll never let you go?"

I look at her and feel my face grow hot.

"You see," she says, "he really means it."

———

I now hold the key to your mystery. It was in the keeping of unspeakable secrets, the dominion of classified information, the possession of special knowledge which thinned the air around you, lending the most translucent glow to your already perfect face.

Finally I understand. It was pain which made your eyes shine, which made red spots stand out in your cheeks.

Although it is far too late, I now understand that it was not information given, but information withheld, which made everyone who laid eyes on you fall in love.

———

Everyone is looking for me. They think I have disappeared off the face of the earth. Little do they know that, in fact, the opposite is true. Each day I become a little less likely to disappear.

My progress is simple, almost indiscernible to the outside world: I have gained a few pounds, I sleep through the night, I no longer have to suppress the urge to hurl myself through Grandpa Jacob's window.

The weeks drift by in the rhythm I have set up for myself. For the first time in a few years, I have a schedule. I know I'm not flying anywhere; I am staying right where I am.

Every day I drive to Connecticut, and every night I watch the ten o'clock news with Myrtle, an enamel tray with two cups of tea, milk and honey set on the coffee table in front of us.

I have not watched the news in longer than I care to remember. I am captured by one story in particular, which I follow from day to day: a Soviet Jew, a dissident named Natan Sharansky is making headlines. He has been held captive in work camps for years, he has staged hunger strikes and has become a focal point for freedom, a prisoner of conscience. He is trying to emigrate to Israel, where he can live the way he wishes, as a Jew.

Myrtle is also taken with Sharansky's plight.

"It never ends, Miss Lucy," she says, shaking her head back and forth in the dark.

"No, it doesn't," I say, but I am thinking that perhaps somehow it does.

Myrtle and I fall into a comfortable silence. We watch the basketball scores, the weather report and the closing credits.

"The state of affairs always puts me right to sleep," she says as she stretches and yawns. "Good night, little one."

She kisses the top of my head and walks toward her bedroom, a small, warm cube of a room off the kitchen pantry.

There is snow predicted tonight, the first snow of the season. The air is full of it, the rich, wet smell. I decide to take a walk down Central Park West, which is still safe this time of night, with its majestic doorman buildings on the west side of the street.

I exit the building and turn right, walking downtown on Central Park West. I have recently purchased a practical coat; I have retired all the fur coats Ben gave me to a locked closet, where I imagine I will only take them out once or twice all winter, perhaps for the opening night of the film.

I bundle the down coat around me, an enormous, white affair, and shove my hands deep in the pockets. Inside, I feel matches, an empty pack of cigarettes, a few loose quarters.

I walk only a few paces away from the building when I see him getting out of a Checker cab at the corner.

"Hello," he says, slamming the door behind him.

I am only frightened for a moment. I knew this would happen sooner or later. Carolyn was right. She warned me. *He meant it when he said he would never let you go.*

"Hello," I answer.

No matter what has transpired between us, I was raised to speak when spoken to. I am always polite.

He grins at me, the willful, predatory grin he uses to secure business loans and mistresses.

"Fancy meeting you here," he says.

"What are you doing here?" I ask. "How did you find me?"

"I have my sources," he says.

I think of Carolyn, and then of Harry Wheeler. It must have been Harry.

How could he do this to me?

I can't even imagine what Ben must have offered him, blackmailed him, bribed him to get this piece of information.

"What do you want?" I ask him.

He walks closer to me. He is carrying a suitcase.

"This is your junk," he says, dropping it at my feet. "I'm delivering it to you, in person."

Ben's voice rises, and the suitcase lands with a thud. A group of teenagers on the corner of Ninetieth Street turns to look at us, snickering.

I stare at him, incredulous. I have never seen Ben this angry, I have never seen him lose control.

"How dare you?" he yells. "How dare you walk out on me like that?"

I don't remind him that it was he who told me that if I left, I'd better not come back.

I don't say anything at all.

It has begun to snow, a few scattered flakes swirling in the air around us. Before I can turn away, before I realize what is about to happen, he reaches out an open hand and brings it across my face hard, and the sound of a slap rings in my ears.

I stand there, paralyzed.

I involuntarily reach up a hand to feel my cheek. As I am doing so, he slaps me again, this time on the other side of my face, so hard I almost fall.

The teenagers have stopped snickering. They stare at us, and I hear one of them asking if they should call the police.

I begin to run.

I am blindly heading for my grandmother's building, where once inside the doors I know I will be safe. I turn around to look at Ben, and as if I am watching from a great distance, I see him lift the suitcase I have left on the sidewalk and hurl it at me with all the force in his body.

It catches me between the legs, and I fall hard onto my knees. I am still looking at him, through a haze of tears and snow. I feel my legs bleeding inside my jeans, blood sticking to denim.

He stands very still for a moment.

"Whore," he spits out at me, "you're a whore."

The words echo in my ears as he turns his back on me for the last time, and walks away.

———

Do you know about winter in Nantucket, the frantic sea gulls, the clear sheets of ice which float just below the ocean's surface? They are dangerous. They are clean and sharp, like blades.

Do you know about Paris in the springtime?

I think of you often. I tried so hard to be just like you, but I went further than I had ever imagined. I wanted secrets. I wanted a life full of intrigue, shadows behind my eyes, the mystery you held in the clean line of your jaw, the silence you kept until you couldn't stand it any longer.

All my life I sought out drama. This was not what I had in mind.

———

Myrtle cleans me up. In the medicine chest there are bottles of antiseptic, Mercurochrome and cotton pads which have probably not been touched in over a decade, but we use them anyway.

She pulls off my jeans, making tiny clucking noises with her tongue; her eyes are dark and wide as she looks at me, not sure what to say. She dabs at my knees with the cotton pads, and as the medicine bubbles and sinks into my cuts, I barely move.

"This is going to sting," she says, wincing herself, as if it is she who is hurt.

"It's all right," I whisper.

"What happened?"

"I'm sorry, Myrtle. I really can't say."

She resumes clucking. Her hands on me are warm and dry. They are strong hands, accustomed to handling the young, the needy, the sick and dying.

"Miss Lucy, you have everything in the world going for you," she says after a while. "You're young, you're nice to look at and you got a head stuffed full of brains. Don't throw it all away over some *man*."

"Why do you assume it's a man?" I ask her.

"Honey, there's only one kind of trouble that causes the look you got in your eye, and that's man trouble," she says.

She tucks me into bed, and sits down on the edge as we watch "The Late, Late Show." *Anna Karenina* is playing. The film is almost over, the final scene.

Greta Garbo stands at the St. Petersburg train station alone, the cold Siberian wind whipping through her fine, pale hair. She is tortured, waiting there for the train to come in.

She is meeting no one. She is meeting her end.

I remember this scene from the book, and can barely bring myself to watch.

Suddenly the train arrives. One car goes by, then another, and another. Soon it will be too late. Garbo's eyes widen, she cannot move, like a deer trapped between a car's two headlights.

Then, in an instant, she breaks the spell. She throws herself onto the tracks and so ends the path of self-destruction on which she had embarked so many years before.

"There, there," I hear Myrtle's voice close to my ear, "it's only a movie," she says.

I realize that at some point I must have grasped her hand, and have been squeezing it with all my might during Anna's death scene.

"Ssssh," she says, stroking my hair back from my forehead, which is damp with perspiration.

"What can I do for you?" she whispers.

"Please stay here until I fall asleep."

I close my eyes and pray not to dream. I want to shut out the world. Just like in the movies, I want the story to be over, I want it to fade to black.

Myrtle hums me an island lullaby as I curl up on my side, facing the wall.

I think I will never fall asleep.

She strokes my head and sings to me, the lovely Jamaican melodies so jarring against the backdrop of this mahogany study high above Central Park West.

After a while, I finally feel myself starting to drift off, comforting myself with the belief that things can only get better.

I am making a dreadful mistake.

I am imagining that the worst has already come to pass.

———

The sky is still dark over Manhattan when the phone begins to ring. I squint in the gray of the room, and stumble to Grandpa Jacob's desk, searching for the receiver.

"Hello?" I say irritably. I am certain it's going to be the wrong number; it's five-thirty in the morning.

"Lucy, this is Aunt Bea," I hear the thick accent over the crackling wire.

"Hi, Aunt Bea," I say.

Why is she calling me here, and at this hour?

It begins to slowly dawn on me that something must be very wrong.

There is a pause on the other end.

"Lucy, the first thing I want to tell you is that your parents are alive."

My legs begin to shake.

"What happened?" I hear my voice say, as if it doesn't belong to me.

"There's been an accident," Bea says.

I watch my legs shake. I push down on them with my hands, but they won't stop.

"What happened?" I repeat. Everything is in slow motion, everything is too slow.

"Lucy, your mother and father are alive," she repeats.

"WHAT HAPPENED?" I scream into the receiver.

"Your father was driving the car—"

"Which car?" I interrupt. This is somehow important to me.

". . . the Audi, and . . . he passed out at the wheel, Lucy."

I squeeze my eyes tightly.

". . . both your mother's legs are broken," she says.

"Is that all?" I ask.

My family has always tried to protect me. They would rather lie to me than have me face the ugly truth. But this is not a moment for delicate phrases, and I am not a delicate girl.

I want some answers.

"No," she says, and then I hear her list what sounds like every bone in the human body. Pelvis, she says, and cheekbone, tibia, several ribs, and she's lost a lot of blood.

"Is my mother going to live?" I ask her.

"We think so," she says.

I sink down into Grandpa Jacob's chair.

"What about my father?" I whisper.

"Lucy . . . your father had a stroke. He hasn't regained consciousness," she says.

"When did this happen?"

"Last night."

"WHY DIDN'T ANYBODY CALL ME?" I scream so loud it bruises my own ears.

"Lucy, I'm sorry," she says, "we didn't know where you were."

———

Have you ever wondered what would happen if your worst nightmare came true? I'll tell you this: outside this window, yellow cabs are creeping slowly through the snow on Central Park West. Early-morning joggers are walking through the dawn to the bridle path, and the Greek deli on the corner is getting ready to open its doors.

Nothing happens, Carolyn. Just as half the world can be destroyed as the other half lives, just as in wartime, your own personal nightmare means nothing in the scheme of things.

But I guess you know that.

Did you wish this on me? Did you shut your eyes tightly, praying for the worst possible thing to happen? Did you create a wax effigy and stick pins into it, until finally something worked?

Let me tell you this: if this is of your working, you could not have done a better job. If this is a test, a mountain to climb, you could not have picked more dangerous terrain.

I am all alone. But I suppose you knew all along, with the wisdom of one who has fallen, that this would eventually be the case.

———

"I'll be there as soon as I can," I say, struggling to stand. My legs have not stopped trembling. They are too weak to support me.

"We'll be here," Bea says. "Overlook Hospital, right off Route 24 in Summit, New Jersey."

"I know where it is," I say woodenly.

"Just ask for Intensive Care," she says before she hangs up the phone.

And so begins a series of phone calls, of arrangements and decisions for which it seems I have been preparing my whole life.

I call Overlook Hospital and ask to be connected with the Intensive Care Unit.

"This is Lucy Greenburg," I say to the charge nurse. "I want to check on the condition of my parents."

"Unchanged," she says.

"How is their condition listed?" I ask.

"They are both critical," she says.

I walk into the bathroom, turning on the fluorescent overhead lights. I splash cold water on my face, then look at myself in the mirror, just to make sure I'm still the same person. A forty-year-old face stares back at me.

I call the garage.

"I need car number 165," I say to the attendant.

"I can't do that," he says.

I take a deep breath.

"This is an emergency," I say, the phrase sounding oddly familiar, echoing in my ears.

"I'm sorry, ma'am. There's a blizzard going on out there, in case you haven't noticed," he says. "We're all snowed in."

"What time can I get my car?" I ask.

"I don't know."

———

I must admit, in that moment of desperation, that I thought of calling Ben. For years, I had believed he could take care of any problem imaginable. He could move mountains, he could stop snowstorms, he could get a garage to open right from the soft leather chair in his office.

He was stronger than Atlas, he could carry the weight of the world on his thick shoulders. He could make lies sound like the truth, he could make hate sound like love.

There was only one thing I know he could not do: that

snowy night my parents were on their way home, safe inside the metal kingdom of their Audi 5000, he could not stop my father's round, bald head from falling like dead weight onto the rim of the steering wheel. He could not stop my mother's screams. He could not stop the rivers of blood which sank into the snow, disappearing into it like flavor sinks into an Italian ice.

I didn't call Ben. Instead, I dialed the number for Silver Hill and asked to speak with you.

There was a long silence on the other end.

"We're sorry, we can't get her for you," they said.

"Why not?"

"Why don't you speak with Dr. Sheidler."

After an interminable pause, Dr. Sheidler got on the phone.

"What's going on?" I asked him.

"I'm sorry, Lucy. Carolyn has gone back to school."

"She has?"

"Yes. You just missed her. Her stepfather picked her up just a little while ago."

———

Several hours have passed since the phone call from Aunt Bea. The sun has long since risen above the Upper East Side, and Myrtle is sitting with me in her bathrobe, anxiously stirring her coffee. She has not stopped shaking her head.

"Mr. Joseph," she keeps muttering to herself, "it's not right."

I have finally found a limousine service which will pick me up as soon as the roads are cleared. Outside, I see plows pushing the snow up along the sidewalks, bundled-up children lugging nannies and sleds on their way to the park.

If something happened to them, if they died, I imagine I would know it. I silently tell myself that I would sense it somehow, perhaps a slight nudge to the back, the way it feels to break the sound barrier during super-sonic flight.

I have imagined thousands of cataclysms, but I have never imagined this could happen to my parents, my safe and solid parents in their safe and solid car, driving exactly fifty-five miles per hour with seat belts crossed over their chests like badges of honor.

Aunt Bea told me that my mother threw herself in front of my father at the moment of impact, saving his life.

"That's why she has so many broken bones," Bea said. "Your father doesn't have a scratch."

I close my eyes and see my mother leaning into my father's soft belly, throwing her arms around him, screaming into his shoulder. She desperately tries to kick his foot off the gas pedal as the speedometer creeps up fast, faster: seventy-five, eighty-five, ninety.

At the moment of impact, there is only white. The white of the snow, the white of the divider, the white of my mother's face. If there were music, it would be Mahler, or Saint-Saëns, or the slow movement of the "Pathétique."

———

"Chaya," my mother told me once, referring to my middle name, "it means life. And you, my beautiful daughter, are going to have the most wonderful life."

———

The snow along the sides of the Jersey Turnpike is still white. I am wearing black. A black stretchy jumpsuit, a black mink coat and black Ray-Bans, all courtesy of Ben. The limousine is black. The driver's hat is black. We are a vision of mourning, of doom and destruction, hurling along the highway past commuters on their way to work.

"I heard it on the CB," the driver tells me. "It was a terrible accident," he says, slowing down as we begin to climb the hill, carefully winding through the snow to the very top, where Overlook Hospital looms, more frightening than any haunted house of my childhood.

I hear my heels click along the antiseptic tile corridor leading to the ICU. I have already begun to learn the language of disaster, and how it applies: ICU, CCU, IV, stat, serious, stable, critical. Disembodied voices swirl around me on the intercom system, paging doctors and nurses. Everything is serious. Everything, on some level, is life and death.

I open the door to the Intensive Care Unit, stopping first to read the sign which tells me not to enter. Instantly, I am in a different world. Everything is quiet. The only sounds are of nurses' whispers and a strange, high-pitched beeping.

The room is shaped like an amphitheatre. In the center, there is a nurses' station. I do not look to my left or my right. I walk straight to the center of the room.

A nurse looks up at me. She is not pleased.

"You're not supposed to be in here," she whispers.

"I'm Lucy Greenburg, my parents are in here," I whisper back. I must look pretty desperate, because this no-nonsense nurse takes pity on me.

"Put these on," she says, handing me a surgical gown, gloves and a hat which resembles a shower cap.

"Which one do you want to see first?" she asks.

"Who's in better shape?" I ask back. My whole body is shaking, but she doesn't seem to notice.

"Your mother," she says, shaking her head.

She leads me behind the first partition. My eyes adjust to the soft light; I swallow a scream. My mother is unrecognizable. Her face is bloated, bloody, her eyes swollen shut. Her nose and left cheekbone are flattened against the swelling. Her lips are distended and dry. The only part of my mother I can identify is her hands, her lovely hands, which are gripping the metal sides of her bed, holding on for dear life.

I approach her bedside.

"Mom?" I softly whisper, bending toward her ear.

Her eyes struggle open. It takes her a few moments to recognize me.

"Lucy . . ." she moans. ". . . I didn't want them to call you."

Her mouth trembles with the effort.

"Sshhh, Ma. Don't try to talk," I say as I brush a few strands of matted hair off her forehead.

She is attempting to say something, but I can't understand.

"Sshhh, Ma," I repeat, but she is determined.

Her mouth twists open again.

". . . your father?" she asks, a tear rolling out of her swollen eye, over the gauges in her left cheek.

"He's alive, Ma. He's going to be all right. You're both going to be all right," I repeat again and again.

Her head nods to the side. She has fallen asleep.

"Your mother is heavily sedated," the nurse tells me. "I can't believe she was able to talk to you at all, in her condition."

I smile at the nurse. I am inflated with hope, puffed up like a helium balloon.

"My mother is a very determined woman," I tell her. "She will survive."

My father lies on the opposite side of the ICU, surrounded by complicated, bleeping machines. He looks as otherworldly as an angel, lying there, his skin so transparent I can see his veins. Wires are connected to every part of him. They stream from his nose, his mouth; they are attached to his chest, his temples, his neck. A thick wire, a catheter, peeks out from below his bed sheets.

I kiss his forehead. His skin is icy. I kiss every part of his face that is not attached to a machine. He does not stir. He is very far away from here, in another land. He is as distant as a sepia photograph.

He looks like history.

He is wearing a neck brace, which pushes folds of skin up around his cheeks, obscuring his closed eyes. The day-old stubble on his face has turned gray overnight. He pulls the hospital air in and out of his lungs with concerted effort; his brow furrows. It is difficult for my father to breathe.

I gingerly lift up the wires lying on his chest, careful not to disturb anything. I rest my head down against him, listening to his heart. I look above me at the EKG monitor, the electronic green peaks, wildly uneven, electronic proof that my father's heart is trapped like a bird in his chest, struggling, beating furiously, burning itself out.

"Your father is a very sick man," the nurse whispers in my ear, "a complicated medical situation."

"What's wrong with him?" I ask, still leaning my head against him.

"We don't know."

And so begins an education, I think, in resistance, in the language of good, stable, serious, critical, and how it applies.

My mother needs an orthopedic surgeon, an ophthalmologist, an internist, a fracture specialist and a plastic surgeon. My father needs a cardiologist, a hematologist and a neurologist.

I walk out of the ICU into the main corridor of the hospital, where suddenly there is noise again.

A white-coated man approaches me.

"Miss Greenburg?" he asks, offering his hand. "I'm Dr. Melman, I'm the cardiologist treating your father."

Dr. Melman looks no older than I do. This does not inspire me with great confidence.

"We'd like to run some tests on your father, but we need you to sign permission," he says.

"Why?"

"Well, these tests run a certain risk, so we ask for permission from the next of kin," he says, not quite looking at me.

"What's the risk?"

"About ten percent," he says.

My knees buckle under me. I lean against a door frame.

"Dr. Melman, I'd like to get a second opinion before I sign anything," I say.

"Miss Greenburg, right now your father has less than a fifty-percent chance to live," he tells me.

————

Could you ever have imagined anything like this? Do you know that white-coated men who spend four years in medical school are able to attach percentages to things such as life and death? They are able to tell us more than God himself. They walk purposefully through the hallowed halls of this hospital, of any hospital; they look absentmindedly not into the desperate eyes of healthy people but at the walls above them, at the clock ticking away. They know time is precious.

He gently places a pen into the hand of a young woman, asking her to sign her father's life away.

"Sign here," he says, glancing at his watch. And she has no choice but to believe him.

"Sign here," he says, and I push my pen across the dotted line, above which the words "CAT SCAN" and "PACE-MAKER" are printed in black and white.

Could you have imagined this? Even in your wildest dreams? Where did you go? And wherever you are, could you find it in your heart to wish me well?

———

I cross off days on the calendar with the hopefulness of a child who eagerly awaits some important event. Each day signifies a greater chance, a lesser risk. A week has gone by.

My mother has been moved into a private room. Her legs hang above her in traction. Her whole body has shrunk; her cheekbones have caved in, her collarbone juts out grotesquely. She refuses to eat.

"The food here, Lucy," she moans, as if culinary delights are her real concern right now, "I can't stomach it."

Every morning, on my way to the hospital to visit my parents, I stop at Zabar's and pick up something to tempt her: whitefish salad, tortellini, fresh warm bagels with chive cheese.

I always stop in my mother's room before visiting my father, who is still in Intensive Care. At least she is able to talk to me. At least she opens her eyes. At least she knows I'm there.

My father is another story. He has been in a coma since the night of the crash. I sit next to him every afternoon, reading to him. I read Dickens, Tolstoy and the Talmud. Friday night, I propped a yarmulke on his head and recited the Sabbath prayers.

Nothing makes a difference. Nothing until today, when I

walk into the ICU, and my father is sitting up in bed, glasses perched on his nose, smiling at me.

I think I am hallucinating.

The nurses stand in their center station, quietly watching. They have grown fond of me during the past week, and allow me access to my father during nonvisiting hours.

They watch as I race to his bedside.

"Dad?" my voice comes out in a croak.

"Hi, dear," he says, as I bend down to hug him.

I hold him tight, oblivious, for once, to the wires surrounding him, the small, angry incision a few inches above his heart.

"Oh, thank God, thank God," I murmur into his warm chest. "Oh, I love you so much," I cry, kissing his gray stubbly cheeks.

I look up at him.

"I love you too," he says, and then pauses, brows knitting together. "Why are you crying?" he asks. "What's wrong, shnookie?"

I look up at him then. My father's eyes are like kaleidoscopes. He is staring at me with all the innocence and guile of a two-year-old.

"Where am I?" he asks.

The realization comes to me slowly, so slowly, the way the cruelest blows are always felt. Inch by inch, my body sinks into it as if I were drowning in a freezing pond.

"Where do you think you are, Daddy?" I ask.

"Home?" he asks.

I shake my head.

"Basketball?" he asks.

"No, Dad. Come on, where are you?"

He presses his mouth together. Then a light bulb goes off.

"Stock Exchange?"

I clasp my arms around his neck. He is drowning, and I am going down with him.

"Where am I?" he asks.

"You're in the hospital, Dad," I say.

His eyes open wide.

"No . . ." he says. He thinks I'm kidding.

"You were in a car crash, Dad."

Suddenly, he tries to bound out of bed. He shoves the IV pole to the side, thrashes helplessly trying to lower the metal guards.

"Where is my wife?" he bellows. "I want to see my wife," he pumps the air with his thick arms.

The nurses come running over.

"Mr. Greenburg, come on, stop it now," one of them says. "Quiet down now, like a good boy."

I turn to her.

"What did you say?" I ask.

"I said—"

"Never mind, I heard you," I hiss. "Don't you ever, ever speak that way to my father again. Do you understand me?"

She stifles a giggle.

"I said, do you understand me?"

She ducks her head into a nod, but I am no longer interested in her. My father is crying. Giant tears roll down his grisly face.

"Where is my wife?" he sobs.

I hold on to him.

"Daddy, she's all right," I tell him. "She's upstairs, in another wing. She has a broken leg, that's all."

This provokes a new wave of tears.

"I want to see her," he cries.

"Soon," I promise him. "You'll see her soon."

I drink a bottle of wine a day. It is my medicine, the way my mother has Demerol and my father has bleeding in his brain. I escape at night, when the lights dim at Overlook Hospital; I take the limousine back to the city, back to Grandma's.

I cannot drive. I am afraid to drive.

I meet people at restaurants with long wine lists, and order something rich and mellow, or cool and crisp. It doesn't matter. I drink it as if it were Triaminic or Pepto-Bismol. I am only interested in whether it works.

My father needs another neurologist; the one at Overlook isn't helping. I call everyone I know. There are specialists at NYU, Columbia-Presbyterian, Mount Sinai.

No one wants to drive out to Summit, New Jersey. No one wants to return my calls. No one, it seems, wants to save my father's life.

Every night, before I go to sleep, I visit Grandma for a while. I sit by the side of her bed as I always have, but I don't talk to her.

I don't tell her that her son is lying in a hospital bed thirty miles away, and that the likelihood she will outlive him grows every minute of every hour. I cannot take the chance that she will understand me.

At least someone can be spared.

In the early hours of morning, when the city is still dark, I invariably wake up and call the hospital.

"Martha, how's my father?" I ask the private nurse I have recently hired.

"He's a live one, Lucy," she says. ". . . tried to climb out of bed three times tonight." She chuckles, as if he were an errant toddler.

I laugh with her. At least she is kind, and she treats him with respect.

I have been told that my mother will live. It is unclear whether she will ever walk again, but her heart is strong, and her body has accepted the transfusions which have been pumped into her like water into a dam. Every day, her face knits more closely back together, as if invisible hands are re-arranging the pieces to a puzzle.

My mother is a very determined woman, I said to the nurse the first day I visited her. She will survive.

I wish I knew the same about my father.

"Dad, who's President?" I asked him yesterday, during our regular quizzes.

"Me," he answered, forceful and rebellious.

"No, Dad. It's Ronald Reagan."

"Oh, shit," he said, his eyes round and dense as marbles.

Yesterday was Saturday, the Shabbos. When I walked into

my father's room, he was circling his face with an electric razor, gazing complacently into a small hand mirror on a tray in front of him. I grabbed the razor from his hand as if it could burn him.

"Daddy, what are you doing?" I asked him. "It's Shabbos!"

I had never seen my father shave on the Sabbath before. It was against the rules.

His hand opened easily. He did not question me.

"So? Let's daven," he said, "let's pray."

I had brought him a prayer book from home, a torn cloth book that had once belonged to his father. He grasped it in his hands, opening it to the correct page for the *Maariv* service.

We began to recite the prayers. My father's Hebrew was flawless. He barely looked down at the book in his hand, he was so secure in the verses, one melody flowing into another in the same clear voice which had recited the prayers for sixty-three years.

It was as if these words had traveled past the blood clotting in his head, sailed past his mangled brain into a part of him where they were safe, where they would always be safe. These prayers were as hard as granite, as deep as the deepest well. They went further than the English language, deeper than his understanding of where he was and what had happened; they transcended his love for me.

"Your father is a very difficult medical case," they told me. "He has a fifty-percent chance to live."

"Your mother is a very sick woman," they told me. "She may never walk again."

"If your father lives," they said, "he will always be confused."

"What does that mean?" I asked.

"He will never be the same."

"What does that mean?"

"Miss Greenburg," they shake their heads in unison, "we cannot answer your questions. We do not know."

———

Cardiology, Hematology, Neurology.

———

"Daddy, Sharansky was released today," I tell him, bounding into his room, sure that if nothing else, he will remember the Jewish Soviet dissident.

"Who?" he looks at me, scowling.

"Sharansky," I say, shot down in my tracks.

"Lucy," he says, sitting up in bed, shaking perspiration off his brow, "I can't stand it in here."

"What do you mean, Dad?"

He points to the curtain, to the next partition.

"This guy," he says.

"Your roommate?"

"Yeah. He's a fucker."

I can't believe my ears.

". . . and he's fucking around with me."

His mouth pulls downward into the valley of wrinkles which has formed overnight. His nurse rolls her eyes at me.

"Aaaah, who cares anyway," he says, and before I can stop him, he throws his bedcovers across the room.

And just as suddenly, he is quiet. He looks at me, and I know he is having a clear moment. Tears roll down his freshly shaven face.

"We're fucked," he cries as he pulls my head onto his naked shoulder.

"No, Daddy, everything's all right," I lie.

"We're fucked," he repeats, again and again.

———

I dream that we are driving north on the Jersey Turnpike, on the way home from the hospital. His cigar smoke fills the car —an acrid, rich smell that I doubt I will ever get used to. Willie Nelson whines on the tape deck as I watch the speedometer creep up past seventy.

"Could you slow down?" I ask.

"Sorry, I forgot," he says, reaching over and squeezing my knee.

"I need to ask you something."

"Shoot, sweetheart."

"I spoke with Carolyn a while back, and—"

"Why didn't you tell me?" he interrupts.

"Let me finish. She told me something, and I need to ask you about it."

His eyes are fixed on the road. The speedometer creeps up again.

"Slow down," I say sharply.

"Sorry. Well, what is it?"

I pause for a moment, frightened.

"Did you ever sleep with her?" I ask.

He smiles. "She told you that?"

"Yes."

"What else did she tell you?" he asks evenly.

"Don't change the subject. Did you?"

Suddenly he swerves, pulling the car to the side of the road, then slams on the brakes.

"Do you believe her?" he asks.

I try to keep calm. "Did you?" I repeat.

His eyes are as large and dark as beetles in this dreamy fluorescent highway light.

"I'm not going to answer that question," he says slowly, measuring out his words as if each one requires a great deal of thought.

We don't speak for the rest of the drive, the rest of the dream. Willie Nelson's voice cracks and shimmers in the space between us, singing of betrayal, and of love.

The nurses are pressuring me. They think it's time for my father to see my mother. They are afraid he will go wandering off into the night, traipsing down hospital corridors in search of her, as bears do for their missing young.

I am afraid. My mother looks far better than she did a few weeks ago, but she still is a terrible sight, with her bloodied face and broken bones. I'm afraid my father won't be able to stand it. And what of my mother, seeing my father? I have tried to explain what he is like, but she doesn't understand. She thinks she still has a husband.

I take a Polaroid of my mother and bring it upstairs to show my father.

"Daddy, this is what Mom looks like," I say. "I just want you to be prepared."

He looks at it, then tosses it across the room like a paper airplane.

"Let's go," he says.

We march down the hall, my father and I, surrounded by a coterie of nurses. One pushes a wheelchair, in case he collapses. Another carries a straitjacket. We enter the elevator, and my father stares at all the buttons. Then, without changing expression, he pushes every single one.

My mother is sitting up in bed, as much as she can. She has put on lipstick, an incongruous pink against her pale skin. The gesture nearly breaks my heart.

Her face strains into a smile when he walks into the room.

"Hello, Wahoo," she says.

My parents have called each other "Wahoo" since their first date, which was a cowboy and Indian movie.

My father stops still when he sees her. His face shatters like glass. His hands reach toward her, but the distance is too great, and he stumbles.

"Come here, Joseph," my mother says.

My father bows his head into her chest, just beyond the cast which ends above her waist. He sobs. His back heaves like a whale, his bald head shiny with perspiration.

"See?" my mother whispers. "Everything's all right. I'm here. We're here," she murmurs, stroking him.

She speaks slowly, she touches him gently. I realize that my mother has understood all along; she looks up at me with a triumphant, tear-stained face.

"You see, Lucy? We're all going to be fine," she says, as I watch my parents cling to each other like two broken dolls.

I wonder whether she really believes what she says. I am

surprised by her hope. I do not have the heart to tell her that once something is broken, it can never be whole again.

————

Most nights I go into the city, but tonight I am too exhausted; I decide to go to my parents' house, just a short distance from Overlook.

It is odd, being here alone.

I turn off one alarm system, then another, until the house welcomes me with a series of clicks, letting me know I am allowed to enter.

There are electronic eyes, there are sensitized pads underneath the plush carpeting, scattered randomly like minefields, yet still I do not feel safe. Our house is the only one in the neighborhood that has not been robbed. No burglar would attempt to enter the brick fortress at 645 Maple Avenue.

I don't know where to sleep in this house which no longer feels like my own. I cannot sleep in my parents' bedroom, beneath the watchful eyes of the Ben Shahn charcoal drawing above their bed. And I cannot sleep in my old bedroom, with its pink-and-orange ruffles, mementos of a girlhood in which nothing was ever supposed to go wrong.

I lie on the couch in the den and watch television. It is the same room in which I spent years sitting next to my father as he hung in traction. It is the same couch on which I first kissed Chris Mulcahy on a hot summer night, when the world seemed full of possibility.

I wander alone around the house of my childhood. Fifteen minutes away, my parents lie in their white hospital rooms, separated by three floors, sleeping farther apart than ever before. My mother lies on her back, her legs in their thick plaster casts hanging above her, disjointed like a marionette's. Her eyes are wide open; she is counting the holes in the perforated ceiling, she is counting the years of her marriage. If she concentrates hard, she can almost count the whiskers on her husband's face, the veins in his arms, the lines on his hands.

In a ward far away, down miles of gleaming corridors, my

father is attached to his bed by a straitjacket. This is "just a precaution." He is not thrashing against the heavy canvas. He is sleeping. His skin is green against the stark white of the straitjacket, and there are deep blue circles under his closed eyes.

He is dreaming. I wonder whether his dreams are coherent, or whether he clenches his fists and grinds his teeth in frustration, because even in his sleep he cannot understand.

———

My father held me in his arms and swirled me around and around. The lawn looked as green as a forest in the dark of the night.

"Daddy, stop! You're making me dizzy," I said, but I didn't really want him to stop. When I looked up at the sky, the stars were dancing.

"I see Grandpa Jacob," I said, "he's doing the rumba!"

My father laughed and laughed. He lifted me onto his shoulders and trotted around the lawn like a horse. Had you driven down our quiet street that night, you would have seen the shadow of a large man, on hands and knees, prancing elegantly on the sprawling front yard of his home, careful not to spill the child who was wrapped around his neck. He knew she was holding on as if she would never let go.

———

I dial the hospital, the number which I now know by heart. "Martha, how's my father?"

"He's having a rough night," she says. "He won't sleep at all."

"Can I talk to him?"

She puts the phone to his ear.

"Dad?"

"Yes," his voice comes faintly through.

"Dad, you going to make it?" I ask for the first time, tightly squeezing my eyes shut.

"No, shnookie," he says.

"Do you know what you're saying?"

"Yes," he whispers, and then mumbles a few other words.

"What are you saying?" I ask, trying not to scream.

"It's no good," he mumbles, "your mother . . . insurance . . . Stock Exchange . . ."

"Daddy, are you trying to tell me about insurance?"

"Yes."

"What about it?" I ask, but I have lost him.

"Five-eighths and three-quarters, left center field," he whispers into the phone as if imparting words of terrible importance.

Martha comes back to the phone.

"What'd you do?" she asks. "He finally fell asleep."

————

Did you ever wonder what would happen if the thing you feared most came crashing down around you in a thousand brilliant pieces, slivers of colored mirror by which to see your nightmare reflected again and again, more clearly than ever before?

I'll tell you this: when you and your pain become one, there is no escaping it. You become a transparent vessel, a bottomless glass. There is no end to it, as you well know, Carolyn.

In the dawn of this day, February the twenty-third, in the year nineteen hundred and eighty-six, life goes on as usual. Mercedes station wagons purr out of the cobblestone driveways of this neighborhood. Tired women pour steaming water into coffee filters, hugging their flannel robes around them. Children slam their lunch boxes against the sides of the bright, yellow school bus.

They scream and yell. They run up and down the aisles, flushed with the anticipation only children seem to have, at the beginning of a new day. They are not aware that on top of a hill, just past their range of vision, a man is dying.

————

I dress up, this morning, as if I am going on a job interview. I wear a black wool skirt, a gold silk blouse, and cover my pale skin with makeup. I look into my mother's vanity mirror and line my eyes carefully, as though I'm drawing a mask. I run a brush through my hair, then bundle it into a topknot.

In the car, on the way to Overlook Hospital, the radio is playing Doc Watson, a jazz melody so low, so throaty it sounds like a human voice. The sun is dazzling against the snow; I wear my dark sunglasses to hide my swollen eyes.

I don't know why I bother. No one is looking.

The driver's name is Ernie, and over the past few weeks, we have become friendly. He has a wife and three kids in Westfield, New Jersey, and wants to open up his own limousine business.

We pull up to the sliding glass doors of the hospital entrance. Ernie will wait for me. Every day he waits, like a faithful lover, for hours and hours.

I visit my mother first. I have continued to do this from the very beginning; her broken bones are easier to deal with than my father's broken spirit.

The door to her room is closed. I peek through the glass, glad to see her propped up in her bed. But then I look more closely. There are people in her room, people I do not know. They surround her in a semicircle. There is a middle-aged woman carrying a clipboard, a white-coated doctor, a priest.

I open the door. My mother turns to me, her eyes seem to fill her whole face.

"Lucy, come here," she says, trembling.

———

Later, she tells me I screamed. She tells me I opened my mouth and wailed, standing in the doorway of her pristine white room.

I wonder what I said, if this is true.

———

"Is he dead?" I ask, burying my head on her chest like I never have done in my life.

"They're working on him," the woman with the clipboard says.

I hate her for saying it, I hate her for the understanding

look on her face. They're working on him. What does this mean?

"His heart is still beating," my mother whispers.

"How long ago . . ."

"Twelve minutes," she says, and for the first time I notice my mother's eyes have not left the clock.

I stroke her face. I push wisps of hair off her forehead. "It will be all right," I say, even as I watch the doctor walk into the room.

"I'm sorry," he says, and I realize it's not a line from an old Cary Grant movie. It is not part of the language of good/ stable/serious/critical and how it applies. I'm sorry is the bottom of the barrel. I'm sorry is the lowest you can go. I'm sorry is the last thing they teach doctors before they graduate from medical school. The inflection. The shake of the head. The sad, remorseful eyes.

When I was a little girl, I used to watch out of my bathroom window when he took his morning swim. I used to observe him conscientiously, to be sure he didn't drown. I imagined his bald head bobbing helplessly in the clear blue water like a plastic beach ball.

One hundred and forty-four laps made a mile in our pool, and I watched every single one of them.

I have prepared for this moment since the day I was born. I have watched my father fade into the distance before my very eyes. I have watched his broad back get lost in a crowd, I have watched his taxi pull away from the curb, always with the fear that I would never see him again.

And now he is gone. My mother's face is a ghostly white, paler than the hospital sheet pulled up to her neck. Her doctor inclines his head at me, and points to the hall.

"I'll be right back, Mom," I say.

"Where are you going?" she asks like a child.

"Just getting some air," I lie.

The doctor rests his hand on my shoulder and waits, as if expecting me to say something.

My mouth is dry, and my skin feels like it's burning. Somewhere in this hospital, my father is lying on a metal table, covered by a sheet. When the human heart dies, does the pacemaker keep ticking? Does it go on forever, even in the grave? Perhaps it is a comforting sound, like a clock.

"Do you want to see your father?" the doctor finally asks.

"See him?" I repeat dumbly.

"Miss Greenburg, do you want to see the body?"

I realize that this is one of those moments in life I can never take back, and never regret. "No," I softly say.

———

And so begins an education in the etiquette of death. (When I was a child, I thought "etiquette" was spelled "edicut," something which sliced sharply, like a blade.)

"I want the funeral here," my mother says.

"But Mom, this is a hospital. I'm not sure they'll allow it," I say.

Her mouth tightens into an expression I know well.

"They'll allow it," she says.

"But Miss Greenburg, we've never had a funeral here before," says the chairman of the board, who is the fifth person with whom I have spoken.

"Have you ever had a situation like this?" I ask him, holding my yellow pad in front of me, tapping my pencil on his desk.

He clears his throat. "No," he says.

"Well, then," I say. "Sir, my mother has a right to attend the funeral of her husband. And she cannot be moved."

He looks at me. I look back.

"The auditorium of Overlook Hospital seats two hundred and fifty people. Will that be sufficient?" he asks.

"Can we have it tomorrow morning?" I ask, keeping my voice steady.

"Tomorrow?" His eyes widen.

"It is a Jewish requirement to bury our dead within

twenty-four hours," I tell him, not knowing how, in my lifetime, I have obtained this information.

———

There are many details, religious technicalities and customs,
which I surprise myself by knowing. There is no reason for
me to have this information; perhaps many years ago my father murmured it into my mother's pregnant belly when she
was asleep, and it entered my consciousness, my cranium the
size of a golf ball.

A plain pine box is required, which remains loosely closed,
to hasten, rather than delay, the process of disintegration.

The body is bathed, then clothed in a white shroud.

The body is buried with a Bible.

The reason mourners, on their way to funerals, leave their
car headlights on is so that they will not lose one another.

After the funeral, each mourner eats a hard-boiled egg. The
egg is a metaphor for roundness. It teaches us that the world
goes on.

———

On February the twenty-third, in the year nineteen hundred
and eighty-six, Smith College is in full swing, in the middle of
second semester. I imagine Carolyn Ward is walking from
class to class, books held loosely in her arms, her face pink
from the fading New England winter.

She smiles at no one. Men look at her, women try to catch
her eye, but she hears only the music playing on her
Walkman; Arthur Rubinstein is performing Chopin's B-flat
Minor Scherzo. The piece is familiar to her, music she
vaguely remembers hearing a long time ago.

She does not hear the phone ringing in her dormitory
room. She does not hear my voice speak into her machine,
even as she hears my music float between her ears. She looks
at the branches of a cherry blossom tree, which are sheathed
in ice. She breaks one off, holding it in her brightly mittened
hands.

"Carolyn, it's me," I speak into her machine. It does not occur to me to identify myself. "Carolyn. My father is dead."

For the first time in my life, the first of many times, I have said the words. I do not need to see his body. The images in my head suffice, torturing me like bats in an attic. Speaking into Carolyn's answering machine, hundreds of miles away, I begin to cry.

"The funeral is tomorrow, at Overlook Hospital in Summit, New Jersey," I say.

I think about saying, Please come. I think about saying, I need you. I think about telling her that it is she I want with me, that I could find all the comfort in the world if I could just rest my head on her bony shoulder, and feel her cool hand run down my cheek.

Instead, I do the only thing I have the right to. I whisper good-bye, and hang up the phone.

————

In the late afternoon, the phone rings in my mother's room, and I rush to answer it. I have been rushing all day, a yellow legal pad under my arm, calling everyone in the world who ever knew my father, calling stockbrokers, rabbis, college friends and neighbors from every place he ever lived.

I have quickly learned to be the harbinger of bad news. It's quite simple, really: first you warn the person to whom you are speaking. You say, "I have bad news," then you deliver it quickly, like a doctor giving an injection. Then you do your best not to listen to the moans on the other end of the phone, the shocked silence, the tears.

I snatch up the receiver.

"Hello?"

"Darling," I hear on the other end.

I am silent, surprised to find that my heart does not turn over. It is broken.

"I just heard. I'm so sorry," he says. "I remember when my own father died, and it's so—"

"Just one question," I interrupt him.

"What?"

"How did you find out?" I ask.

"Carolyn," he says, "she called me in London. I'm over here on a business trip, and—"

"Thank you for calling," I say, keeping my voice even, trying not to upset my mother, who is lying flat on her back, looking up at me.

"Please do not call again," I say, placing the receiver back on its hook, severing the connection between us.

———

Perhaps this is one of the moments in my life I will never understand. Were you trying to help me, when you picked up the phone and dialed London? I would give almost anything to know what went through your beautiful, complicated head.

Or were you trying to stir up trouble.

Either way, you and I both know that it doesn't matter. There is only one road out, Carolyn. And in the matter of my dreams—yes, I still dream—there are only ghosts.

———

It is unseasonably warm on the morning of Joseph Aaron Greenburg's funeral. People I have not seen in years filter through the sliding glass doors of the hospital, looking somber and uncomfortable in their black woolen suits, fur coats draped over their arms.

I avoid them as I make my way up to my mother's room. Her doctor stops me before I enter.

"Miss Greenburg, stay close to your mother's side today," he says, steering me into the waiting area. "She is a very sick woman."

I feel faint. I must begin to sway, because the doctor hands me a container of orange juice.

"Drink this," he says.

I take a sip.

"Drink the whole thing. You need to keep your blood sugar up."

He watches me until I finish. It is the kindest gesture I have seen him make, this man to whom death is part of a day's work.

We enter my mother's room together. She is lying flat in bed, and is wearing a silk robe of my father's, which was sent down from his room.

I am afraid to touch her. She looks as delicate as the blown glass she has collected from Jerusalem; if I touch her, she may turn to dust.

"Are you ready?" I ask her. There are attendants standing by to hoist her onto a stretcher.

"Come here, my baby," she says, reaching out her arms, "my little Lucy, all dressed in black." She bites her lip. Her skin is cool as I lean forward to kiss her.

I have worn black all my life, but the clothes I am wearing today are different; the same black pleated skirt, the same silk jacket have taken on the shape of my grief, as though they could walk away by themselves and there would be no question as to whom they belonged.

My mother is lifted gingerly onto the stretcher, her legs held in traction. We wheel her down the hall carefully, like a breakable object, like a carton labeled "This side up."

The day after the accident, she gave me her wedding ring to wear, for safekeeping. Until today, I have worn it on a chain around my neck. As we enter the elevator, I unclasp it and place it in her hand.

"I'm here, Ma," I bend down and whisper in her ear.

"What are we going to do?" she moans.

She looks up at me with her enormous, sunken eyes.

"Hold my hand, Lucy," she says with all the dignity she can muster. "Hold my hand and don't let go."

The auditorium is packed with mourners. This cavernous room is not meant for a funeral. The walls are covered with gold-plated plaques honoring doctors. My father's coffin lies in the center of a podium which, until this day, had only been used for hospital dinner dances and testimonial luncheons.

People descend upon us as we wheel my mother's stretcher into the room.

I wave them away.

"Stick close to your mother's side," the doctor had said. "Your mother is a very sick woman."

Dark, dark men with long beards and top hats surround the plain pine box covered by a black cloth, the Star of David. They encircle it, murmuring Hebrew words and swaying back and forth. The pitch of their voices rises and falls like the tide. The prayer books in their hands are only for comfort; they know the words by heart.

Snatches of conversations, of high-pitched whispers can be heard all around.

"A terrible accident," says a woman with a thick German accent.

"Who was driving?" asks her companion.

"I think the daughter," she says, pointing at me, "and look, not a scratch on her."

There is no music at Orthodox Jewish funerals. There are no flowers. There is no stained glass. There is nothing of beauty here in this room, where everything is black and white.

We move my mother's stretcher down to the front row. She stares at her husband's casket and grips my hand tighter. The casket is closed. She will never see him again. My parents are both shattered. In the distance between them, in the few yards between my mother's warm hand in mine—her bruised face, her useless legs, her veins filled with transfusions of someone else's blood—and the pine box in which my father's body lies, I think I will never again see so clearly the fine line between life and death.

The rabbi looks familiar. I stare at him until I realize that I recognize his face from family photographs. He married my parents, he buried Grandpa Jacob, and now he is burying Jacob's son. I wonder how it all balances out: are there more joyous occasions, more weddings, bar mitzvahs, the ritual of the *bris?* Or does he spend his life in rooms like this one, participating in the steady unabashed wailing, the discreet white handkerchiefs, the thick, undiluted air of death.

I see Carolyn walk in. She is alone as she stands just inside the entrance to the auditorium, scanning the room, and I have never seen her look lovelier. Her hair is pulled back off her face, swept beneath a navy blue hat; she is wearing silver hoop earrings, a dark silk suit, heels, and a single strand of pearls. A camel's hair coat is slung over her shoulders.

After growing accustomed to seeing her in standard-issue pajamas all fall and winter, for a moment I almost don't recognize her.

I think she is more of an actress than I.

She spots me, then raises one gloved hand. It falters in the air, then drops. She doesn't know what to do.

I cannot go over to her; I promised I would not let go of my mother's hand.

Carolyn sees Harry Wheeler seated in the last row, and makes her way toward him through the crowded room. She drapes her coat over the back of a chair, and smiles the pained smile which people adopt at funerals, a cross between "How are you?" and "Isn't this tragic." He leans over and kisses her as she sits down with him.

I keep my eyes on my father's casket, barely visible between the top hats, pale faces and swaying backs of strangers. This religious ritual is foreign to me, as strange and outlandish as if it were a funeral pyre. This is what he would have wanted, I think to myself, this is what he would have wanted, I try to convince myself again and again.

———

The loudest sound I have ever heard was on the day of my father's funeral. First, the rabbi cut a small vertical path in the thread of my black silk jacket, then signaled silently to me, miming a downward motion.

"You must rend your clothing," he said to me.

"Why?" I asked.

"Because it is written."

So I grasped onto the ends of the fabric and jerked my

hands quickly, and oh, the sound of it. You must have heard it halfway across the room. You would have heard it halfway across the world. To this day, I can hear it ringing in my ears. I wanted to continue to rip my clothing, I did not want to stop until everything was in shreds around me.

It was the sound of the ending of a life, Carolyn. It was the sound of the tearing of a heart.

———

My father is buried in the family plot, at the feet of his father, the great scholar Jacob Greenburg. On this warm February day, my high heels sink into the crusty ground of the cemetery.

The grave diggers have opened the correct grave. They still remember the events of more than twenty years ago, and if not, the uneven mound of earth is there in the family plot to remind them.

It takes eight men to lift the casket onto the white canvas straps. There are holes in the bottom of the casket, so that my father's body will disintegrate as quickly as possible. How long does it take? How long does it take for dust to return to dust?

The rabbi hands me a shovel.

"You first," he says, gesturing at the small hill of dirt next to the grave.

I am alone in this crowd of people who profess to love me. My mother is lying in her hospital room, an hour's drive away, and my father is lying in the place he will never leave.

The dirt is surprisingly heavy. I let it trickle from my shovel, and it seems to take forever until it hits the pine box six feet below. I want to jump in after it, but somehow I don't. Somehow I control the urge to scream, to beat my fists against the frozen ground like an old Russian peasant woman, like an ancestor of mine might have done in another time and place. Instead, I shovel the next mound of dirt, and the next, each time hearing a thud so final it seems to thin the air.

One by one, my relatives join me, pale men and women wielding shovels ferociously, as if they were instruments of war. The definition of what "forever" really means seems to be written on the quickly disappearing lid of my father's coffin, as the rest of the crowd joins in, and we bury one of our own.

Shiva

*G*randma's apartment was filled with people all day long. For seven days it was like this; we were observing the ritual of sitting shiva. The door was left ajar. People poured into the marble foyer, hanging their winter coats on a special metal rack set up for the occasion.

I knew you would not walk through that door, Carolyn. You had attended the funeral, which was more than I could have possibly hoped for. A few times during that week, I thought I smelled you. I turned around quickly, surprised, and each time I saw a stout older woman, a friend of Grandma's who was wearing Shalimar.

Have you ever paid a shiva call, do you know what it entails? Do you want to know? Well, this is how it was: twice a day, the rabbi from Lincoln Square Synagogue came over to conduct the religious services, *Mincha* and *Maariv*. Usually a rabbinical student is sent over to do this, but in our case the chief rabbi himself attended. After all, he told me, it was the least he could do; it was the death of Jacob Greenburg's only son.

Morning and night we sat on folding chairs in Grandma's living room, twenty-one stories into the sky. We faced east, toward Fifth Avenue, toward Jerusalem. Always, there was a *minyan*, a gathering of the ten men required for prayer. Early in the morning, strangers came, men from the synagogue who were doing *mitzvot*, good deeds, by being a part of the services. They let themselves in quietly, these men. They nodded at me, sympathetic, dismissive, as they took their proper places under the massive portrait of my grandfather.

I sat on a low bench, lower than the rest of them. It was a mourner's bench, reserved only for immediate family. I was the only immediate family present. The two other women who should have been there were both lying in hospital beds, one in New Jersey, the other behind a closed door, down a long, narrow corridor in that same apartment.

As we were leaving the cemetery after the services, the rabbi came running after me.

"You must wash your hands," he said, pulling me away from the limousine.

"Why?" I asked.

"Because it is written."

I just looked at him.

He placed a hand gently on my elbow, guiding me toward the main building.

"You must wash the death away," he said, "and get on with the business of life."

I did not bother to tell him that I could swim the English Channel, I could cross the Atlantic Ocean, and that no amount of washing away, no religious symbolism could ever rid me of the thin, invisible layer of pain which now coated me like a second skin.

Yet I let the water trickle over my hands into the cracked white basin at the cemetery. I thought of how many hands must have trembled beneath that faucet, how the plumbing beneath must be eroded with shattered faith.

I remember how the Manhattan skyline appeared before me through the tinted window of the limousine as we approached the city after the burial, like the biggest possible reminder that the world goes on.

In bars and elegant restaurants, music was playing, glasses were clinking, people were laughing. In office buildings, messengers were pushing carts full of mail, switchboard buttons were lit up with phone calls. Even people who had attended the funeral that morning were going about the rest of their daily lives, pinched around the edges, perhaps, but whole and untouched.

You were on your way somewhere, that afternoon. Where were you going? I saw you getting into the limousine with the personalized license plates, Carolyn.

Did you want me to see?

There were sixteen other obituaries in the *New York Times* on February the twenty-fourth, in the year 1986. My father was not the youngest; AIDS had begun to hit the young homosexual population of New York City. Tragedy was everywhere you looked.

There was a quarter page taken in the *Times*, and in *The Wall Street Journal*. "The Governors of the New York Stock Exchange mourn the loss of our dear friend and colleague, Joseph Aaron Greenburg" was printed in irrefutable black and white.

I think this is when I started to believe it. If it was printed in the *New York Times*, it had to be true.

I keep these obituaries and mementos in a box labeled "Greenburg Estate," buried way in the back of my closet, right in front of a box labeled "Broadhurst." I pull out the clippings from time to time. I dust them off like heirlooms, which in some sense they are.

This is what remains of my father: I have two pairs of his cuff links, star sapphires and gold coins. I have a ratty orange sweater of his, a terrible color for me, which I wear all the time. I have old photographs with perforated edges from a trip to Miami he took with the City College debating team of 1939. The photos have captions beneath them written in ink: "Greenburg is busy looking at coeds instead of debating," the handwriting says, or "Greenburg is making eyes at the coed behind the palm tree." This is written below a picture of my father standing at the prickly base of a tree, his arms crossed akimbo, a head full of wavy hair blowing in the hot Miami breeze. He is smiling a broad, devilish smile—an expression which is unfamiliar to me—and a young woman, the coed in question, is passing in the background, unaware of the fuss being made.

I also have my father's *tefillin*, and a World War II prayer book for Jewish soldiers and sailors. I have an assortment of letters he wrote his mother from summer camp over fifty years ago, and a tape made at his bar mitzvah which I have never listened to in the year that has passed since his death.

I am surrounded by memories.

I carry his key ring, a cracked leather pouch with the initials J.A.G. imprinted in gold leaf lettering. On the walls of my new apartment, I have framed photographs of Grandma, my father as an infant, my parents at their wedding. He became a part of me in death, in a way which was impossible when he was alive.

He liked you, you know. My mother didn't think much of you, but my father liked your spirit.

"That Carolyn Ward," he would say, shaking his head back and forth, "she's a pistol."

I think you reminded him of all the coeds in the world, of dark blurs behind palm trees, the world of incalculable risks and potential rewards.

My father's life ended, for all intents and purposes, on the concrete divider of Route 24, near the Short Hills Mall in New Jersey.

This is something which defines me, the same way having

red hair, or long legs, or a genius IQ defines other people. I wear it like a badge of courage; it has taught me that I am a survivor, because if I was ever going to go down, it would surely have been on that snow-filled dawn a year ago.

Why was it we were only able to come through for each other during moments which were life-or-death?

I really didn't expect you to come, though I had hoped you would. I would have survived that day without you. I would have put one foot in front of the other and walked through that day, and eventually it would have been over.

You knew that. You knew more about pain than anyone has a right to. There are a few things in life which cannot be shared, and grief is one of them.

All you did in your quiet, composed way was to stand in the background behind the flurry of activity surrounding death, and to keep an eye on me when no one else would, as if to say, *Despite everything, I am here.*

Where did you find the courage? What was it that kept your feet on the ground that day, your eyes focused, your back erect and proud? You were the most fragile person in that room, Carolyn, yet you were my strength.

Just tell me this: are you glad to have met me, or would you take it all back, starting with the moment you walked in that door at Smith College with your soft leather suitcase in hand, with Ben to your right, and your mother behind you.

And what about the snowstorms in Northampton, the endless cups of tea laced with whiskey, the whispers which hung in the room between our two beds, in the dark?

I cannot go on.

I have only one regret. I never meant to hurt you, but this is, of course, a moot point.

It is winter again. The snow is pushed up along the sides of the Upper West Side street where I live. Outside my brownstone window I have hung a bright red bird feeder, which is filled with grains and seeds, the only color against the white-covered trees, the bare branches in the garden.

This is my life: four mornings a week I take the subway at Seventy-ninth Street up to the gates of Columbia University, where I have enrolled as a transfer student. I grasp the *New York Post* in my brightly mittened hands, reading first the headline story—this morning it was COP SLAYS MOM; SAVES KID —then the gossip page and the horoscopes. I still have a habit, I cannot help it, of reading not only the prediction for my day, but for yours and Ben's as well.

I find out what Ben is doing from the covers of *Fortune* and *Forbes*. I know he is alive, healthy and thriving.

What about you? I know you have not married, because I read the society pages. And I know you are alive, Carolyn, because I read the obituaries every day. I live in dread of seeing yours. I have already seen it in my mind's eye: your name in bold italics, **Carolyn Ward, 22.** It would give a vague, cursory cause of death, and would ask for contributions to be sent to Memorial Sloan-Kettering, in lieu of flowers.

On the subway I read the *Post* and sip coffee through a hole punched in the plastic lid of a cup. Once I get off at Columbia, I go to a coffee shop on the corner of 117th Street and Broadway. I'm a regular there; they know me. When I walk in, one of the Greek brothers behind the counter waves at me and calls out, "Hello Lucy," his thick accent spilling over my name like the syrup he hands me to pour over my order of pancakes.

"The usual," he says with a flourish, as he places my food in front of me, along with a small glass of fresh orange juice.

"Yes," I answer, still so relieved that there is anything at all in my life which could be called routine.

There are people who recognize me on the street. Most times they can't figure out why I look familiar, and just stare at me quizzically for a moment or two.

Sometimes they come up to me.

"Did you go to Scarsdale High?" they will ask me, or "Weren't you a counselor at Camp Hilldale?"

Actors who do commercials have a funny sort of celebrity. People recognize our faces, not our names. Commercials enter the brain sideways, become lodged under "Miscellaneous."

Once or twice I have been recognized from the film I did, which was released a month after my father died. It rarely happens, because I look quite different now, with my hair pulled back into a ponytail, my plaid parka, the books I hug to my chest like a shield.

I am taking French, nineteenth-century literature and a technical course on Mozart. It is not a full course load, because I have a whole other life, different from the life of a student.

In the afternoons I go visit my mother.

I was my father's daughter. What does that make me, now that he's gone? Everywhere I look, there are women. They stride in white uniforms down the shiny corridors of the rehabilitation center where my mother lives. They sit quietly in wheelchairs, gazing out their windows at the traffic below. They stand next to me at the Korean market, squeezing bruised tomatoes, expertly picking out the ones least likely to spoil.

It seems the world has depleted itself of men, as if the absence of my father has wiped out half the population. Everywhere I look there are women with strong hands, women with lined cheeks and sturdy legs. All except my mother, whose legs have atrophied to twigs under the mohair blanket which is always on her lap.

My mother has maintained her sense of pride. She will not allow anyone to see her legs, not even her nurses. Only I am allowed to rub the pungent, oily lotion into the thin skin of her calves, which are narrower than my wrists.

Do you remember when we were young?

We are young, you might say, in the endless conversation I continue to have with you quietly, when no one is listening.

Do you remember when disaster was something we courted, something we were able to pick and choose? I no longer have a choice. It is as permanent as my mother's shattered legs, my father's headstone planted firmly in the ground.

Who had a choice? I can almost hear you tap your fingers impatiently. *We did what we did, Lucy.*

I'd like to believe that. But some things are no longer possible.

I imagine you're with him. I know that wherever you are, you will not be safe until you escape him for once and for all.

Don't be a fool, Lucy. He'll never let you go, you told me once, your wrists as thick and white as a snowman's.

No, Carolyn, it is you who has the rocky road ahead. It is no wonder that you sought your deliverance with the sharp edge of a razor blade, the tepid water in a cracked, white tub.

My life has allowed me to go on. Ben can no longer touch me. I have an unlisted phone number, and very few people have my address. I spend my time in the Columbia University library, Greek coffee shops, city buses and the Burke Center for Rehabilitation.

I do not frequent four-star restaurants, or spend time in hotel lobbies or the first-class lounge at Kennedy Airport.

Chances are our paths will not cross anytime soon. I've always hoped I would somehow know if you were in danger, but that clearly has never been the case. Besides, I do know you're in trouble; I knew it the moment I saw you fold your long legs into the back of that black limousine a year ago.

What I'm trying to say is this: in acting, there is something called the trust exercise. It involves closing your eyes and falling backward, believing that someone will be behind you to catch you before you hit the ground.

I was not behind you in the past, and you almost broke your skull, you fell so hard.

Know that I will be there for the rest of my life.

Every Friday afternoon, before the Shabbos, I pay a visit to Grandma. I sit by her bedside, stroking her hand, reading her the Sabbath services from an ancient, tattered prayer book. I wander around the apartment, picking up photographs of cousins with whom I have nothing in common. They stare at me from the recesses of their silver picture frames, dark-eyed rabbis and rabbis' wives; they are earnest, solemn members of a society in which it is meaningful to be a grandchild of the great scholar Jacob Greenburg.

Sometimes I spend the night at Grandma's, though I live only twenty blocks away. I have grown accustomed to sleeping in the gold-and-black study, or doing my homework safe under the watchful eyes of Grandpa Jacob's leather-bound books.

In the pale blue light before sunrise, often I perch on the windowsill looking down at Central Park. There are people jogging around the reservoir, and the trees are still lit up at Tavern on the Green, remnants of the night before.

After dawn breaks, taxis begin to crawl through the icy transverses, mothers and children make their way down Central Park West, walking hand in hand through the snow. Homeless people get up from the doorways where they have spent the night huddling away from the cold.

Today is Saturday, and visiting hours at the rehabilitation center are extended all day long. I stop at Zabar's on my way to the garage, and pick up a quarter pound of Norwegian salmon, fresh cheese and bread.

Perhaps my father sees me now, as I wind my way up the Hutchinson River Parkway on my way to see my mother. I am driving his Citroën and listening to a recording of Schumann's Symphonic Études. I am not a happy woman—he might see that—but he would also see that I am hopeful and proud, which he always told me was more important.

I can almost see him shaking his head at me, sad that I am so alone, but he would know that my heart is stitching back together more slowly than my mother's broken bones, that someday I will be able to look up at the colony of stars and point out his face to a little girl who will be tightly holding my hand.

"Look, Mommy, it's Grandpa Joe," she will say with all the wonder in the world.

"He's smiling at us, he's winking at us," she will whisper in my ear. And I will twirl her around and around until she screams with delight, sure that I will catch her in my arms.

Dani Shapiro was born in New York City and grew up in Hillside, New Jersey. She received a B.A. and M.F.A. from Sarah Lawrence College, where she is cofounding editor of *One Meadway*, a national literary magazine. She lives in New York City where she is at work on her second novel.

BOOKMARK

The text of this book was set in the typeface Janson by Berryville Graphics, Berryville, Virginia.

It was printed on 50 lb. Glatfelter, an acid-free paper, and bound by Berryville Graphics, Berryville, Virginia.

DESIGNED BY GUENET ABRAHAM